"You can't do it, can you."

"What?" Roya asked.

"Trust men," Nick replied.

"After Bud? I don't think that's possible."

"It has to be sometime," he said.

"Why?"

He ground his fingers into her shoulders ever so slightly as he fought the impulse to shake her, make her come to her senses. *Because if you don't trust me, we'll never have a chance.*

He wanted to kiss her then, kiss her deeply. Bring her to tears the way he had the first day they'd met. He wanted her to move his soul again. He'd never felt like that before or since. It had been hell working with her every day— watching her struggle against Bud's screwups, his addictions, his mistress's greed.

But Roya did it and never complained to anyone.

Nick admired her for that. It was just one more reason why Roya had gotten under his skin.

Lanigan's "vivid characterizations will make you cheer and cry."

CATHERINE LANIGAN

IN LOVE'S SHADOW

MIRA®

MIRA

ISBN 1-55166-435-6

IN LOVE'S SHADOW

Copyright © 1998 by Catherine Lanigan.

All rights reserved. Except for use in any review, the reproduction or utilization of this work in whole or in part in any form by any electronic, mechanical or other means, now known or hereafter invented, including xerography, photocopying and recording, or in any information storage or retrieval system, is forbidden without the written permission of the publisher, MIRA Books, 225 Duncan Mill Road, Don Mills, Ontario, Canada M3B 3K9.

All characters in this book have no existence outside the imagination of the author and have no relation whatsoever to anyone bearing the same name or names. They are not even distantly inspired by any individual known or unknown to the author, and all incidents are pure invention.

MIRA and the Star Colophon are trademarks used under license and registered in Australia, New Zealand, Philippines, United States Patent and Trademark Office and in other countries.

Printed in U.S.A.

For DH,
with all the love and prayers in my heart.

IN APPRECIATION

Even though MIRA means "brightest star," the
bearers of light have always been angels.
My Guardian Angels take care of the heavens.
On earth my angels are named Dianne, Martha,
Katherine, Stacy, Amy, Jodee and Lissy.

1

The air was thin, brittle and still. It was the kind of winter evening that allowed sound to travel unimpeded. Bud knew it was a fact he should remember as he pulled his Mercedes into the drive of his Schaumburg home.

The sun hung just above the horizon, but already the temperature had plummeted to below zero. It was going to be a bitter night, he thought as he walked up to the front door, snow crunching under his shoes.

The neighborhood was unusually quiet. Bud assumed most everyone was shopping for last-minute Christmas gifts just like his wife, Roya.

Roya.

He stopped abruptly and looked at the house he'd built in the late seventies. For the first time, he was seeing it for what it was, what Roya had always said it was, "a monstrosity."

But then, I didn't build it for Roya.

He'd wanted so badly for it to be a replica of the grand estates he'd seen on the East Coast when he'd visited his sister, Daria, one summer in New York while she was attending Vassar. He'd wanted to fit in with her elegant society friends, women with aristocratic bone structure and impeccable clothes. Above all, he'd envied the careless ennui with which they viewed life and themselves.

For Bud, life had always been an intense grapple between himself and the forces that continually tried to beat him into submission. A battle that, for the most part, the forces had won.

He gazed at the house. It was a corruption of good taste, its ostentation counterbalancing its classic Greek Revival lines. It shouted what Bud was, what he despised about himself and what he'd sought a lifetime to cure—his Polish heritage.

This is the last time I'll walk through this door.

Once inside, Bud glanced at the stately mahogany grandfather clock Roya had given him for his fiftieth birthday, four years ago.

"Impeccable taste." He remembered his friends commenting on Roya's gift and the black-and-white formal party she'd given him as a surprise.

"So elegant. Refined." He'd heard those words, too, used to describe his beautiful and much younger wife.

Even now, it was the only thing Bud found to smile about. Those were precisely his reasons for marrying Roya. She was class. With a capital C.

Intricately tuned chimes rang out four o'clock.

"I have to hurry. There isn't much time."

Bud flung his black cashmere overcoat on the burgundy brocade settee in the foyer. It missed its mark and puddled on the white-and-gold marble floor.

"White and cream would have been a better choice, Bud. Gold is overdone," Roya had said when he first showed her the house. She'd been eighteen.

"I thought it looked rich."

"Flashy is not rich, Bud," she'd replied with the innate confidence he'd always lacked. "Gold is Las Vegas and we're Sutton Place." Even her smile was measured for the correct impact. Not too bright, yet not weak, either.

He knew then he needed her. Needed her to make him look good when they went out in town. Needed her to smooth his rough edges. Needed her to wash away the stench of poverty and fear that clung to him.

He unlocked the door to his study. Bud didn't trust anyone, not his wife and certainly not his two teenage daughters, Lucienne and Cynthia, in this, his most private domain. Even the cleaning woman who came twice a week was barred entrance. Bud cleaned the room himself. He knew better than to leave anything to chance.

He unlocked the drawers and searched them frantically.

"Shit."

Then he unlocked each of the three file drawers next to the desk. Shoving his hand to the flat drawer bottoms, he found nothing.

"How can it be missing? No one's been here."

He slammed the last drawer shut just as the phone rang.

Startled nearly out of his leather desk chair, he reached out and carefully turned up the volume on his answering machine.

Thank God I never went to voice mail.

The connection was clear, too clear for the caller to be using a cellular phone. A single breath was all he heard before the caller hung up.

He couldn't tell if the caller was male or female. But it didn't matter.

Both were just as deadly to him.

"Shit! How could I not have seen this coming?"

His nerves were raw as he shoved his hands through his thick white hair. He needed more time. Time to think. To plan. To escape.

"Christ, Bud. You stupid, stupid Polack! Escape to where? To what? This has been there all along and you didn't see it! Just how dumb can you be?"

He spied the closet door and was on his feet in seconds. He flipped on the light, yanked the door open and scoured the interior.

"It's gotta be here!"

Frantic tears burned angrily in his eyes. He tossed doctored old company files and foreign car magazines to the floor as he moved farther back into the closet. High school yearbooks, scrapbooks, a small wedding album and photographs of a Caribbean vacation with his mistress, Kitt, formed piles of debris at his feet.

His fingertips brushed against cold metal.

"Thank God."

He clutched the revolver, a prayer of benediction escaping his lips. He stretched his arm to the very back corner and found the box of bullets he would need.

He kicked the photographs of Kitt to the back of the closet. "Bitch!"

He turned out the light and shut the door.

Headlights from the street pirouetted across the paneled study wall.

"God! Not already!"

His fingers trembled as he jammed the bullets into the chamber. He sank to the floor, hiding in the increasing shadows as the last of the sun's rays died.

He could hear the car outside. Was it in his driveway or the one next door? He strained to hear his children's voices, but there was nothing.

He couldn't be sure the car door had even opened yet.

Fear paralyzed him. Were they coming for him? Or did he still have time?

He crawled along the carpeted floor close to the wall, through the doorway and out into the foyer. He could see through the narrow windows on either side of the front door that the car was not Roya's. It was small and dark, a compact of some sort parked between his house and the neighbor's on the street. Its headlights were off and the driver was watching the house. Waiting.

"Shit!"

Not for a second did he think they'd sent only one man. There had to be an accomplice. Or two.

Bud scrambled along the foyer floor to the back of the house where the kitchen overlooked the backyard, empty swimming pool and snow-covered redbrick terrace. He didn't dare turn on a light in case they were in the backyard.

His heart hammered against his chest. He couldn't catch his breath. Then he realized he was crying.

He was going to pee his pants.

"Oh, God. Oh, God."

His eyes shot to the backyard. He knew every inch of the land he owned, possessed it with pride. Against a screen of tall evergreens that Roya had strung with crystal Christmas lights, he saw a figure walk through the shadows, making its way across the yard.

Then he heard the front doorbell ring.

Terror clawed at him.

He fought for control and cocked the gun.

"This is one dumb Polack you'll never get!"

The doorbell rang again.

Another car entered the cul-de-sac, its headlights illuminating the front steps of the Pulaski house where the lone figure dressed in black stood, his hand gripping a metal object.

The winter air cracked with the gunshot blast.

Bud had been right; the sound traveled for miles.

2

Roya scanned the roomful of people, wondering why she'd even come here.

To please my family…again! That's why.

Her sister, Adrienne, had landed a job with a new PR-and-marketing firm at the end of August. For the past four months, Adrienne's voice literally trilled with enthusiasm about Freddie Lambert's persona, his penthouse apartment, his business savvy. Roya accepted the Christmas party invitation hoping that, once she met Adrienne's infamous boss, his mystique would be dispelled.

Judging by the sumptuous down sectional sofas slip-covered in white, Egyptian-motif-embossed fabric, the Lalique coffee tables and the hundreds of white roses, calla lilies and dendrobia bouquets resting on Roman pedestals, Adrienne's description had been understated.

Ordinarily, Roya would be fascinated with every nuance of decor, the food and the guests. But not today. Her despondency clashed with the holiday cheer, creating a combustible elixir.

A waiter offered her an oversize glass of white wine.

"Thanks," she said, thinking that it hurt to smile.

She swallowed deeply.

She should be window-shopping, dropping off the trunkful of old clothes for the Salvation Army, even seeing a shrink. Anything but this.

Then she saw Adrienne waving to her.

Her own arm felt like lead, but she waved back. And

drank more wine. "You can do this. You can do this," she told herself.

"Hello, darling!" Adrienne's beautiful, animated face bussed her cheek.

"Merry Christmas," Roya replied.

Is that really my voice? So flat. So lifeless.

"I didn't see you. Did you just get here?" Adrienne deposited her empty wineglass on a passing tray and skillfully retrieved a full one.

"Yes, just."

"You look lovely," Adrienne said.

Roya was used to Adrienne's compliments. She only said them in order to elicit one for herself. "And you're stunning. Is that new?" she asked, referring to the elegant black velvet coatdress Roya knew had been tailor-made to skim Adrienne's long, slim body.

Adrienne nodded. "Cost me my last commission. But it was worth it. Freddie told me I was the only woman here who had any style. I told him it was in my genes. Being born in Paris as we were."

Roya didn't hear her. She'd learned to tune Adrienne and her chaotic life problems out a long time ago.

Odd, she's not complaining about anything. I wonder when she gave that up?

Adrienne was still rambling. "Isn't this incredible! Do you have any idea who these people are?"

"Uh-uh," Roya replied, looking over the rim of her wineglass at the guests for the first time.

"Chicago's hottest media crowd. These are the shapers of what we'll see, think, buy and lust after next year. I think it was absolutely darling of Freddie to let me invite you."

"I shouldn't be here, Adrienne. I don't have any connection to these people."

"Are you nuts? I damn near sold my body to get this invitation. I need your support, Roya."

"My what?" Roya was confused.

"Freddie's top clients are here to be schmoozed and to schmooze. You handle this social kind of thing with more aplomb than I'll ever have. I figured you could take one half of the room and I'll take the other half." She laughed nervously, realizing she wasn't getting through to her younger sister. "Roya, if I show Freddie that I can get one of his new writers, or maybe the Indian psychologist who just hired us, placed on 'Oprah' or 'The Jenny Jones Show,' he'll be kissing my ass."

"As opposed to the other way around?"

Adrienne pulled up the back of her black velvet collar. "Damn it, Roya! This is my career. My future!" She paused a moment and then continued, "But it's Christmas, so I'm not going to take offense at what you just said."

Roya's cheeks flushed with embarrassment. "I'm sorry, Addie. I shouldn't be here. I'm in a foul mood and I needn't inflict myself on you."

"Can my ears be hearing right? Roya, Miss Sunshine herself, is *not* in a good mood?"

Roya belted back another slug of wine. "No." Her voice was riddled with an anger she'd never heard in herself before.

What's the matter with me? Serenity is my middle name.

Adrienne's eyes were filled with empathy and a touch of curiosity. "Well, blast away, little sister. It's not like I've never done that to you."

"You're different."

"You mean, I'm a bitch and you aren't," Adrienne said coolly.

"I didn't say that. And don't put words in my mouth."

Adrienne observed Roya for a long moment. "Okay. Then spit it out."

"What? Here? Now?"

"Why not? Who's to care? These folks are cutting deals...both for business and for who's gonna get laid tonight."

"God, Adrienne!" Roya glanced away at the crush of people standing near the floor-to-ceiling, wall-to-wall lake-view window. A tiny unwanted tear settled in the corner of her eye. "Must you always relate everything to sex?"

"I don't...always." Adrienne lowered her voice, then placed her hand on Roya's arm. "You're really upset. I'm sorry. This is unusual for me. You're the one who's always in control. In charge."

Roya removed the tear with the pad of her index finger. "Yeah. I know."

"So, what is it? Something with one of the girls?"

"It's not the girls."

"That only leaves Bud, and that's impossible. He's Mr. Perfect."

Another tear sprang in Roya's eye. She hugged herself and looked away.

"Shit! That's it, isn't it." Adrienne was aghast. "Not that I don't believe Bud can be a horse's ass, but I don't believe you'd see it."

"Just shut up, Adrienne! You have no right to talk! Your whole life has been trouble with men. And don't think I didn't see that new rock on your hand. When did you get it?"

Adrienne looked at the enormous square-cut diamond. There was neither elation nor disdain in her expression. She merely examined it for what it was—jewelry. "Last night."

"Congratulations."

"Thanks."

"So what number is this?"

"Fuck you!" Adrienne whirled around and was starting to walk away when Roya grabbed her arm.

"I'm sorry, Addie. Please, let's not fight."

Adrienne took a deep breath, then dropped her shoulders. "Okay." She turned back to Roya. "We really got off on a bad foot."

"I told you I didn't want to be here."

"But you came, anyway." *I should have known it wouldn't be for my sake.* "This tells me you *do* need to talk. What's he done?"

"Nothing."

Adrienne clenched her jaw in frustration; her words barely hissed through her teeth. "Okay...so what has he *not* done, then?"

"He...he doesn't sleep with me, for one thing."

"Well, I wouldn't worry about it. A couple weeks here or there—"

"Four months," Roya said, cutting her off.

"Shit."

"He comes home late. I can't find him at the office or on the loading docks during the day. He doesn't answer his cell phone."

Adrienne took a step back. "This isn't good."

"I think he's having an affair."

"Well—" Adrienne bit her tongue. Nothing would have pleased her more than to shoot down her brother-in-law, but she didn't. She remembered all too well how she'd felt when she'd discovered her first husband was sleeping with her college roommate.

Roya had had no sympathy for her then, no understanding. Not even a kind word. *"You picked him, Addie,"* Roya had said. *"You knew he had a reputation for womanizing when you married him."*

But Adrienne had chosen to love her sister despite her inability to empathize. Roya was seven years younger than herself and had married Bud Pulaski when she was eighteen—just a baby. What could she possibly know about life?

"Roya, just because it may look like he's having an affair, doesn't mean that he is. You've been married to the man for twenty years, for God's sake. He's never strayed, now, has he?"

"No."

"Well, then. There you are. It's probably nothing. Maybe he's doing something special for you and the girls for Christmas."

"Four months, Addie. He hasn't touched me in four months. Not a hug, a kiss, a touch of his hand. I feel like I'm all dried up, my blood turned to powder. I even have nightmares about it."

"Look, Bud is fifty-four. You're thirty-eight. Maybe he doesn't have the old drive anymore. Maybe he needs to see a doctor."

"Maybe." *Maybe not.* "But wouldn't he want to hold me, kiss me, even if he were…impotent? Wouldn't he want to make me feel wanted?"

Adrienne shook her head. "Sorry, it's hard for me to think of Bud ever being like that."

Roya scowled at her sister.

"Hey, I apologized before I said it." Adrienne glanced up and saw Freddie approaching. She flashed a charming smile. "Here comes Freddie. Please, buck up. For me?"

Isn't that what I always do? Buck up for you. Mama. Papa. Dad Pulaski? The girls. Why must I be the family caretaker while you go to parties, gathering men like Madame Bovary?

"Okay," Roya said, looking up at the short, trim man dressed in an expensive Italian black wool suit. He balanced an oversize martini glass in one hand and an Arturo Fuente cigar in the other. He switched the cigar to his left hand, took Roya's hand and kissed it in a courtly, theatrical manner.

"You bless my home with your beauty," he said, with an efficacy that belied his short stature.

He popped his head up and around like a cockatoo, checking on his guests and the service, his eyes orchestrating his employees' moves like a seasoned coach. But strangely, Roya did not feel neglected in the least. His magnetism was addictive.

"Thank you," Roya replied sweetly. "Your home is more than elegant, it's…" She was at a loss for words.

"Feng shui," he said, nodding approvingly. "You feel it, don't you? That comfortable, harmonious feeling? Proper alignment of energies in the home is key. Key!" Enthusiastically he pointed across the room. "The far northeast area is my money corner, ergo the ficus tree and white-satin-covered table. To the south is my happiness corner. I had a lot of fun with that. My feng shui designer told me I was lacking in one of my chakras. I needed alignment. So we settled on the frosted orange ornaments on the flocked tree. Just to get me through the holidays. And of course, I keep all the toilet lids closed."

"Excuse me?" Roya snapped her mouth shut. "I mean, why is that?"

"It's the key to my financial success. Otherwise, all my money would go down the drain, as it were."

"Oh." Roya's expression was blank.

Freddie leaned closer. "You don't reside in the city, do you, dear?"

"No. Schaumburg."

Freddie turned to Adrienne. "What I couldn't do with that face!"

Adrienne jumped in before Roya could speak. "She's not a model, Freddie. She's a housewife."

Freddie's face was incredulous. "It's positively a sin to waste our country's natural resources." He jerked his head at Adrienne. "Lou Hastings just arrived. It's show time, Addie. His book is sinking fast. Think you can keep him afloat?"

"I know I can," Adrienne said confidently.

Freddie puffed his cigar, smoke billowing over his head, and made his way through the throng looking like the little engine that could.

Adrienne squeezed Roya's arm affectionately. "Don't run off. This won't take too long, I promise. Besides, I want you to meet Gavin."

"Gavin?"

"My fiancé."

Roya looked into Adrienne's glittering blue eyes. "You're going to marry this one, aren't you, Addie?"

"Nah! I just wanted the excitement for the holidays. You know, wear the ring to midnight mass and all."

"But you don't go to church anymore."

"Not true! I always go to Christmas and Easter services."

"Addie, you will give him the ring back, won't you?"

"Of course! There's always more where it came from." She grinned mischievously. "Tiffany's." Then she laughed.

Roya shook her head. "I hope you don't hurt him."

"Gavin? Never. He's a heartbreaker. So beautiful it hurts my eyes to look at him. Trust me, I'll be getting out before he has a chance to hurt me. Isn't that what I always do?"

Roya sighed heavily. "Yeah, Addie. Always."

"There's an incredible buffet over by the windows. Try the marinated crab fingers. Outstanding." Adrienne glided away, her deep strawberry blond hair looking like wildfire against the shoulders of the black velvet, and all the while she was unaware of the admiring glances she harvested as she crossed the room.

Lake Michigan reflected rose-and-lavender-colored light from the setting sun as Roya approached the window. She realized she'd finished two enormous glasses of wine on a very empty stomach. If she was to meet her daughters in an hour at Water Tower Place for the last of their Christmas shopping, she'd be wise to fill her plate.

Standing at the end of the buffet table, with his back to the room and his cellular phone plastered to his ear, a tall, dark-haired man flung both arms high in the air in response to what he'd just heard at the other end of the line.

"I'm out! You hear me? Consider my contract canceled!" He gestured wildly again and angrily punched the end button.

"Oh, my God!" Roya cried out as her plate clattered to the highly polished hardwood floor.

He turned around.

The impossibly elegant woman with moonbeam blond hair gaped at him.

"Look what you've done!" she scolded.

"I?" He blinked his eyes, clearing the anger from them. "Oh, shit!"

Roya was covered from neck to waist with linguine in olive oil and basil, crab claws, salmon, and butter-and-caper sauce. "My dress is ruined!"

Quickly, he grabbed a linen napkin from the buffet table and anxiously, clumsily, began wiping down her chest. "I'm sorry. I didn't see you standing there."

A clump of smoked fish hit the floor.

He tried to catch the pellet-size capers with his left hand and grasped Roya's breast instead.

The olive oil and melted butter had seeped through the gold organza bodice, and the fabric had matted to her bare skin. She could feel the heat of his flesh against her as if she were naked.

Indignation transmuted to desire in a millisecond.

Roya held her breath. Too much wine had made her light-headed. She flushed.

He stopped abruptly, his words caught somewhere between the smoky intensity in her blue eyes and the hardening nipple he held in his hand.

There was only one thing he could think to do.

He kissed her.

He'd meant for it to be a segue to his offer to pay her cleaning bill. It was supposed to be a trifling peck, a holiday greeting no more binding than sending a Christmas card to a client.

He was a man of numbers, an accounting genius, a businessman's man. He'd never been married, not even engaged. Romance was an illusion, just like movies and fiction. He was firmly based in reality. Kisses meant nothing to him. Until now.

It wasn't her full lips, nor their slight tremble that turned his insides out. Nor was it the spice-and-vanilla scent she wore somewhere between her full breasts that invaded his mind. It wasn't her beauty, classic and flawless though it was.

It was the salty tear trickling down her cheek that sucked him from his world into hers. He drank it, consumed it. Harbored it, knowing she was part of him now.

He pulled her into him, mashing her body against his, forcing her to meld with him. His hands splayed her back, needing to memorize every inch of her.

He slanted his mouth over hers, invading her with his tongue. Claiming her. He needed to know her taste, her texture, her responses as he forced himself deeper, then deeper still.

He filled his lungs with her breath. When she moaned softly, he swallowed her submission. He would bring her into his world, just as she'd captured him...so effortlessly.

His mind was altered. Totally. Completely. His thoughts were garbled; he fought for clarity and could find none.

His hand tightened around her breast. She pushed her flesh against him, filling his palm, overflowing his fingers.

She was a stranger.

And yet, nothing had ever seemed more natural to him than filling himself with this woman.

Bits of conversation and sprinkles of business nomenclature fell upon Roya's ears. Vaguely, she remembered she was at a party. But what kind and where, she didn't know.

She'd lost her mind. She'd been transformed into a mass of physical, chemical, sexual response.

It made sense to her. It all made sense to her.

She'd been starved for affection, attention and sex for so long that her body had gone into a kind of sexual hypoglycemic shock. She craved this sweet man's kiss. Not even when she'd first met Bud had he ever kissed her with such possessiveness, such insatiable need.

This stranger kissed her as if she were the last woman on earth and he was going to die in the morning. The taste of her lips, the heated press of her breast against his hand, would be the last thing he remembered before death.

There was no other explanation.

Roya knew that no man in his right mind kissed like this. This wasn't simply a kiss; this was the death of the soul and then its rebirth.

For the rest of her life she knew she'd never forget this moment, never forget this man and his tumultuous passion.

She wished the kiss could last forever, but it couldn't—she was married to Bud.

"I think we should stop," Roya said, pulling away, relinquishing her need for more while hoping he would not agree with her.

His breath came in deep pants and his eyes refused to focus. He cupped her face because he didn't want to see anything beyond her lush swollen lips.

He kissed her lower lip and suckled it, feeling an odd sense of pride at realizing he was responsible for the satin-soft lights in her eyes.

"I'll buy you a new dress."

"That's impossible."

"Nothing is impossible," he breathed seductively.

"I bought it in Paris. It's an original."

"Yes, of course it is." He couldn't take his eyes off her face. He didn't give a damn about the dress, unless it was completely off her body. Which, at this moment, was what he wanted to do with it. Too easily he imagined her naked. It was an eerie sensation because he thought he knew exactly what she would look like. Every flaw. Every mole. Everything.

She took a step away but he pulled her back to him.

She let him.

Roya knew she was drunk. It was the only explanation for the heightened sensations she was feeling. She'd gone all her life without ever paying attention to the staccato beat of her heart or the slow ripple of heat that surged from the center of her body through her limbs to her face when she blushed. She'd never realized a nerve at her jawline jumped when she was anxious and she couldn't remember ever getting wet between her legs by just looking at a man.

"I have to go...." Roya said.

"No!" He cleared the passion from his throat. "I mean...I'll have it cleaned. I'll help you."

She took the napkin from him. "I'll do it myself." She looked around. "Do you know where I'd find the powder room?"

"No, I've never been here before."

"Me, neither." She didn't want to look at him any longer. It was too dangerous. She took a step backward, then two.

His arms were tense, the muscles tight. He wanted to hold her close. He took a deep breath and released her. "You're coming back?"

Reality hit her like ice water. She had to leave. Right now. If she didn't, she'd be to blame for what happened next. And something would happen. She knew it in every bone in her body. She was more than vulnerable right now; she was pissed at Bud. She was hurt and neglected. She needed someone. It was no wonder she'd reacted to this man the way she had. She was starved for affection and desperate for attention.

An hour from now, she'd be back to her old self.

"Sure, I'll be back. You'll wait here, won't you?" she asked him.

"I'm not moving an inch." His smile was sincere. Open. Warm.

He was the most lethal man she'd ever met, the kind of man who could *matter* to her.

"Great," she said, then turned and left.

Roya dabbed at the oil-soaked bodice with the napkin as she made her way through the crowd. She found Adrienne just breaking away from her client.

"I have to go," Roya said anxiously, glancing back to see him watching her.

"What the hell happened to your dress?"

"I'll tell you later. I have to meet the girls. Will I see you for Christmas dinner?"

"Sure. It's okay I'm bringing Gavin, right?"

"Huh?" Roya could feel his eyes on her. She had the oddest sensation that somehow he knew she was ducking out.

That's crazy. He can't read my mind. We're strangers....

"My fiancé?" Adrienne was clearly agitated with Roya's lack of interest in her engagement.

"Was I mistaken or is the powder room next to the front door?"

"It is."

"And where is my coat?"

"In the closet next to the door. The valet will help you. Thanks for coming." She clipped off her words.

Roya kissed her sister's cheek. "I'm dying to meet Gavin. Really. It's just that I'm flustered over my dress."

"Yeah, sure," Adrienne replied. "Hug the girls for me, okay?"

"I will." Roya forced a smile and rushed toward the closet.

Nick watched her move through the crowd, stop for a moment and discuss something with a strawberry blond woman and then move toward the powder room. Without taking his eyes off her, he grabbed two flutes of champagne from a waiter. He was already wondering if he shouldn't call for dinner reservations. Rosebud on Rush was close.

He lifted the champagne to his lips and abruptly halted. "Damn it. No!"

He bolted through the crowd.

The front door opened, then closed. She was gone.

He finally made it to the front door, then rushed to the outer hall, then to the express elevator. But he was too late; the elevator had already reached the street.

He went back inside the penthouse and made his way carefully to the wall of windows. He strained to catch a glimpse of her exiting through the front doors to catch a cab, but no one emerged.

He realized she'd driven her own car.

Quickly, he scanned the crowd, looking for the strawberry blond his moonbeam goddess had spoken to just prior to leaving. But there was no sign of her so he surmised she must have left as well.

He sank into the down sectional and stared at the view of Chicago's Magnificent Mile. Christmas lights twinkled as streetlights came on. This high up he had the impression he was suspended in space.

Or heaven. That's what it had felt like kissing her.

He shook his head and derisively laughed out loud. The twenty-something redhead sitting across from him looked at him as if he were nuts.

He wasn't crazy. He'd just screwed up his whole life in the matter of one hour. Not only had he quit his new job over a matter of principle, but he'd let the woman of his dreams slip in and out of his life like a vapor.

No, he wasn't nuts. Not yet, anyway.

3

Roya stood at the Marshall Field's cashier's station thinking about the stranger who'd kissed her less than an hour ago. She touched her bottom lip with her tongue; a small blister had risen where he'd pressed her lips too harshly against her teeth.

It wasn't a dream. He was real.

Her hand was trembling as she wiped a thin veil of nervous perspiration from her upper lip.

What's worse, my feelings were…are…real.

"Ma'am?" A woman's voice broke into her thoughts.

Roya gave the saleswoman a bewildered look. Then she realized what the woman had said.

"Of course my card is good. I just used it downstairs not twenty minutes ago."

"I'm sorry, ma'am." The woman looked over the rim of her bifocals. "It happens at this time of year. Purchases add up quickly, you know." She handed the store credit card back to Roya. "Do you have another card? Visa, perhaps?"

"I didn't know Field's took Visa," Roya said with relief.

"What's the matter, Mom?" Cynthia asked.

Roya smiled at her nineteen-year-old daughter. "Just a mix-up, I'm sure. Where's your sister?"

"Looking at the sale sweaters," Cynthia said. "Her baby-sitting money is burning a hole in her pocket." Placing her hand over the sage green blouse and matching suede vest, she asked, "Do you think Aunt Adrienne will like this? She's so picky."

"She's discerning, dear." Roya smoothed her daughter's blond bangs out of her eyes and laughed. "At least that's what she tells me all the time."

"So, tell us about her new fiancé. You met him, right? Is he gorgeous? Or no? Did you like him? Is she bringing him for Christmas dinner?"

Roya rolled her eyes. "Please, Cynthia, one question at a time. I swear, it seems I've been saying that since the day you opened your mouth."

Cynthia huffed. "Mom, is he coming or not?"

"Yes." Roya looked up as the saleswoman picked up the ringing telephone. She could tell from the woman's perplexed expression that something was wrong.

"Do you think she'll marry this one, Mom?"

Roya didn't like the way the woman picked up her Visa card between her forefinger and thumb, as if it had lice. "Why don't you ask her, dear?" Roya replied halfheartedly, her eyes glued to the saleswoman's face.

"I'm sorry, this isn't working, either."

"I don't understand," Roya replied, looking askance at her credit card.

"You might want to call them when you get home. The card has been denied."

"Denied?" Roya hadn't a clue what the woman was talking about.

"You're either over your limit or the card has been canceled for some reason."

Cynthia signaled to her sister, Lucienne, who quickly joined them.

"What's up?" Lucienne asked.

"Mom's credit cards are maxed," Cynthia said, as if she'd owned dozens and knew quite well what her mother was experiencing.

"Is that all?" Lucienne pulled out her wallet. "How much do you need, Mom?"

"I doubt you have enough to pay for this," Roya replied, and looked back at the saleswoman. "Could you hold this for me until tomorrow when I cash a check? It's a surprise for my sister."

"Sure. Just write your name and number here. I'll hold it for twenty-four hours, but then it will have to go back out on the floor."

Roya's smile was grateful. "Thanks. My sister told me explicitly that this was what she wanted."

I owe her at least this much for being so short with her. And for my behavior this afternoon. God only knows what she's been told by now!

"It's lovely," the saleswoman replied. "And quite expensive." She winked at Roya. "It's nice to give something special at Christmas."

"Yes, it is. Thank you for understanding."

"You're welcome, Mrs. Pulaski," the saleswoman said, and attached Roya's name card to the hanger.

The girls huddled around their mother as they walked toward the down escalator.

"You must have spent a bundle on us for Christmas, huh, Mom? Fess up. What did you get us?" Lucienne laughed, elbowing her mother.

Shaking her head, Roya replied, "That's what I don't understand. I was so busy helping out at church this year and the Cancer Christmas Ball that I didn't buy anything yet. Your formal for the Christmas dance was your big gift, Lucienne, which we discussed. I was going to give Cynthia money for next semester because that's what you asked for, right?" She turned to her eldest daughter.

"Right," Cynthia replied. "Maybe Daddy got you something smashing like...pearls or a fur coat! God! I hope he didn't actually do it. My activist friends will be horrified."

"Oh, who cares about *them*," Lucienne replied, her eyes brightening at the thought of the white mink coat her father had been promising her mother for years.

"I've explained to him that I'd be uncomfortable in a

fur these days, but he's so old-fashioned," Roya said as they reached the main floor. "My black wool is practical."

Lucienne cringed. "Oomph! You didn't use *that* word, did you?"

Cynthia's chin lifted indignantly. "And what's the matter with being practical? It seems to me that everyone in this family could use a little more practicality."

"Speak for yourself," Lucienne quipped. "Just because you're taking accounting this semester doesn't mean you can dictate how I spend my money!"

"Don't argue, girls. As soon as we get home your father will straighten out this mess. I'm sure it's nothing."

Just then Roya's cellular phone rang and she stopped to answer it.

"Roya, where are you?" Adrienne asked.

"At Water Tower. We were just leaving. I have to get home and fix dinner...."

"The hell you do! We need to talk. Now. I'll meet you for coffee."

"But, Addie, dear, I have the *girls* with me."

"Forget the camouflage. I'll meet you at the Bistro on Ten."

"Okay," Roya agreed reluctantly, and hung up.

"What's going on, Mom?" Cynthia asked.

Oh, nothing much. Your mother just made a spectacle of herself in full view of every journalist in the city, that's all. You'll probably see my face on the cover of Chicago Magazine *kissing a strange man. That's all.*

"Adrienne wants to meet us for coffee. We'll leave the car in the parking garage and take a cab. It'll be faster."

Adrienne drummed her red lacquered nails on the pink linen cloth. Because she was seven years older than Roya, there were things Adrienne knew about men, life and herself. For instance, she had concluded that it was not the institution of marriage that was at fault for her two failed marriages, but that her "men picker" was on the fritz. On her fortieth birthday, after ten years of being divorced, she'd become engaged. She broke up with Henry the next day. Every year since, Adrienne got engaged, then backed out. Now that Gavin had asked her to marry him, she was feeling flat-out petrified.

It bothered her that Roya had picked up on that fact without even meeting Gavin or seeing them together.

Adrienne was the family fuck-up. Roya, on the other hand, had been nominated for sainthood the day she'd married Bud. Roya was the one with the stable marriage, the suburban mansion—ugly as it was—the two perfect children and a life that all the women's magazines of the nineties catered to. Back in the eighties, Adrienne's career-oriented life-style and unattached marital status had been in vogue. Suddenly, the world changed, the pendulum swung, and marriage and babies were back in. The world was *committed.*

Adrienne felt out-of-sync. And just a bit lost.

She'd been so used to chastising herself for her erroneous decisions, that Roya's problems hadn't impacted her until *after* her sister had left the party.

Adrienne was a permanent student in the school of hard knocks, but Roya was an innocent. She hadn't a clue what real life was about. And from the rumors floating around Freddie's, Adrienne realized her little sister was in a great deal of trouble.

Cynthia and Lucienne dashed out of the taxi, waving jubilantly at Adrienne through the garden window.

"God bless 'em," Adrienne said with a wistful flicker of awe. "They still love me. No matter what."

"Aunt Adrienne!" Lucienne swooped into her outstretched arms. "I've missed you!"

Adrienne embraced each of the girls. "My God, I don't know which of you is prettier!"

Cynthia pushed her wire-rimmed glasses up the bridge of her nose. "Don't say things you don't mean, Aunt Adrienne."

"Sorry, I forgot. Let me ask…a four point?"

"You got it!" Cynthia slapped Adrienne's high-five sa-
lute.

"Amazing there's that many brains in our family,"
Adrienne joked, looking at Roya's pride-filled expression.

"I never doubted it for a minute," Roya said with a
knowing smile on her lips.

"Mom says you're engaged. Are you gonna keep
him?"

"Oh, God! Lucy!" Cynthia rolled her eyes.

"Well, I want to know." Lucienne playfully slapped
her sister's forearm, then turned back to her aunt. Her
eyes filled with anticipation.

"I'm…I'm thinking about it." She kept her eyes riveted
on Roya. "What with marriages falling apart the way they
do, it makes me wonder if it's worth the bother."

Roya pretended to study her menu.

"So, what's it like knowing so many men want you?"
Lucienne asked, planting her elbow on the table and
plopping her chin in her hand.

"Lucy!" Cynthia groaned.

Just then the waitress came to take their order. The girls
wanted to see the dessert tray, which gave Adrienne a
chance to sequester Roya in the ladies' room.

"I suppose you want an explanation," Roya said sheepishly.

"Actually, no. What you do with your life is your business. However, I just want to make a comment and then
I'll shut up until such time as you seek out my advice."

"You're going to tell me I'm a married woman and I
had no business…"

"No, that's not what I had in mind at all."

Roya's eyes were huge. "You're kidding! That's what
I'd say to you."

"I know. But you give lousy advice." Adrienne smiled.
"Look, you've got some problems with Bud. Big ones, I

think. If it's possible, and I'm not saying it is, try to work that out first before you go any further with your affair."

"I'm not having an affair."

"That wasn't your boyfriend today?"

"No! I never saw him before in my life. I don't even know his name!"

Adrienne's eyes were skeptical. "Some guy is practically swallowing my sister whole in front of half of Chicago and you expect me to believe you just met him?"

"Yeah."

"You never saw him before?"

"Not till Freddie's."

"Well, shit, girl. What do you do with guys when you've been introduced?"

"Addie..." Roya cast her a warning glare. "I'm not in the habit of having lovers. There's only been Bud. Until today. And that was just a kiss."

"*Just* a kiss? From what I heard, you two coulda steamed clams." She put her hands on her hips. "When are you seeing him again?"

Roya threw her hands in the air in exasperation. "I don't know him! I'll never see him again. Don't want to see him again. It was a mistake. I was drunk."

"Two glasses of wine does not make anyone *that* stupid, *that* fast."

"It was my empty stomach."

"Try your empty heart."

Roya's eyes held her sister's. "Okay. That, too," she replied glumly. "I don't know what to do."

"For now, go home, give Bud a blow job and try to get him to come around. Guys are weird. He'll snap out of it. Maybe he's stressed because of business."

"That's impossible. Things have never been better, he tells me."

Adrienne didn't like what she was hearing. She'd heard it too many times before. Lived it herself. She knew she shouldn't do it, but she stepped out on thin ice and asked, "Have you caught him with anyone?"

"No. It's just a feeling."

"I know that kind of feeling. There's only one way to get over it. Hire a private investigator."

"Oh, God. This is all too…"

"Real?"

"Yeah," Roya groaned. "Addie, mind me asking something?"

"Shoot."

Roya took a deep breath. "Do you know who that man was today?"

"The kissing bandit? No. But I'm trying to find out how he was invited. Somebody had to know him. He's not in the media. Freddie said he invited reps from a variety of up-and-coming local companies to broaden our client base. It was a long list. Don't worry, we'll find out."

"Thanks, I appreciate it." She looked at her reflection in the mirror; her gaze penetrated the glass, seeing inside her own soul. "Nothing like this has ever happened to me before."

Adrienne watched her sister. *And I've never seen you like this before. Not even when you first met Bud.*

As if transported back in time, Adrienne remembered the night Roya was standing on the stage at the Blackstone Theater wearing a black-and-white gown, radiantly beautiful, accepting the audience's applause.

"Please, there is no need for all this," she said into the handheld microphone. "Your accolades for the actors are warranted, but not for me," she said. "I have failed you and Jimmy Johnson."

Jimmy Johnson was the six-year-old boy Roya had read about in a neighborhood newspaper. Jimmy needed kidney dialysis and his parents had no insurance or money to pay for his medical care. Roya's heart had gone out to the boy; it had been her idea to put together a fund-raiser to help defray Jimmy's medical costs. The family had readily agreed. Roya coerced and cajoled her high school drama club into putting on a show. Addie had made her debut into the world of public relations and promotions, and boasted that she knew the owner of the Blackstone and could get the theater for free. Maybe she could get some of the new kids and comics at Second City to donate their time. Roya jumped on the idea, both naiveté and dauntless courage driving her.

"How do we get people to come?" Roya had asked Addie.

"We send invitations to every wealthy theater buff in town. To business owners trying to break into society. To attorneys, and especially to doctors. This is what I do. I have my hands on the best lists in town. Man! Who would ever have thought addressing all those invitations last Christmas for the Heart Foundation Ball would come in so handy?"

"You have their list?"

Addie nodded. "I copied it."

"Isn't that illegal?"

"Nope." Addie grinned. "Just unethical."

It had gone so well—until the final tally of expenditures and ticket sales backstage that night. "We're short," Roya announced sadly.

"Impossible!" Addie had replied.

"We only raised ten thousand dollars and the Johnson's need much more. Just to pay their back bills they need five thousand more this month. And it's all my fault."

"How can you say that? Look what you did. What you accomplished! For someone fresh from her high school graduation four months ago, I'd say you did darned good!"

Roya's eyes were sad as she lifted her chin determinedly. "There's only one thing to do. I'll have to tell the patrons the truth."

"What?"

Roya whisked away from Addie before she had a chance to stop her.

"No!" Adrienne yelled out after her. "Don't do that! Lie to them. They'll never know the difference!"

The audience had quieted down as Roya told them the dismal results. "I'm afraid that, as your chairperson, I have failed you and the Johnson family. It was my job to help them. But it wasn't enough."

"How short are you?" a man's voice from the audience asked.

"Five thousand," Roya blurted. "A hundred thousand," she said more softly.

The man rose to his feet. "Then I'll donate the five thousand you need."

Addie was watching from the wings and gasped aloud.

Roya's hand flew to her throat. "You can't be serious, Mr., er, uh…"

"Pulaski," Bud said, smiling charmingly, adjusting his black tuxedo tie. "And I'm most serious." He reached in his jacket pocket and withdrew his checkbook. He held it high and looked around at the audience. "I challenge every person here to dig a little deeper. What do you say?"

Another man stood. "I'm with you. I'll give a thousand."

"I don't have much, but I have a hundred," an elderly woman said.

Addie and Roya couldn't believe it. Another two dozen people stood up shouting contribution numbers as if they were at an auction. The energy in the room was electric.

And Bud Pulaski was in the center of it, making it happen.

After the crowd had left, Bud came up to Roya and handed her his check.

"How can I thank you?" Roya asked, clearly still stunned at the turn of events.

"Have dinner with me."

"I beg your pardon?" Roya asked.

He'd glanced at Addie, then back at Roya. "Your sister needs to tell you how this fund-raising world works."

Addie was immediately on the defensive. "It certainly doesn't work like you're thinking," she sneered.

Roya leveled cool eyes on Bud. "Adrienne needn't tell me anything, Mr. Pulaski. You've told me all I want to hear. Thank you for your contribution. We'll send you the pertinent paperwork tomorrow for your files." She started to walk away.

"You have me all wrong. My intentions are honorable," Bud called out.

"Really?" she asked, looking back at him over her shoulder as if she'd forgotten him already.

"I plan to marry you," he said boldly, with a flashing smile.

"Preposterous!" Addie shouted at him, then quickly looked at her sister. "Any man who says something so insane has ulterior motives, Roya."

"And do you know anything about my motives?" he challenged.

"I certainly…well, no, I guess I don't."

"Addie, you're behaving so strangely. Do you know Mr. Pulaski?"

"Know him?" Addie fumbled a split second, then regained her control. "Not at all."

Roya was as cool as a spring breeze off the lake and nonplussed as she faced him, gently clasping her hands at her waist.

Addie was taken aback with Roya's coyly played poker hand.

"You seem quite sure of yourself, Mr. Pulaski, considering that I'm only eighteen and you're almost twice my age."

He chuckled. "Old enough to know what I want."

Adrienne waited for the fireworks between them to erupt, for sexual signals and gushes of excitement to be sent from one of them. But Roya seemed to accept Bud as if he were her fate.

"You'll need to meet my father, then," she said simply.

"Fine. How about tomorrow night? Say eight-thirty at the Pump Room? You'll all be my guests, of course."

"Of course," Roya replied.

"Good." He smiled and then walked away.

Adrienne realized her own heart had stopped beating. "Are you out of your mind?"

"No," Roya said with a smile.

"But, but...you don't know this guy from Adam. You know nothing about him. What if you don't get along? What if he's not Catholic? What if he's a crook? What if he's a bad kisser, for God's sake?" Adrienne gestured excitedly for emphasis.

"Calm down." Roya glanced down the center aisle to see Bud leaving through the exit doors. "He knows everything about me, can't you tell? He knows I was looking for a knight in shining armor. He knows how to please me. He knows I want to help others with my life. He knows I like the theater and that I'm good at what I do. He knows I'm eighteen and capable of taking on a strong challenge like this fund-raiser. Best of all, he owns a tuxedo," she said, laughing.

"You're nuts!" Adrienne said, grabbing Roya by the shoulders. "You're really considering this man's proposal."

Roya sighed wistfully, her first sign of attraction to Bud. "Yes, I suppose I am. It's quite flattering to have an older, more worldly man interested in you, isn't it?"

Addie let go of her as if burned. "I...wouldn't know. Don't care to find out, either. I like 'em young and energetic, and with a heck of a lot more romantic fiber than that guy!"

"Addie, you're getting awfully worked up over my love life."

"Roya, this was a proposal. Not a love life."

Roya was beaming. "To me, it's a love life."

Addie shook her head. "All these years I've waited for someone, something, to rattle your cage, and even when you get proposed to, you act like nothing has happened. Mama is right. You're unshakable. A real rock."

Until now, Adrienne thought, looking at the plethora of emotions in her sister's eyes. This man today had rattled Roya's cage but good.

Adrienne knew she was pushing things, but she willingly stepped farther onto the ice. "It was just a holiday kiss, Roya. Mistletoe stuff. No big deal, right?"

"No. It wasn't. I can still feel him holding me." She touched her mouth; her fingers trembled. "I can still taste him. It's like he's still here with me." She hugged herself. "Like he's holding me."

Adrienne dropped her head and shook it. "I was afraid of this."

Roya hugged herself tighter to ward off Adrienne's warning. "I'll forget him, won't I, Addie?" There was desperation and sadness in her eyes.

Adrienne wished she could gather Roya in her arms, but her sister wouldn't have understood the gesture, having never been one for affectionate displays. It was a curse of the entire Monier family. Adrienne had always been the misfit, wanting and needing affection by the bucketfuls. Therefore, there didn't seem to be any harm in adding a lie to her list of misdemeanors.

She looked at Roya, pretending a hope she didn't feel. "You'll forget, kid. We all do."

4

The roses arrived; they were red.

Kitt took the vase from the delivery boy and tipped him a dollar.

"Thanks, ma'am," the red-haired teenager said. "Is it your birthday?"

"No," she replied dourly.

"An anniversary, then?"

Glaring at him, she said, "Get outta my face, will you?"

"So-o-ory," he said, screwing his face into a gnarled mass of discontent.

Recognizing his expression as mimicking her own, Kitt slammed the door. "Asshole!" she muttered.

She put the flowers in the center of a glass-topped coffee table where she'd already cleared a place. Kitt knew Bud would send her roses today. It was his way of making up after a fight. Bud was so painfully predictable, he often crossed the edge of boring. She'd never tell him that, though. She wasn't stupid.

"Sixteen, seventeen, eighteen..." She began counting the expensive South American roses. She always demanded these particular flowers because it took over a week for the buds to open to dramatically large burgundy blossoms. They reminded her of the full-blown, sexual flower that she was. It meant a great deal to Kitt that Bud thought of her like that. Red, open, bursting with orgasmic pride. That's how it had always been with them since the day she'd lost her virginity to him when she was sixteen and he'd been eighteen.

"Twenty-six, twenty-seven…"

Back at Our Lady of Mount Carmel High School on Chicago's West Side, Kitt had been the prom queen, beautiful, popular and crazy mad in love with Robert "Bud" Pulaski. He was the star quarterback, and in those days no one dared call him a "dumb jock." They were devoted to each other.

Even the nuns knew they were screwing. Hell, they couldn't take their hands off each other in the halls between classes. She dreamed of only one thing—being Mrs. Bud Pulaski.

When Bud graduated and the clamor of football fame grew silent, he quickly realized that money bought adoration. While Kitt finished high school, Bud drove a truck for his father's small company. He wisely invested his salary back into the company, building it, expanding the number of trucks and delivery routes.

Kitt began a lifelong career of waiting for Bud.

For thirty-six years she had waited. She was fifty-two years old and she was still waiting to become Mrs. Bud Pulaski.

Their argument last night had been their most violent to date. He'd slapped her, and she'd landed a few blows herself. But that was nothing new for them. Neither was the nearly sadistic lovemaking that always followed the name-calling, tears and apologies.

Only this time had been different. This time Kitt had done what she'd promised herself she'd never do. She'd played her trump card, and she'd miscalculated.

Instead of falling to his knees in awe at the ironic twist of fate that had kept their lives entwined for more than three decades, Bud had left. He told her that he would never see her again, that he despised her, hated her. That he hated himself.

"Thirty-four, thirty-five, thirty-six." Kitt counted the last rose. "One for every year of our lives together. God, in heaven, he forgives me!" Her hand was shaking as she plucked the envelope from the center of the roses.

"How odd." The envelope was not the usual florist's enclosure card, but blue stationery with a wax seal on the back stamped with a *B*.

An ominous feeling descended upon her like a dark cloud. She instantly sat on the sofa as she opened the note.

Kitt,
In all these years I've never written to you and now find myself struggling over how to begin this letter. I cannot call you "dear" because there is nothing dear about you—yet you are the only person I can turn to now. I keep asking myself, "What twisted game has God been playing with us?" My answer, of course, is that God had nothing to do with any of it. All this was your doing. And yet, I love you. Therefore, I cannot fault you. You have pushed me beyond my limits, and we all have limits, Kitt. Even you. I cannot do as you ask. I cannot marry you. Ever.

I refuse to hurt my wife. She's done nothing to deserve the heartbreak or pain a divorce would cause.

All I can say is that I have made my choice. I hope you will forgive me. I hope God will forgive us both.

I have loved you...always.

Bud

Kitt read the note three more times, but none of the words registered. Bud never meant what he said. That was one of his most endearing qualities. A million times he'd vowed he'd never come back, but he always did. Bud was a creature of habit, a man of superhuman desires. He would come back with his tail between his legs, begging her to take him back. And she would. She always did. She was a creature of habit, too.

Crumpling the note in her hand, Kitt walked to the picture window. She looked down on the city of Chicago and out to the glittering lake beyond.

She knew how to get to Bud and he knew how to turn her screws. That's the way it was for them. What was it he always said to her? *"We're just two peas in a pod."*

Kitt's life with Bud had always been a nightmare, but it was the only dream she had.

5

→ ←

Blood was everywhere.

It looked to Roya as if some evil phantom had painted a mosaic of blood and bits of flesh on the sliding glass doors, ceiling, walls and floor underneath the kitchen table where Bud's body lay.

The only thing not red was the gray metal of the .357 Magnum lying next to what remained of Bud's head.

"Da-a-ady!" Cynthia screamed.

"Mo-o-omy!" Lucienne covered her ears and dropped to the floor, curling up into a fetal position.

"Bud? Bud?"

Is that you, Bud?

Roya's shock was immobilizing her, forcing her to stare at the bloody mess around her.

She felt suspended in a place of nightmarish emotions and horrific surroundings. She was not of this earth; she was in hell.

She realized Adrienne was right. She'd forgotten all about the kiss. Even the stranger's face was obliterated by the sea of blood and brain matter on which she stood.

She didn't think to call the police. What good could they do?

Roya felt her current life ending. It was as if she were being sucked into a dark vortex, with unfamiliar emotions whirlpooling around her. She was Dorothy about to meet the Wizard of Oz.

She realized Bud had created this chaos. *What were you*

thinking, Bud? Were you trying to punish me? Destroy yourself?

Unbelievable as it was to her sense of logic, she reached out into the space around her, thinking she could touch the emotions and thoughts that had led him to take his life.

Dark, clawlike shadows hung from the ceiling. She recognized them as despair.

Panic was a thick brace of cold, steel gray light that clamped around her heart, strangling her soul.

Just as she believed she would die from the intense cold she felt, white-hot fires of inexplicable anger—Bud's anger—funneled toward her, bent on burning her to a cinder. She wanted to kill, yet be killed.

His dying thoughts surrounded her as if she were the enemy. She could almost hear him sobbing and cursing.

How could your life be so terrible that you would want to leave me, Bud? I've always thought our life together was heaven.

Until recently.

And this anger. Was it directed at her? And if not, who? Didn't he know he had options? Why choose suicide? Why now? Why? Why?

"*Why!*" Roya screamed as loud as her lungs would allow.

The spinning stopped abruptly as she was pulled back to reality by the invading sound of Cynthia's demanding sobs.

"Mom! What's happened to Daddy?" Cynthia shook Roya's shoulders. "What's the matter with you? Why can't you hear me? Talk to me, Mom!"

Roya heard both her daughters' pleas and cries of disbelief.

"Daddy…" Lucienne's voice warbled like a dying, fragile bird. "Da-a-ady!" she screamed, and threw her hands over her head.

Roya grabbed both her daughters and pulled them out

of the kitchen, away from the deathly sight and smell, into the foyer and around the corner to Bud's office.

I can do this. Be calm. Keep yourself together, Roya. Think of the children. Don't think about Bud...not now. Maybe later.

Her hand was trembling as she picked up the phone and dialed 911.

She was stunned at the calm steadiness in her voice, as she said, "This is Mrs. Bud Pulaski at 415 Orange Blossom Lane. My husband has shot himself. Send someone...anyone...right away."

"Did you check the body for vital signs?" a husky, female voice asked.

"No."

"Can you tell if he's alive?"

"No. Bud's dead."

"I'm dispatching an ambulance and police unit immediately."

Roya could hear the woman giving codes and her address to someone over a radio. She heard their disjointed crackling response. The intervening moment yawned in front of her.

Bud's dead. I won't be able to talk to him.

This is so crazy, Bud! How could you do this? Leaving me here alone? Leaving the girls like this? Without any warning. How goddamn selfish can you be?

She wanted to rail at him, vent an anger she'd never known before. But she couldn't. The woman on the other end of the phone was asking more questions.

I must stay alert.

"I have a few routine questions to ask you, Mrs. Pulaski, for your safety. Are there any signs of a stranger in the house?"

"No." *But then I didn't look.*

"Did you notice any sign of forced entry?"

"No." *The back door was unlocked. Bud always locked the back door. Did he know them? Just who were these people?*

"Stay calm, Mrs. Pulaski."

"I am." *I'm numb.*

"Stay on the line, Mrs. Pulaski."

"I will," Roya replied, and clutched Cynthia's hand.

Lucienne turned away from her mother and vomited on the Persian rug. "Oh, God."

"It's all right, sweetheart. Cyn, help your sister to the bathroom."

Lucienne tried to reach for Cynthia's outstretched hand, but her arm remained at her side. Panic riddled her body. "Mommy...I can't move!" Lucienne cried. "I can't feel anything! Am I dead, too?"

Shock. We're all in shock. That's what it is. I must remember that. Lucienne is alive. Cynthia is alive. I am alive. Bud is dead. That's right. Bud's dead.

Putting her arm around Lucienne, she pulled her close. "You're fine. Really. You don't have to go to the bathroom if you don't want. Stay here with me."

The woman on the end of the phone came back. "Mrs. Pulaski, there's a squad car not far from you. He'll be there in less than five minutes. Don't touch anything. Stay calm. Do you want me to remain on the line with you?"

"No. My daughters are here with me." Her voice cracked with fear.

"How old are they, Mrs. Pulaski?"

"Nineteen and sixteen," Roya answered, knowing the woman had been carefully trained to handle shock victims. She noticed how practiced and cool the woman's voice sounded. She continued asking Roya questions that didn't seem important to Roya under the circumstances, but perhaps they were. Maybe she was taking notes. Maybe Roya shouldn't be talking with the woman at all. Was she supposed to call an attorney? Maybe she should call Dr. Winston for the girls. Did they need a sedative? What if they weren't all right? What if they were severely traumatized by this? What if none of them ever recovered?

God damn you to hell for doing this, Bud Pulaski! God damn you!

Whirling blue-and-red lights from two squad cars mingled with the festive Christmas lighting of the neighboring houses. It was an eerie juxtaposition of the blessed and the profane. Only the Pulaski house was still dark.

"They're here," Roya said into the receiver, and hung up. *Oh, I forgot to say goodbye.*

Cynthia walked over to the floor-to-ceiling study window. "We forgot to turn on the Christmas tree, Mom," she said with frightening placidity. She went to the living room and plugged in the crystal lights on the ten-foot tree. "That's better," she whispered to herself.

Roya watched the front lawn as uniformed men bolted from the cars and raced to the front door. The strobing white lights of an ambulance followed and another official car followed it. The cacophony of sirens sounded the alert to the neighborhood. The Jamisons' front door opened first. Mari and Paul dashed down the steps still holding their white dinner napkins in their hands. They raced down the snowy sidewalk and across the cul-de-sac.

One of the policemen held Mari back, but even from a distance, Roya could see confusion and horror in Mari's face. Paul put his arms around his wife and held her close to him.

It was a common gesture between husband and wife. Roya remembered it well.

They just want to help. Like I would want to help them if they were in trouble. Trouble? How could we be in trouble? I'm Mrs. Bud Pulaski. We've never had any trouble.

Cynthia's tears dried first. Being the eldest, it was her responsibility to help her mother through this crisis. Her father had always had high expectations for her, and her sterling academic record proved she'd always been up to the challenge. He would want her to fill his shoes, be an adult. She just hadn't realized she would have to do it so fast. An hour ago she was a college freshman. She suddenly felt old, very old.

Cynthia opened the front door for the police. "Good evening, Officers," she said robotically. "My mother is waiting for you in my father's study." She motioned to her left.

The men seemed like giants as they walked by her, their uniforms, patrol sticks and gun holsters contemporary armor against ancient evil. She felt oddly secure, as if their strength and authority could put her life back together again.

Before she closed the door, two paramedics came up the walk with a stretcher. They were followed by a stocky man dressed in a business suit and wool coat. A strong wind wailed through the bare tree branches, making a deathly sound. It seemed an appropriate song for this night, Cynthia thought, looking into the deeply lined, bleak face of the dark-haired man in front of her.

"I'm Lieutenant Dutton. Homicide." He extended his hand.

Placing her hand in his, Cynthia was surprised not to feel the press of his flesh against hers. "My father killed himself."

"It would seem so." He dropped her hand and signaled with a slight nod to one of the paramedics. "This one feels like ice."

Cynthia shook her head. "I'm not cold."

"Did you make the phone call?"

"No, my mother did. She's in there with the others."

One of the policemen walked out of the study. Roya was a step behind with Lucienne huddled next to her like a nursing kitten. "Lieutenant, this is Mrs. Pulaski. She says the body's in the kitchen."

"I'm Lieutenant Sam Dutton, Mrs. Pulaski. How are you doing? Do you want one of the paramedics to check you out?"

"I'm fine, really," she lied. "The girls…"

"I understand."

Cynthia was having none of it. "I'm perfectly okay, Lieutenant," she said indignantly.

The lieutenant turned to the officers and whispered orders to them. One man went into the kitchen with the paramedic, while the other went outside the front door, speaking into a handheld radio.

The first paramedic returned from the kitchen, looked at the lieutenant and shook his head. "I'll get a bag."

Lieutenant Dutton nodded. "The coroner's on his way." He turned back to Roya. "I'll need a full statement, Mrs. Pulaski. My men will be going over the area pretty thoroughly. It may take a few hours."

"Going over? For what?"

He shrugged nonchalantly. "It's all routine, but quite necessary in case it's not a suicide."

"Not a—" Roya paused as realization dawned on her. "Oh, my God. You're talking about a murder? That's the craziest thing I've ever heard. No one would want to murder Bud! He didn't have an enemy in the world."

"I'm sure he didn't, Mrs. Pulaski, but please try to understand. Mine is a nasty job, because I have to always assume the worst, play the devil's advocate. I have to ask questions that might be painful, but to protect you and your daughters, I have to ask them. And they have to be answered truthfully."

"I understand."

"While I check out the kitchen, I want you to call your parents or a relative, someone who can pick up the girls for the night. They don't need to be here for all this." He placed his hand gently on her shoulder and gave it a slight warning squeeze.

The girls.

Roya looked at Lucienne's crumbled, tear-streaked face. Her blue eyes were filled with confusion and terror, and she was clinging so tightly to her mother that Roya's ribs had started to hurt. Selfishly, she didn't want to let the girls leave. She needed to hold them as much as they needed to touch her; her daughters were her only connection to normalcy. But when she looked into Cynthia's violet eyes and saw resolute hopelessness, Roya flung her own needs aside. "I'll call my mother right away."

"I'll get them a mild sedative before the paramedics leave."

"Thank you," Roya said, and went back into the study to the telephone.

"Mom, I don't want to go to Grandma's," Cynthia said stalwartly. "I can help you with the questioning."

"Cyn, I think the lieutenant is right. You and Lucy should get away from here and get some rest."

"Mom, I'm staying," Cynthia replied sternly.

Roya had never experienced either of her daughters negating her wishes. She took Cynthia's hand. "Please. You'll help me most by watching over Lucy. The police need my attention and I can't do both properly."

Lucienne tried to stop crying, but all she could see was blood and only half of her father's head. *Weren't we enough for you, Daddy? How did I fail you? What did I do wrong? Why did you want to leave me? Leave us?* Lucienne burst into hysterical sobs.

Cynthia put her arms around her sister, hugging her mother at the same time. "Okay, Mom. I'll take care of her."

Roya kissed both her daughters, and with her arm still around them, she punched out her parents' number.

"Mother? Hi. I need to ask a favor."

6

"I can't believe this!" Marie Monier said to her daughter Roya. "Bud would never kill himself."

Etienne Monier dropped his soup spoon. "What the hell is going on?" He rose from his chair, his cotton napkin falling to the floor. "Give me that phone!" he demanded, yanking the receiver out of his wife's hand.

"Papa?"

"This is Christmas, not Halloween. What's going on over there?"

Roya's voice quavered. "Bud's dead, Papa. The police are here. I can't talk long. I just wanted to know if you and Mama could come get the girls. I don't want them to see...but then—" she swallowed hard "—they already have."

"Police?" Etienne's eyes narrowed. Since his childhood on the streets of Paris, he'd always been wary of police. To him they were the enemy, bent upon entrapping him for the minor thefts he pulled to feed his empty stomach.

Marie's eyes glassed over. She turned away from Etienne and hugged herself protectively.

"Roya, have you called your attorney?"

"What for?"

"Police can't be trusted. Don't tell them anything. And for God's sake, don't let them take you anywhere."

"I'm not leaving the house, but they suggested I get the girls out of here." She glanced back to the kitchen. "Papa, there's blood everywhere."

"Blood?"

Marie's eyes were enormous orbs. "What?"

"I told you. Bud killed himself."

Etienne shook his head. "I thought you meant…"

"What?" Roya shouted angrily. "That he died in his sleep? No, Papa. He did it up big—real big. There's brains all over the door wall for God's sake!"

"Roya! Don't shout at me. I'm your father."

"What is it?" Marie asked.

"Bud shot himself," Etienne said, putting his hand over the receiver. Then he turned his attention back to what Roya was saying.

"Then come help me!" she pleaded while fighting an intense need to let go of her self-control.

Marie huddled into the corner, shaking her head at her husband. "I…I can't go. I couldn't face anything like that."

Etienne put his hand over the receiver. "What about the girls?"

"Maybe Adrienne could pick them up and bring them here."

He nodded. "Roya, we think you should call your sister. She could pick up the girls and bring them here. Mama is very upset by all this. I don't want to leave her."

"Mama's upset? *Mama?* What about me! Bud's left me this horrid mess to clean up! Papa, please come help me!"

Marie had turned white. Panic filled her eyes. "Don't leave me, Etienne. Please…"

"Mama's hysterical, Roya. I think I may have to call the doctor. She…doesn't look so good. Call me back after you talk to Adrienne."

Etienne hung up the phone and went to his wife, who collapsed in his arms.

Roya stared dumbfoundedly at the receiver. The dial tone was the coldest, most heartless sound she'd ever heard.

"This isn't happening to me!" She slammed the receiver down.

"Mrs. Pulaski, we need to speak with you as soon as you finish," Lieutenant Dutton said.

She looked into his brittle eyes. Nothing here tonight disturbed him in the least, it seemed, and she surmised that he'd seen it all before. People blown apart, lives strewn on the floor.

She wished she could be as cynical, but this was her first time dealing with crisis. Dealing with anything more consequential than a dead car battery had been Bud's domain. Taxes, braces for Cynthia, downturns in the economy, social injustice—all Bud's domain. Or so he'd told her for twenty years.

"*It's not your job to worry,*" he used to say. Her job was to care for the girls, bring the difficult decisions or problems to him and always, always, look happy, be happy, be carefree. After all, she was Bud Pulaski's wife.

"Do I need to call my attorney?"

"By all means if you feel you should."

"Am I under arrest?"

Lieutenant Dutton's face was placid. "At the current moment, no."

"But I could be considered a suspect."

"It's possible."

"I didn't kill my husband, Lieutenant."

There was only silence.

Roya picked up the phone. She ground her jaw to hold back an unfamiliar yet powerful rush of adrenaline. She realized it was courage. "Excuse me while I call my sister. I need to take care of my children first."

"Sure," he said, and walked away.

Adrienne lay naked beneath a fresh Norwegian pine tree decorated with romantic ribbons, lace and sentimental ornaments from her childhood.

Gavin Baker bent his elbow and propped his head on

his hand, his eyes still unfocused from their passionate
lovemaking. He leaned over and kissed a taut nipple.
"Have I told you today that I love you?"

"Yes. But I'd like to hear it again." She smiled, reaching
up and pulling his mouth to hers.

"I thought you'd never be able to leave that stupid
party. I've had a hard-on for three hours."

Adrienne giggled happily. "That's not my fault."

"Oh, yes it is." He slipped his arm under her back and
rolled her on top of him. His smile was broad, the lights in
his eyes too searingly emotional to be a reflection from the
Christmas tree.

He touched her cheek with his thumb and held his
breath as he peered deeply into her eyes.

"You really love me, don't you, Gavin?"

"You have no idea how much," he said softly.

"It's almost painful to see that much love," she whispered, a tear threatening the deepest, farthest corner of
her eye. A tear she didn't dare ever let him see.

"What an odd thing to say. Love...painful?"

She tried to look away, but he turned her face back to
him. "It's always been like that for me."

"Always? How long is always?"

"Back to being a kid, I guess."

He rolled her onto her side with her back to the Christmas tree and he curled his long body around her, forcing
her to accept his protection from the cold.

She nestled her face against the hollow of his chest. She
could smell his cologne and the musky scent of their sex.
Timidly, she touched the dark hair on his chest, realizing
she barely knew anything about this man to whom she
was engaged to be married. But she'd been playing a
game, a familiar game in which she'd always positioned
herself to win.

But something had happened in the last ten minutes to
change everything and she hadn't the slightest idea what
it was.

He lifted a lock of her hair, held it to his nostrils and slowly inhaled her perfume, as if its scent was *important* to him. His voice was husky yet honeyed with concern. "I'll be meeting your parents tomorrow night…after mass. If you don't get along with them, tell me now. I don't want to get off on the wrong foot."

She was taken aback that he cared about pleasing her enough to ask about her ground rules. "It's no big deal. I told you, they're just ordinary parents."

"Ordinary parents do not teach their children that love hurts."

"They never said that."

"Obviously they didn't have to. They got the point across, now, didn't they?"

Her protests were stillborn. "I…see what you mean."

"And how did they do that?"

"By always pointing out my mistakes. By putting Roya on a pedestal so high not even a saint could knock her off."

At the mention of her sister's name, Adrienne's cheeks flamed with anger. She was shocked at the acid she felt in her throat. She wanted to say other things about Roya, hateful, awful things, but she kept silent. She'd always kept silent; she didn't want to hurt Roya.

But in the process of not emoting, Adrienne had hurt herself. Sabotage, subterfuge—she'd used them both to make certain she continued to live up to her parents' low opinion of her.

"What mistakes?" Gavin asked.

"Huh?"

"What was the first mistake your parents said you made?"

Adrienne had blocked so many of her memories about family that she now realized she'd forgotten most of her childhood. "I don't remember."

"That's tough," he said, kissing her ear. "But all that's over for you now, isn't it?"

"How do you figure that?"

"You have me now. My job is to fill you with so much love that you forget all the pain." He touched the edge of her eye and uncovered the hiding tear. "I have a great deal of affection and attention I want to give you. I want you to wake up every day satiated from being with me. More than anything, I want to take away those dark slivers I see in your eyes."

"The what?"

"Those shadows I see whenever you try to convince yourself that you don't love me, those seedlings of fear."

"I'm not afraid."

"Yes, you are. You're afraid of being abandoned. Two husbands cheated on you, then left you. My guess is you felt abandoned by your parents, as well."

She huddled closer to him, his body heat necessary to her.

She saw slices of moments in time, of the past she'd believed she'd effectively erased. "I don't ever remember my father, or my mother for that matter, holding me. I used to beg to be held, to be picked up. But they wouldn't do it. Mama said her back hurt. Papa said I was too grown-up to be held. But I was only two…or less."

Her tears chose to hide no longer.

Gavin pressed her nape so that her face was close to his heart. "I'll hold you every hour of every day. All you have to do is ask. I'll never turn you down."

She was curled inside his embrace. Deep sobs grew inside her, demanding to be released, but she swallowed them. She was too embarrassed to let Gavin see her vulnerability.

"Can I ask you a question?" he whispered.

She nodded.

"Did they hold your sister?"

Her instant response was to say yes, but then another scene vaulted across her mind. She'd been eight or nine, Roya only two. They'd been rollerskating and both had fallen and scraped their knees badly. Adrienne had been told not to take Roya out on the skates, but Roya had begged Adrienne so sweetly that she'd given in. Roya's knees had been ripped apart by the sharp gravel along the side of the street.

"My God! She'll need stitches!" Marie had screamed.

"I'll drive them to the emergency room," Etienne had said.

"I can't take this," Marie had replied. "You'll have to go alone. This is just too much for me," she'd said, rushing away from her crying daughters.

"But, Mama! I'm not that bad hurt!" Adrienne had said. "Please just come be with us. Hold my hand till the doctor comes."

Marie had stopped abruptly on the staircase, looked at Adrienne, and said, "Why on earth would I want to do that?"

"Because you love me, Mama," Adrienne had replied, but her mother was no longer listening.

Adrienne lifted her arms and slipped them around Gavin's neck and pulled him toward her. It was a gesture she'd never made before with him. With anyone. "No," she said. "They didn't hold Roya, either."

"Darling, baby girl..." Gavin replied softly as his mouth took hers in a tender kiss.

Adrienne was lost in the kiss, feeling an overwhelming flood of emotions. A quiet glow burned inside her heart. It was as if she could feel her heart opening, accepting Gavin, accepting herself. Elation roared through her. She wanted to run up to the rooftop and shout to the world....

"Joy," she said.

"Hmmm?" Gavin kissed her forehead.

"I...I feel joy!" she elaborated, her voice full of wonder. "I've never felt like this before, Gavin." She was breathless with awe as she looked inside herself, liking what she saw, what she felt.

"Thank God," he said, and covered her face with kisses.

Then the phone rang. Adrienne didn't hear it, but Gavin did. "Let it ring," he said, planting kisses down her throat.

"Let what ring?" Adrienne asked, then heard the phone on the next ring.

Gavin moved his lips to her breast, filling his mouth with her flesh. Adrienne moaned.

The phone continued ringing.

After the tenth ring, Gavin groaned aloud. "Who could possibly be so insistent that they don't get the hint?"

"Roya," Adrienne said, getting on her knees and sliding across the carpet to the telephone next to the sofa.

"Oh, thank God you're there, Adrienne. I need you."

Adrienne had just experienced the single most important moment in her life. She'd realized she'd fallen in love with the man she'd agreed to marry, and was about to *promise* herself to him. The last thing she needed was one of Roya's silly errands. "No can do tonight, hon. Call me in the morning, okay? We'll talk about it—"

"Bud's dead."

"What?"

"He killed himself. We think. The police aren't sure. They haven't found a note yet."

"What kind of a joke is this?" Adrienne sat bolt upright.

Gavin sat up with her, sharing the earpiece.

"You think I'd joke about brains blown all over my kitchen?"

"Good God!" Gavin exclaimed.

Roya's voice cracked as hysteria wedged its way back inside her. "The police might even suspect me of murder! Can you believe that?"

"Do you want me to call Gary Bledsoe for you? You should have an attorney, Roya."

"I don't care about an attorney right now." Roya found

no logic in her mind, only emotion and a fierce need to protect her daughters. Like a trapped animal, she knew survival was paramount.

"What do you need me to do, then?"

"I want you to come over and get the girls and take them to Mother's for me. I've got to get them out of here. You should see this place, Addie. It's hell."

Adrienne could picture it, could feel the warm blood as it left Bud's body and turned cold, could smell his death. She started shivering, then began to shake. Her own blood turned ice-cold. "Bud...shot himself?" Her eyes rolled back in her head and she fainted in Gavin's arms.

He picked up the receiver and said, "Roya? This is Gavin. We haven't met, but Adrienne just fainted. I'll have to call you back."

He replaced the receiver and pulled Adrienne into his arms, rocking her like a baby.

7

Kitt had fallen asleep watching the movie-of-the-week and didn't realize the ten o'clock news had come on. She thought she'd been dreaming, hearing the newscaster's voice repeat Bud Pulaski's name twice in less than ten seconds. Her eyeglasses were cockeyed across the bridge of her nose, making focusing impossible. But there was nothing impaired about her hearing.

"Police are investigating the shooting of Bud Pulaski, a prominent Chicago businessman. Interviews with the neighbors have revealed that Mrs. Pulaski returned home around suppertime to find her husband dead in the kitchen from a gunshot wound. Though we are told appearances point to a suicide, homicide has not been ruled out by investigating authorities here at the site. Back to you, Walter," the on-scene reporter said.

Kitt slammed her hands over her gaping mouth. "Oh, God."

She closed her eyes.

"This is a dream."

She opened her eyes, but the newscast was real.

The reporter was clearly standing on Bud's front lawn, the swirling lights from police cars behind him looking like fireworks. Christmas lights from the neighboring houses cast a surreal glow over the darkly dressed onlookers who crept like vultures toward the house for a closer view of the bloodbath. Yellow plastic tape imprinted with black lettering, Do Not Cross Police Line, was strung around the perimeter of the yard like orna-mentation.

"Kent, do the police have any indication about motive if this was a murder?" the anchorman asked.

"No, Walter. They're tight-lipped on just about every-thing out here. I saw the forensics crew taking footprint impressions in the backyard, and when I asked one of them about it, he said that the tracks were recent and were not those of the deceased. Unfortunately, I have nothing else to report at this time. We'll be staying out here in Shaumburg to keep you and the viewers informed."

"Thanks, Kent," the anchorman said, turning his gaze back to face the camera.

Kitt had watched Walter Jacobson report the news on WBBM most of her adult life. She never once dreamed he would be the one to tell her that her life was over.

How silly of me to think it would be someone else. There is no one else in my life. There is only Bud. Was only Bud.

And now he's gone. I never became his wife, we never became a family. And now there is no one, not even a reminder of him for me to hold on to.

Her fingertips were icy as she dragged them down her dry cheeks. She realized she'd been holding her breath so long that her heart felt as if it had stopped beating.

She felt as if she were dead, perhaps she was.

No, not dead. Alone. I'm alone now.

Walter had gone on to more important business—the weather.

How strange that the world should go on spinning. That things like the weather are important anymore.

Kitt shook her head.

"What am I doing?" She laughed frantically to herself.

She felt around the satin sheets, down comforter and piles of pillows for the remote control. Grabbing the black plastic pad of buttons, she hit the channel changer.

Her smile was crooked, askew, as if she'd put her lip-stick on wrong. *I was just dreaming. Bud isn't dead. He cer-*

*tainly would never, ever, kill himself. After all, we'd just had a
real meeting of the minds. For the first time ever, we were on the
same page. All he needed was to cool off. That's all.*

She switched to Channel 7, WLS-TV.

Horrified, she saw an even more gruesome live-cam
shot of Bud's body being zipped into a plastic bag. Two
men lifted the bag onto a gurney. The cameras shot past
two young girls, their faces tear-streaked. They quickly
turned their backs to the camera and were ushered to another room by a blond woman.

"Roya," Kitt said in hushed, reverent tones.

The announcer went on to chronicle the events, stating
much the same as Walter had reported.

Bud is dead.

Kitt depressed the power button so forcefully, she
knew she'd broken the remote. "You son of a bitch, Bud!"

She bolted out of bed, her black-satin-and-chiffon negligee trailing off her shoulder like a showgirl's boa. "How
could you do this to me?"

Icy fingers raked her black, teased hair. She wanted to
scream but didn't. She pulled on her hair, hard, until the
pain brought tears to her eyes.

She was alive. Bud was dead.

"I swear to God, Bud, I will hate you for the rest of my
life for doing this to me!"

She untangled her hands and gnarled them together at
her waist as she started toward the bathroom. She tripped
on the negligee and fell to the dirty white carpet.

Tears streamed down her face. She wailed like a banshee, pounding the floor with her fists until she knew
she'd bruised herself. She was knocking on hell's gate, but
she didn't care.

How many times had she lain on this floor and cried
her eyes out over Bud? It was her makeup that had
stained the carpet. How many nights had he left her
alone? How many promises had he made and broken
without a single thought of how much he'd hurt her?

She should be happy he was dead; her pain and abuse would be over. But she wasn't happy. She felt as if she'd been drawn and quartered.

Her body was cold and her heart was frozen. She knew she'd never feel another emotion for a single human being for the rest of her life.

Her sobs came in heaving gasps, sounds bellowed from a part of her soul she hadn't known existed. Pain shredded her psyche, shucking away all tenderness and caring and leaving only heartbreak and bitterness.

Behind her closed eyelids, Kitt stared at the abyss of the darkest night of her soul.

Decade after decade Kitt had kept her adolescent dreams alive. She could see them dancing before her like brightly colored pixies on a crystal lake. She saw herself in her wedding gown, looking not a day over eighteen, her hand entwined with Bud's. He was telling her that he loved her.

She saw herself as a young mother with two adoring children and Bud at her side. Again, he told her that he loved her.

She saw a plethora of holidays—Christmases, Easters, birthdays—spin around her like a galaxy of stars, and in their midst she stood with Bud.

Then she saw it vanish.

She saw Bud's coffin.

Kitt screamed at the top of her lungs. "Don't be dead, Bud! Be anything, but not dead!"

Suddenly, she knew what it was like to kill in order to eat, maim in order to protect. But she had nothing to protect now that her dreams had died with Bud. Still, her instincts were to maim.

She had to pull herself together if she was to safeguard her sanity.

Think.

"How could this have happened?" she wondered aloud.

She wiped the tears from her face with the palm of her hand.

There was no question Bud would never have killed himself. He had too much to live for. He had her, didn't he?

But who would have murdered him?

The vision of Roya guarding her precious daughters from the camera lens shot across Kitt's mind.

"Of course she did it!" Kitt scrambled to her feet. "It all makes sense now." She leaned on the vanity and stared at the streaks of black mascara on her cheeks. "Bud and I argued. He went home and told Roya it was over between them. He told her that he loved me. That he's always loved me."

She took a deep breath to slow the torrent of thoughts charging through her brain, then rummaged impatiently through the dozens of inexpensive cosmetics, cleansers and lotions that filled her countertop. "Where the hell is it?" Finally, she clamped her hand over a white jar and unscrewed the plastic lid. She smeared cold cream over the mascara and wiped it off with a tissue.

"Roya couldn't take it. She freaked out. She threatened him. Bud's got a gun in the house, or at least he used to. She went for the gun. They struggled. It went off and she killed him rather than let him go."

Kitt's eyes were steel reflections as they stared back at her. "Bitch."

Her mind played out the scenario. It made perfect sense. Roya had lied to the police, which of course, she would have to do. Kitt would expect no less from her.

"She thinks she can get away with murder and maybe she can. Lots of folks seem to be doing that these days. If they have money. And connections. It shouldn't be all that hard for her, either."

Kitt peered at herself more closely. "But she won't get away from me. I'll make her life hell. I'll make her wish she was never born. Her and those two precious girls of hers.

"They don't know what it's like being out in the world. The real world. The cold world. But I do. I could teach them some lessons. Ones they would never forget."

Kitt chuckled to herself. "Maybe in the end, that's what my mission in this life has been about—teaching others. Sounds downright noble, now that I think about it."

She picked up her brush and tried to smooth her sleep-rumpled hair, but the bristles became snarled in the rat's nest at her crown. Cursing, she freed the brush and tossed it into the drawer containing fake hairpieces and falls. She yanked the negligee up over her exposed breasts, displeased with the tawdriness of the portrait. Carefully, with shaking fingers, she managed to tie the satin ribbon at her throat, knowing she looked just as elegant as Roya.

"*Elegant.*" Bud's voice echoed in her memory.

Just as she turned from the mirror, Kitt was struck by Bud's bitingly vivid words.

"Why won't you leave Roya?" Kitt had asked him for the millionth time. "You tell me you love me."

"I do love you. I crave you. I am obsessed with you," Bud had said.

"Then what's she got that I haven't got?"

Bud had shrugged his shoulders cavalierly. "She's elegant."

"Elegant?"

"She makes me look good to the people who count."

"That's it?" Kitt had asked incredulously. "You would give up a life of loving me, being loved by me, all that we are to each other because she is elegant?"

Bud had sniffed at her as if she were less than insignificant. "You worry too much. It's nothing. You and I will always be together. We're two peas in a pod, you and I. Now, Kitt, baby, tell me you love me."

And she had.

Kitt had always done what Bud had told her.

But now that tragedy had shifted her perception and her plans for the future, it altered the landscape of her past as well.

Is it possible that Bud never intended to marry me at all?

In nearly forty years of loving Bud Pulaski, Kitt Cabrizzi had not once ever dared to ask herself that question.

It was bad luck. It was blasphemy. It was against the laws of right and wrong.

Of course Bud had always intended to marry her. Kitt knew it as much as she knew her own soul.

But what if he hadn't? What if he's been using me? Playing with me the way I thought…assumed…he was always playing with Roya? What if it was me he was fooling? What if I've been wrong about him, about us, all my life?

Kitt looked again into the abyss that negated life, negated the past and negated her future.

She decided right then and there that she had no choice but to fight back.

8

It was Daria who rescued Roya.

She'd only heard the words "Bud's dead" and she was out the door.

She hadn't bothered to tell her father that his son was dead. Oscar Pulaski had Alzheimer's; he wouldn't have understood.

The scene outside her brother's house looked like something out of a movie. A dozen police cars, all with their lights flashing, formed a barricade at the end of the cul-de-sac. A throng of neighbors impeded the paramedics and the arriving county coroner's van. She parked her car a block away, bundled herself against the cold and the curious stares, and went to the front door.

"I'm Daria Pulaski. His sister," she told the police guard at the door who let her in.

Daria thought she'd prepared herself on the drive over. She was a fan of "on the spot" police dramas and had watched action movies since she was a kid. She was the only girl on her block who owned a G.I. Joe before she got her first Barbie. She always told herself she was of a militant mind-set, but she'd never been emotionally involved before.

The walls reeked of death and pain. The faces of the police were glacial-looking, like androids. They marched past her as if she were invisible.

"Can you believe this shit, Jess? In Schaumburg?" one officer remarked to another as they passed by her in the foyer.

"Would you look at this place? My wife would give her eyeteeth to decorate like this. It's all she talks about," the middle-aged, overweight cop answered.

"What I couldn't do with this kinda money, and this guy blows his brains out. It makes no sense."

His partner laughed derisively. "I think that's the point."

They left through the front door.

Daria couldn't stand it—strangers passing judgment on her family.

She searched the living room; the place was a wreck. Roya's Dresden doll collection was askew on the tables where forensics had dusted for fingerprints. The honey-colored raw silk sofa cushions had been upended, and gold-tasseled throw pillows had been tossed on the floor. Lamp shades were cockeyed and paintings were off center, making her feel as if the house were listing.

"Roya?" she called, and went into Bud's study. Suddenly, she halted, remembering that he'd barred her from entering his study for more than ten years. She'd forgotten what the room looked like.

Bud had always been egotistic and possessive about his belongings and this place where he kept them; even his thoughts were under lock and key. He'd barred all of the women in his life from seeing its interior.

Looking at the sparsely filled bookcases—which in her own room were stuffed with literature, self-improvement books and biographies of world shapers, philosophers and great metaphysicians—she was appalled by the insignificance of his fiercely guarded prizes.

A high school football trophy sat alone on the bottom shelf, testimony to the shallowness of his psyche. She remembered that the day after he'd gotten the trophy, he'd gone joyriding in a GTO and wound up in jail. Oscar had been furious when he'd bailed Bud out, calling him a "dumb Polack." No further accomplishments graced the shelves, not even from a hobby revealing later-life expertise.

Daria wasn't surprised by this. "Bud always sabotaged himself. Runs in the family," she scoffed aloud.

All her life, Daria had lived in Bud's cold shadow. Nothing she did could measure up to Bud's glory in her father's eyes. Nor in Bud's.

She'd tried to please them both, learning the trucking business to work alongside Bud when he took over from their father. But it was never enough.

Her valedictorian status in high school landed her an acceptance at Vassar, and for a short period of four years she'd earned Bud's respect. For a brief moment in time he'd let her believe he needed her. Then she realized Bud was *using* her.

Daria had landed a job as a photographer's assistant at *Glamour Magazine* that summer with a little help from her roommate's New York connections. The job paid little, but the prestige was enough to keep her closely tied not only to her Vassar girlfriends but to the new wave of young models, actresses and rock stars that filtered through New York City the summer of 1970.

She wrote to Bud and her father about her triumphs— photographing Cybill Shepherd, hanging out with Cheryl Tiegs, even meeting Gloria Steinem, whom she instantly idolized to the point of obsession. She'd been to parties on Long Island and a wedding in the Hamptons. She was accepted.

Bud was incredulous when he received her letter. So much so that he telephoned her.

"Daria, you don't need to make up stories to impress Dad and me."

"I'm not lying to you, Bud. Everything I wrote is true."

"No way! Those blue bloods aren't going to let a Polack like us...like you...be their friend."

"You're so full of bull, Bud. You believe what you want. You're the only one who cares about that stuff.

You're the one with the chip on your shoulder. Nobody gives a damn in New York. Really."

She failed to tell him that she never engaged first in conversations about religion or backgrounds. Racism and bigotry were part of their parents' world, and all of her crowd disregarded it along with their virginity. She didn't tell him that her friends only cared about women's liberation. They were apostles to the new faith, the new freedom. And Daria's New York life-style screamed *freedom*.

"I'll bet they wouldn't give me the time of day," Bud had said.

"You're wrong, and I'll prove it. Get your butt on a plane. Come see how I live. I'll show you."

"You're on!"

Bud flew in that weekend.

It was the first time Daria had ever impressed her older brother with anything about herself, her life.

He liked the flat in the Village that she shared with two other girls. He took a room at a small hotel on Thirty-eighth near Grand Central Station, but he needn't have bothered. He never slept.

The weekend was a constant party. Daphne Hutton's wedding had been that Saturday, and the festivities surrounding it were nonstop. Though Bud had always dreamed of going to Harvard, then to law school and living in New York himself, one too many twists of fate had kept him in Chicago, driving a truck for his father's company just as he'd done since he was fifteen. But that summer, Bud's hard labor had produced a taut, toned body that made Daria's friends drool. They wanted him. No one asked about his heritage.

Daria was more than proud to show off her tall, handsome brother. It was the first time she'd felt a camaraderie with him. He was relaxed and eager to be a part of Daria's new life.

Wedding champagne flowed from noon till dusk. Once

Daphne left on her honeymoon, the guests became more raucous as they danced to a rock band on an outdoor terrace of the Hutton mansion. The drinks got stiffer and joints were rolled by the pool. Vodka laced with acid turned up the volume.

With dawn only an hour away, Daria's crowd left the mansion lawns and headed for Fire Island, ten and eleven crammed into convertibles and sports cars.

Girls ran naked into the surf. Couples had sex in plain view of one another. Then they switched partners. Then they switched again. Bud stopped counting how many times he'd come, and with whom, he'd told her later.

Then they switched partners again. Daria found it was the first time she'd ever really been turned on. As dawn broke, she realized the head between her legs belonged to a man she'd never seen before. It scared the hell out of her.

Bud sobered the instant a Harvard grad grabbed his head, trying to force him into taking part of a "daisy chain."

Bud grabbed his pants and his sister and marched toward a red Mustang with the keys he'd stolen from the owner's pants.

He slapped Daria across the face. "No sister of mine is going to turn into a—"

"Shut up!" she raged at him.

"The hell I will. I'm taking you back to Chicago."

"I won't go!"

"Oh, yes, you will!" He pushed her into the car and drove them at breakneck speed back to the Village. While Daria sobbed, still half high, still turned on, Bud packed her clothes, record albums and cosmetics in the suitcases he found in the storage area.

"Those aren't mine," she said, pointing to the matching set of American Tourister bags.

"You think I care? I don't. Consider it payment for the

sex you've been giving them. No wonder they like you so much. No wonder they don't care if you're a Polack!"

"I haven't slept with anybody, Bud!"

"Don't give me that crap!" He slapped her again. "How would you remember? I've never seen so damn many drugs!"

She started to protest, then looked away. She knew he was right, and it both frightened her and made her angry. Now Bud had more control over her than ever before.

"That's what I thought." He grabbed her by the hair, hauling her up to his face. "You think I'm being mean, don't you."

"You're a bastard!" She pummeled his chest with her fists.

"On that count you're right." His voice was hard and razor sharp.

She knew instantly he spoke the truth. "What?"

He released her.

She stumbled backward from him, her eyes wide, her mind cold sober. "What are you saying?"

"I am a bastard. I was adopted."

"I don't believe it."

"It's true." He turned away from her and went back to throwing her things in a suitcase.

"Dad...never told me. Then you're not really my brother. You're probably not even Polish."

He turned to face her. "The world thinks I am. So, that makes me what they think I am." His twisted smile was derisive. "Double whammy, isn't it. A bastard and Polish to boot."

"So, you've chosen to hate the world," she said softly.

"It hates me. I hate it back."

Their eyes met, occupying the same intellectual plane. Something clicked in her head, and Daria knew in that moment Bud envied her. She was the legitimate one. She had the East Coast friends. She had the education he craved. She was everything he wanted to be. And due to her growing addiction to drugs, she was pissing it all away.

Bud was right—she was stupid. But, best of all, her stupidity got his goat. He was angry. Daria loved having this power over her brother, she just didn't know how long she could make it last.

"Fine! Then leave me the fuck outta your life!" She grabbed a fistful of her underwear out of the suitcase. "You can't make me leave."

"The hell I can't. I may not be your brother by blood, but you're my responsibility. If you stay here, you'll throw your life down the drain. I'm not going to let you do that. It would kill Dad."

"I don't care! It's my life!" She screamed so loud she scathed her vocal cords.

"You're an addict. You're going back to Chicago to get straightened out."

Daria hated him then. She continued hating him during the six months she spent getting off pot, LSD, coke, hashish and the dexies she took to stay thin like her model friends. She had lost her freedom.

When she got sober she discovered she was academically intelligent, but stupid about life. She found she had zero self-worth and set about trying to find some.

Now she was forty-nine years old and she still hadn't found it. She'd spent her life working alongside Bud, building the family business into the largest trucking company in the Midwest and one of the ten largest in the nation.

Bud took all the credit and most of the money, but Daria didn't care about the money. It meant nothing to a person who didn't have a life, anyway.

"Roya?" Daria called out again, leaving Bud's study. She saw the two policemen lingering by the front door. Their words stuck in her head. *"It doesn't make sense."*

Senseless? Bud has never done anything senseless in his life. He calculated everything.

Daria had to agree with these men. Bud Pulaski would not kill himself.

"Roya? Roya!" Daria called.

Roya appeared at the top of the massive curved staircase and leaned over the balcony. "Daria! Thank God you're here!"

Roya rushed down the stairs, and though her face was suffused with shock and anger, Daria was struck by her grace and poise. Roya's family had always claimed royal blood. Named Roya for it, in fact. Daria had thought their French haughtiness appalling, but now she realized the meaning of the old saying "blood will tell."

Roya was coping; she was in control. Daria couldn't help but admire her for it.

"Daria, I don't know what I would have done if you hadn't come," Roya said, embracing her sister-in-law.

"Of course I would come. He is…was…my brother."

Roya's eyes were shot with pain which she tried to hide. "That's more than I can say for my own family."

"They turned you down?" Daria was incredulous.

"Mama won't come. She said this—" she gestured shakily around her "—was too much for her. However, she and Papa will keep the girls for me. When I told Adrienne over the phone, she fainted dead away."

"Fainted?"

"She was with her new fiancé. Gavin told me he'd call back." She looked away, tears welling again. In a soft almost distant voice she said, "I haven't heard from him."

Daria couldn't help thinking Adrienne's reaction was overly strong. But then, Daria had always thought Adrienne was just as spoiled, just as pampered by life as Roya.p "I want to see Bud," Daria said. "Where is he?"

"In the kitchen."

Roya grabbed Daria's arm as she started toward the back hallway.

"You don't really want to see it, Daria."

"The hell I don't! I want to see for myself that Bud would take his life," she replied angrily, breaking out of Roya's hold.

"Well, he did!"

"They're going to have to prove it to me. I know my brother, damn it! Bud's strong like me. He's taken some hard knocks before. Nothing in this world could have pushed him over the edge. Bud doesn't believe in edges and neither do I."

Daria trounced stubbornly toward the kitchen.

She smelled it before she saw it.

"Don't touch his head, Stevens! The photos aren't completed yet," Lieutenant Dutton shouted. "And tell me those blood samples are finished!"

Men scraped the floor with scalpels and tongue depressors.

"Get that tape off the phone recorder."

Colored powders were dusted on every surface not splattered with blood, creating mushroom-shaped clouds above sweeping brushes.

The smoke from a cheap cigar fouled the air. Urgent commands pummeled her ears. It wasn't the blood, the bits of flesh or even the stench of brain matter that struck her. It was the acid smell of cryptic indifference from the men in the room that burned her nostrils. Their eyes were pitiless as they glanced at her, then turned back to their work.

Bud's body was being shoved into a black plastic body bag. He looked like so much refuse. She couldn't see his face—there wasn't much left—but she noticed that his hair glistened in the incandescent light as if he'd just been to the stylist. His arm flopped outside the bag, powerless to hit her, harm her again.

Odd, she didn't feel anything for him. No sense of loss,

no sense of injustice overwhelmed her. This man who had forced his rules upon her most of her life would no longer be shaping her future.

She felt the icy shroud of his shadow lift off her shoulders.

Daria took a deep breath, trying once again to remember her glory days of freedom in New York. She'd thought perhaps she'd be elated now that Bud was dead.

But she wasn't.

She didn't feel sad. She was not in shock. She was not filled with sorrow. Nor was she glad.

Then she realized she was scared.

All her life she'd blamed Bud for her problems. Now she was on her own; she was alone.

And she didn't like it one damn bit.

＿＿＿•＿•＿

9

Roya felt as if she were underwater; sounds came to her in distorted garbles.

"I'm so very sorry to hear the news, Roya. I'd offer to help, but, well, our family is leaving today for our annual Florida trip."

"But you're so young, Roya. And beautiful. I'm sure finding a husband won't be difficult for you."

"Nothing like this has ever happened in our neighborhood, and to think it was Bud who brought this down on us. Can't you do *something* about the news trucks? My kids can't play in the cul-de-sac."

From what Roya could discern, it was just as well she didn't know what they were saying.

Her body acted as if she'd been the one shot. Her limbs were heavy, her arm movements leaden, and her legs carried her only in slow motion. People came to the house— some she knew, some she didn't. Their faces had appeared pulled and oddly rounded, as if she were seeing them through a fish-eye lens. She didn't recognize anyone.

She realized that she was dreaming and this was a nightmare.

"Roya, what the hell do they have you on?"

"On?"

"Drugs, Roya. What kind of tranquilizer did they give you?" Adrienne asked the next afternoon.

"Addie, is that you?"

"Of course it's me. Don't you remember? Gavin and I got here about eleven just as the police were finishing."

"I thought you said you weren't coming." Roya's eyelids felt like anvils.

"I never said that. I...I was just a bit overwhelmed, is all. Suicide isn't an everyday occurrence in our family."

"No. I suppose not," Roya replied, looking down and seeing she was dressed in an apricot silk negligee. "When did I go to bed?"

"You were dressing for bed when I got here. Don't you remember? I helped you. The paramedic said he gave you something. What was it?"

"I don't know." She looked around her bedroom. The cream-colored walls trimmed with elaborate white molding and the French antiques seemed familiar. "I remember people. Lots of people. They were talking to me."

"Some came last night, some this morning and then some this afternoon. You were lucid for a while. You said you wanted to see them."

"I did?"

Adrienne's eyes filled with concern. "You're worse off than I thought. Where are those pills?"

"I don't have any..."

Adrienne reached behind the pillow and retrieved a pharmaceutical company's sample packet. "Seconals?" She eyed her sister. Then she stuck her hand farther behind the pillow and found Zanex. "How many have you taken?"

Roya started crying. "Don't be mad at me, Addie. I only take them when it hurts." She touched her abdomen, then her heart. "It hurts all the time."

"Okay, that's it!" Adrienne slipped her arms around her sister and dragged her from the bed.

"Where are we going?"

Adrienne pushed open the mirrored French door to the bathroom. The white marble gleamed, the golden brass fixtures sparkled. Their reflections danced around them in the honeycomb of two-foot-wide beveled mirror panels that surrounded the room.

Addie shook her head as she led Roya to the black marble shower stall. "This room would drive me nuts."

"It was Bud's favorite place to…"

"I can imagine. Nothing would have pleased him more than seeing himself from every angle."

Roya chuckled. "Yeah, that's what he said."

Adrienne didn't bother to strip Roya of her expensive nightgown. She turned on the cold water full blast.

Roya didn't flinch. She let the pulsating showerhead blast her body. Her blond hair matted to her head as she stretched her arms out, palms flat on the cold black wall.

Adrienne went to get two towels.

Roya remained in the shower for ten minutes, clarity returning with every second.

She pulled the spaghetti straps down over her shoulders and let the gown fall in a clump at her feet. She turned off the water and took the towels from her sister, wrapping one around her head, the other around her body.

"I feel terrible."

"You should. Your husband just died."

Roya went to the vanity and sat on her gold metal makeup stool. She stared at her face. Mascara streaked down her cheeks, her eyes were red and her bottom lip was still swollen from having kissed a stranger less than twenty-four hours ago.

"What a mess."

"Makeup will cure half of it," Adrienne reassured her.

"I didn't mean my face," Roya said sarcastically.

"I know," Adrienne replied, walking to the tea cart Roya kept stocked with coffee, herb teas, a coffeepot, powdered cream and sweetener. "I made coffee."

"The first pot is mine."

"You got it."

Roya cleaned off her mascara and tossed the tissue in the waste can. "Have you seen the girls?"

"No, but Mama says they're fine."

Roya slammed her fist on the counter. Perfume bottles rattled. "Damn it! Their father is dead! They are not fine."

"Okay, doing as well as could be expected. Which means they probably ate breakfast and went to the bathroom. That's all Mama knows about people, anyway."

"I'm sorry," Roya said compassionately.

"Don't be." Adrienne handed Roya an oversize cup of steaming hot coffee. "You should be royally pissed, outraged to the max! Your husband just pulled the most selfish stunt known to man! Even I want to wring his ghostly neck!"

"Not a bad idea," Roya said, drinking deeply.

"At least your sister-in-law is venting her anger in a positive manner."

"What's Daria doing?"

"She demanded an autopsy. She claims that since there was no suicide note, Bud was murdered. She's pretty adamant about it, too."

"That's ridiculous. Who would kill Bud?" Roya snorted skeptically.

Adrienne was silent as she stared at Roya's reflection.

Roya's eyes popped up. "Me? She thinks I would murder my own husband?"

"Don't worry, she'll drop the idea when she calms down."

"But for her to think that...even for a second. I love Daria! I love...loved Bud!"

Adrienne shook her head. "You're just now figuring out that she hates your guts?"

"Since when?"

"Come off it, Roya. You know this."

"I don't know this! Answer me!"

"Since the day you took her big brother away from her."

"What?"

Adrienne put her hands on Roya's shoulders, leaned closer to the mirror and spoke to Roya's reflection. "You really are like Cinderella, aren't you? Don't you know anything that's going on outside these castle walls?"

"Obviously not."

"Even on your wedding day, Daria couldn't get enough jabs in. Remember those rumors that you were preggers?"

"Not Daria?"

"Yep. And the looks she gave you? Turned me to stone."

"I never saw..."

"Maybe you didn't *want* to see."

"But I liked her. As a person, I mean. I was always kind to her," Roya replied, confusion clouding her eyes.

"Just because you want to play with all the kids in the playground doesn't mean they all want to play with you."

Roya's face fell to her hands. "Why does it have to be this way? Why can't we all just get along? We're family, for God's sake."

Adrienne laughed, a cruel edge to her voice. "Roya, darling, when are you going to learn that it is precisely because we *are* family that we can never get along."

Roya shook off her sister's hands. "Sometimes I really hate you, Addie!"

Adrienne stepped back as Roya went to the dressing room. "Yeah," she replied, staring coldly at her countenance in the mirror. "I know what you mean."

10

The funeral was well attended by the press, their numbers overflowing the church, making the scene look as if Bud Pulaski was loved by hundreds. In reality, fewer than eighty relatives, friends and colleagues came to mourn him. Of that number, three-fourths were employees from the Pulaski Trucking Company Bud had co-owned with his father.

Oscar arrived in a wheelchair, though he didn't need one and had never been infirm a day in his life. Daria had insisted upon the conveyance so that she could put a seat belt around his middle, keeping him constrained should he be inclined to "wander."

"I have more than my share of lucid moments, Daria," Oscar had said to his daughter an hour before leaving for the church. "My mind may take off for hell and back, but I'm not going to walk out of my son's funeral."

"Dad, do this for me. I'll be seeing all our friends and I can't keep an eye on you every minute."

"Since when have you been doing that?"

"Every day for the past fifteen years," she said bitterly.

"That's not true. You go to work every day. I'm here by myself most of the time."

"Mrs. Early is here all day with you."

"Who the devil is Mrs. Early?" he asked, his bushy white eyebrows cocked in surprise.

"I rest my case," Daria said, throwing up her arms.

Oscar yanked his tie, forcing the knot to straighten. "Roya takes care of me. More than you do, I'd say."

Daria's eyes slithered across the room to him. Jealousy thinned her lips. "Roya hasn't done shit for us and don't you forget it!"

"That's not true," he replied calmly. "I don't know who Mrs. Early is, but Roya brings me lasagna. Bakes cookies and brownies for me. She takes me to church on Sunday because you won't go anymore."

"Religion is a travesty."

He jabbed his gnarled finger at her. "You'll go to hell for saying that!"

Daria rolled her eyes. "There is no hell, Dad. Everybody knows that."

"Sometimes I wonder if you're even my daughter...the things that come outta your mouth. Your mother must be rolling over in her grave."

Daria turned her back on him. "I've got to finish dressing. Try not to burn the house down while I'm gone."

"Are you crazy? I'd never burn the house down! You think I'm stupid?"

She stopped abruptly on the stairs, refusing to face him. "Yes, I think you're stupid. You might want to look at the sofa in the living room before you make that statement again." She raced up the stairs and slammed the door to her bedroom.

Grumbling obscenities at his daughter once she was out of earshot, Oscar wheeled the chair around to face the living room. He gaped at the burgundy brocade sofa with its two charred cushions.

"When did that happen?" he exclaimed.

Daria watched as they wheeled her brother's casket down the aisle and out the door of the church. The pallbearers were Bud's employees, drivers mostly. Only Jim Bentley from accounting came from the main office. She'd personally called Bud's neighbors and company executives, asking each if they would like the "honor" of being one of Bud's pallbearers.

They had all declined.

She wasn't surprised; Bud had a lot of enemies.

That's why she believed he'd been murdered. Nobody could go through life twisting people's lives to suit his own needs, desires and passions the way Bud had and get off scot-free. Surely there was someone out there who hated him as much as she did, someone with enough balls to do what she'd wished she could do—put a gun to his head and watch the life drain out of him.

Bud's end was deserved.

She'd been right when she told her father she didn't believe in hell. Life was hell. Anything after that was heaven.

The first shall be last and the last shall be first.

Kitt Cabrizzi stood at the back of the church, waiting for her chance to bring the Biblical tenet to bear upon the here and now.

All her life she'd been relegated to second place in Bud's life. She was about to change that.

Bud had taught her long ago that planning and orchestration were the keys to success.

It wasn't "right" thinking or being positive. It wasn't being a do-gooder, a nice person or voting Democrat. It wasn't patience, for the stress of waiting for something to happen could kill a person. It wasn't charity, an invention to assuage a rich man's guilt for being wealthy, nor was it chastity devised by fathers of daughters who didn't want to lose power over their offspring.

Calculated moves insured one of being a winner, and Kitt wanted to be a winner.

Believing she could beat Roya when it came to fashion, Kitt wore a classic designer black wool suit that hugged her voluptuous figure. Her hat was broad-brimmed, but not too wide, so that the cameras could zoom in on her face. She chose her veiling carefully, desiring one with open chain work that gave full access to her face. Her makeup was impeccable, though her lips were bloodred, the color Bud liked best. There was no evidence of tears, nor would there be any.

She made certain the press was behind and to the side of her. Their support and attention was very important. She watched the ceremony like a general holding his troops back until the very last second. Her attack would be swift, sure and unexpected. She knew all too well she had only one chance to wield her power.

Power.

That's what life was about—who had the power, who used it, who gave it away.

Bud had had power. He'd used it like a club over her, forcing her to submit to him and ultimately addicting her to him. She'd known for years her only escape from Bud was through death. Either his or hers. It didn't matter.

Against his wife, Bud seldom had to use much power; she was so easily conned. He'd told Roya that he loved her and she'd believed him. But Kitt knew he hadn't. He'd lied to Roya, telling her that he wanted children. He'd never played with them and seldom talked to them, though he displayed them for public "show and tell." They were two darling little trophies. They had served their purpose, Kitt thought.

In Kitt's opinion, Roya had made two fatal mistakes. She'd fallen in love with Bud and she'd believed what he told her. Bud didn't give a damn about his family. He used his wife and children to make himself look good in the community and to his clients.

Hell, he only went to church to gain more power over his friends. They thought he was a model husband and father. He donated large sums of money to the church and became a hero. But Bud didn't believe in God; he'd believed in the devil, saying often that's who he was.

Bud had told Kitt all these things over the years.

Kitt had tried to break it off with Bud, but he knew she was bluffing. He told her not to worry, that the day would

come when she could dance on his grave. When she'd
agreed with him, he'd told her to make sure she was naked when she did.

Today she was going to dance. Today she was the one
with the power, power to annihilate lives. Power to shat-
ter dreams just the way all these people had taken her
dreams from her.

She'd wanted only one thing in life—to be Bud's wife.
But as long as the elegant "Princess Roya" lived, Kitt's
dream could never come true. Bud had chosen refinement
and beauty over Kitt's passionate devotion.

Now it was Roya's turn to find out what it felt like to be
on the outside looking in.

The casket rolled to a stop in the vestibule, where the
funeral director and his assistants removed the rolling
legs. The pallbearers would then carry the casket out the
door and down the steps, to place it in the hearse.

Roya, Cynthia, Lucienne, Marie, Etienne, Adrienne,
Gavin and Daria, with Oscar, stood and filed out of the
front pews.

Kitt watched Bud's family approach her, their eyes
bloodshot from tears.

She nearly laughed aloud, knowing their tears had only
begun.

She waited patiently as they came closer. Roya's eyes
met hers; her gaze was blank as she looked at this
stranger.

Kitt stepped from her position at the end of the pew
into the aisle in front of Roya.

"The last shall be first," Kitt said aloud, but to herself,
as she was now first in the procession behind Bud's casket.

"See here!" Etienne said, reaching out to tap Kitt's
shoulder.

Kitt shucked off his hand with an exaggerated twist of
her shoulder. "Don't touch me!"

A quick-witted photojournalist snapped a succession of

shots. Suddenly, the press came alive, their eyes recording the scene.

"What are you doing?" Roya asked in a soft whisper.

"Doing?" Kitt whirled around theatrically, her veil floating around her face like smoke. "Taking my rightful place with Bud."

"Excuse me?" Adrienne pulled her nieces behind her.

Gavin clutched his fiancé's hand. "Darling, I don't think..."

"Look at all of you!" Kitt blared. "High and mighty shits every one of you."

"Who are you?" Roya demanded.

"I'm Bud's lover. His mistress. Kitt Cabrizzi. The only woman he loved for nearly forty years. I'm the one who should have been his wife."

"Oh, my God!" Roya felt her knees go weak, but she held her own.

"Christ!" Etienne exclaimed.

Marie gasped, as did everyone around them, everyone except for the tall, dark-haired man who appeared out of nowhere. His blue eyes bore down on Kitt like a bird of prey. He clamped his hands around the fleshy parts of her upper arms and squeezed very hard. "Excuse me. I think you've got the wrong church," he growled menacingly at her.

"The hell I do..."

He lifted her straight off the floor, her high-heeled shoes dangling at the ends of her toes.

"You're hurting me!" she screamed.

"That's the idea," he said gruffly.

Flashbulbs popped. Journalists craned their necks, then turned and headed for alternative exits.

The stranger moved Kitt swiftly around the casket, through the vestibule and out of the church.

Roya's face blanched. "It can't be..."

Gavin pulled Adrienne close. "Who is that guy?"

"I haven't the slightest idea."

Marie looked at Roya. "You know him?"

Roya's mind was filled with the memory of a stunning kiss. Even with Bud's death, she'd dreamed about that kiss last night. She'd needed to feel his arms around her again, to make her believe there was an afterlife.

She touched her lip; the blister was gone. "No. I've never seen him before."

The press was buzzing. A cub reporter for the *Chicago Tribune* turned to Jim Bentley, one of the pallbearers, and asked, "Did the company hire a bodyguard?"

"That's not a bodyguard. It's our new general manager. Nick Petros."

11

Though only a hundred people came to the house for the meal after the burial, to Roya it seemed like thousands. No matter which way she turned, she was followed by Adrienne, her mother, her father. Even Oscar. Their presence was stifling, their gazes like surveillance cameras.

They thought she had known about Kitt Cabrizzi and Bud having an affair, but she hadn't. She hadn't suspected a thing. At least not until the past four months, when the signs were so blatant she couldn't have missed their inference. But even then, she hadn't had actual proof.

Had they always been there, those signs, alarms she should have seen and heard? Was she too stupid, too trusting or too preoccupied to see? Or was it her pride that blinded her to the truth?

Maybe Bud had been a consummate liar. Or an actor. One thing was for sure, he had been unfaithful.

If he'd always had Kitt in his life, even before they were married, then he'd never been true to his wedding vows to begin with. Perhaps she hadn't seen the signs of an affair, because he'd always been having one. Of course, nothing had changed drastically, because Bud's behavior hadn't altered in the least.

The rage inside her burned like hell's inferno. She didn't simply hate Bud, she despised him. Silently, she cursed his ghost. She prayed there was such a thing as reincarnation and that he would come back as a woman married to a man just like himself. Nothing could be more fitting. She wanted him to feel this riot of destructive emotions. She wanted him to know what it was like to be pushed to the edge of one's control. She wanted him to be stuck in the same situation she was, pretending to be the grieving widow, when her shock and outrage told her to smash everything he'd ever touched in this house.

She wanted to burn his possessions, throw acid on his clothes, cut his face out of every family photograph ever taken. She wanted nothing of his to remind her of him. Ever.

Lucienne appeared out of nowhere.

Bud's daughters. My daughters.

Roya realized the children were her greatest joy, but looking at them would also be bittersweet because Bud remained alive in them.

She vowed she must never let them know the depth of her pain, the intensity of her hate.

"Mom, do I have to hang around here all day?" Lucienne asked, a distinct whine to her voice Roya hadn't heard since childhood. "I don't know what to say to these people."

"That's okay. They don't know what to say to you, either."

Lucienne heard the determination in her mother's voice. She'd almost forgotten the clipped brevity of tone over the past few years. Her mother had become easy to manipulate, especially over the past four to six months, Lucienne thought. It was as though she'd been in another world, preoccupied, distant.

Lucienne watched her, studying her mother's poise, noting that her hands trembled just enough that she chose to hide them firmly clasped behind her back. "Did you know her, Mom?"

Roya knew it was only a matter of time before both girls asked the questions that her adult friends were too polite or afraid to ask. "No. I've never seen her before in my life."

"Do you think she was a kook?"

Roya hadn't been prepared for this eventuality. She'd assumed both girls would believe Kitt's claims. There was no sense in avoiding the inevitable. "No, I think she's a slut."

Lucienne sucked in her breath but didn't laugh. "She is, isn't she?"

"Of course."

"So what does that make Daddy?"

Roya's eyes were brittle as ice when she looked at her daughter. "Untrustworthy."

"An adulterer," Lucienne replied flatly.

Roya didn't see the rigidity set her daughter's face like drying concrete. Lucienne felt it, though. It was as if her entire body had turned to stone. Hard, impenetrable. All her life she'd been warned, told, informed and threatened with damnation if she ever committed adultery.

Yet her father had.

He'd done it with some slut for more than thirty years. Even after she was born, her father had been screwing the brash-looking whore. He'd taken precious time away from her mother, herself, to be with that woman. He'd chosen sex over family.

Lucienne could not remember a time when she hadn't looked up to her father. He was more than a king to her. He was the kind of Prince Charming she was looking for in the boys at school. She'd wanted them to be tall, handsome, self-made businessmen like her father. She'd always thought it was sweet and endearing when her father brought home pretty necklaces and bracelets for their mother. As Lucienne got older and the business made more profits, the small gemstones became diamonds and emeralds. Mikimoto pearls graced Roya's ears, and she had Rolex and Piaget watches, both of which she seldom wore.

Suddenly, Lucienne realized each of those gifts was in payment for a night he'd spent fucking his mistress.

Yet he'd paid off his wife as if she were the whore.

Lucienne's confusion was cataclysmic. Every tenet she'd been taught had instantly been destroyed. She didn't know what was the truth anymore. She didn't know who to believe.

Roya replied, "Yes, Lucienne, an adulterer."

Lucienne looked at her with eyes that were suddenly much older. "Thanks for not denying it."

"You're welcome."

Lucienne walked away, searching for a corner to be alone.

Roya hadn't the slightest idea whether she'd handled that well. Somehow, it didn't seem to matter. They were still in the eye of the maelstrom.

"I wish all these people would go home," she said to Adrienne, who came to stand beside her. "I need time to think. Things are happening too fast. I can't tell if what I said to Lucienne was the right thing or not."

Roya rubbed her forehead viciously. "Damn him! You know, if he weren't already dead, I'd shoot him myself!"

Adrienne slipped beside Roya and handed her a glass of white wine. "Drink this. It'll cool you down."

"Thanks." Roya drained half the wine. "Why is it you seem to know what I'm thinking before I think it?"

"I've been there, remember?"

They exchanged a profound, knowing look that in a single instant altered their relationship.

Roya reached out and touched Adrienne's arm. "My God, Addie. How did you live through it? I feel so...betrayed. I hurt physically. I feel as if my insides have been sliced open and drained dry. And I'm really, really angry. God! I would relish watching him die. I hope he was in pain. A lot of pain. Torturous pain." Spittle rained from her mouth as she spoke.

"But you know what the worst part is? The humiliation. I feel so stupid! I'm an intelligent woman; I should have known!"

With each of Roya's words, Adrienne's long-healed wounds threatened to open. She willed them shut. "I know."

Roya placed her hand over her solar plexus. "I didn't know anything could hurt so much." Her eyes flitted across the room nervously. She was convinced everyone was staring at her, pointing fingers as if she were a sideshow act. "How long do you think they've all known? Thirty years, like Kitt said?"

"Probably not. One thing I did learn when it happened to me was that people aren't so much concerned as curious. Once the novelty of the initial shock wears off, they move on to the next juicy story. You're the one left to deal with it. They have their lives. *This* is your life. No one can go through this but you."

"How can you be so understanding? So sweet to me, when I didn't help you at all."

"You know, at the time, it hurt me—your distance. Your never wanting to listen to me. But as I got older I realized you couldn't empathize with me because you hadn't been there. How could you give me advice? Rhetorically speaking, you were still in diapers."

"Thanks for the support, Addie, but the truth is, I was self-centered. I could have comforted you. I don't have to break a leg to know it hurts."

Adrienne shrugged her shoulders. "Maybe. Maybe not. I don't think very many people *do* understand what it's like to be betrayed. It's an emotional pain, invisible and easy to ignore. And I also realize that other people are afraid when they hear stories like ours. They're afraid that if they get too close, that pain, that betrayal will happen to them. They close themselves off emotionally out of fear." Adrienne looked down at her wineglass. "What's that saying, 'All we have to fear is fear itself'? Once it's happened to you, it's almost better. Sorta like having chicken pox. Now you'll be immune."

Roya's voice was infused with awe as she asked, "Can you ever forgive me, Addie?"

Adrienne paused for a long moment, realizing she *hadn't* forgiven Roya. She'd harbored a resentment for years. It had grown into a bitterness that had separated them. Adrienne had missed out on many family functions, birthday parties for her nieces, outings, even simple shopping trips with her sister because she'd wanted Roya to pay for her sin of omission.

She dropped her glib smile and replied, "Yes, Roya, I forgive you." And she meant it.

Roya hugged her.

Adrienne was shocked at the sense of release she felt. It was as if her bitterness was washing right out of her body. She'd underestimated its pervasiveness.

Adrienne blinked back a tear and changed the subject. "Brian Connolly is here. He wants to talk with you about the reading of the will."

Brian Connolly was Bud's attorney, CPA and sole confidant. To her knowledge, Bud had never had a best friend, though she doubted Brian would classify himself as Bud's friend. Brian was "class, just like you, Roya," Bud had said every time he mentioned the Irishman. Bud had respect for Brian, but Roya doubted the feeling was mutual.

"I was hoping we could wait on that kind of thing."

Adrienne shook her head. "Brian told me after the burial service that there was some urgency about the reading."

Roya's skin crawled. "You think it's because the police might arrest me?"

"Don't even think such a thing! The police aren't going to arrest you."

"It can happen. Especially now that the news has that crazy woman, Kitt, on videotape. What if they think I killed Bud for revenge?"

"Roya, it's impossible. You were with me all afternoon

at the party. Then you went shopping with the girls. They're witnesses. And then you were with me again before coming home. You all have iron-clad alibis."

Listening to Adrienne, Roya's thoughts went back to the afternoon of the party. She immediately thought about the stranger who now had a name. Nick Petros.

"Alibis." Corroborators. Witnesses. Was that why fate had put Nick Petros in her life? Brought him into Bud's business? Was it just coincidence they were together that afternoon? Or was it more than that?

She couldn't help thinking that the nuns in school were right. We all have guardian angels that move us around like pieces on a checkerboard, protecting us, putting us in the right place at the right time.

Perhaps that was all Nick was to be in her life. A knight protecting his queen. And now with Bud dead, the game was over.

She spied him lifting his coat off the foyer settee and heading for the front door. Funny, she hadn't known he was in the house. He was leaving without saying a word to her. She'd been in shock, seeing him at the church. Then he'd saved her. She'd heard Jim Bentley's voice explaining who he was, and impossible as it might have been, Nick's betrayal of her stung even more than Bud's.

"Addie, tell Brian I'll meet with him after everyone leaves."

"Okay," Adrienne said, and walked away.

Roya quickly walked toward Nick. She caught him just as he'd opened the door. "I'd like a word with you, if I may. In private." Her anger rumbled like an earthquake below her polite surface.

"I really can't," he said tersely, a nerve in his jaw twitching.

"Please," she said haltingly.

"Okay," he finally agreed.

She glanced to her left. "There's no one in the study." She motioned with her arm for him to precede her.

He shifted his weight. "Fine."

His expression was granite. His eyes, chips of ice.

Hers were flame.

Roya closed the door behind them as Nick moved to stand by the windows, holding his coat in both hands in front of him.

"What are you doing here?" Roya demanded.

"I work for your husband. *Worked.*"

"Did he hire you to seduce me?"

"No."

"What then?"

"I'm the general manager."

"I've heard. But I've never seen you at the office."

"Bud hired me the first of December. I quit the twenty-third."

"The day I met you," she said.

"The day he died," he retorted bitterly.

"I know very well what day it was. What I want to know is why you followed me."

"I wasn't doing anything of the kind. I was there by invitation."

"Ha!" She crossed her arms over her chest.

He exhaled his anger through his nostrils. "Look, maybe you pick up the rest of your lovers that way..."

"Excuse me?" Her head jerked backward at the impact of his barb.

He shifted his weight and glanced out the window, wondering how far he should go. *All the way. What have I got to lose?*

"I resigned from your husband's employ because I found out about the way he conducted his life. Not that I'm all that judgmental about people, or a moralist. But when his extracurricular activities affected my efforts to conduct business, it also affected my reputation. I'm a hired gun, on a contract. I'm not bound to him. Frankly, I don't normally give a shit what others do. Now that I've

seen you, I realize that you and Bud were…well, of the
same caliber. I wash my hands of the both of you."

He started toward the door.

"Wait!" She put her hand on his chest to stop him.

He looked down at her hand as if he'd been touched by
a leper.

She retracted her hand. "I didn't know who you were."

"We've established that."

"And…at the party? You didn't know I was Bud's
wife?"

"No. I just thought…"

"What?" Her eyes beseeched him.

"I made a mistake. That's all."

*A mistake? Was that what it was, Nick Petros? Or was it
something else?*

Odd, she didn't remember seeing these shadows in his
eyes at the party. She did remember the flutter of his long
lashes against his cheeks when he closed his eyes to kiss
her. And his moan of surrender when she gave in to him.
She remembered the taste of his tongue against hers and
the sweet, subtle power in his arms. She remembered a
different man.

Her voice was filled with humility and gratitude when
she spoke. "You saved us today. My family is indebted to
your quick thinking. Your courage."

"You're welcome," he said flatly, and walked to the
door.

She watched his back. "I want to apologize for my behavior at the party. I wasn't…myself."

His lips curled into a snide grin as he glanced at her
over his shoulder. "Really? Well, the next time you go
slumming, Mrs. Pulaski, you might want to check out
your victims a little better. Good day."

He closed the door quietly.

Roya grabbed the crystal desk clock and flung it after
him. It broke on the floor. She stared at the shattered

pieces. She'd lost control. Totally.

She'd never felt better in her life.

Nick Petros slammed his car door and rammed his key into the ignition switch. He turned it. It sputtered, but refused to connect.

"Son of a bitch!"

He floored the accelerator. He turned the key again, still ramming his foot against the pedal. The engine ground, gurgled and died.

He'd flooded it.

He hit the steering wheel so hard he hurt his hand.

"Damn!"

He exhaled, inhaled and exhaled again to calm himself, then turned the key slowly. This time the engine came to life.

Nick peeled away from the curb, spewing snow and slush.

He was racing away from Roya's house, but the farther he drove the more he thought about her. The mess he'd made of things was thick and putrid with powerful, negative emotions.

Emotions. God! He hated them. Always had. Always would.

"Well, it doesn't matter anymore because I'm done with all of them."

Fate had stepped in and saved him. He supposed he should be happy about that. If he hadn't gotten into an argument with Bud the afternoon of the party and resigned over the phone, he'd still be working for Pulaski Trucking Company. This way, he would be starting out the New Year on a fresh note.

Granted, it would take a month or more to secure another contract, but he wasn't worried. He was good at what he did; all the headhunters said so.

Nick was good because he always kept a cool head. Most businesses got in trouble because of poor management, which translated meant "emotions." Hearts don't belong in business; that was Nick's rule.

The thirty days spent investigating Bud Pulaski's business had told him more than he ever wanted to know about the man and his mind-set.

Nick had gone into Bud's office at nine on the morning of the twenty-third. Bud had seemed anxious, placing phone calls that didn't go through. His anger was apparent.

But then, so was Nick's. "I can't solve your problems unless I see the missing records and files I requested."

"Missing?" Bud waved him away with his hand. "Everything's there. Just do your job."

"I can't, Bud. I don't have the records I need."

"I can't help that. Ask Daria. Or Marjorie, my secretary."

"They're no help. Only you know where you put them, Bud." Nick's voice held accusation and blame.

Bud slammed the phone down. He shoved his fingers through his hair, staring blankly at the desk in front of him. Perspiration clustered at his temples.

"Christ...what to do?" Bud's whisper was frantic. He rose from his desk, patting his jacket pockets as if searching for something.

Nick couldn't help thinking that Bud was acting as if Nick wasn't even there.

"Bud."

"What?" Bud jumped. "Shit. You still here? Look, I'm busy. I...I have an appointment." He went to the coatrack and grabbed his trench coat.

"But we need to get this straightened out. You want me to meet with these marketers, and the first thing they'll ask for is our promotion budget. If I don't know what you spent over the past five years, this whole thing is a waste of time."

"Oh, hell, I don't care. How much do you think? Fifty thousand?"

"Get real," Nick guffawed. "I need triple that."

"Okay. Triple. Just bring in some business. Okay?"

"Have you got that much, Bud? I don't want to be the guy out on the limb when you can't back me up. These people remember things like that. It's my face, my word they deal with."

Bud threw him a sarcastic smile. "Then cover your ass."

"Excuse me?"

Bud's face was flushed. The sweat trickled down his cheek. "You haven't got a clue what it's like to really be out on a limb, do you? You've never owned your own company. Know why? It takes balls. Guts. You've always worked for someone else. Let them pay your taxes, insurance, fund your 401 retirement program for you."

"I don't know where you got that idea. I'm a hired gun. I go where I want to go. I'm just as much my own business as you are."

"The hell you are!" He pointed angrily out the window. "See those loading docks? Those guys, the drivers, the shippers? I'm responsible for them. That secretarial pool out there? I pay their wages. I've got fifty-seven employees I worry about every damn day. If I don't make this place run, they starve."

"Is that so?"

"Yeah, that's so."

Nick didn't back down. "Then if you're so concerned about their welfare, why is it I've come across over a hundred grand in expenditures I can't account for?"

"Impossible." Bud's face went from red to blue.

"That's the money I need to promote you, to bring in more contracts. To get the revenues up to where they should be."

"It's my money. I needed it," Bud said, taking two long strides toward the door. He flung it open. "I have to leave. And so do you."

Nick shrugged his shoulders. "This is crazy. You're crazy, but it's your funeral."

Nick's argument with Bud had continued over the cellular phone. Bud couldn't, and wouldn't, give him a concrete budget. Freddie was pressing Nick for a number; they couldn't formulate their marketing strategy without it.

Nick remembered flinging his arms in the air and telling Bud he quit. And that's when he'd knocked Roya's plate out of her hand.

His anger at Bud, his embarrassment over having ruined this woman's clothes and his utter shock at the impact of her eyes on him had impelled him to do something he never would have done if he hadn't lost all his control to emotions.

He'd kissed her.

Just thinking about the way she'd felt in his arms gave Nick a headache. He rubbed his forehead, then pinched the bridge of his nose.

In his entire thirty-nine years he had never acted so ridiculously irrational before. He remembered thinking thoughts that were more than just uncharacteristic of him, they were bizarre. That was the only word for it.

Not only had he been consumed with passion, he remembered thinking that all the crap he'd heard about destiny and soul mates over the years was true. He'd wanted Roya sexually, to be sure. The chemistry between them even today in her home had been so explosive, he'd rushed out of there to avoid making a fool of himself again.

Only this time, his reaction to her had been even more intense. This time he knew what kissing her was like. Kissing was the least of the things he wanted to do with her.

Christ! He was losing his mind.

Sorry, lost. Past tense. I lost my mind playing Sir Galahad at the church. And where did that impulse come from? Since when have I ever been the one to step in the middle of someone else's shit? Nick "Avoidance" Petros is my name.

The stricken look on Roya's face, at the moment Kitt Cabrizzi had shouted that she was Bud's lover, was his motivation. He remembered thinking he wanted to stuff a rag down Kitt's throat to shut her up. Rage altered his personality.

But where had the rage come from?

He didn't know Kitt, didn't really know Bud.

But I know Roya. Inside and out. It's as if I can sense her every thought, her needs, her desires.

"Impossible, buddy! She's a stranger. Totally! Things like this don't happen. You don't just meet somebody out of the clear blue and know everything about her."

He rubbed his forehead. "This is not happening to me."

He turned onto Lake Shore Drive and headed to his high-rise, back to where life was normal. Back to where his life had been before Roya's kiss.

He parked his car, hit the automatic lock button on his remote and rode the elevator to the fifteenth floor.

He unlocked the door and flipped on the lights. His keys clattered against the mahogany Chippendale table-top in the entry. He crossed the living room to the kitchen, sat on a bar stool and hit the play button on his answering machine.

"Hi, Nick. It's Mom. Just checking to see if you've decided to join me for New Year's. I understand about that funeral you had to go to, but I would love to see you. Give me a call. Love you."

"Hello, Nicholas." Cassie's voice caused Nick to hold his breath. "I'll bet you didn't think you'd hear from me, did you? What the hell, it's Christmas. It seems weird, leaving a message. I know you won't call me back. But I just wanted you to know I was thinking about you. I hope you're happy, Nicholas. I really do. I'll always love you. I wish it didn't have to be this way between us. Merry Christmas, darling."

He snapped off the recorder.

Cassie. Hell.

He went to the freezer, pulled out a bottle of frozen Absolut and made a dry martini. Olive, no pimento. Straight up.

He went to the window and looked out over the frozen city. After that call, he thought he'd reminisce about his ex-fiancée, who'd dumped him eighteen months ago for a river-rafting guide with no money but a passion for adventure and the outdoors.

Instead, he realized, he was reliving Roya's kiss. Again.

"Christ! It was only a kiss, not a weekend romp in the sack! It would be different if it was the best sex of the century, but it wasn't!"

Angrily, he turned away from the window and flopped in one of the wing chairs. He stared at the empty fireplace.

It was Christmas, and he hadn't done a damn thing about it. Hadn't bought a tree. Hadn't even burned a fire.

He always had a fire burning in the winter. But not this year. This year he didn't care.

He drained the martini, saving the olive for last.

Salty…like a tear.

The memory of the kiss assaulted him. He was beginning to think he would never escape it. It was as if she were in his arms again. He felt her breast in his hand. He could hear her nearly inaudible moan. He smelled her perfume.

"Christ! I wasn't like this even with Cassie! And we were very nearly married."

But you didn't marry. She left you. Or did she?

Was it possible fate had stepped in and altered his path? Was he led to Roya for a reason?

The specter of their lovemaking was relentless, playing itself over again in his mind's eye.

Nick Petros was not a metaphysician. He didn't know

why his life should have changed so much in the span of one afternoon. But it had. And now he had to deal with it. Logically. Not emotionally.

Easier said than done.

The best course of action he'd taken was accusing her of slumming, because that's just what she'd been doing.

Nick had stumbled onto the fact that Bud had a mistress. It was natural for Roya to want to lash out at her husband by taking lovers. Married women did it all the time.

She was definitely not the kind of woman he could trust, he decided.

Odd, though, how innocent her eyes seemed to him when he looked at her. She appeared to be genuinely hurt by his rejection of her.

It makes no sense.

Obviously, the woman was a consummate actress. She'd made him feel like he was the first man who'd ever kissed her the way a woman should be kissed.

Somehow she'd elicited a floodgate of emotions in him. At the time he hadn't cared. He'd even wanted to feel everything he was feeling.

Now, he just wanted to be numb.

He got up from the chair and went to the bedroom.

"Sleep. That's what I need."

He slipped naked between the sheets and punched his pillow three times with his fist as he always did, then turned out the bedside lamp and closed his eyes.

He tossed and turned for hours. Finally, exhausted, he fell asleep. In his dream he made love to Roya, forcing himself to exorcise the demon. But she came back to him. Over and over again.

The alarm went off as usual at six-thirty.

He awoke hard as a rock and covered with sweat. He shot out of bed and turned on the shower, pacing back and forth while the water warmed.

"This is nuts."

He continued pacing. "Let's look at this logically," he said to himself. "Something has happened. We've established that. A cathartic alteration due to the expanse of time since my breakup with Cassie. Yes, that's it. Eighteen months is too long a time to hold in my anger."

He snapped his fingers in the air. "That's why the kiss was so emotional. It was a release of anger. Nothing more! And once I clean my things out of my office at Pulaski Trucking, I'll never have to see Roya again."

Smiling to himself, he stepped into the shower.

It all made sense to him now. Roya wasn't a person so much as a reaction, his final emotional release.

He was proud that he'd been able to logically explain his behavior to himself.

In time, he'd forget Roya just as he'd forgotten Cassie.

The water pelted his face and slaked down his back.

He waited for relief to flood him, but it didn't come.

Behind his closed eyelids, he saw Roya's face.

It was beginning all over again.

How much time does forgetting take? A day? A night? Or will I feel like this always?

12

The aftermath of a funeral was much like that of any family celebration, Roya thought as she surveyed the wreckage. Dishes were scattered everywhere, food stains left trails on the carpets throughout the house, flowers were wilting in their vases, and she was physically exhausted. The difference was that this time Bud would not be there with her, discussing the success of the party, sharing their guests' anecdotes.

"They love you, you know," Bud used to say. "They don't come because of me, they come because they love you."

"What a silly thing to say, Bud. They're *our* friends."

"I can tell they don't like me." He would kiss her cheek as she put food away. "You're so beautiful and sweet to them. You make everyone feel special."

"That's because they are special to me, Bud. They're my friends. I'd do anything for them."

"They know that, too. You have a heart of gold, Roya. It shows."

"So do you, Bud," she would say.

"No, I don't, Roya. That's why I married you."

Invariably, Bud always said the same thing after all their parties. For more than twenty years, he'd told her that she was loved and he was not. She'd never understood those words, but now she did. She'd never paid any attention to them. Suddenly, she wished she had.

Could it have made a difference? Would things have turned out differently? Would he have been faithful?

* * *

"Roya," Brian Connolly said, his voice breaking through her thoughts, "I've asked the girls, Daria and Oscar to meet us in Bud's study."

"His study?"

"For the reading of the will."

Roya felt cold. It seemed so final, so utterly conclusive. "Must we do this now?"

"I think it's best to get it over with." He took her elbow, leading her out of the living room toward the foyer and the study beyond.

She looked at his broad Irish face. She'd never seen him look this glum. "Is there something wrong with the will, Brian?"

"With the will? No. Not exactly."

"Brian…"

Daria looked up as they entered the room. She'd finished adjusting Oscar's wheelchair so that he sat far away from the window and any possible drafts. She noticed that Brian was empty-handed. "I thought you were going to read the will."

Brian glanced at his hands sheepishly. "I'll have a copy sent to each of you. It's not long. Bud left his entire estate to Roya. The business, of course, was Bud's.…"

Daria suddenly cut in. "That's not true. It's jointly owned by Dad and Bud. Bud's share would revert to Dad."

Brian looked at Oscar, who hung his head.

"Bud bought out your father five years ago."

Daria looked at her father. "It's not true, is it?"

"I'm afraid so."

"But why?" Daria's voice cracked with indignation.

"I didn't want to be a burden to anyone. I knew how bad off my mind was. Bud couldn't afford to have me as a voting member when I was out of it half the time."

"But…I thought you were willing your share to me!" Daria's eyes were wide with shock.

"In a way, I am. What's left over in the bank will all be yours."

"But I don't want it!" Her eyes were frantic, her voice harsh. "I've put my blood and sweat into that company. I thought I was building my own future! I never would have done it if I thought you two were screwing me out of my inheritance!"

"Daria, I don't think either Bud or Oscar intended that," Roya said.

"Shut up! I don't want to hear it! All my life I've kow-towed to Bud. Sucked up to him. Done his bidding. But I knew all my work was for my future. I was working to-ward something, damn it!"

"Daria, I know how you feel...." Roya said.

"The hell you do! Don't try to patronize me. I got screwed and you know it!"

I always get screwed. Why is that? Why is my life turning to ashes?

Daria's face was crimson with fury, but she refused to let a single tear fall.

Brian stepped over to Daria. "I think you should wait to hear what I have to say before you start a family feud."

Roya looked at Brian. "I don't think I'm going to like this."

He shook his head. "You won't. The fact of the matter is, there's no company left."

"What?" Roya was incredulous. "Bud has always made money, long before I met him."

"I'm sorry, Roya."

"There's been a mistake. Bud put money away...."

"He put it back in the business," Brian explained. "That was his nest egg, his retirement fund."

"What about insurance? IRAs?"

"He cashed them in," Brian explained.

"I don't understand. Bud hasn't increased my house-hold allowance in over five, no, six years. It didn't seem to me that he was all that extravagant."

Brian nodded. "He was if you consider the company revenues have been dropping steadily over the past two years."

"Mom, what does all this mean?" Cynthia asked suddenly, feeling a chill sweep over her. It was the first reaction she'd felt since finding her father in the kitchen. It was as if she'd been asleep for the past three days. She wasn't sure she wanted to wake up.

"Bud, the company and, by virtue of that, all of you are bankrupt," Brian said quickly.

"I don't believe this!" Daria protested.

"My son is a fine businessman. He'd never go bankrupt. You've made a mistake."

"Mom? Is it true?" Cynthia's eyes were filled with dread. She didn't know much, but she did know that no money in the bank would mean she wouldn't be going back to college. She'd worked all her life to get good grades in order to go to college. She'd focused on nothing else.

Cynthia felt cold from the inside out.

Roya's thoughts were frantic. She remembered the woman's voice at Marshall Field's. "Sorry, this card isn't working." Then, "This card isn't good, either."

Bud had canceled her credit cards. She knew it now. Then she heard Nick Petros's words. "I was a client at the party." Why would Bud have sent Nick to discuss promotion and marketing with Adrienne's new firm unless...

Bud needed the business.

Roya's eyes met Brian's. "He was losing it all, wasn't he?"

"Yes," Brian said flatly.

She looked away from Brian, ashamed she'd been incognizant of Bud's predicament.

Is this why you killed yourself, Bud? Over money? Didn't you think I would understand? Did you know me that little? Trust me so little?

Roya looked around the room at the eyes leveled on her. Cynthia trembled from the impact of her shattered dreams. The confusion and fear in Lucienne's eyes told Roya that she was catching on quickly. Even Oscar's face was anticipatory.

It hit her that subconsciously they had placed her in the patriarchal role. She was the head of the family now, whether she was prepared or not.

Okay. So my marriage wasn't the best in the world. I didn't even share equal status in Bud's eyes. That was then, this is now.

She looked at Brian. "I want to know exactly where I stand, Brian."

"The business is on the verge of collapse, but it hasn't officially dropped off the deep end," Brian explained.

"Then there's a chance I might save it!" Daria brightened.

"I'm afraid it would take more than one person's efforts. Frankly, it's a mess and beyond hope, if you ask me."

Roya's mind was racing. "But it's not a lost cause yet."

"It might as well be," Brian said tersely.

"I'm not going to let it go," Roya said. "Not without a fight."

Daria was incredulous. "What the hell are you talking about? You don't know a damn thing about the business. Nothing about what Bud and I have built, except how to spend his money."

Roya's eyes were determined, but not damning as she said, "I doubt we have the luxury of a family feud at this moment, Daria. So, I'll forget you said that. By law, Pulaski Trucking Company is mine now. I can do with it what I want. I could let it go under, but one thing I always respected about Bud was his loyalty to his employees. Those were the only people who came to his funeral. I saw their faces, the fear in their eyes. I knew what they were thinking—'What happens to us now?' They didn't have to say it, I could feel it. If the business isn't officially bankrupt, then we still have a chance to turn it around."

"Don't play Joan of Arc with our lives, Roya," Daria said.

Roya put her hands on her hips. "Okay. What would you suggest?"

"Obviously Bud brought in Brian's expertise and he's suggested bankruptcy. It's a dead horse. Let it lie. Later I'll pick up the pieces, give it a new name and start over."

Let me be the savior. Just this once. I can do it. I need to do it. I need you to look up to me, since I don't know how to respect myself. Daria caught herself in her own thoughts. She didn't understand what she was thinking or why. Something was changing inside her. But why now? And what purpose did it serve?

She tried to keep her mind on the proceedings, on the interplay of powers around her. She had to keep her wits to win. After all, winning was everything, wasn't it?

Roya turned to Brian. "What did you advise Bud to do, Brian?"

"Actually, Bud was taking the right steps. He just didn't... Well, never mind. I suggested filing chapter eleven—reorganization. Bud did bring in Nicholas Petros, who has some brilliant plans to bring in more contracts. Given enough time, and not having to pay the creditors, I think it is possible to beef up the revenues and put the company back on its feet. But, Roya, I have to agree with Daria. You're a housewife. What do you know about business?"

Roya knew what they were saying. She'd bitten off more than she could chew. Sure, she'd run a few household accounts, looked for bargains when shopping and saved money on the side to pay for special presents. But what did she really know?

She knew she was a hard-working person. She'd handled four major charity events last year—no mean feat. She'd been active and that had to count for something. Besides, she was not so egotistical that she wouldn't ask questions of experts when she didn't know the answers.

She was overwhelmed with the sense that she was doing the right thing. For everyone. She was gambling with their lives, the careers of Bud's employees and the futures of both her daughters. Part of it was her need to assuage her guilt over Bud's suicide. He'd copped out, but she wouldn't. The other part was that Brian had given her the thumbnail sketch of how to proceed—file the reorganization papers and convince Nick Petros he should stay.

"I know all I need to know, Daria. I own Pulaski Trucking Company. It's mine to do with as I please. If it's already lost, then I'll be wasting my time, but I believe we still have a chance."

Daria glared at her, her face intractable, her shoulders stiff and defensive.

She was losing again. It felt like coming down from drugs. She was half out of it, yet struggling desperately for control.

Suddenly, it hit her why she had disliked Roya so intensely all her life. It wasn't that Bud had replaced Daria with Roya. No, it was Roya's strength that caused her jealousy.

Daria was not a strong woman. All her militant, women's lib, placard-waving years had done little to produce any deep-felt courage. She was a braggart, a phony, and had conned no one but herself.

Suddenly Daria saw the reality of her life—her foundation had deep fissures running through it. Her childhood had broken apart when her mother died, leaving her alone to deal with a father who was incapable of showing her any positive emotion and no affection. She thought she'd dealt with his penchant for belittling her in front of Bud at every turn, but she'd been wrong.

Roya, on the other hand, had come from a loving family environment.

Daria almost couldn't believe her own shallowness.

She'd been jealous of Roya because Roya had drawn a longer, luckier straw.

Daria knew if she didn't leave, she would embarrass herself even more. She needed time to think.

She wrapped a white-knuckled grip around Oscar's wheelchair handles. "We're getting out of here," she said, her face down, pushing Oscar toward the door.

"Please, Daria, don't be like this. I want what's best for all of us. Say you'll work with me. Help me. I need you."

These were the words she had desperately wanted to hear, but her learned behavior was hard to overcome.

"You know damn well that by rights the company is mine. I put my life in it. You're only doing this to give yourself something to do now that Bud is gone. You're so full of yourself you haven't thought about the workers or us." She gestured around the room. "Why, you're more egotistical than Bud, and that's damn hard to be."

She turned Oscar's wheelchair toward the door. "No, Roya. I won't help you. You're not helping me. Only yourself. You wanna look good to your girls and to Brian here. Well, you can't fool me. You can rot in hell before I'll lift a finger to help you!"

She pushed Oscar through the door, her anger leaving a wake of heat behind her.

"Why are we leaving?" Oscar asked, his eyes rolling from side to side, the Alzheimer's claiming his mind again.

"We aren't leaving. We got kicked out," Daria replied, and closed the front door behind them.

13

Kitt Cabrizzi flipped through the channels. She had to be on television, she just had to be.

But she wasn't.

She rifled through the papers, both morning and evening editions, and found not even the first mention of her name, nor her glorious stand at the Sacred Heart of Mary Church.

"Shit! What the hell's the matter with these bastards?"

She'd had her shot at her fifteen minutes of fame and she'd blown it.

What good had waiting around on Bud Pulaski's ass for almost forty years gotten her if not a couple of lines in a short column?

"Oh, to hell with it," she grumbled, and threw the newspapers in the trash masher.

It would have been fun to see herself in the news, but that wasn't the fish she was baiting.

Kitt wanted one thing and one thing only—revenge.

She wanted Roya Pulaski to personally pay for every minute she'd spent as Bud's wife. Roya was a usurper, an evil witch who had used her youth and beauty to steal Bud from Kitt.

Bud had proposed to Kitt when they were in high school. He'd told her the night he'd taken her virginity that one day she would be his wife....

"I don't really want to do this, Bud," Kitt had said as Bud unhooked her bra in the back seat of his father's Impala. "I'll go to hell. The nuns said so."

He kissed her then, making her mind turn to mush.

She broke away. "Or I'll get pregnant," she added, struggling to get up and away from him.

Bud slid his hand around to her breast and squeezed ever so slowly. "God in heaven, Kitt, you have the biggest boobs in school. You're magnificent. Not even Marilyn is this big."

Kitt preened, temporarily sidetracked from her fear of damnation. "I'm two inches bigger. I read her size in *Movie Time Magazine*."

Bud was breathing like a caged animal. He lifted her sweater. "I have to see for myself. Both of them. All at once."

His eyes smoldered with appreciation. "Christ! You're the most beautiful thing I've ever seen. I adore you, Kitt." He clamped his mouth over her nipple, massaging her flesh, building a liquid heat inside her.

She was stunned at her body's reaction. She'd been told sex was painful, dirty and evil. But she found it to be nothing of the sort. She was flushed from head to toe, a languid drowsiness coming over her, relaxing her muscles, turning her bones to water. She fell limp against the back of the seat as Bud licked her nipple, then pinched it. He gripped her flesh with his strong fingers and pulled on her breasts. She'd thought he would hurt her. Instead, a tickling pang blossomed between her legs. She moaned as Bud filled his mouth with her other breast. The tickling increased until the sensation moved inside her, pulsating.

Bud tweaked her nipples. She gasped and the pulsing continued. Her ears began to ring. She arched her back as a heat like she'd never known spread inside her body and erupted on her skin. She realized she was sweating. The wetness between her legs was embarrassing.

She opened her legs and felt Bud's erection against her thigh. His narrow hips were gyrating against her, forcing her to take up his rhythm, though neither of them had stripped.

She knew she should stop him. She was a virgin, a "good Catholic girl." She'd never led a boy on in her life.

But Kitt loved Bud.

She'd loved him for two years before he'd even asked her out. They'd been going together for four months now. They'd made out before, but always just necking, certainly not petting—until tonight.

It seemed it was all happening in a rush. She didn't have time to think about things or make decisions. She knew she loved Bud in a romantic, innocent way, but tonight he'd changed all that. Tonight he'd seen her breasts for the first time. He had only touched her there once before, and she'd done the right thing and pulled away. He'd done the right thing and apologized.

Kitt had gone to confession about it. Bud had not.

"Bud, we have to stop," she urged him. "You…you don't have any rubbers. We should use rubbers."

"Next time," he groaned, and slipped his hand under her poodle skirt and crinolines. She was wearing only cotton panties which he pulled down in one motion.

He sucked on her breast with a smacking sound that turned them both on.

His finger slid easily inside her. "God, you're so wet, Kitt. I never knew anyone could be that wet."

Having Bud's thick finger inside her was the most delicious feeling she'd ever felt. She felt her walls clamp around him, pulsing against him.

In that instant she knew she was going to like sex…a lot.

"Put another finger in, Bud…just to see."

"Are you sure, Kitt?"

"Oh, yes, Bud. Very sure."

It was divine. It was what she knew she was made for. She wasn't one of those tight, prissy girls. She was going to be open and ready for him, no matter what size he was. She didn't know anything about men, not having any brothers, but judging from the size of the erection he was rubbing against her leg, she thought he would be big.

"I want you, Kitt. I want to stick myself inside you so bad, I can't stand it."

Kitt opened her eyes and looked at him. He'd taken off his letterman jacket and shirt and had unzipped his jeans. He was magnificent. His broad shoulders and sculpted muscles glowed in the dim street lamp light half a block away.

Kitt knew she hadn't seen anything more beautiful in her life than Bud Pulaski naked.

He started to pull off his underwear.

His penis bulged against the cotton.

Kitt's eyes widened with anticipation. She held her breath.

"God, Kitt, you'll always be my only girl."

Her eyes shot to his face. She blinked, then looked back at his engorged penis.

"I can't do this!" She burst into tears.

"What?"

"Something bad will happen to us. We'll go to hell. I'll get pregnant. You'll leave me."

Bud gazed at her silently. Then he took her hands from her face, forcing her to look at him. "I'll never leave you, Kitt. Ever. I'm making you my girl tonight. For good and always. If you get pregnant, I'll marry you. So there. They can't say anything about that, can they? And you're not going to hell, because I love you. We're sorta engaged now, wouldn't you say?"

"We are?"

"Someday I'll buy you a big ring." He kissed her lips eagerly. "Be my girl. Tonight."

He placed his hands on her knees and spread her legs apart. "Let me see all of you, Kitt. Let me feel all of you."

She let him enter her.

That's when she knew that everything the nuns and her parents had told her was bullshit, flat-out lies. And that they'd been trying to manipulate her life by putting the fear of God in her about sex.

Bud filled her up. He was thick and long and strong. He sensed her body's every rhythm, her every need. The best part was that Bud liked being inside her so much that he forced himself to wait a long, long time before he came.

Bud had made love to her for nearly three hours that night, the majority of that time inside her. Kitt wasn't the least bit sore when she walked up the concrete steps to her parents' house. In fact, she was still pulsing and already planning for the next time when they could do it again.

Kitt was glad she'd carefully guarded her virginity, saved herself for the boy she loved. And it had been worth it, because tonight Bud had proposed.

She was Bud Pulaski's girl now. They were engaged.

Someday he would marry her and she would be his wife.

That was the way it should be.

If Bud had married Kitt instead of Roya, she would be the "good Catholic girl" she once was.

Marriage would have washed away her sins, legitimized her. Would have given her status in society. Would have made her a lady.

But Bud reneged on his promise.

He'd cheated her out of the future she'd planned for, lived for, dreamed out, since she was sixteen.

Kitt could have dumped him as well, but she wasn't a welsher. Neither was she a strong woman. She couldn't remember a time when she didn't lean on Bud. He was the man, the strong one. She was a woman, dependent and frightened to death of life without Bud. She loved him that much.

Kitt had promised Bud she'd love him always. She'd promised him that she was "his girl."

For Kitt Cabrizzi, love was eternal.

Her love for Bud was all-consuming. She couldn't turn it on and off like tap water. She was Bud's girl and always would be, no matter who tried to come between them.

And Bud had loved her the same way.

Kitt knew that Bud had married Roya because he wanted a wife with class, but she also knew that he would tire of the blond ice maiden.

And he did.

But he had trapped himself, and found he couldn't get a divorce without causing flak in his business and social standing.

Kitt had tried to warn him when Roya started volunteering for charity events soon after they arrived home from their honeymoon. In less than five years, Roya had made a name for herself in Chicago society—and she kept moving up.

Kitt warned Bud about the web Roya was weaving, but he laughed it off. Bud was enslaved all the same.

Kitt demanded he get a divorce nearly once a week for eighteen years. And twice a week, Bud insisted he "was working on it."

But the divorce never materialized. And now Bud was dead. Kitt would never be Bud's wife. She'd lost her bid for legitimacy.

Kitt wished to hell she could be like the younger women she knew around Chicago. They ordered men up like take-out food, not caring if they were married or not. They didn't ask for commitments. They didn't lose their hearts. They took sex for what it was, had a good time and moved on.

But Kitt was fifty-two years old. She was a throwback to another era. She wasn't raised the way the twenty- and thirty-somethings were raised. Nor did she have a fulfilling career like her "fortyish" friends.

Bud had been Kitt's career. Bud had been Kitt's life.

Bud was all Kitt had ever planned for, dreamed of and lived for.

Roya had stolen Kitt's dream; Roya was a thief.

Kitt knew it was a sin to steal.

Roya would have to be punished.

14

Roya awoke to crashing sounds coming from downstairs.

Her first thought was that the house was being broken into. She opened the bedside table drawer and withdrew the .38 she'd moved recently from Bud's study. She'd always felt uneasy about guns in the house, especially because of the children, but Bud had told her she was silly and naive.

Now her world was different. She had to protect her family from all harm, and if there was an intruder downstairs, she would have to use this gun.

Bud had used a gun—though not this one—to kill himself.

She stared at it, realizing that now she'd have to draw her own conclusions about guns and their use. Bud was dead. His opinion, his wants and needs were no longer applicable.

The effacement of Bud Pulaski had begun.

Cra-a-ash! Glass shattered, then popped.

Roya bolted out of bed, grabbing her robe on the way to the hall.

"Mom!" Lucienne rushed up from behind her. "What's going on?"

"I don't know."

The sound of more glass breaking assaulted their ears as they ran down the spiral staircase.

"It's coming from the living room," Roya said.

Then they heard someone crying. Another crash. Smash. Pop.

"Oh, my God!" Suddenly, Roya knew. "Cynthia!" she cried out as she rushed into the living room.

Cynthia was hysterical as she swung again at the half-pulverized Christmas tree with her old softball bat. "I hate you! I hate you!"

Cynthia made a wide arc with the bat over the grouping of family photos on top of the baby grand piano. Several of the frames sailed off the black-lacquered surface and clattered to the floor.

She stomped on the photograph of herself and her father on her graduation day. "Stinking coward!"

"Cynthia!" Roya shouted as she rushed up to her.

Cynthia was oblivious to her mother and sister. Anger clashed with adrenaline in her head like titans. She heard nothing, not even her own sobs. "How could you leave me? I never want to be anything like you!"

Roya tried to put her arms around Cynthia from behind, but failed. Cynthia shucked her off, and in so doing, barely missed hitting her mother in the face with the bat.

Cynthia's eyes were glassy, as if she were in a trance. "I despise and detest you! I wish anybody had been my father but you!"

Lucienne took up the flank. "Get the bat from her, Mom! She doesn't know what she's doing!"

"I figured that!" Roya guessed Cynthia had blocked out everything except hate. She circled to her front, forcing Cynthia to see her, then grabbed Cynthia's shoulders.

Lucienne went for the bat from the side.

The ploy worked.

"What are you doing?" Cynthia asked, her voice coming in hard pants. She stared wild-eyed at the bat.

"Helping you," Roya said, taking the bat from Lucienne.

"No, you're not!" Cynthia screamed, and reached for the bat. "You can't stop me. Nobody can!"

Suddenly Roya lifted the bat and swung at the tree, knocking half a dozen ornaments to the floor where they exploded on impact.

Lucienne gaped at her mother. "Are you crazy?"

"No." Roya smiled. "Just angry as hell." She looked at her eldest daughter. "Right, Cyn?"

Cynthia's eyes lost their flame. Her breathing slowed. She wiped the sweat from her forehead with the sleeve of her nightgown. "Yeah, right, Mom."

"Well, I'm angry, too, but I'm not smashing the tree up!" Lucienne flung her arms in the air.

Roya handed her the baseball bat. "Go for it."

Lucienne looked at the bat and shook her head morosely. "It won't bring Daddy back."

Roya dropped her arm. "I'm not so sure I'd want him back."

"What?" Lucienne's look was incredulous. "You don't mean that!"

"I don't wish he were dead, that's true. But frankly, I've learned a lot about my husband in the past four days. I'm beginning to wonder if I ever really knew him. Facts are facts. He killed himself, despite what Daria believes. He was always selfish and I knew that. What I won't forgive is not only his abandoning you girls, but leaving us with no way to pay for your educations. That's what is eating at you, isn't it, Cyn?"

"Yes," Cynthia replied bitingly. She rubbed her upper arms, surprised that they ached. "Daddy said he put the money away for us. How could he lie to us like that? I was counting on him."

"It might not be a lie. He may have at one point in time. But he pulled it out. Used it for…"

"His mistress?" Lucienne asked.

Pride pulled Roya's shoulders back. "Yes. There's no sense denying it at this point. You were there, you saw Kitt. You heard her."

"Yes, we did," Cynthia said, glancing at her sister.

Roya looked to the ceiling, anger smarting her face. She didn't even have the luxury of lying to her children about his sordid "other" life.

"It makes me so very, very angry that Bud did this. Not only did he have his priorities screwed up, but he just up and left this god-awful mess for us to deal with. He didn't care what you girls thought of him. He just wanted out. He was such a bastard."

Cynthia and Lucienne exchanged a look.

"We've never heard you talk like this, Mom," Cynthia said.

She looked at her daughters. "Why should you have? I was never in this position before. I was living a fantasy. It wasn't real. Any of it. This—" she hit the bat on the floor "—is reality. The blood, guts and horror of it."

"God..." Lucienne slammed her hands over her ears. "I don't want to hear this."

Roya dropped the bat and took Lucienne's hands away. "I want you to hear it, Lucy. I don't want you to be as ill-prepared for life as I've been. I want you to know what you're up against."

Lucienne stared at her mother in disbelief. "You need a Valium, Mom."

"Taking a pill won't make it go away, Lucy. Avoidance will only make it worse. Maybe all this is happening to us now so we can learn just that."

Lucienne's face crumpled. She was on the verge of tears.

Roya could tell she was trying to be strong for everyone's sake but her own. She wished she wouldn't try so hard—it wasted time and energy she would need to tackle problems. That was a lesson Roya was learning very quickly.

Finally, Lucienne exploded. "There's no way you can make me feel good about this."

"That's not what I was—"

Lucienne cut Roya off. "I didn't ask for this crap to happen to me! Neither did Cyn. Neither did you! It's shit! I heard everything Aunt Daria said, and I figured out real quick what Mr. Connolly was saying. We're gonna have to sell our house. Maybe move out of the area. That means I'll be losing all my friends, all my chances at the student council and getting on the pep squad and a million other things I was aiming for. This is a crappy, lousy thing Daddy did to us! But hey! He didn't give a shit, did he? He took the easy way out. Makes me think maybe I should do the same thing!"

Roya slapped her.

Lucienne gasped.

Roya retracted her hands, clamping them over her mouth.

God, what have I done?

Lucienne's eyes were enormous with shock as she stared at her mother.

Roya had never laid a hand on either of her daughters. She was stunned that she'd done so now. But deep inside she felt her action was warranted. "You'll do nothing of the kind, Lucienne Pulaski. You're still the same sweet, intelligent, beautiful girl you were last week. You will not end your life. Don't even think such a thing. You're better than your father."

Roya burst into tears and pulled Lucienne into her arms. She smoothed her hair and kissed her forehead. "You're better than all of us put together."

"Really?"

"Yes, really. Promise me you'll never say that again."

"I promise."

Roya's voice was edged with a determination she'd never heard or felt in herself before. "I'm not going to let this destroy us. I won't."

Cynthia bent over to retrieve a wooden ornament she'd remembered painting in grade school. She flicked away a piece of glass and straightened the red-and-green-plaid ribbon.

"Cyn, you were right to smash the tree," Roya said.

"I was?"

"Uh-huh." She motioned for Cynthia to join in the hug—which she did. Roya kissed her. "It might not have been the ladylike thing to do, but it was the right thing. You feel better, don't you?"

"Sorta."

"Well, that's a start."

Cynthia looked at the tree. "Actually, it was pretty dumb. Lucy and I made a lot of these things."

"Yes, you did," Roya said, inspecting the mangled tree. "I suppose it would have been better if you'd asked Lucienne's permission to break her things as well."

Cynthia pushed her glasses up the bridge of her nose. "I'm sorry, Lucy."

"Don't do it again," Lucienne said in a half-warning, half-consoling tone.

"I won't," Cynthia agreed.

Roya looked at both her daughters. "The worst is behind us, girls. We'll get through this just fine. I know it," Roya said confidently.

"I hope so, Mom," Cynthia replied with uncertainty.

Lucienne avoided their eyes.

"We'll clean this mess up in the morning. We're all exhausted. After a good night's sleep, we'll handle things better."

They walked up the stairs, each immersed in thought.

Roya turned out the light from the crystal chandelier that hung over the foyer. Lucienne was silent as she went to her room and closed the door.

How many weeks do I have left in this beautiful house?

Cynthia paused just before she opened her door and looked at her mother. "I'm sorry I broke Lucy's ornaments. I didn't mean to hurt her. But I'm not sorry for how I feel, Mom. I really hate Daddy right now. I'm not sure I'll ever stop."

"Oh, Cyn, you don't really mean that, do you?"

Her eyes were implacable. "I've never meant anything so much in my life."

"I wish you didn't feel that way."

"Sorry, I do."

"It's not good to hold resentment. The bitterness will eat you alive."

A cynical smile curved Cynthia's lips. "You can't mean that you don't hate Daddy right now."

Roya glanced down, then back at her daughter. "Frankly, I've never hated anyone or anything as much."

"That's what I thought." She opened her door, and without looking back, she said, "Good night, Mom."

"Good night, Cynthia. I love you."

"Love you, Mom."

Roya closed the bedroom door and leaned against it, feeling a thousand years old.

Trust. What an idealistic, nonsensical concept it was.

She'd trusted Bud since the day she'd met him. She would have fared better trusting Attila the Hun.

"Roya Pulaski—the fool. The idiot. The trusting soul. The unsuspecting wife."

If it all hadn't been so clichéd, she would have felt better.

Thousands of women, maybe millions, had been betrayed by their husbands. How did they deal with it? She'd watched daytime television talk shows. She knew what they all said. It was the stuff of soap operas.

She realized her initial shock was wearing off like Novocain. Even her anger masked the abiding pain roiling within. She was empty, hollow. And yes, a bit frantic.

She wanted answers, but the only ones she found made her feel worthless.

It was the most debilitating emotion she'd ever known. All her life she'd thought she'd done the right things—helping her family, doing things for others when she didn't want to or need to. She thought of the times when Bud had made her feel good. To her surprise, she realized he'd given her attention and tokens of affection, but only in public. Their hours alone had been punctuated with his accomplishments, his victories. When she began relating her day to him, her triumphs for a charity, like when she'd coerced the City of Chicago to underwrite an art showing with the proceeds going to the city's homeless, Bud hadn't acknowledged her coup at all.

Rather, he'd snapped his fingers and said, "That reminds me! I've got to call Central Builders about their contract." Then he'd left the room.

As her memories catapulted through her head, she realized that during most of their quiet personal times Bud had ignored her. He was always on the phone, preparing for a meeting or going out the door. Leaving. Bud forever seemed to be leaving.

She hadn't been abused or misused. In fact, she hadn't been used at all—at least not as a human being. Not as an equal. And certainly not as a wife.

"My God, you look fantastic tonight!" he'd said on their tenth wedding anniversary. "I have a surprise for you."

"The Cape Cod Room? I love that place. It's so nostalgic that I…"

"No way. It's too dark. No one will see us there. I want to show my girl off! I didn't tell you before but tonight just happens to be the Chamber of Commerce awards banquet. I found out through the grapevine that I'm receiving one of their top awards."

She remembered pretending that it didn't matter—that she was happy for him, proud of him. She remembered putting away romantic fantasies of dancing till midnight, then driving down the upper Gold Coast area, maybe stopping at one of those late-night coffeehouses. She'd wanted to talk with him.

She flung her hand to her forehead. "My God, that was nearly a decade ago. Even then I was desperate for attention, wanting to share my feelings with him."

That night came back to her. She'd wanted to cry, but had swallowed her pride and shoveled her need for a partner deep inside. She'd even convinced herself this was what all marriages were like.

Now she wondered, were they really?

Or had she duped herself for so long, she wasn't sure? She knew what she'd wanted from her marriage when she was eighteen. Bud had seemed so charming, accomplished and sexy then.

Perhaps she was guilty of allowing babies to usurp her husband's place on her priority list.

When she thought back to her honeymoon, to those first months of moving into this house, she realized Bud had virtually patted her on the head, telling her to be a nice girl, just as her parents had done, and then he'd left.

She'd told herself that a successful man *always* worked long hours. Even weekends at times.

Was he with her, even then? Loving Kitt? Not loving me?

"Yes, Roya," she said, answering her own question. "He was."

She immediately went to the bed, stripped back the expensive down comforter with its silk duvet cover and yanked at the white damask sheets. She balled the top and bottom sheets, tossing them in a corner. She took Bud's pillow, his white monogrammed terry-cloth robe and his slippers, and shoved them under her left arm. With the sheets under her right arm she went out to the hall, down the stairs and into the kitchen. She stuffed two plastic garbage bags full, tied them, walked barefoot out the frozen back steps and deposited the bundles in the garbage can.

She retraced her steps, quietly shutting her bedroom door.

She went to the bathroom, found a can of Lysol disinfectant spray and coated Bud's side of the padded mattress cover.

She leaned over and sniffed. "Good," she said aloud. "Now he's really gone."

She capped the spray, lay down on the bed, crossed her arms beneath her head and stared at the ceiling.

She had a lot of thinking to do.

15

Daria went to her old neighborhood—Clark and Rush. When Bud had brought her back from New York, she'd tried to break away from him, his overzealous, macho-possessiveness nearly strangling her. She moved to Old Town, along with hundreds of others of her flower-power, psychedelic, antiwar, anti-anti-generation.

She refused to move back home with Bud and her father; she couldn't take Oscar's continual put-downs.

"You can't cook for beans. Didn't your mother teach you anything?"

"Not enough, obviously," she would say, and bite her tongue to keep both bitterness and tears of grief from escaping.

"Why can't you iron like your mother? Sew like her? Dress like her?"

Be her. It didn't matter what she did for her father, it was never enough. Daria couldn't raise the dead.

Daria wished they could all put her mother to rest, but by using his wife as a yardstick, Oscar kept her memory alive.

Looking around Old Town tonight, remembering her childhood, Daria finally began to understand her family dynamics.

"How strange that Bud's death has brought mother's death back to me."

A cold blast of wind swept down the alley behind her, pelting the back of her neck. She shivered, feeling a deep pang in her belly. She lifted her face to the night sky as tears stung her eyes. "Mama. I miss you. I really, really miss you."

The pain in her midsection spread and furrowed deeper. It had been nearly forty years since her mother's death, and Daria had never addressed her loss. She'd been walking through life with her emotional shields up, thinking to keep herself armored against all mankind because she couldn't abide loving just to be abandoned again.

Bud's death should have been a relief to her. Instead, it shadowed her like a spy, and in her anxiety of trying to elude it, her vision of the past was becoming clear.

Upon her return to Chicago in 1970, the liberal arts major that had landed her an editorial job in New York didn't so much as open a rest room door in Chicago. Lake Michigan's industrialized, steel-oriented coast was over-populated with high school graduates filling every secretarial job available. Business had unilaterally issued a moratorium against hiring college graduates that year. Too many baby boomers like Daria were chasing too few jobs. Times were tough.

Daria adjusted. She settled. Forced by fate and circumstances, she did the one thing she'd sworn all her life she'd never do—she went to work for Bud.

Her position as assistant to the operations manager paid her enough money to keep her small apartment in a post World War II redbrick apartment building on the Near North side. She could walk the streets on Sunday morning, slip into a coffeehouse and lose herself, or find herself, whichever felt appropriate.

Daria had loved spending her weekend nights at Mr. Kelly's with Angela, the girl who lived next door and who'd introduced her to some of her friends. When Daria had first moved in, Angela took her to the hippie boutiques up and down Rush Street. She'd bought cheap white dishes out of a wooden crate at a quaint shop called Crate and Barrel. She'd stocked up on incense at Moonlight Lady and had her palm read in a basement bookstore specializing in the occult.

Angela had been a blast to be with. But a year later, she had decided to leave Chicago, marry a Vietnam vet and move to Wisconsin to raise dairy cows.

For all Daria knew, Angela was still there.

Lost in thought, Daria started across the street. Because it had begun snowing fiercely, she didn't see the approaching car.

The honking horn caused her to jump back, slamming her backside against her car.

"Are you crazy? Damn druggie!" the man in the car shouted, rolling the window up as he drove away.

Daria watched his taillights vanish behind a wall of snow.

Too easily she remembered other nights on this street, stumbling out into the traffic, nearly getting killed and others shouting obscenities at her.

"At least these folks are more polite."

But I'm not on drugs. I'm just sad. And terribly alone.

She walked through the falling snow, thinking how much she'd always hated the snow.

Heartless clumps of airborne ice.

But tonight the snow looked different somehow. Felt different. Was it possible it was warmer? Like a goose-down comforter, covering the earth, sheltering it from worse indignities.

"God, what's the matter with me? I've never been poetic before."

She squinted as she looked down the block at the old coffee shop where she used to hang out. Then she saw a golden puddle of light on the fresh snow.

"It's still there!" A wave of nostalgia washed over her.

Shuffling her feet, she carefully treaded the icy sidewalk and entered the shop.

She waved to the owner.

He nodded courteously but did not stop drying one of the oversize cappuccino cups she remembered so well.

"Sol. You don't remember me?" She went up to him, her hand extended.

"Should I?" He peered at her, trying to remember.

He was older now, looked nearly sixty. His middle was huge, his hair wisping a nearly bald head like silver lacework. But he still retained his good looks.

"No, you shouldn't." She chuckled lightly. *It would have been nice if you had.* "Daria Pulaski. I used to live here."

"Yeah? How long ago was that?"

"I moved here in 1970. I left in '79. Then about nine years ago, I moved home to take care of my Dad when he got sick."

"Geez, that's tough, kid."

"Yeah." She looked around the nearly empty shop. "Pretty stupid to move, huh? I could have had some great real estate if I'd stayed."

Sol was looking at her more closely. She could see him leafing back through time. Then he snapped his fingers.

"Cappuccino and *pain au chocolate*," he said proudly.

"You do remember!" Daria's face lit up.

He put the cup down and shook her hand, holding her forearm against his mighty onslaught. "Damn, baby, but you haven't changed much at all!"

"You think so?" She was stunned at the elation she felt.

"I do. You've fared a lot better than most of the old crowd. 'Course, most of them never kicked the drugs. Shame. They look worse than me!"

"Oh, Sol, you're just trying to make me feel better."

He peered at her. "Don't get mad if I say this, but it looks to me like you could use some cheering up."

"It shows that much?"

"Yep." He paused, then picked up the cup. "How about one of my new concoctions? It's got chocolate and mint for the holidays. I have to keep up, you know. The competition is rough."

"I hear you." She smiled. "I'd love some cappuccino."

Sol went to work whistling an old Three Dog Night tune. Daria hadn't heard the melody in ages. It took her back, making her feel comfortable.

"So, you haven't seen anyone I'd know, huh?"

"Sure I have. Jerry McNully? He's an attorney now. He and his wife moved back just last year, bought a brownstone not too far away. Said he got a steal on it for eight hundred thousand. Now that his three kids are finished with college, he's gearing down his practice a bit."

"Three kids? I didn't know he'd married. I didn't even know he'd finished law school. He was such an anarchist. For heaven's sake, Jerry was my connection for pot." *My God! Did everybody build a life but me?*

Sol laughed. "Yeah, I never figured Jerry for the domestic type. He says he was just screwed up until he met Mary."

Daria untied her wool scarf feeling more claustrophobic than warm. "Mary. Sounds like a nice girl."

"She's sweet. I like her." Sol placed a gargantuan cup filled with foamy milk and strong coffee in front of Daria. He leaned on the counter, his eyes unnervingly frank.

"So, what about you? Any kids?"

"No. Actually, I never got married."

Sol straightened. "A girl as pretty as you? I find that hard to believe."

Daria couldn't believe flattery could be so compelling. "No one's called me a girl in a very, very long time."

"Why not? To me you're just a kid," he said with that jolly manner of yesterday.

"You used to call me that."

"I called you 'kiddo.'"

"Yeah!" She snapped her fingers. "That was it."

"I remember," he said, looking down sheepishly, a distinct crimson blushing the ridge of his round cheeks.

"You flatter me too much, Sol."

He pulled a chocolate biscotti from a huge glass container and replaced the lid. "I remember everything about you, Daria. I just didn't expect to see you walking in here tonight."

Daria felt the conversation turning intimate, and it made her uncomfortable as all unfamiliar situations did. "I shoulda called first, huh?"

"Funny about time," Sol said. "You being here now, it all comes back to me like it was still happening. I remember you coming in late at night. Just like this. You'd sit over there in the back, by the window. You'd stare at the snow for the longest time. I thought you were the prettiest girl I'd ever seen. You looked like…I don't know, one of those Kennedy women. So polished, like you were a Hyannis Port misfit or something. You always wore white on the weekends. White wool coat. White pants, white muffler. White mittens. Not gloves—never gloves. You said you wanted to feel your fingers. I thought that was such a sensual thing to say.

"When everyone was gone, I'd pour you coffee and we'd talk. I remember thinking how smart you were, how well read. You used to read a lot then."

"I still do," she said.

"That's good." He smiled. "You don't remember spending time with me, do you?"

"No, I guess…"

"I just wasn't there to you," he offered.

A pained expression crossed her face. "That's not true."

"Sure it is. It's okay, too. You had a lot on your mind."

"I don't remember."

"Your brother, what was his name?" Sol asked.

"Bud…"

"Yeah, that's it. You were white-hot mad at him nearly every time you came in here."

"Was I really?"

His eyes were steady. "Consumed."

Have I wasted my entire life being mad at Bud? Have I thrown away the years that foolishly? It's not possible! I was building a life at the company. Wasn't I? I was planning for my future, I thought.

But now Bud has taken even that from me.

Then another thought struck her. *I'm doing it again! Blaming Bud.*

"Daria, are you all right? You look pale."

"Sol, Bud's dead."

"What? How?"

"I think someone murdered him. Everybody else thinks he killed himself. He didn't leave a note, though. That's kind of weird." She looked down at the floor. "He cut me out of his will."

"How do you feel about that?"

"Angry. Hurt. Rejected."

"Understandable. Especially when he was your life."

"Bud wasn't my life."

"Sure he was." Sol's eyes pierced her. "Remember those nights when you'd come in here. Sometimes we'd talk."

"Vaguely. I guess that's why I came here tonight. I was remembering. Hoping your shop would still be here."

"Back then, Bud was your sole motivation for everything you did. You smoked dope to piss him off, hoping he'd catch you. You told me so yourself. I asked you why you did that and you said it was because he didn't stand up for you against your father."

"I said that?"

"You said you thought older brothers were supposed to be protectors. When your father picked on you, Bud sided with your father. You could fight one of them, but not both. Bud failed you. He became a parent, instead of being a brother, which left you feeling alone."

The pit of her stomach yawned. It ached. She clutched at it. "Oh, Sol, that's how I do feel. So alone." Her hand flew to her forehead. She could feel perspiration breaking out on her forehead.

"Lots of us feel that way, Daria. I do."

"You? But you have…"

Her eyes met his crystal grays. She felt as if she were looking into his soul. It was the most intimate thing she'd experienced in her forty-nine years on earth.

He took her breath away.

"You don't look so good, kiddo." Sol reached out and touched her shoulder.

Daria wiped her forehead, trying to hide her feelings. "I'm fine. Must be a caffeine rush."

He realized she was uncomfortable, and that was the last thing he'd wanted. "I make good stuff, huh?" Sol chuckled.

"The best, Sol." She smiled up at him. Her eyes ached, looking at his heart sitting out there for her to see.

"Say! I've got something very special a friend of mine gave me for Christmas. This will make you feel better!"

As he scurried off to the far end of the counter where he kept pastries, breads and chocolates, Daria realized that Sol liked catering to her. It seemed he couldn't do enough for her. His eagerness was childlike. Odd, she'd never liked effusive people. She'd always felt uncomfortable when someone wanted to please her, believing they had ulterior motives. But Sol changed her opinion.

Why now? Why this moment? Why here with Sol? What's happening to me?

"Try this," he said.

"It looks like a truffle."

"It is. But it's from Ecuador. In the Andes. The filling is called *maure.*"

Daria bit into the chocolate. "It's fantastic. Like watermelon, raspberry and cranberry, all in one."

Sol nodded excitedly. "I'd make a fortune if I could import them."

"Why don't you?"

He shrugged his shoulders. "No way to transport them. I've looked into it. Cargo goes by ship and the chocolate melts too fast. FedEx could work, but the price is too high. So, it'll just have to be a once-a-year special treat when my friend smuggles them in for me."

"Too bad. I've never tasted anything like it."

"I know. Something like that would give me an edge over my competition." He leaned back and grinned widely. "Maybe even make me famous."

Daria laughed.

"See that? You're feeling better already. Must be magic in that there chocolate."

She licked her fingers and smiled at him. "I don't think it's got anything to do with candy, Sol. But yes, I feel it's magic all the same."

"Daria, I have to lock up in fifteen minutes. Would you keep me company?"

Daria felt a warm glow filling her insides, where only a little while ago there had been pain.

Sol smiled at her. "What do you say?"

She was amazed at how handsome he was when he smiled. Suddenly, she remembered him when he was young, and it was as if the days in between had never passed.

"I'd like that, Sol. I'd like it a lot."

"I'm glad," he replied.

16

Nick Petros sat across the beveled glass-topped table from his mother, Antigone, stirring down a thick blanket of foam on his cappuccino.

"Are you going to tell me about it or should I pretend I'm not seeing this maelstrom in your eyes?" Antigone asked her son.

"Mother, must you be so dramatic?"

"I'm Greek. It's allowed."

Nick laid the gold-plated demitasse spoon on the cobalt blue china saucer. He lifted the cup to his mouth; the coffee was ice cold. He had no idea he'd been lost in thought this long. He put the cup down after one sip. "I hate it that you know me so well."

"I'm a mother. It's my job." She smiled indulgently.

"Few mothers are like you," he said, and was struck at the profundity of his comment.

Antigone Petros had no equal. To everyone who knew his mother, she was the embodiment of creativity, sensitivity and classic elegance. She was tall, carrying her still-slender body erect, and though her face was showing the webbing of her fifty-nine years, she was beautiful and ageless. Her intelligence fascinated Nick. Where he used logic to decipher life's dilemmas, his mother employed a mix of ancient Greek philosophy and metaphysics to draw the same conclusions.

Nick knew she tolerated his deductive reasoning solely by virtue of the fact that she loved him. With others, Antigone pressed a magnanimous smile upon them and wrote them off as lost causes, not worth her time or breath of spirit to reform.

Antigone was not a rescuer, though Nick was.

Antigone sought to change the world by bringing hidden talents to light. Since Nick's father's death twenty-one years ago, Antigone had traveled around the world twice collecting unknown artists' works for her private showings. She sold these works at fair prices to her international set of not-so-wealthy friends who embraced her enthusiasm for discovering talent. Antigone's taste was unsurpassable when it came to any or all intellectual or pleasurable life pursuits. She wore her joie de vivre like a brightly colored scarf.

Nick, on the other hand, didn't have time for art, travel or joy. He was too busy altering the course of his clients' histories by cleaning out the sludge of their businesses, burning off the deadwood of passé systems and then re-seeding the fallow ground with extreme measures necessary to produce profits.

"Women like me generally choose not to become mothers, Nicholas," she said, brushing her hand against a thick wave of expertly colored auburn hair. "I like that part about our relationship. I've never quite seen myself in the maternal role. I've always fancied myself more your friend."

"Thank God," he interrupted.

"Which is why," she continued, her dark eyes beaming, "I have allowed you to bumble through life as you have, virtually unassisted."

"I would hardly say that, Mother."

"That's because you haven't the slightest idea what it's like to have a possessive parent. Greek mothers are notorious for smothering their children. God knows my mother did. I wanted to be nothing like her in the least."

"And you've succeeded admirably," he complimented her as he rose from the table and stared out the window at the panoramic view of Lake Michigan.

It was as clear a winter night as Chicago could offer. The lights of north Lake Shore Drive ribboned below, headlights streaming past. Sights like this made him sometimes wish he were a poet.

Fortunately, such moments were rare. They detracted from the mental processes by which he made his living—his handsome living.

Antigone rose gracefully from the French brocaded chair, crossed the antique gold-and-cream Aubusson rug she'd found in a flea market outside Deauville, France, fifteen years ago and looked up at the portrait of her dead husband, Constantine.

She waited for illumination to hit her son.

"Bumble?" He cocked his head around to stare incredulously at his mother. "I haven't bumbled a single step since I was born and you know it."

Antigone clasped her hands in front of her and smiled fatuously.

"I hate when you look at me like that," he grumbled, walking toward her. He rubbed the back of his neck where the hairs were standing on end. He always felt like this when his mother was about to impart her peculiar wisdom, which he never wanted to hear and which always came to bear upon his life. "Is this going to be like that time you told me Cassie and I would never fit?"

"I never said anything so banal. I said you were an implausible match, if I remember correctly. She wasn't the one, I could tell."

"The one. And what does that mean?" he said, lifting the lid of a burled wood humidor, inspecting the illegal Cuban cigars and then closing the lid again.

Antigone rolled her eyes. "I hate it that you never listen to me."

"Mother…"

She exhaled with frustration. "Cassie was not your soul mate."

Nick eyed the humidor. "Please, Mother. It's Christmas. Isn't that enough fantasy for one week?"

Antigone stood in front of Nick, lifted his chin to her face with her fingers and said, "You're my son. An imbecile sometimes. But still, my blood. I know when you're in trouble. And this time, you're in up to your shoulders. Why don't you want to talk about her?"

"Her?" He swallowed.

"The woman who has occupied your thoughts since the moment you walked in the door."

"This is ridiculous!" he said, taking his mother's hand and squeezing it affectionately. "I'm thinking about the job I no longer have."

"I think not," she replied sadly. "I know the look you have when you are challenged by work. I know when you're winning your battles and when you are losing. I know when you are sick, in lust or just plain tired. This faraway fire in your eyes is the same look I saw in your father's eyes the first time he saw me."

"Shit." Nick looked at the floor.

"You don't have to talk about it if you don't feel comfortable. But you're thirty-nine years old, and if you think you are going to live all your life without being forced to taste living at some point or other, you're mistaken. Humans were not meant to live via remote controls, Nick. If you don't jump in and *feel* life soon, it's going to kick you in some very unpleasant places."

"I know you're trying to help."

"What else would I be doing?"

"Please try to understand. I remember the pain you felt when Dad died. You were more than distraught. You were inconsolable. I thought your world had ended."

"It had."

"See? That's exactly what I'm trying to say!" He stood.

"Nick, you can't tell me you're running from love because you're afraid of losing love like I did!"

"What's wrong with that? How can I miss something I never had? It's much safer my way." *Painless. Perfect.*

"My God. I had no idea you felt this way, no idea I hadn't conveyed my sentiments to you more explicitly."

"I know what I need to know," he said, shoving his hands resolutely in his slacks pockets.

Antigone's eyes were strained with irreparable sorrow. "Nick, my precious. What I had with your father, our love, is immortal. I will always have my memories. I will always have your father with me. There has never been another man for me because Constantine was everything I ever dreamed of in a man, in a person and more. He's not dead to me." She placed her hand lovingly over her heart. "He lives with me in every breath I take. I never forgot him. I never let a day pass without talking in my mind to him. Love does not die. It lives on!"

Nick couldn't stop the look of pitiable indulgence he gave her. "Maybe you should give up his ghost, Mother, and build a life for yourself instead of trying to run mine."

For the first time in her life, Antigone Petros looked at her son with disdain. Then she quashed the negative feelings inside her. She loved her son too much to fight with him.

She watched the blood drain out of Nick's face when he realized the import of his blasphemy. "I'm sorry, Mother. I didn't mean that."

"I know, darling."

He came to her and held her close, in silence.

Antigone couldn't help thinking that in one thing she was right—Nick had met someone, an important someone. And he was shaken to his core over it.

She had faith in him. Nick would come around. Life had a way of making wise men of fools, given enough time and experience.

"Nick, all I'm trying to say is that I'd like to be your friend and, if you need me, I'm here to help."

Nick kissed her cheek, continuing to hug her.

What was there about his mother that made him nuts so fast? How could she be so right about his feelings? And what the hell were his feelings, anyway?

How could he possibly discuss Roya Pulaski with his mother when he didn't know what she was to him?

Definitive columns of white halogen lights lit the pre-dawn highway as Roya drove with her groggy eldest daughter to the offices of Pulaski Trucking Company.

"Could we hit a drive-thru for some coffee, Mom?" Cynthia yawned.

"And just when did you start drinking coffee?"

Ever since the blood. Since Daddy turned my life guts-side-out and put this confusion in my head. I only wish coffee were enough.

"I think I need it," she said, looking her mother squarely in the eye. "I hope we aren't going to make this five o'clock thing a routine."

"Chances are," Roya replied, her mind whirling with anticipation and fear of the unknown, the least of which was the knowledge that she would be seeing Nick Petros this morning. She wanted to be prepared. She wanted to have a strategy in mind when she pleaded with him, ordered, cajoled him into staying with the company. But just how would she do that?

Nick despised her, thought she was a slut. And now she needed him.

Roya's frown was intense.

Cynthia cocked an eyebrow. "How is it you're so wide awake, Mom? I heard you up and down all night. Don't you have any more sleeping pills?"

Roya clenched her jaw. *I was thinking about Nick. About a kiss. About the untenable situation I'm in.* "I don't have time to sleep anymore. I have one heck of a learning curve in front of me trying to save this company."

"Save our butts, you mean."

"That especially."

Cynthia turned up the heater a degree. "So why did you volunteer? You could have let Aunt Daria take it over. She knows what to do."

Roya shook her head. "I doubt it. Ownership for Daria would be the trophy. It would have meant she had won her battle with Bud. I'd never really seen her bitterness before Addie told me about it, but when Brian was reading the will, I saw in her eyes what I should have seen years ago."

"Saw what?" Cynthia sat upright, ears pricked.

"Envy."

"Aunt Daria? No way."

"In a self-serving way I'm glad you didn't see it, either. I don't feel quite so blind. But I decided last night that I don't want you or your sister raised like I was, thinking the world is full of nice people only waiting for a chance to help others. There are some things your father was right about. God helps those who help themselves first."

"I can't believe you're saying this, Mom."

Roya cast her a sidelong glance that shot through Cynthia like winter wind. "The difference between your father and myself is that I'm not doing it just for me, but for us. I will not let both you girls suffer due to one man's stupidity and cowardice. Even if he was your father."

"And you believe Aunt Daria is just like him?"

"How can she not be? No, darling. I love Aunt Daria, but she wouldn't have fought for us the way she would need to. She's never had children. She doesn't know what it means to put someone else's life before your own."

Cynthia's mouth gaped. "And you do?"

Roya was shocked her daughter knew her so little. "Make no mistake, Cyn, I would take a bullet for you and Lucienne." She gripped the steering wheel with a strength she'd known she possessed but had never been

forced to use. "No one is going to take my children's live-
lihood from them."

"Not even Daddy?"

"Especially not your father."

Cynthia put her hand on her mother's coat sleeve, feeling the rigidity and strength in her forearm. "I think I like
knowing this side of you."

"What side is that?"

"Genghis the Mom."

Pulaski Trucking Company occupied four acres of Illinois prairie when Bud relocated it from its original site on
Cicero Avenue in 1972. Sprawling like a giant concrete
spider, its multiple docks spoked out from the main offices, it lacked style and design. Nick Petros had never
seen anything uglier. But it was efficient. He had to give
Bud credit for that.

In the brief month he'd worked for Bud, Nick had
learned a great deal about the man who'd built a family-
owned trucking company into a national concern. Bud
had done it by being a maverick.

There was nothing on earth Nick respected more than
mavericks. He was one himself.

In the early seventies, unions ruled the country. The
Teamsters were more powerful than God when it came to
venting wrath on commerce and the retail industries of
America. No one dared hire truckers that were nonunion.
But Bud Pulaski had done precisely that. Nick could only
venture that, at the time, Bud's vision hadn't been as large
as his later reality proved to be. Perhaps Bud had come
into his fame and fortune by chance. Whatever the case,
Bud had devised the unique idea of joint-venturing with
his drivers. The drivers were independent contractors in
the beginning, providing their own trucks. As time
passed, more trucks were necessary and Bud proposed

buying the trucks with the drivers, using their salary to pay the debt service on the trucks. Once the trucks were paid off, the driver was the sole owner of the vehicle. This partnership mentality with his drivers instilled a sense of pride that no union could provide.

Bud Pulaski's drivers were bonded to him for life. They were loyal and fiercely devoted to Bud—their friend and partner. They often spoke of defending Bud to the death.

Nick had discovered that fact within days of coming to Pulaski Trucking.

He was even getting used to Bud's employees acting like pilgrims to Bud's Mecca.

Bud Pulaski was one of a growing legion of small employers to follow the Sears Roebuck style of employee benefit programs that allowed even the lowliest clerk to purchase stock in the company on both a weekly payroll payment basis or by investing his annual Christmas bonus back into the company.

Nick found other employee benefit incentives that Bud had used in the early days when he was building his company. All of them were well intentioned, visionary and helped establish strong employer-employee relations.

Somewhere between 1995 and 1997, Bud's private demons had surfaced. His arrogance, self-centeredness and horrific lack of self-esteem cost his loyal partners and employees as much as they did Bud.

It was that truth Nick Petros had unearthed and it disgusted him.

Nick had never known poverty, but he had known hard work. He knew what it took to make a buck and save one. These people never even spent their Christmas bonuses on toys for their children, all in the hopes of one day owning valuable shares of Pulaski Trucking Company. When Nick realized that Bud's staff would lose everything—their savings accounts, their credit union funds, college funds and most important, their trust in their god—he felt physically ill.

The end of Pulaski Trucking Company was an American travesty. It was unnecessary and it was one man's fault.

"Son of a bitch," Nick thought as he placed his personal belongings in a small cardboard box.

He had always made it a practice to travel light. Other than the engraved brass day calendar his mother had given him more than a decade ago, there were no photographs, no special coffee mugs, no sentimental paintings or even a holiday plant from a friend. Nick's office was as clean and neat as a hospital room—and just as sterile.

"No sentiments. No losses," he said to himself as he traced the engraving of his mother's inscription on the calendar, thinking of their dinner discussion the night before.

Nick, my eternal portrait of love. Mother.

It crossed his mind how unlike his mother's ideal his life had turned out to be.

Even more ironically, he'd spent nearly forty years seeking emotional oblivion and now suddenly found himself wondering if he was missing something.

He looked down at the date.

It was Monday, December 29. Only a few days left of the year. Then he'd start a new year fresh.

Fresh? From what? Close it out, Nick.

But something inside told him it wouldn't be that easy this time. Something was changing, something he didn't understand.

Perhaps he'd brushed his mother's words aside too quickly. Perhaps he shouldn't have rushed away last night. Perhaps he should have leveled with her.

He put the calendar in the cardboard box. "I better call Mother," he said, not realizing Cynthia was standing in the doorway watching him.

"Does she get up this early, too?" Cynthia asked, pushing her glasses to the bridge of her nose.

"Who...?" He stopped in mid-motion.

"Your mother. I didn't know anyone got up as early as my mother."

"What's she doing here?" he asked, unaware of his indignant tone.

"She owns this place," Cynthia retorted, matching his pomposity with her own hauteur. She had to admit to herself she was fascinated with the handsome man who had come to her rescue, or rather, the family's rescue, the day of the funeral.

Nick dropped his hands to his sides and glared.

Cynthia smiled. "She's in her office. She said you were going to have a meeting with her this morning." Cynthia looked down at the box. "Seems you two have your signals crossed."

"I was not informed of a meeting. Besides, I don't work here anymore." He turned away.

"I think that's what she wants to talk to you about."

"We have nothing to discuss," he said flatly.

Cynthia pushed herself off the doorjamb, stuck her hands in her slacks pockets and shuffled away. "Whatever."

Nick shot to the doorway. "Hey! Come back here!"

Cynthia continued strolling nonchalantly down the corridor.

"You tell your mother if she wants to see me, she knows where my office is," he shouted, but Cynthia kept

walking, a wave of her arm over her head signaling her
apathetic response.

Nick slammed his fist against the doorjamb.

She sent her kid to do her bidding?

"That tears it. I'm outta here!"

17

By six-thirty in the morning the docks were filled with workers loading cargo and drivers double-checking inventories. The offices were illuminated, computers were booted up and the smell of fresh brewing coffee filled the halls of Pulaski Trucking Company.

By all sights and sounds, it was just another day of business, no different from the thirty odd years that had preceded this one.

For Roya, it was like no other day in her life. Not even the late afternoon of Bud's death.

This morning was a beginning and an awakening.

She felt a perception she'd never known before. Her nerves were piqued but not frayed. Her mind was on alert but sensed no danger.

How ironic. In the aftermath of Bud's death, when I should be grieving, I feel as if I've just come alive.

She'd never thought of this building as anything more than a facility in which Bud worked, a place she only visited upon Bud's request for an errand run or a meeting with their CPA.

Now it would be the seat of her learning, her college, her life for God only knew how many years to come. Possibly forever.

If I don't screw up.

Entering Bud's office, she crossed the floor as if encountering a minefield. The room reeked of desperation and failure. It had that same finality to it she'd sensed in their house only moments before finding Bud's body. This office was the past—Bud's past. It was certainly not her future.

By the time she reached his desk, stood behind it, then sat in the chair, she realized she couldn't possibly work in his space.

She quickly left the office, went across the hall and opened the door. The room was filled with cardboard boxes stacked atop an old wooden desk. A single secretary's chair, upholstered in a faded gray Herculon, stood in the corner. The window was covered with a rust-and-blue rolled shade she remembered throwing in the garbage fifteen years ago when she'd remodeled the den in their home.

"Marjorie," Roya called to Bud's secretary.

"Yes, Mrs. Pulaski?" Marjorie hustled up to Roya.

"Whose office is this?"

Puzzled, Marjorie looked at the dirty walls and dusty corkboard. "It's a storage room."

"No one's ever used it?"

"Not that I know of."

"Good," Roya said, pushing up her sweater sleeves. "It's mine now."

Marjorie gasped. "But Mr. Pulaski's office is much nicer...and warmer."

Roya instantly grabbed a box of file folders. "Any idea what this stuff is?"

"Outdated files. Old customers we no longer service."

"Old customers?" Roya looked down at the box as if it contained gold. She plopped it back on the desk. "Great. Then I'll start here."

"Start?"

Roya smiled. "Yes, calling these customers first."

"But—" Marjorie's confusion was behemoth. "I thought you came to clean Mr. Pulaski's office...." She looked across the hall.

"Hardly. I'm taking my husband's place."

Marjorie's eyes rounded with shock. "But Miss Daria

was planning to take...I mean Miss Pulaski..." she stammered.

"Yes, I know," Roya said. "But the truth is that Bud left everything to me."

"But you don't know anything about..." Marjorie clamped her hand over her mouth to keep the words from spilling out. "I'm sorry. I forgot myself."

"I'm sure there will be a lot more said about my new position throughout these halls and bays before the day is over, Marjorie. The fact is, I have a mess on my hands, and you're right, I don't know anything about the trucking business. But I've listened a great deal over the past twenty years to Mr. Pulaski when he was discussing the business. By osmosis alone, I think I've retained enough to keep us afloat until the year is out."

"But that's only three days."

"Precisely my point. How badly can I screw up in three days?"

Marjorie's smile was wan, lacking support or confidence.

Roya didn't blame her.

The fact of the matter was that Roya could screw up plenty in only one day. She had more than a plateful.

Today she had to deal with Nick Petros. If she lost him, she might as well shut the company doors.

Damn if I will!

Cynthia turned around the corner and Roya saw the smug look on her daughter's face.

"I was right. He is here."

Cynthia nodded. "He's here, all right. But he's packing."

Roya's face showed no surprise. "Did he say anything to you?"

"I told him you expected to have a meeting with him this morning."

"You did what?" Roya rocked back on her heels.

Cynthia shifted her weight and put her hand on her

hip. "He was leaving, Mom. I didn't want him to go. I thought I'd give him a reason to stay."

"You thought wrong," Roya said, pushing past her and rushing down the hall.

Cynthia looked at Marjorie. "I hope Mom doesn't expect me to work in this dingy office."

"No," Marjorie replied, heaving her chest forward imperially. "She said this is to be her office."

Cynthia's mouth gaped as Marjorie went back to her desk. "My mother wouldn't be caught *dead* in a room like this."

Nick backed out of his office and right into Roya. The cardboard box nearly slipped out of his hands.

"Sorry," he apologized.

"I was hoping to talk to you," she said.

"So I heard." He frowned.

"Ordering you up to see me was Cynthia's idea. Not mine. I had no meeting scheduled."

"Nor will you have. I don't work here," he said, stepping aside.

Roya blocked his path. "Please, Mr. Petros. Could we talk about this?"

"No."

"Look," she said as anger smudged the edges of her composure. "I'm prepared to carry through with the terms and conditions of the contract you signed with my husband. You'll get your money."

"Gee, thanks. You make me sound like a mercenary."

"I didn't mean it like that and you know it. Why is it you have to turn my words around? I'm not trying to hurt you. I'm trying to help this company."

"Yeah, right."

He didn't know how she managed it, but there was just enough sincerity to her words to make him believe her.

"Truly," she said.

"Look, this isn't a Joan Collins movie. Just because you

inherited this place doesn't mean you suddenly know how to run a business."

"I know that."

"Do you? I doubt it. Ego has no place in a failing business. It's blood-and-guts time."

"I can handle it." *I've seen blood and guts. Have you, Nick?* "How?"

"By convincing you, one way or another, that Pulaski Trucking is worth fighting for."

"Why? So you can go shopping with your kids next week?" He nearly bit his own tongue wondering where this acidity was coming from. He didn't want to hurt her. Not really. He just wanted to be away from her, to forget.

"No, dammit!" She wanted to cry. Lord, it would have felt great, but she couldn't afford tears—strategically or emotionally. She'd cry later, when there was really something to cry over, not this silly frustrating man. "You're right, I'm doing this for my children's future. Where they are concerned, I'll go the limit. But there are people here I've known since the day I married Bud. I've helped them through illnesses, family crises, divorces and deaths. They stood beside me at Bud's funeral. He didn't deserve their loyalty, but in their way they were telling me that I did. I owe them. Now, are you going to help me or do I have to fight dirty?"

"Dirty?"

Her eyes narrowed as she scrambled for arguments, options. "Push me and I'll take you to court over your contract."

Nick was incredulous. "You don't have the time or money," he parried.

"The hell I don't! My legal advice is free, a trade-off with Brian. He'd do anything for me."

"Shit. You've already discussed this with him, haven't you?"

"I have," she lied. She wished she could cross her fingers behind her back.

Nick was impressed. He'd underestimated her.

Roya continued. "According to Brian, this company has not received a resignation letter from you. I have no acknowledgment of your defection from my husband, verbal or otherwise."

"You know damn well he died shortly after I quit!"

"I know nothing of the sort. All I have is your word. And for some reason you are hell-bent on reneging on our contract. Brian says I could even get a settlement out of you. Seems you have more money that I've got."

"How the hell do you know my financial status?"

"The Internet. My daughter is a hacker," she said flatly. Nick didn't miss the steeliness of her tone. "I need you, Mr. Petros."

I need you. I need you. I need you.

Her words seemed to reverberate in the hallway around him like an echo bouncing off the ancient rocks of the Greek Isles. Nick had never heard those words in his life. Never thought he wanted to hear them. Never thought they could alter his thought patterns so drastically. He hated the way they riveted him to the spot, then painstakingly chipped away at his resolve.

Roya took his silence as a sign he was weakening. "I know every single one of my faults, Mr. Petros. I know my shortcomings, my ignorance, but I'm willing to do anything and everything it takes to keep myself and this company out of bankruptcy. My life is at stake here. Please, won't you help me?"

What the hell was there about her that made him feel like a knight in shining armor? He'd never entertained such fantasies before. He was a man geared for the twenty-first century.

He had very much liked the person he'd been prior to meeting the then-married Mrs. Pulaski.

But Roya, the woman, was another matter.

She reminded him of a flower about to open. And in

that opening he could see more pain, heartbreak and anguish than he'd ever bring upon himself.

He should teach her to be hard, callous the way he was. She needed a shell but was too naive to know it.

Christ! She's enough to bust my heart open.

His every instinct told him to put one foot in front of the other and get the hell out. Instead, he heard himself say, "Nine months is all I'm obligated to under the contract. It's not much."

Roya beamed. "Are you kidding? I created a child in nine months and I was only nineteen." She held out her hand. "We have a deal, Mr. Petros?"

He shifted the box under his left arm and shook her hand. "Deal."

Roya felt oddly shy holding his hand. Believing she'd effectively placed him in an unemotional cubbyhole in her mind, she wasn't prepared for the comforting wave that washed over her.

"Thanks," she said, stepping away from him.

She'd thought of nothing for three days except how to keep Nick Petros at Pulaski Trucking. She remembered all too well his moral blasting of her. She supposed in a way she'd deserved his intractable derision.

Being honest with herself, she had not thought it possible she'd win this victory. She'd prepared herself for his rejection.

She didn't know where the notion of a lawsuit had come from, but her bluff had worked.

She would remember this Achilles' heel of his. She might need the knowledge in the future.

18

Daria didn't like the tumult of emotions inside her as she drove up to her parking space at the front of her office building. She was confused, hurt and terrified.

It wasn't Bud's mysterious death that upset her most, despite the fact that she'd professed to the police she believed he was murdered. Nor was it Bud's betrayal of her. And it wasn't even Roya's fatuous stupidity at wanting to take over the company that tied her belly in knots.

Daria didn't like change.

She hadn't ever realized this about herself before, but that was the bottom line.

Her comfort zone had been destroyed. She was being forced out into the world, to look at her life and make a new beginning at a time when she should be entering an era of downloading, downsizing her expectations of herself.

Daria had hoped by this point in her life to be taking it easy, but that wasn't an option anymore.

Daria slammed the car door and locked it. Zipping her down-filled parka against the winter wind, she hauled several canvas bags out of the trunk, along with two cardboard boxes, and entered the building for the last time.

Daria's rubber-soled boots squished against the faded linoleum as she walked past Marjorie's desk.

"Good morning, Daria," Marjorie said brightly, then, seeing Daria's dour look and the boxes, instantly dropped her smile. "Uh, will you be needing help?"

"No," Daria snapped, and marched into her office.

Marjorie was out from her desk in seconds, nearly flying to Roya's door. She tapped lightly.

"Yes, Marjorie," Roya's voice said from the interior.

Marjorie opened the door.

Roya was standing on a step stool, taking the roll shades down from the window with a screwdriver. Her platinum hair was cobwebbed with dust and pieces of brown-painted plaster. She wore a smudge of dirt or carbon on her cheek. Beads of sweat trickled from her forehead. Her white cashmere sweater had been swiped with bands of dirt from metal shelving in the closet. Marjorie had never seen Roya without every hair in place and her beautiful clothes cleaned and pressed.

"You wanted me to tell you if Miss Pulaski arrived?"

Roya's eyes widened. "She's here?"

"Yes, just walked in."

"Hallelujah! That's a good sign!" She jumped down from the step stool, bringing the shade crashing down with her. Plaster ripped from the wall along with the bracket she'd been extracting.

"You won't think so when you see her. She brought boxes. I think she's leaving."

"Oh!" Roya looked down at her filthy hands. "I was afraid of that."

Marjorie was confused. "Why would Miss Pulaski be leaving? She's as much this company as Mr. Pulaski is. Er, was."

Roya knew better than to discuss the specific terms of Bud's will with her secretary. Marjorie wouldn't believe Bud's seemingly calculated negligence toward his sister.

I hardly believe it myself.

"I'll talk to her," Roya said, dusting off her hands. "Would you mind calling the phone company and having jacks installed in this room? Take the phones out of Mr. Pulaski's office and use them in here."

"Do you want me to have his furniture moved in here as well?"

"No. I'll bring some of my own things from home."

"But what should we do about Mr. Pulaski's things?" Marjorie asked her, confusion over the changes mounting by the moment.

"Put an ad in the classifieds. We could use the income," Roya replied, and left a stunned Marjorie behind.

Daria's eyes were filled with tears when Roya walked in.

"Daria, I'm so glad to see you," Roya said, going toward her.

Daria put her hands up to stop her. "Don't come near me," she demanded. "I'm just getting my things."

"I want you to stay."

"Who gives a shit what you want?"

Roya suddenly realized she'd spent too much time worrying about dealing with Nick Petros and not enough strategizing how to approach Daria. "I need your expertise."

"Tough." Daria pushed past her, grabbed a stack of manuals from the bookshelf and shoved them in her canvas bag.

"Put those back," Roya said.

"What?"

"That's company property, and if you take them, I'll have you arrested." Roya's eyes were flinty as she stared at an unrelenting Daria.

"Fine." Daria put the books back.

Roya exhaled. "I don't want it to be like this."

"It's not your choice. I'm calling the shots on this one."

Roya flinched at Daria's venomous blast. She remembered Adrienne's counsel that Daria was envious of Roya. At the time she'd hardly believed it possible. Now the truth coiled around her like a deadly python.

Watching Daria's strong arms lift heavy picture frames off the walls, her movements expedient and obviously well calculated to take as little time as necessary, Roya barely glimpsed the woman she thought she'd known for twenty years.

Though Daria worked swiftly, Roya was excruciatingly aware of the glints of hatred that shot from Daria's eyes like flying glass.

"I didn't murder your brother, Daria," Roya said.

Silence.

Roya's mouth gaped. "How could you think I would do such a thing? What motive would I have?"

"Isn't that obvious?" Daria snorted.

"Not to me."

Daria whirled toward her like a banshee swooping down from the highlands. "You couldn't wait to take over this company. Look at you! Bud's only been in the grave a few days and you're here tromping around like Little Miss Dictator. Ordering people around. Ordering me."

"Where do you come up with this nonsense? Being part of the business world is the last thing I'd ever conjure up as an ideal life-style for myself."

"Not the way I see it. You don't want me around here and you know it. This begging and pleading act is for show. You know damn well I'd be a fool to help you. What the hell do I get out of it, anyway? Bud made sure I got nothing. Well, I'll take my nothing and start over someplace else. I've spent all my life working for family and I ended up with zip. No more. No *mas*, baby."

Roya decided to try another tack. "Your expertise is imperative for the life of this company. Don't you care about the people here? Marjorie?"

"Hell, no," Daria spat.

"I don't believe you."

"What?"

Roya stood firm. "I don't believe for a single minute that you really think I murdered Bud. Or that I'm trying to screw you out of your inheritance. If we were profitable, I'd make damn sure you were compensated for all your years with Bud."

Their eyes met.

In that moment Daria wanted to believe her sister-in-law. She wanted to believe that Roya would treat her fairly in the end, but she couldn't allow herself that luxury.

After all, look where trusting Bud had gotten her. Bud had not been loyal to her, so why should Roya?

"Do you know why I never liked you, Roya?"

Roya was taken aback. "I...didn't know that..."

"Sure you did," Daria cut in. "It was because you had it easy. And Bud was the one who made life a piece of cake for you. He didn't do that for me. He made me work twice as hard as other employees, because he didn't want them to think he was showing favoritism to family. Or so he said.

"Do you know why I didn't come to your fancy dinner parties or show up at the charity balls when you got me a free ticket? I was working overtime. Oh, I know I said most times that I had plans. Like I had another life. A life. Ha!

"The fact is, I would have loved to go to the country club or on a sail across the lake. But Bud always managed to plop a pile of paperwork on my desk at six o'clock. Stuff that had to be done by the next day. You see, he was embarrassed by me. My behavior wasn't acceptable, he told me. He was afraid I'd cut loose. Light up a joint or drink too much. Or whatever it was he was so petrified I'd do. Hell, who knows. But the point was, he used the carrot of my inheritance to dance his jig for almost thirty years.

"You never had to work for anything, Roya. Not even at landing Bud. He just fell in your lap. You even got your engagement ring on your second date. It was no sweat for you. And your parents lapped it up like honey. They offered you up like a sacrificial lamb, if you ask me. No questions asked. Bud told me once he just flashed his money and they practically shoved you into his arms."

Roya felt tears in her eyes as Daria's words struck a chord. She held herself in check.

"All you ever had to do was dress up like a dolly, spend his money and keep the kids out of his face. Now, how tough was that?"

"It wasn't," Roya said over the lump in her throat. For the first time, she felt Daria's shoes fitting around her feet. She felt terribly guilty about Bud's treatment of his sister. She wished she could say something, do something, to turn Daria's attitude around, but at this moment, Daria was filled with vengeance. Frankly, Roya felt as if she had a right to it.

Roya knew she would feel exactly the same if she were Daria.

"I wish you would stay, Daria," Roya said softly.

Daria lifted a heavy canvas bag over her shoulder. "I can't."

"I know." Roya shoved back her shoulders valiantly. She was almost proud of Daria at that moment, standing up for herself.

Daria fought an onslaught of emotions as she hoisted a cartonful of animal figurines she'd collected for years.

"I'm not giving up on you, Daria," Roya said.

Daria knew she didn't have to go. She could cave. She'd done it for Bud for years. Roya did need her. Needed her badly.

But isn't that acquiescing again? What if this is my last chance to take charge of my life? I must stay focused on myself. I have to be tough.

"Nick is extremely competent. You're in good hands. You don't need me anymore so I'll be punching out."

Daria's shoulder hit the doorjamb as she lumbered out the door, but she didn't flinch.

She didn't curse. She didn't look back. She just kept going.

* * *

Word of Daria's resignation spread through the halls and across the bays of Pulaski Trucking like a firestorm.

"Marjorie overheard Daria accusing Mrs. Pulaski of murdering Bud," one of the drivers said to a keypunch operator.

"What the hell is Mrs. Pulaski doing here, anyway? She don't know dick about hauling."

"I wouldn't worry about it. Soon as she breaks a fingernail, she'll be back in the beauty shop where she belongs."

One of the dispatchers turned to a secretary at the watercooler. "Yeah, Mrs. Roya Pulaski won't stick it out the week. Daria will be back and we'll be back to normal."

Marjorie overheard the conversation and was spurred to add, "Don't kid yourselves, guys. Bud Pulaski is dead. Nothing will be normal for us again."

Roya drove a twenty-four-foot truck home from the docks with Cynthia following in the family car.

She pulled up to her house and found nearly every light on, though she knew the house was empty.

"What's going on?" she said to herself as she engaged the emergency brake and hopped out of the cab.

Cynthia parked the car at the curb and rushed up to her mother. "You're looking a little too natural behind that wheel, Mom," she joked, and followed her mother's concerned gaze. "Lucy must be home."

"I hope not. I told her I wanted her to stay with Mother."

Roya had no more spoken the words than the front door opened and Marie Monier appeared in the doorway, wearing a white apron tied around her slender middle. She folded her arms across her chest the way she always did before a fight.

Roya hung her head. "Not tonight."

Cynthia peered at her grandmother. "What's she doing here?"

"Making a stand. Can't you tell?"

Roya approached her mother.

"It's about time you got home. It's after eight. And what is that contraption doing here and why are you driving it?"

"It's a truck, Mother, not a contraption. I've got to move some furniture to my new office. I thought my desk from the bedroom..."

Roya kissed her mother's cheek.

"Are you out of your mind?"

"Probably." Roya looked past her into the foyer. "Where's Lucienne?"

"In the kitchen with your sister."

"Addie's here? I didn't see her car."

"Your father brought us all over. He went to the store for me. The situation in your pantry is deplorable, Roya. How can you cook with so little?"

"Preparing dinner hasn't exactly been on my mind lately, Mother."

"Hi, Grandma," Cynthia said, hugging Marie, hoping to stall the confrontation between her mother and grandmother.

"Hello, dear. Come get out of the cold," Marie said, closing the front door behind them.

"I thought we agreed that Lucy was to stay with you and Papa for the next few days."

"You and your father agreed. I had no say in the matter and neither did Lucienne. The fact is, there is nothing for the child to do at my house but get into trouble."

"Trouble?"

Cynthia leaned her mouth to her mother's ear.

"Bored."

"Oh, yes. Well, that's probably true. Then you don't mind staying here with her?"

"Mind? Of course I mind."

Cynthia rolled her eyes.

Here it comes. Roya clenched her jaw against the onslaught.

Marie's delicate hands settled firmly on her hips. "I'd like to know if all this nonsense Lucienne has been telling me is true."

"Nonsense?"

"That you've decided to run Bud's business," Marie replied.

"Bud's dead. He left the business to me in his will. Or what there is left of it."

"It's bankrupt, Lucienne told me."

"Not quite," Roya said. "There's a chance to save it. Slim, but still a chance."

Marie shook her head. "I don't understand what's gotten into you, Roya. Your place is in your home, taking care of your children. When you chose to become a mother, that responsibility was for a lifetime." She had to look away from her daughter as a tear sprang to her eye. "I thought I raised you better than this."

"This?"

"Abandoning your children. And especially during this time of mourning. Why, it's not…not civilized, the way you dump Bud in the ground and then go traipsing around—" she glanced out the front window "—in a truck!"

Roya's impatience erupted. "I refuse to have this conversation with you, Mother. It serves no purpose."

"You owe me an explanation," Marie said as unfamiliar anger steeled her resolve.

Roya was incredulous.

Has everyone on the planet lost their mind today?

"Owe? I owe a lot of things, Mother. Money to the creditors. Time to my children. An apology to Daria. A debt to Nick Petros for agreeing to work with me. Not to mention a curse or two to my poor dear husband who not only cheated on me, but blew his brains out when the heat in the kitchen got too hot. I'm a lot of things, Mother, but I'm not a coward. I won't hide behind these walls while my life and my children's financial future crumbles around us because your need for cultural protocol has not been met!"

Marie's mouth fell open, and she quickly snapped it shut. "I don't know what's happened to you, Roya. You've never treated me like this. You've always been so…"

"What? Easily manipulated? The faithful servant doing your bidding? Driving you to the hairdresser's on Fridays, to the grocery on Tuesdays, to the bank on the first of the month. And you know, I have to ask myself why I did that for twenty years. You're a healthy woman. You could take driving lessons and probably pass with flying colors, considering all the back seat instructions you've given me all my life. But then I think to myself—" Roya tapped her cheek with her forefinger "—what's mother so afraid of? The driving itself? Then I think, no, that's not it. She's self-centered. Just the way I was until Bud died.

"Well, I don't have time for selfishness anymore, Mother. But you're right about one thing—I have changed. Drastically. And I have no intention of reverting to the vapid, ignorant woman I used to be. I like this person I'm turning into."

"Well, I don't."

Roya watched her mother's implacable expression and found herself filled with empathy for this rigid woman who was never meant to be a part of the modern world. For the first time in her life, Roya saw her mother not as a parent, but as a woman, afraid of her own shadow, afraid of living, and impossibly clueless about how to alter her world. Marie lacked accomplishments of her own. She'd lived life through her children, and as bizarre as it seemed, Roya realized that she'd been nothing more than a fairy-tale princess to her mother.

Marie had never let her daughters forget that royal French blood surged through their veins. The world Marie wanted for her daughters was caught in mists of history and tradition, with little reality.

Adrienne had always been the rebel. Not Roya.

Roya could see that even in Adrienne's misconduct—her divorces, many fiancés and exciting career—Marie had subconsciously supported Addie's behavior. Marie had needed the excitement. Marie had needed the chaos, turmoil and pain to balance her mundane, middle-class life.

Marie's stand against Roya today was the most courageous and proactive behavior she'd ever displayed.

Roya smiled inwardly with admiration.

Marie didn't know it now, but in time she would. They were all changing.

She slipped her arm around her mother's shoulder. "Oh, you'll like me, Mother."

They walked toward the kitchen where Adrienne had

come to stand in the doorway.

Marie wriggled out from Roya's arm and marched stone-faced past Adrienne. "I don't have to do anything of the sort."

Roya expelled a leaden sigh.

"Good going, sis," Adrienne chuckled. "That took balls. More than I ever had. I didn't know you had it in you."

"Neither did I," Roya said, slipping her arm around Adrienne's waist.

"Well, I for one do like the new you. I always knew I had a sister."

Roya's eyes met Adrienne's.

In the midst of the chaos around her, Roya felt a love so deep and endearing it awed her. In her heart, she knew she'd done nothing to deserve Adrienne's love. It was unconditional and boundless. It was a miracle—and it was hers for the taking.

Roya gathered the love in her hands like a bouquet, knowing she would remember this moment for the rest of her life.

19

Kitt Cabrizzi's legal documents flowed over the fax machine at Pulaski Trucking Company in full sight of three employees. Marjorie had been too late to retrieve the heinous flow. The gossips latched onto the substantiations of the rumors that Bud Pulaski had been banging his high school sweetheart till the day he died.

"How could he have done that to poor Roya?" Alma Masterson said to Linda Peters in the secretarial pool.

Linda slicked her pinkie finger over a thickly drawn black eyebrow and closed her compact. "Bud was no saint. Roya was stupid for not seeing him for what he was. Stupid is as stupid does, if you ask me."

"She did not deserve to be betrayed just because she loved her husband, trusted him and believed in him. Lots of us trust our husbands."

Linda smacked her lips together, spreading lip gloss into the creases. "I don't."

Alma's smile was smug. "You shouldn't."

"Mom, are you listening to me?" Cynthia asked Roya, who was poring over the stack of new faxes Marjorie had just brought in.

Roya's eyes felt as if they'd fall out of her head.

This is impossible. Utterly, insanely impossible. Surely there's a mistake. Surely Brian missed something.

"Mom, I've been through this whole box of files. Called every company we used to do business with. Half of them were disconnected phone lines. That must mean they are

out of business now, huh? Or moved, maybe." Cynthia
yawned and leaned back in the upholstered boudoir chair
Roya had brought from her bedroom. The chair looked
silly in the tiny, unventilated office, but Cynthia had to
admit, with the long hours she and her mother had been
working, the chair was damn comfortable.

Roya had stayed at the plant on Saturday night painting the walls an eggshell white and installing the yellow-
and-white-striped draperies she'd removed from the
master bath.

At first Cynthia thought the idea of making over the office with her mother's favorite French pieces was a waste
of time.

However, Cynthia had never bargained for the incredibly long hours her mother would be at the office. Roya
had told Cynthia she'd wanted to make her office
uniquely her own and that it had to be a home away from
home.

That was exactly what had happened.

Roya's office was a symbol of her commitment. But to
the staff, it was yet another point of ridicule. Too often
Cynthia had stumbled onto a trio of workers plotting subterfuge.

"If you were smart like me, you'd be ducking out at
lunch to look for a new job," one of the computer opera-
tors said in the women's rest room while Cynthia eaves-
dropped from her stall.

"You're right. With Daria gone, the handwriting's on
the wall. This place is history."

Cynthia hadn't told her mother about the daily grum-
blings she was hearing. Her mother had too much on her
mind as it was.

"How about I order us a pizza for supper, Mom."

"Fine." Roya kept reading.

"Maybe throw in a couple of seven and sevens." Cynthia leaned forward to see if her mother was listening.

"Sounds good."

"Maybe Tiffany's would deliver a silver tray for us to serve it on. How's that?" Cynthia chuckled to herself.

"Uh-huh."

"Earth to Mom!" Cynthia shouted, and clapped her hands.

Roya jumped in her chair. "What?"

Cynthia's laugh stopped cold in her throat on seeing the stark terror in her mother's eyes. "God, Mom. What are you reading?"

Roya's hands were frozen and shaking at the same time. She didn't know if she wanted to hit, throw or crumple the papers in front of her. It didn't matter what she did to them. There were more papers just like them sitting in Kitt Cabrizzi's attorney's office.

Roya reached for the telephone and punched out a number.

"Brian?"

Upon hearing the name of the family attorney, Cynthia sat bolt upright, all thoughts of food fleeing from her, along with what felt like the blood in her veins.

She and her mom were in trouble. Again.

"Tell me this isn't true, Brian."

Just then there was a knock on the door, and, without waiting for an answer, Nick Petros opened the door and walked in. "Roya, I just—"

"Shh!" Cynthia held her fingers to her lips in warning.

Roya had not looked up and was unaware of Nick's presence as she continued speaking with her attorney. "Are you trying to tell me that my husband set up a trust fund for Kitt Cabrizzi and none for his daughters? And that Kitt's claim to her inheritance is legal?"

Roya raked her fingers through her hair as she listened.

Nick knew he should leave. This was none of his business. He didn't want to hear anymore about Bud Pulaski's twisted actions. He wanted to steer clear of dangerous intersections when it came to anything about Roya.

But Nick stayed.

He listened as intently as did Roya's eldest daughter.

Roya felt as if her breath were being cut off.

"She's got enough money to feed her, clothe her, send her to Europe if she wants! Do you know what this means? It means Cynthia will have to drop out of college. I pay her tuition per semester, not by the year. Do you know how much college means to her? She's bright. Far more intelligent than I ever was or will be. This is a waste of a young woman's life. And for what, Brian? I ask you!"

Passing her hand over her upper lip, she wiped away nervous perspiration.

"I don't believe this! What can I do? Sue? Contest the will? How much would that cost?"

Cynthia bit her thumbnail.

"And where would I find that kind of money?"

Roya's head came up and hit the back of her chair.

It was then that she saw Nick.

She blushed.

Nick's eyes bore into Roya's.

I'm here for you. He wanted to say it aloud, but didn't dare. Cynthia would take it the wrong way. Or worse, the way he intended it. Roya would read too much into it. He couldn't risk letting her know she could depend on him.

Yet, once again, he felt like Lancelot to her Guinevere. He was unused to wearing armor. It shocked him how comfortable it felt.

Roya's blue eyes were filled with dismay, fear and pleading.

Nick held his breath as he willed his strength into her.

Roya couldn't have stopped the flood of emotions inside her if she'd tried. All she knew was that at that moment, Nick looked like the Second Coming.

Cynthia's eyes went from her mother to Nick and back again.

She felt an energy in the room she'd never experienced before. It reminded her of her high school chemistry class.

When magnet meets steel.

Cynthia wasn't sure what it meant, but she knew one thing. Her mother had never looked at her father the way she was looking at Nick Petros, and her father had never looked at her mother like this, either.

Cynthia bolted out of her chair. "Excuse me. Gotta order a pizza," she said, rushing past Nick, bumping his forearm in her haste out the door.

"Brian, I want to meet with you in your office first thing in the morning. Don't give me that. I'll come in at six. I don't sleep much these days as it is. Fine. I'll see you at eight."

Roya hung up.

Nick expelled his breath. "I'm sorry." He motioned toward the door. "I should have waited outside until…"

Roya waved away his objections. "Forget it. I'm surprised you haven't heard about it from one of the women in the office."

"No, I don't hang out with them much."

"Oh." Roya rubbed her eyes. They were wet. She looked at her fingers.

Shouldn't anger be hot and dry?

"Lousy break," he said, instantly regretting his flip tone.

She glared at him.

"Is there anything I can do to help?"

"What's this? Nick Petros offering to help without the threat of a lawsuit?"

"Thanks, I deserved that."

"I know," she said, looking at the fax. "What kind of justice is there in a world where a mistress can claim nearly a hundred thousand dollars and I'm forced to sell my house?"

"You want justice? Go to a movie," he said, sitting in a wing chair, the only one in the room large enough to fit his lanky frame. "Are you really going to sell your house?"

She nodded. "I have to. I need the money to meet next month's payroll."

"I see."

Roya heard respect in his voice. She felt as if he'd just handed her a national award. "Thanks."

"For what?"

"I dunno." She paused. "Yes, I do. Thanks for working as hard as I do. Harder. At least you know what you're doing."

"That I do," he said, taking a sheaf of papers out of his folder. "I think I've come up with an idea to get some business in here without spending a lot of money."

"Define 'a lot.'"

"Nil. Hardly any. Only ten thousand."

Roya clasped her hands on the top of the desk. "I didn't sleep last night going over the books. According to the figures I have, I don't have a dime to spend on ads of any kind or venue."

"Remind me to talk to you about those books when I finish."

Roya was intrigued. "Tell me now."

"One of the reasons Bud and I were fighting that day—" he cleared his throat awkwardly "—was because I knew a great many bookkeeping records were missing."

"Missing?"

"Yes. I needed an accurate budget to give to Freddie's company in order to launch our ad campaign. Bud kept fudging. One minute he held my feet to the fire. The next he gave me the moon. I knew he wasn't making any sense."

"You're right. It doesn't make sense. And Brian said there was a hundred thousand not accounted for," she said, remembering her conversation with the attorney on the day of the funeral.

"You think that's Kitt Cabrizzi's trust fund."

"Stands to reason. It certainly bears looking into. I'll

talk to Brian about it in the morning. At the very least, it is an odd coincidence."

Nick frowned. "I don't believe in coincidence."

"Really? Neither do I."

"There's always a reason for everything." Nick smiled to himself. "My mother told me that."

"She's right."

"She means it metaphysically."

Roya smiled. "I like her already."

Nick stuck his finger in the air. "Which leads me to this," he said, holding up the folder.

"Okay. Tell me your idea."

"To put your mind at ease, I never said you would have to put out money."

"But you said 'ten thousand'…"

"Trade out," he said, pulling a fistful of newspaper clippings out of a second folder.

Glancing over the desk, she realized she was in each of the photographs.

Why, those are my charity photos. The Heart Ball. The Cancer Society… They're all there!

"Nick?"

He jabbed his finger at the clippings. "You made some damn strong connections in this town, lady. I never realized it until my mother gave me all these."

"Your mother again?"

"Antigone's a piece of work. But anyway, it got me thinking. All these charities take donations, right?"

"Yes."

"We need exposure. A lot of it and fast. It's January. High season for the social set, I understand. You get on the phone and you offer our trucking and moving services to each of the charities, say a thousand dollars' worth each, in trade for an ad in their program or maybe a blip in the columns the way you did with this jeweler here," he said, handing her an article out of the *Chicago Tribune*.

"Not only that, but we get the tax write-off as well," she said brightly.

"Now you're getting the hang of it," he said, pride radiating from his eyes.

"Why didn't I think of this? I've thought of it for a hundred other people."

"Preoccupied, I guess."

"Just a little," she agreed, glancing at Brian's fax.

Nick had expected her to pause with her heavy thoughts. But she hadn't.

She'd raised her face back to his a millisecond too quickly.

That was how she saw the longing in his eyes.

She didn't turn away. She didn't flinch. She didn't rebuff him.

Instead, she gave it back to him measure for measure.

She wants to kiss me as much as I want to kiss her.

Nick felt his emotions spilling out of him. For weeks he'd managed to keep them under control. He'd even conned himself into thinking that he wasn't attracted to her, wasn't interested in pondering what - would - have - happened - if - she - hadn't - been - the - boss's - wife kind of thoughts. He'd pretended they were co-workers and that was all.

Nothing could have been further from the truth.

He knew it.

She knew it.

The door flew open.

"Mom, I ordered two large pizzas and three sodas," Cynthia announced, looking at Nick. "I figured you for a whole pizza, Nick."

Nick tore his eyes from Roya and swallowed back his lust. "You figured right."

20

Lieutenant Dutton showed up at Pulaski Trucking Company unannounced.

Seeing his face coming down the hall toward her scared the hell out of Roya. All her life she'd never understood why innocent people would run from the truth, from justice. But at that moment, as guilt-free as she was in the murder or suicide of her husband, Roya wanted to run as far away as she could and never look back.

The lieutenant's face was grave.

Behind him was another man in uniform carrying a box.

"Lieutenant," Roya said, extending her hand to him, wondering how she was able to move or talk.

"Mrs. Pulaski, I tried to call you, but your telephones here have been busy for hours." He smiled at her.

It was a good sign.

"Thank God for that," she said. "Please, won't you come into my office?"

"Thanks," he said, and followed her to the small room.

Lieutenant Dutton looked around, his surprise obvious on his face.

"Is there something wrong, Lieutenant?"

"I had thought…well, expected something more grand," he said.

She chuckled to herself. "I know what you're thinking."

"I doubt it." He coughed.

"Most men would feel as if they were walking into a Barbie dollhouse."

"That's exactly what I was thinking," he said, eyeing the diminutive chairs and settee. He glanced at the porcelain china teacups, teapot, sugar bowl and creamer. He couldn't help wondering what Alice would do in this wonderland.

And if she had a single chance of surviving.

"I came to let you know you're off the hook," he said flatly.

Roya felt a rush of relief. She was innocent, but it was melodious hearing that the law thought so as well.

"Thank God that's over. You've determined it was a suicide then?"

"I didn't say that." He shook his head.

She was incredulous. "But that's...why not?"

"Frankly, we've found a great many disturbing factors that all point to murder."

Enemies?

Roya felt her legs go wobbly. "Please, sit." She motioned to the wing chair where Nick always sat.

It fit the lieutenant well.

She folded uneasily into her desk chair. "Tell me, if you may."

"Sure you want to hear this?"

"Definitely." She braced herself, knowing more of Bud's sludge was about to be rooted out.

"Your husband had mob connections."

"That's preposterous." Visions of herself, Bud and her young daughters in church flew across her mind. She saw Bud holding Cynthia's tricycle for her. Bud showing Lucy how to hold a tennis racket. Bud on Christmas morning, coffee in hand, waiting patiently for everyone to open the lavish gifts he'd given his "little women." Bud holding her. Bud kissing the girls good-night.

There had been many reasons Roya hadn't seen this

tempest coming. Her corner of Bud's world had been protected, sane and, by her yardstick, loving.

She'd been too busy to grieve, too scared of losing what little she still owned. She'd been fighting battles with her family, her employees and what seemed like legions of factions all bent on destroying her.

She'd been angry with Bud over his affair. She'd been bitter and determined. But she hadn't been sad.

Until now.

She put her hand to her heart, hoping it wouldn't burst through her chest. The pain was unbearable.

Lieutenant Dutton saw her pain.

"Maybe we should do this some other time. Do you want me to leave?"

"No." She closed her eyes slowly, then opened them again, prepared to hear the truth. "Go on."

"According to our sources, your husband was an occasional user. Bought good stuff. Expensive stuff from dealers with strong Colombian connections. And over a very long period of time. Thirty-some odd years, as far as we can tell."

Roya felt herself drowning again.

This man was telling her Bud had been a cocaine addict. She'd never seen any evidence of drugs. No powders or pills or straws or whatever those things were she'd seen in the movies. Roya's knowledge of drugs extended as far as the ibuprofen she took for menstrual cramps and the Seconals she'd taken after Bud's suicide.

God, she had a lot to learn about life.

About Bud.

What amazed her most was how he kept everything secret, at least from her. It was as if he had lived parallel lives.

What had that been like for him? And which life had he preferred—the one with her and the children, or that other one filled with intrigue, danger and nefarious people?

She shuddered.

"You okay?"

"Fine." She steeled herself.

"We have a few more angles we're checking into. Nothing concrete yet, though. I'll keep you up to speed."

"Angles?"

"Leads. My man is meeting with his snitch tonight. We'll know more then."

Snitches. Coke. Mobsters. And Kitt Cabrizzi. My God, Bud, I never knew you at all.

"I'd appreciate anything you could tell me."

"I was hoping you could tell me something," he said.

"Sure. What?"

"Anything that comes to mind along these lines. A phone call you might have misunderstood at the time. Unfamiliar names he might have dropped. Records we missed. Meetings with no apparent connection to the business. Stuff like that. We've found that, after the crisis of the initial murder has passed, family and friends remember a great deal more than they'd anticipated."

"I'm sorry, Lieutenant. It's just that I'm having a hard time taking all this in. I suppose I'm guilty of convincing myself that Bud committed suicide, so the concept that someone murdered him just hasn't registered with me. You see…I'm the one who found the body."

He had his gun in his hand. There was no sign of a struggle. Wouldn't I have felt it somehow if Bud thought someone was going to kill him? Wouldn't I have at least known that much about my husband?

My God, what am I thinking? I was insensitive to the fact that he wanted to kill himself.

Lieutenant Dutton watched her trying to make sense of the senseless. "Things aren't always what they seem, Mrs. Pulaski. I don't know if you follow this kind of thing in the papers, but back in 1982, a famous Italian banker with close ties to the Vatican was murdered. At the time, his death was made to look like a suicide. It took Kroll Associates, the best detective agency in the world, to break that case."

She shook her head. "I didn't hear about it."

"It was in the news here quite a bit. What with Chicago's close Catholic community. Newspapers. Television."

Roya's mind clicked. "I see what you're saying. Bud's enemies might have remembered those details as well. Used the same methods."

"Precisely," he said.

"Frightening. To think the blueprint for murder is televised for public consumption."

"Happens every day. Recipes for making bombs of nearly every magnitude are published on the Internet daily."

"I'd heard that. But when it strikes in your own backyard, it's terrifying."

"No one is immune to violence."

"I'm finding that out, Lieutenant."

"You have my card if you need me?"

"Yes."

"Good. I'm hoping to put a closure to this investigation soon, Mrs. Pulaski. I don't like loose ends."

"Neither do I. But, Lieutenant, I have to say once again, I'm still convinced my husband killed himself."

"Frankly, Mrs. Pulaski, initially I'd thought the same thing. But we had reports that your husband was followed home that night. There's no question there was someone else in your yard that night. We have footprints to prove it."

Roya's shock was evident in her gasp.

Murderers? In my backyard? What if we'd been at home? Would they have killed me as well? Cynthia? Lucienne?

Roya felt her pulse stop.

She'd never in her life let herself think she or her daughters were vulnerable.

How dare Bud place us in such a precarious position?

How could he be so self-centered?

There it was again, she thought. Bud thought of Bud. Bud cared about Bud and no one else.

Whether he died by his own hand or someone else's suddenly didn't seem all that important a riddle to solve.

Frankly, she didn't care anymore.

She'd wasted enough emotions, good and bad, on Bud Pulaski.

Lieutenant Dutton droned on with his explanation. "Those footprints don't match your shoe size, nor those of your daughters, sister, mother or father."

Roya's mind clicked again.

What about my sister-in-law?

Roya couldn't believe she was thinking such traitorous thoughts. Daria? Impossible. Yet, Daria had accused her of killing Bud. What if Daria had made a big show to throw suspicion off herself? But what would her motivation be?

Envy.

Adrienne's words haunted Roya like a ghost.

"Hell."

"Pardon me?" Lieutenant Dutton's keen eyes were riveted on her. "Did you remember something?"

"Not really."

"Please. It may be insignificant to you, but it could be just what we're looking for."

Roya wasn't prepared to throw out her damning suspicions. At least not yet.

She suddenly remembered something else.

Pulling out her desk drawer, she lifted the fax she'd received from Brian. "Kitt Cabrizzi had her attorney send this to me. Maybe you should look into it."

He took the papers and read them.

Roya watched as his eyes stopped dead center in the page where the hundred thousand dollar amount was mentioned.

He looked at her. "Is this for real?"

"More real than I want to admit."

"I'll check it out. Thanks," he said, standing. Suddenly he remembered the officer behind him.

"I almost forgot, Mrs. Pulaski. These are some things we took from your husband's study. Bullets. Papers. Photos. We're finished with them now. It's your property. You might need them."

The officer put the box in the corner, nodded and stood on the other side of the door.

"Thanks," she said, looking at the container as if it contained a cobra.

Lieutenant Dutton shook hands with Roya. "I'll keep in touch."

"Please do," Roya replied.

The lieutenant left quietly, like a phantom.

21

By Valentine's Day, Roya had sold it all: the house she'd never liked, the elegant furniture, Bud's Mercedes, his clothes, his gun collection, the grandfather clock she'd so painstakingly searched out for his fiftieth birthday, the patio furniture, the junk in the basement and the heirlooms in the attic.

Roya sold her past for profit.

Every family member she could count despised her for it.

"You've lost your mind, Roya Monier Pulaski. Pure and simple," Etienne said as he watched her move cartons of meager necessities she'd retained to get herself and her daughters through the next few years.

"It's my stuff, Papa. I can do whatever I like with it."

"Many of these were gifts from us. We intended them to be heirlooms for the girls."

"Cynthia needs college tuition, not a silver tea service."

"But these are irreplaceable!" he retorted.

"They are things!" Her eyes bore into him.

Adrienne entered the kitchen. "Whoa! You sure know how to clean house! Did I get here in time to buy the *Bois de Boulogne*?"

Roya shook her head. "Sorry."

"Roya! How could you? You know damn well I've always wanted that painting!"

"I knew nothing of the sort. You never said you even liked it," Roya replied, shocked that Adrienne was turning on her as well.

"I would have killed for that painting."

"Really?" Roya cocked her eyebrow.

"Don't look at me like that," Adrienne warned.

Roya felt like arguing, she who'd made a practice of never arguing because it was a waste of time and breath. But suddenly, it seemed the right thing to do. The only thing to do.

"If the shoe fits," Roya said.

Adrienne was taken aback. "You don't mean that."

Their eyes locked like battering rams.

They both had the right to their emotions. But they were both wrong.

"I don't," Roya said. Then she motioned over her shoulder with her head toward counters filled with kitchen utensils, dishes and stainless waiting to be packed. "Help me, please. I don't need more grief. I've got to get this stuff out of here, and I've got two girls upstairs who want to lynch me at sunset."

"I can imagine. New house, new school, new friends."

Roya's eyes were filled with pleading as the front door opened and yet another delivery service arrived to cart off more goods. "Addie?"

"Okay," Adrienne answered, looking past Roya to Etienne's irascible face.

As the one-and-only authentic French Impressionist painting was removed from above the living room mantel to be delivered to a society matron friend of Roya's, Marie's eyes fluttered, signaling she was about to faint or vomit.

"*Mon dieu*, Etienne. Does she have to sell that painting? I don't think I can stand it." Marie raised her hand to her forehead, then cupped the other hand over her mouth.

Roya looked at her sister.

Adrienne shrugged her shoulders.

Neither Roya nor Adrienne could ever tell which attention-grabbing reaction their mother would choose.

They both ignored Marie and nothing happened.

"I'll see to the delivery man," Roya said, leaving the kitchen.

Adrienne began packing boxes.

"You're not helping Roya do this?" Etienne asked.

"This?"

"Uproot the children," Marie blasted indignantly.

"They'll survive," she said as she stacked pots and pans, the bread machine, a fifteen-year-old toaster oven and a hand mixer in a box. "Sometimes you gotta go with the flow." She looked around. "Did she sell the big Kitchen Aid?"

"Yes," Marie groaned. "To a neighbor."

"Guess she won't be baking cookies for Oscar anymore."

"That's another thing!" Marie retorted. "What about her duties to her father-in-law?"

Roya came back in the room. "Maybe he'll get well."

"Don't be so flip, missy." Etienne shook his finger at Roya.

"I don't have time for charity. Besides, Daria has plenty of free time to take care of her father."

Adrienne's hand stopped in midair. "What are you talking about?"

"She quit."

"Since when?" Adrienne was incredulous.

Roya rubbed her temple. "I thought I told you. She followed through on her threat to leave. She walked out the day I walked in."

"Shit."

Marie gasped. "Watch your tongue, Adrienne."

Adrienne tuned her mother out. "Roya, how in the world are you managing? I mean, Daria was..."

"My lifeline?"

"Yeah."

"Why do you think I look like this?" she asked, pointing to the dark circles under her eyes. "I've been working night and day, not only to learn what went wrong and how to fix it, but to just keep the daily fires put out. I'm doing Daria's job as well as Bud's."

"Why didn't you tell me? I had no idea it was this bad. I mean, I understand selling the house. I would have sold it even if I didn't need the money. Bad memories."

"Bud didn't build this house for me." She lowered her voice. "Knowing what I know now, I think it's Kitt's house."

Adrienne's eyes rounded. "Impossible."

"I've thought about it a lot. She had to be living here with him while it was under construction. Then he met me and kicked her out."

"Where do you dream up these things?"

"It's fact. When Lieutenant Dutton returned Bud's things from his study, I found a stack of photographs of Bud and Kitt. She was here. In this house. She chose the bathroom hardware and the countertops and the marble floor."

"Oh, God." Adrienne put her hand on her sister's shoulder. "I have to hand it to you, I'd be a lunatic at this point."

"Going nuts is a luxury for me right now. I have to keep it together." Roya's eyes swam with tears and she balled her fists. "I won't let my kids suffer because of all this crap."

"I understand. Still, you were lucky it sold so fast, what with there being a suicide here and all...."

"I dumped the house. The owners got a good deal and couldn't care less about ghosts. Fortunately, the second mortgage Bud took out wasn't large."

"Thank God."

"So, I have enough to cover the basic payroll and expenses for at least six months. I'm realizing that business is not a matter of winning, but of staying in the game."

Adrienne whistled softly. "You are learning fast."

"Even with Daria gone, I've got an ace in Nick Petros."

Adrienne sealed a carton with strapping tape. "How so?"

"He's nearly as driven as I am. He works like a Trojan and he's come up with some incredible ideas," she said, explaining Nick's strategy with the charities. "We've already contracted with two new companies. With Cynthia's help on the telephones almost daily for the past two months, we've rekindled our relationship with at least a dozen of our old clients. We have work, Addie. Honest, bill-paying work." Roya smiled proudly.

"I can't believe I'm hearing what I'm hearing, seeing what I'm seeing."

"What?"

"You." Adrienne smiled at her sister. "You love it, don't you?"

"Love it?"

"All these years I envied you this perfect life out here, being treated like a princess, not struggling with bills, deadlines, subordinates, bosses...the unemployment line. I always thought you had it easy."

"I did—"

Adrienne put up her hand to interrupt. "But what I found was that all those headaches were the challenges. They were the things that made me feel alive. Put adrenaline in my system. Chills on my skin. I discovered I liked the thrills, the accomplishments, the creativity. And now that's what you're discovering."

"It's true."

"Damn, you're more like me than I'd thought."

"We are family, after all," Roya said.

Adrienne was thoughtful for a moment. "As such, why is it that you haven't asked me to help you?"

"Well, I..." Roya looked down sheepishly. "Truth is, I didn't know how to ask."

"You're kidding."

"I'm not. Frankly, I was, er, am intimidated by you. Your clients are savvy and global and, well, glamorous.

I'm a trucking company for God's sake! And there is the point that you're one of the most expensive agencies in town."

"There is that," Adrienne mused. "Working with Freddie wasn't what I had in mind."

"It wasn't?"

"What I meant was moonlighting."

Anticipation filled Roya's face. "How 'light' are we talking?"

"Very. As in free."

"Oh, Addie." Roya threw her arms around her. "You can't know what this means to me. Nick will keel over. He was so impressed with Freddie at the party."

"Party?"

"Sure. Your Christmas party—" Roya stopped.

Adrienne put two and two together and they clearly equaled a kiss. She glanced over at the very open ears of their parents.

She grabbed Roya's elbow and dragged her sister to the foyer.

"Roya, are you saying what I think you're saying?"

"I...thought you knew. You said you'd ask Freddie who he was."

Adrienne shook her head. "I dropped it. What with Bud dying and the funeral. And then you never said anything more about it. I figured it was just a stranger, someone who remained that way. But Nick Petros?"

Roya could feel the blaze in her middle igniting. It was always like that when she thought about Nick...*that way.*

Adrienne watched her sister radiate like a small planet.

Adrienne had been in love only once in her life—with Gavin. She'd known what it was like to lust after a man, need a man, be desperate for a man. Want a man.

But loving a man was different.

It went deeper, further and was more pervasive to one's personality than any single factor.

Love had changed Adrienne's perspective on just about every issue she could imagine.

If her guess was right, love was more to blame for the immense changes in her younger sister than her commitment to her daughters and their future welfare.

Adrienne held Roya's shoulders as she peered at her. "Tell me you are just working with this guy."

"I am."

"That's all?"

Roya nodded. "I swear."

Though I wish it were more, so much more.

"This is not good—what I'm seeing in your eyes, Roya."

"I don't know what you're talking about. Nick is my employee. Actually, he wouldn't say that. He's on contract."

"Don't give me that. You're in love with this guy and you shouldn't be."

"First of all, I'm not in love. And what's wrong with that, anyway?"

Adrienne expelled a deep sigh. "You're vulnerable right now. You're a widow. Not just any widow, but one dealing with murder investigations, infidelity and daily potshots from our loving parents, your kids and God only knows what else. You're shark bait, Roya."

"I'm what?"

"Listen, honey. We don't know this guy from Adam. Where's he from? Is he married? Got kids? Skipped on his child support? Is his driver's license valid, for heaven's sake? We have to check him out. I mean, for all we know he could be a fortune hunter."

"Yeah, right. I suppose he's after my canceled credit cards."

"Roya, this is serious."

"You have no idea how serious," Roya said quietly.

"So, tell me. Have you slept with him?"

"No, it's nothing like that. In fact, he wouldn't touch me if his life depended on it."

Adrienne smiled. "A gentleman? I'm liking him better already."

"That's not what I meant, though he is a gentleman. Nick Petros thinks I'm about as close to a whore as…Kitt Cabrizzi."

"Ha!" Adrienne stuck her finger in the air. "He's not the one. He doesn't know you in the least. Forget him."

"I've tried. I thought I could work my way through it, but being around him every day has made it worse for me. I can't sleep, and when I do, I dream about being with him. Kissing him. Like we did at the party."

Adrienne remembered advising friends, who complained of the same emotional ailments as Roya, that a kiss was only a kiss. It didn't mean much.

Now she knew better.

A kiss meant everything. A kiss was the key to the soul.

"Roya, that was a month and a half ago."

"I know," she replied sadly. Then, just as quickly, she put her emotions away. "You really have nothing to worry over, Addie. Nick is—how does everyone say that now?—emotionally unavailable to me. I won't get my heart broken. I'm being a good kid, taking care of business, and that's all. Nick will finish his contract and I'll never see him again. It's as simple as that."

"Roya, if you believe that, you're in for a dose."

"If you're serious about advising us on our marketing, then you'll meet him, and when you see us together, you'll see for yourself."

"Hmmm." Adrienne chewed her bottom lip thoughtfully. "Just so you understand, it's not that I don't want you to have a guy in your life. I truly want you to be happy. It's just that I've made so many mistakes with men, and I wasn't nearly as vulnerable as you are. And I…"

"Addie?" Roya interrupted.

"Okay. Okay. I'm being overprotective. I admit it. But I've just found this incredibly wonderful person I've been stupid enough to overlook in the past, and I swear, I'll tear the eyes out of anyone who hurts you."

Roya hugged her sister. "I love you, Addie."

"I love you more."

22

Daria's days were too long to endure alone. After caring for Oscar and getting him settled for the day in front of the television, she grabbed the employment section of the *Tribune* and drove into Old Town.

"Hi, Sol," she said brightly after waiting in line to place her order.

"Daria," he replied with a mellow rush of air. The sound made her heart skip. "I didn't expect to see you. Not today."

"I shoulda called," she joked.

From behind her, she heard a young man say, "Hey, lady. Speed it up, okay?"

"Sorry," she said, glancing over her shoulder. She was glad for the interruption. She hadn't realized how much she'd come to enjoy her short visits with Sol. Ever since they'd become reacquainted, she'd made a habit of coming into Old Town to see him at least twice a week. She'd found it was best to drive in later at night, after business was winding down.

She was amazed that he had energy to open the shop early in the morning, stay through lunch, walk to his nearby home to rest for an hour or two, then return and stay until after ten at night. She felt guilty for the couple of nights when she'd kept him until midnight chatting away about nothing in particular.

At first they talked about books they'd read or were reading. She found that he liked to haunt the local book-stores just as much as she did. Sol owned a rare-book collection and said he'd been going to estate sales and auctions for thirty years.

Daria wished she'd done anything for thirty years—anything except work for Bud.

No matter how hard she tried, she still couldn't shake the betrayal she felt, couldn't find solace in the mantra "what was meant to be was meant to be."

She didn't see any pattern of positivity in the fact that her career had ended as abruptly as Bud's life. It just didn't make any sense. She would be fifty this year—no time to be starting over like some college grad. She felt horrendously cheated.

Yet, when she came here to see Sol, he always made her feel better. Everything about him brightened her day.

The aroma of the coffee, the steamed milk and the cinnamon buns in the oven brought her youth back to her. The wood floors creaked in the same way they had in 1970. The glass door with its tinkling silver bell was just the same. The bentwood chairs and tiny round tables were the same. Even Sol seemed the same.

But she had changed—drastically. She was jaded now, skeptical and frightened. She didn't like being any of these things, but she was.

Life scared her now.

Daily, she was reminded of how precarious life was. How it could end in a blast of gunfire, or slowly, inch by inch, like Oscar's painful deterioration. She despised death, though she knew she would have to accept it.

She wished she could stop time from advancing. Perhaps that was why she liked the coffee shop so much. Here she was timeless. She felt young again and free. She felt hopeful. It was a good feeling.

"You look good," Sol said.

"Thanks," she replied. "So do you."

The impatient patron behind her said, "Lady, puh-leeze!"

Sol smiled.

Daria hadn't realized how much his smile meant to her. "The usual, Sol."

"I'm way ahead of you," he replied. "Stand over there by the window. There's a table coming free and Melanie is just out back. She'll take over for me in a second. I'd like to talk to you."

"Great," she said, moving out of the line.

Sol handed the coffee orders to the redheaded boy at the cappuccino machines. In moments Melanie returned to take orders and Sol was free.

"Wow, business sure has picked up for you," Daria said approvingly.

"Yeah. It's my mocha-macho supreme. I put hot fudge in the hot drinks. It's really gone over. That and my Valentine's Day special. Buy one, get a certificate for free coffee on Valentine's Day."

"My God, the place will be packed, judging from what I see today."

Sol chuckled to himself. "I feel good, Daria. Like I'm finally giving the chains a run for their money."

Daria looked over at his two-person crew. "They look tired, Sol. And so do you. I think you're working too hard."

Sol tapped the newspaper with his index finger. "And you aren't working at all."

She shook her head. "I can't seem to find anything."

"With the employment picture the way it is? I find that hard to believe. Everyone I know is singing the same song. Good help is so very hard to find," he crooned to an old Paul Anka song.

She laughed. "Okay, so I haven't exactly been pounding the pavement. I miss the plant, frankly. I miss everybody there. The action. The headaches. The clients. I miss...Bud."

"That's a heavy-duty admission."

She put her hands to the sides of her face, thinking to wipe away her shock. "I can't believe I said that. Where did that come from? I don't miss him. He was a bastard. He cheated me."

"But he was your brother. You had karma with him. You had a relationship with him. His passing left a big void. It's okay to miss him. It makes you feel vulnerable, doesn't it, when you realize you put so much of yourself into someone else."

"Yeah, it does."

"Life is for seizing, Daria."

"What?"

"Life isn't just something to get through. It's to experience. The pain and sorrow will always be there, but you have to take a chance, be courageous enough to go for the pleasure."

"What exactly are you saying, Sol?"

"Only that you think death is something to fear. It's like you're holding your breath until it gets here."

"I do do that. But what other way is there?"

"Try biting off some big chunks of life. Do it all. See it all."

She stared back at him.

Sol smiled slowly. "Do those words sound familiar?"

"A bit."

"Good. I heard them from you. You and I were sitting at that table over there. You said you were going to Europe. You were going to write and paint and draw and own a vineyard someday and you were going to drink every kind of coffee in the world."

She laughed freely and without censure. "I did used to say stuff like that." She shook her head. "I guess everyone says that kind of thing as a kid."

"I believed you," he said, reaching for her hand.

She looked down at his enormous fingers crossing over hers like armor, shielding her. She felt warm inside again. She realized she was starting to feel that way every time she was near Sol. He was giving her the one thing she'd always wanted from Bud—a feeling of being protected.

Her face felt hot as tears pierced her eyes.

Sol put his hand on her shoulder, and Daria dropped her head so he wouldn't see her cry.

He massaged the tension he found. "It's okay to miss your brother. You loved him. He just didn't love you back, is all."

"Yeah," she sniffed.

"I'm glad you came here today."

"Me, too," she replied, and squeezed his hand.

He reached behind him and took a paper napkin from the stack on the service counter.

Daria blew her nose.

"Why don't you go back to the plant?"

"I can't."

Sol nodded. "Too much pride, huh?"

"Yeah." She looked away from him out through the window. She wasn't used to dwelling on such deep emotions, though Sol appeared to be more at ease with them and with life itself than she. She wiped her tears and changed the subject.

"I like your Valentine decorations, Sol."

He smiled knowingly and didn't press the painful issues for now. He glanced at the hearts and cupids Melanie had plastered all over the glass. "Makeshift stuff." He looked at Daria. He thought he'd never seen anyone quite so lost. "Think you could do better?"

"Huh?"

"I was thinking, since I'm doing so well and I'm too busy to really do that kind of thing right, maybe you could come down tomorrow and work with it a bit. Maybe put some of those ivy vines in the window like I've seen at the florist across the street. Maybe you might help me out behind the register. All those folks wanting their free drinks. It will be a madhouse. I don't pay much over minimum wage, but it's better than nothing."

Daria looked up at him and smiled. "Why, Sol, are you asking me to be your valentine?"

"Oh, no. I'd never...I mean. Well, yeah. I guess I am at that."

"Thanks for being my friend, Sol."

"I thought you could use one," he replied.

"I could." Daria folded the newspaper. "I'll check out the ads next week. It looks to me like I've got a part-time job."

"I should say you do." He grinned back at her.

23

"What a bummer," Lucienne said, wrinkling her nose at the small ranch house on the West Side of Chicago her mother had rented.

"It's sturdy, has a new furnace, new toilets and new carpeting. We'll make it charming," Roya replied brightly as they walked up the snowy sidewalk of the three-bedroom, two-bathroom redbrick house.

"We sold all the good stuff. There's nothing left to make it charming with, Mom."

"We'll buy new things. For our new life." Roya kissed her daughter's cheek.

"Mom, you said we were broke."

"I don't intend to stay that way forever, Lucy. This is just a temporary thing. Nothing ever stays the same. Not even bad times. Besides, it's not bad, exactly. Just different."

Lucienne cast a sidelong glance at her sister.

Cynthia hoisted an armful of bed linens. "Different, Lucy."

Roya turned on the lights in the living room and adjusted a dimmer over the fireplace.

Lucienne grabbed her sister's arm. "I can't believe Mom is happy about this. I don't get it."

Cynthia sighed heavily. "It doesn't matter what we think. This is the way it is."

Lucienne didn't like one single thing about her "different" life. She especially didn't like the fact that her old friends proved they'd never been friends in the first place.

They'd treated her like a pariah after her father's suicide. None of them said anything directly, of course, but Lucienne got the distinct impression one parent too many had heard the rumors about her father and his mistress. She hadn't dared tell her mother about her problems with her friends; she was too busy these days to listen. There always seemed to be yet another crisis her mother had to handle.

Somehow, Lucienne's struggles continued to grow and neither her mother nor her sister seemed to notice that her telephone no longer rang, party invitations did not come in the mail and she was no longer included in after-school activities.

Lucienne felt as if the world had flung her aside.

"What do you think of your room?" Roya asked from behind Lucienne, who was staring at her room from the threshold.

"Fine."

"Don't you like how the wallpaper you picked turned out?"

"Yeah, sure," Lucienne replied numbly. In reality, the pink rosebud paper looked stupid to her now. She did not feel like a little girl anymore. She felt like a misfit.

Besides, with no friends, who was to care if her room was pretty or not.

"I think it's lovely!" Roya beamed.

Lucienne's patience hit its limit. She tossed bed linens on her twin-size bed and said, "It's juvenile, Mom. I must have been in a zone when I picked it. In fact—" she put her hands on her hips "—I hate it!"

Roya stepped back. "Take it down then."

"Do what?"

"Steam it, strip it, paint over it, for all I care. It's just paper."

Lucienne's eyes narrowed. "I don't get this act of yours, Mom."

"Act?"

"Yeah. How can you be so happy about this…crappy little house in this really crappy neighborhood?"

Straightening her resolve, Roya replied, "Because for the first time in my life, Lucienne, something is mine. All mine. It was my decision to sell the old house. I probably could have struggled on. Could have dumped the company, let it go bankrupt and found some simpleton job somewhere to keep me occupied. I didn't have to bite off half the world and incite your wrath, Daria's anger and my parents' criticism. I never had my own apartment or went to college like Cynthia or did anything for myself. I went from high school to being a wife.

"I'm sorry you don't like this place. I do. I'm trying to make the best of our situation. So is your sister. The way I see it, you have two choices. You can change your sullen attitude and enjoy what we do have, or you can go on being angry or hurt or insensitive, or whatever it is you've decided is best for you. But while you reside under my roof, I would appreciate it if you would at least make an effort to understand what the rest of us are going through."

Rage coiled inside Lucienne. Though she was looking in her mother's eyes, she didn't see anything familiar about her. Her mother had changed so drastically from the person she'd always known that Lucienne was unable to discern whether the changes were good or bad.

Her new mother was headstrong, energetic and apparently had abandoned her quiet, selfless ways.

Well, if she can transform herself into someone new, then so can I.

"The paper is fine, I said," Lucienne finally replied.

"I wasn't talking about the paper," Roya answered.

"Neither was I." Lucienne looked away from her mother and into the room. "I'll try to make it work, Mom."

"That's all I ask." Roya put her arms around her daughter, a smile warming her face.

Cynthia walked down the hall at the precise moment her mother and Lucienne hugged. Roya's back was to Cynthia, so she didn't see her mother's expression, but she couldn't miss the acrimonious languor of Lucienne's embrace and the indulgent roll of eyes.

Cynthia was about to confront the situation when the doorbell rang.

"Are you expecting anybody, Mom?" Cynthia asked.

"No," Roya replied, going to the door.

"Nick!" Roya gasped with surprise. "What are you…"

From behind his back he produced three small floral bouquets. "Happy Valentine's Day."

"Happy? Oh, God! I'd forgotten," she said, taking the flowers. Of all the people and all the acts of kindness she might have expected, Nick Petros bearing daisies had never entered her mind.

"There's one for each of you," he said. "I figured with the house being new and all, it might need brightening up."

Hearing a man's voice at the door, Lucienne instantly pushed past Cynthia and rushed to the door.

Cynthia knew Nick's voice well. She heard it every day at the office. Shoving her fists in her jeans pockets, she sauntered slowly toward the door, making her expected appearance.

"Look, girls. Nick brought you flowers."

"Cool," Lucienne said, greedily taking the flowers from her mother's hands.

"Won't you come in?" Roya asked him.

"Actually, no. I just wanted to deliver those."

Cynthia walked up. "Hiya, Nick."

"Cynthia. How's the move going?"

"Fine," she replied as Lucienne whisked by.

"Wow!" Lucienne exclaimed. "I've never had Valentine's flowers."

Cynthia followed her toward the kitchen. "You've never had any flowers, period."

"Neither have you," Lucienne retorted.

Nick took a step backward. Jabbing his thumb over his shoulder toward his parked car he said, "I'll see you tomorrow."

"Nick, this is silly. Please come in and have some coffee with me. Let me show you around."

Cynthia hung just inside the kitchen doorway, far enough away from her mother and Nick that they would not suspect her of eavesdropping. With her back against the wall, she slowly rolled her head back toward the front door. She was unable to tear her eyes off her mother's animated face.

Roya reached her hand out to Nick. "I insist."

She smiled.

Nick smiled back.

He looked down at the snow and made an arc with his toe. "Just half a cup. Then I should go."

"You have other plans?" Roya asked, a catch in her throat.

Cynthia watched the dance between her mother and their general manager. She'd had her suspicions about her mother's feelings, but until now, Nick was nonparticipatory in the situation.

Cynthia was more than a little curious about this change—if there was one at all.

Nick's presence seemed to fill the house, Roya thought. Suddenly, the ceiling appeared lower, the walls more confining and the cheap new carpet tawdry.

She realized that she wanted to impress him and there was nothing about her home that was extraordinary.

"Let me take your jacket," she said, feeling childishly awkward, as if this were her first date in high school.

"Thanks," he said, slipping the expensive navy suede off his arms.

His eyes scanned the living room where a fat sofa faced a mundane fireplace devoid of the brass andirons and elaborate screen he remembered from the Schaumburg house. Only two small chairs and a lamp table finished out the room. Glancing at the walls, he realized the rumors he'd heard at the office were true.

Hanging his jacket in the coat closet, Roya glanced over her shoulder at him. Suddenly, she realized what Nick's trip here was about. She shut the closet door.

"Satisfied?"

"What?" He answered abruptly, turning to face her.

Cynthia instantly straightened, her ears pricked.

Lucienne appeared behind her sister, holding her breath, eyes glued on her mother.

"You didn't come over here to bring flowers to us, did you, Nick?"

"What are you talking about?"

"You're checking up on me. Just like my parents did. Just like Addie. They all think I'm nuts."

"I don't think anything of the kind."

"Sure you do," she said, approaching him, indignation firing her eyes.

Unconsciously, he spread his feet a few inches farther apart, as if taking a stance against danger. Or an enemy. "Okay. So I heard a lot of stories. I heard about the car and the house. That was to be expected. Then I heard that even the drivers were buying your furniture. The stories got wilder. I heard you would have sold your own kids if you thought they'd bring an extra buck."

"I can't afford sentiment right now. You needed the money for the ad campaign."

Pursing his bottom lip, he nodded. "I was afraid that was what was going on. This is all my fault."

Roya's arms fluttered in the air. "You think I don't know how important it is to get that campaign off the ground? It's paramount, Nick. It could mean our survival."

"Not to the exclusion of your life, Roya. You have to have a balance, not this extremism you seem to think is the key to success."

"You're a fine one to talk! You work just as many hours as I do. If I had a video monitor in your apartment, I bet I'd find you're still working even after I'm asleep."

"Well, thank God, you don't," he said. "No, Roya. I put in my time, but I also have a personal life. And I don't use excuses like ad campaigns to mask grief."

"I'm not doing that."

"The hell you aren't."

She crossed her arms, holding herself together.

Nick continued. "Look, I didn't come here to beat you up. I did come here hoping to find some truth about what's been going on."

"What does it matter how I get the money?"

"People talk, Roya. They talk among themselves, among companies, among industries. I make my living by certain ethical standards. It was bad enough when your husband's—" He glanced at Cynthia and Lucienne, cleared his throat and went on. "Your methods reflect on me. My next contract depends on how well I perform with you."

Roya had to fight to keep her jaw closed. "That's what this is all about? You? Your reputation?"

Nick realized he'd made a mess of things. "I didn't mean it the way it sounded. It's just that—"

She cut him off. "Oh, I think you've been quite clear, Mr. Petros. You don't approve of my methods. Frankly, I don't give a damn what you think. You'll get paid just like everyone else."

"It's not the money."

"Oh, but it is the money. It is precisely the money. That and the control. I have the control and you want that, too? Is that it?"

"You're blowing this out of proportion."

She threw her hands in the air. "I hate it when people say that to me."

"Heard it before, have you?" He couldn't resist the barb. It was worth it to watch this incredibly poised woman lose it. He thought he'd never seen anything so natural. Or as beautiful.

He stopped his thoughts dead in their tracks.

He was doing it again—using anything and everything as an excuse to have an exchange with her. Which was more than stupid, it was insane.

If ever in his life Nick had met a woman who should be poison, Roya was it. He shouldn't have come here. True, he had wanted to know the truth. He had needed to know if it was his marketing proposal that had caused her to give up practically everything she'd ever owned.

The truth was brutal. It made him feel guilty as hell.

Nothing was worth this. He wasn't worth it.

"I think you'd better leave," Roya said, her angry lips in a thin white line.

"So do I," he agreed.

He went to the closet and took out his jacket.

He glanced at Roya and her glare hit him like a rock breaking glass.

Lucienne boldly stepped into the room. "Thanks for the flowers. They're really pretty. I like mine," she said, offering a quick look at her mother's intractable face.

Cynthia clasped her hands behind her back. "Yeah, Nick. That was thoughtful. See ya tomorrow." Cynthia retreated down the hall to her bedroom.

Reluctantly, Lucienne followed.

Roya inhaled then exhaled, but her anger continued to bite her insides. "Next time, don't waste your money on flowers."

He went to the door. "I won't."

He left.

"Ungrateful son of a bitch!" Roya pounded her fist against the wall, stormed down the hall and slammed her bedroom door.

24

Kitt Cabrizzi stood down the cul-de-sac from the empty house in which she'd once lived for two years. The windows of the neighboring houses backlit Valentine's hearts and cupids, creating silhouettes of romance and love.

Appropriately, Bud's house yawned in the darkness, its lack of electrical power testament to its vacant status.

Blasts of wind slapped the real estate sign in the front yard. Tree limbs rattled and a squirrel raced across Kitt's path.

She'd loved this house. No mansion could ever have served her better. Bud had moved her into the yet-unfinished shell in 1975, shortly after he finished building the new plant. Bud was riding high back then and he was more than eager to please Kitt.

He succeeded. It was one of the few times in Kitt's life when she'd been happy. It wasn't the house itself, it was Bud who had made her feel like a queen.

"Can we afford gold towel bars, Bud? They're so classy."

"Baby, I'm not Onassis."

"Not solid gold. The fake stuff. Plate. You know what I mean."

He'd begun tearing off her clothes with his teeth. "Anything you want, baby. You're the one with class."

"Do you think so, Bud? Really?"

He'd kissed her ravenously. "'Course I do. Besides, who ever heard of a Polack with class?"

"Oh, Bud," she'd moaned as he made love to her.

From the rust-and-navy draperies that fell in heavy pleats from the ceiling and the multicolored shag carpet to match for the den, to the latest Far Eastern-influenced patterns of Congoleum for the kitchen and breakfast room, Kitt had chosen it all.

She'd had a blast.

For months she hadn't thought anything could cap her happiness. But she was wrong.

Bud asked her to set a wedding date.

Kitt wanted six bridesmaids. Bud told her to have ten. She wanted a huge church wedding so that everyone from Our Lady of Mount Carmel High School could see that Kitt Cabrizzi had finally gotten her man. Finally, she would put to rest the slurs about her "putting out for Pulaski" she'd overheard in the boys' gym. She wanted a wedding so classy, so spectacular, that every tight-assed, Goody Two-shoes in school would envy her.

Bud told her the sky was the limit. He wanted a sit-down steak dinner with champagne at the new Ramada Inn. He told her to rent a limousine, four limousines for all the wedding party.

He didn't care about the cost.

He just wanted her to be happy.

Kitt's intuition told her it was a perfect time to die. This much bliss couldn't last.

She'd been devastatingly right.

Kitt had been sitting at the new rattan kitchen table when Bud arrived in the middle of the afternoon.

"You're home early," she said, looking up from a decorating magazine. She held up her cheek for a kiss.

There was none.

She felt the room chill instantly. "What's wrong?"

"Just about everything," he said, reaching in his inside blazer pocket and withdrawing his checkbook. "But I know how to make adjustments. I hope you do as well."

Confusion rumbled through her insides. She was uneasy.

She'd never heard this indifference in Bud's voice. Never seen his eyes look like marble. "Adjustments?"

He scribbled her name on the top of the check. "I want you to get your clothes and things out of here this afternoon."

Kitt knew she was dreaming. This wasn't real.

She laughed.

He glared at her and continued. "I'll hire some people to help you if necessary."

"Help me?"

"I want you gone by the time I get home at seven." He ripped the check off the pad and handed it to her.

"What's this?"

"What does it look like? Fifty thousand dollars. In a year, I'll give you another just like it. A hundred grand should make you happy."

Kitt's mouth was numb, as if she'd been shot up with Novocain. No matter how much she tried to move her tongue, no words formed. She sat frozen in her chair, staring at him.

Bud capped his pen and slipped it, and the checkbook, back in his blazer pocket. "It's over, Kitt. Today I met the girl I'm going to marry."

Today I met the girl I'm going to marry.

Kitt knew Bud's words would echo in her soul for all eternity, and they would always slice through her being like a guillotine.

"I'm the girl you're going to marry."

"Not anymore."

He started to walk away.

Kitt shot out of the chair and grabbed his arm. "Just like that? You think you can get rid of me with a check? You think I want the money?"

"No," he snarled. "I know you want me. But you can't

have me. In a day or two, you'll want the money. Take it, Kitt. You deserve it."

"You selfish son of a bitch!" She slapped him.

He stared coldly at her. He didn't flinch.

She slapped him again.

This time he clamped his huge fingers around her wrist. "I told you, Kitt. It's over. Don't fight with me. There's nothing you can do."

"The hell there isn't. I'm not leaving."

"Fine. I'll have the sheriff escort you out. You're trespassing on private property."

She gaped at him.

Where was the boy she'd loved? Given her virginity to? Loved beyond all reason?

The man who looked at her with abhorrence glinting his steely eyes was a stranger.

For Kitt, that was the day Bud Pulaski died.

For the rest of her life, she was incapable of resurrecting him.

She'd left the house in less than two hours. She didn't cry a single tear. The shock to Kitt's nervous system rendered her incapable of little more than staring dumbly out the picture window at her mother's house from dawn to dusk for almost two months.

When she'd reached consciousness once again, she telephoned Bud and demanded a monthly stipend. "I need rent, food and gas money, Bud. The utilities, too."

"What the hell did you do with the fifty grand?"

"I put it into a savings account. I'm talking to an investment broker tomorrow about stocks. That money is for my retirement."

"Retirement? You're only thirty years old. Hardly ancient."

"I don't think you understand, Bud. I'm damaged goods. No one will marry me now."

"You've been listening to your mother too much. Remember 'free love'?"

"It was never free for me, Bud. Maybe for you, but not for me."

"I meant you're being old-fashioned. It's stupid."

"I thought you knew at least that much about me, Bud. I'm exactly that. True blue. One man all my life. I'm not a sleep-around."

"Fine. How much money do you want?"

"Fifteen hundred a month."

"Shit! Where are you renting? Marina Towers?"

Kitt stood her ground. She got her money, but never her wedding band. Never her dream.

Kitt stood in the cold shadow of the house she'd built with Bud.

It stood to reason Roya would abandon it. It had never really been hers to begin with. Kitt had put a curse on the house the day she'd walked out.

That was the good thing about curses—they lasted a lifetime.

Roya knew it. Maybe Bud had even known it. But best of all, Kitt knew it and it gave her comfort.

25

"Your name's Lucy, isn't it?" the gangly, dark-haired boy asked, leaning over the top of Lucienne's locker door as she retrieved her books.

For nearly a month Lucienne had been attending Our Lady of Mount Carmel High School and no one had said more than "Hi" to her. Startled that anyone was speaking to her, much less knew her name, Lucienne was instantly suspicious.

"Lucienne," she corrected him, keeping her eyes on the vacant locker interior. Sidelong glances informed her that this was Brad Eastman, captain of the undefeated basket-ball team, a senior, and according to the conversations she'd overheard in the lunchroom, Brad had his pick of at least a dozen college scholarships. The word was that the offers were pouring in as their team entered the regional championships. Brad Eastman, along with last year's winning team, had played in a charity exhibition game with members of the Chicago Bulls.

Brad Eastman was a legend in the making.

Lucienne had heard he was equally as notorious with the cheerleading squad. There was no question in her mind he was talking to her now solely because she was the new kid in school.

He probably thinks I don't know about his reputation.

Brad leaned his face closer to Lucienne. "Yeah, I heard it was something foreign."

She immediately crouched to the bottom of the locker,

pretending to straighten her gym shoes and socks. "French."

"Really? Where in France are you from?" He smiled broadly, revealing perfect rows of white teeth. His green eyes sparkled through longer lashes than Lucienne's own.

"Schaumburg."

"Oh," he replied, hiding his embarrassment by waving to a friend. "Jason!"

"Hey, Brad. How's it going?" Jason winked at Brad.

Lucienne caught Brad's return wink.

"Great," Brad replied to Jason, then closed the locker door for her. "At least I hope I'm doing great. Am I?"

"I don't know what you mean," she said politely but coolly. She leveled her eyes on him, showing him she wasn't the least intimidated or impressed with his approach.

Brad held his breath as Lucienne stared him down. He knew what she was doing. Girls always tried to play hard to get with him. But they all wanted a date with Brad Eastman. Dating had been child's play for Brad all through high school. He'd never thought much about the whole process. He didn't belabor calling girls or talking to them. He just did it. He never got nervous or anxiety-ridden like some of his friends. Not over a girl.

A game, yes, but never a girl.

Fact was, he laughed about guys who couldn't control their girls. Brad didn't have the time for complications of any sort. He was on his way to being a professional ball player. He ate, slept, dreamed and lived basketball.

His father said he'd been born with natural talent. The Mount Carmel coaches agreed. So did the spotters for top colleges, sports announcers and even the scout for the Bulls he'd met with just last week. Brad had his priorities straight.

Career first, last and always.

At least that's what he'd thought before this moment.

Looking into Lucienne's blue eyes, he struggled to understand precisely what was different about her.

Blue-eyed blondes were rampant at Mount Carmel. Her heart-shaped face was soft, yet her squared-off chin gave her strength.

But there was something different about her.

Something that put goose bumps on the soles of his feet. He felt as if he'd been blindsided from behind by a baseball bat. There had to be some reason he'd suddenly gone stupid.

"Not great, huh?" he finally managed to say.

Lucienne shrugged her shoulders, adjusting the strap of her shoulder bag. "I'm gonna be late," she said, and walked away.

Brad gaped after her dumbfounded. One minute he'd been talking to her and the next she was gone. "Hey! Wait up! I'll walk you to class."

She kept going.

He raced up behind her. "I'm Brad Eastman."

"I know," she said, keeping her eyes straight ahead.

"You don't like me, do you?"

She bit her tongue to keep from smiling. He was galloping beside her like a puppy. "I'm just late, is all."

He snapped his fingers. "You're not into jocks."

"I didn't say that." It was getting harder to keep a straight face.

"It's basketball you hate."

"Not true. I'm a Bulls fan all the way. I used to go to the games when my Dad was alive."

"Geez, I'm sorry. I didn't know."

She felt a bite at the bottom of her stomach. "He didn't take me. He got free tickets. My Aunt Adrienne took my sister and I."

As she spoke, Lucienne realized that her grieving over her father was not due to his death, but rather to the end of her needing and hoping to have a relationship with him. She understood now that no matter how hard she had tried to get her father to love her, pay attention to her, have a relationship with her, it never would have happened.

Not in a million years.

For affection she would have to look elsewhere.

"Are you...coming to the game tonight?" he asked hesitantly.

"I wasn't planning on it." She stopped at the door to the chemistry lab.

"I have to be back here an hour before the game so I couldn't pick you up. But I'd like to take you out for a taco after we win."

The corner of her mouth crept upward, and she saw his eyes sparkle like fireworks. "Confident, aren't you?"

"About winning? I don't know any other way to think. So how about it?"

"I have a lot of homework, but if I get it all done, I suppose I could go," she said with a flip shrug.

"Great!" He brightened, taking no offense at her lack of enthusiasm. "I'll see you then."

The class bell rang.

He dashed down the hall so quickly he didn't hear Lucienne say, "I'm not making any promises."

Roya brought home sandwiches from the deli for supper that night. Cynthia peeled off the tops of diet sodas and scooped large helpings of coleslaw onto paper plates.

"I never thought I'd see the day when I'd be using paper plates," Roya groaned, eyeing the cupboardful of prettily painted ceramic dishes. She remembered the plethora of compliments she'd received after luncheons and parties for the ingenuity of the tables she set. She shoved them back to the past where they belonged.

"Lucienne, what are you doing in that bathroom?" Roya called, hearing the blow-dryer blast for an inordinately long period of time.

"I'm coming!" Lucienne yelled through the closed door, but didn't appear.

"Mom," Cynthia asked carefully. "Do you think I could bring that old Mac home? The one the graphics department replaced last fall?"

"What's a Mac?"

"That computer. The one I've been talking to you about all month. The one I've been tinkering around with at work on my lunch hour." *The one I've fallen in love with.*

"I'm sorry, darling. My head just hasn't been in the right place. Why do you need it here?"

"If it was at home, I could spend nights working on some ideas I've got for the ad displays Nick was talking to me about. Weekends, too." Cynthia sat down at the kitchen table.

"Nick?" Roya's attention was instantly focused and centered squarely on her daughter.

Lucienne exited the bathroom. She had lightened her honey blond hair with streaks of platinum much like her mother's color and curled it softly around her face and shoulders with hot rollers. She wore a red plaid kilt, black turtleneck, black tights and black flats. She was the picture of a teenage goddess, but her parent and sibling hadn't noticed her new hair color or style.

She picked up a turkey sandwich and smiled smugly to herself. It was rather fun having a secret from them. She didn't know what her mother would think about her going on her first unofficial-official date. She'd always thought everyone would make a big deal about it. Sort of like Cynthia's senior prom, which she attended with that dreadful, dull-looking computer nerd. But Cynthia had liked Charlie.

Lucienne tried to understand Cynthia, but the girl was just too cerebral sometimes.

"Yeah," Cynthia continued. "We were thinking about a new company logo. Something more twenty-first centuryish. Futuristic."

Roya dug into her coleslaw. "That's the dumbest idea yet. Did Nick come up with that?"

"Well, yes. But I have some really cool ideas, Mom. We gotta think global, Nick says. We have to use the new buzzwords and keep our thoughts expansive. I'm really excited about this campaign you're trying to launch, Mom. Since I had to drop out of college indefinitely, I've been feeling as if I, er, we weren't going anywhere, till now. I was starting to think we really were going to lose the business and I'd never get the chance to finish my education. Then Nick got me switched over to advertising. And everything in my head just clicked, Mom. It's been the most amazing discovery."

"I wish he'd told me some of this," Roya replied.

"I'm telling you now," Cynthia said proudly.

Roya instantly caught her inference. Cynthia was feeling overlooked, overshadowed at work. Nick, in his subtle way, had given Cynthia an important role in an important project. He was making Cynthia feel worthy.

Roya felt ashamed at the jealousy she was feeling right now. Nick was doing a more successful job of parenting her daughter than she was at the moment.

"I mean, I've never thought of myself as a creative person, you know, Mom?"

Cynthia was talking so fast, Roya could barely keep up. But she did. It was imperative.

"Of course you're creative," Roya said. "Remember your music lessons and ballet?"

"That was kid stuff and I never liked either. Lucy is better at fine arts than I am."

Roya looked to Lucy.

Lucy chomped away at her sandwich, smiling with her cheeks full of food. The look Roya gave her made Lucy feel as if her mother would pat her on the head, the way she did when she was three. Lucy closed both eyes, then opened them.

Roya sighed happily and looked back at Cynthia.

She hadn't seen the sparkle of anticipation in Lucienne's eyes. But Lucienne could feel it crackling around her head like shots of electricity. She'd never felt so alive.

She had Brad to thank for that.

Lucienne glanced at the wall clock and stuffed the last bite of sandwich into her mouth. Swallowing, she said, "Mom, can I take the car tonight?"

"Where are you going?"

"Library. I have a report due next week, and if I don't check out my books before the weekend, the good ones will all be gone."

Roya nodded. "I understand. The keys are in my purse."

"Thanks, Mom," Lucy said, kissing her mother's cheek as she rose from her chair.

Roya didn't take her eyes off Cynthia while Lucienne put on her coat. "What else do you and Nick have in mind for my company that I don't know about?"

"A lot, Mom." Cynthia's voice flooded with excitement.

Lucienne looked back at her mother and sister. They were so intent on their exchange they didn't hear her say goodbye, nor did they hear her leave.

"You were good, Brad," Lucienne said to him after the game as they entered Vinny's Pizza Parlor, a neighborhood establishment since before World War II.

"I was playing lousy until I saw you in the stands," he said, sliding into a leather booth. He dug in his jeans pocket for a quarter, slipped it into the tableside jukebox and punched out J-4.

A classic Rolling Stones song began to play.

"You can't like the Stones," she said with surprise.

"My dad plays this stuff on old 33^1/$_3$'s. My older brothers hate it, but I love it. The Beatles, too."

"Me, too," she said. "My dad liked Chicago and Three Dog Night."

A group of senior classmates passed the booth, stopped to congratulate Brad on his winning basket. Brad introduced Lucienne to his friends.

Lucienne thought she'd freeze to death from the icy looks she got from the two dark-haired girls. When they left, she asked, "Are they your old girlfriends?"

"Melissa and Annie? No."

"Then they'd like to be."

"Not a chance. Melissa has been Frankie's girlfriend since freshman year. Annie and Steve are a serious couple. They're going to Northwestern together next year. They're inseparable."

"You could have fooled me. I've never had anyone look at me with such…hate, almost."

Brad reached across the tabletop and took Lucienne's hand. "They're jealous. But it has nothing to do with me. You're very, very pretty tonight."

"Thanks," she said, refusing to allow the compliment to go to her head. "You don't have to suck up to me, you know."

"I wasn't doing that."

"Sure?"

"I was telling the truth, is all." He leaned forward slightly and lowered his voice. "So, if I don't have to give you compliments, that must mean I'm finally doing great with you, huh?"

"No." She shook her head, throwing him a coquettish glance she'd never practiced, but which came naturally to her. "What I meant was that it won't do you any good."

Brad's grin filled his face and he laughed. "Fantastic!"

"Are you not following me here?"

"If I'm not doing great, then I have to work harder, right? That means more time with you. More dates." He leaned back in the corner of the booth and propped his right leg on the seat. "So, where do you want to go Saturday afternoon? A movie? To a museum? In-line skating?"

"On ice? I don't think so." She shook her head as the waiter appeared to take their order.

Brad ordered a large supreme pizza and two sodas.

When the waiter left, Lucienne said, "I have plans this weekend, Brad."

"I know you do. With me. This weekend, next weekend and every one after that."

She was intrigued by his persistence, not put off. "I think you've been sniffing sweat socks too long. I'm trying to tell you that I'm not interested in you, Brad. I'm a very busy girl. I have—"

His eyes locked on hers with determination and sincerity. His voice was hard and clipped when he spoke.

"Then why did you change your hair for me? Why did you put makeup on? Why do you look at me like you do? Why did you come tonight?"

"Curiosity."

With a mischievous grin, he dug in his pocket for another quarter and put it in the jukebox. He punched H-7. "I don't think so, Lucienne. I think it's because you know as well as I that from today there's only one thing that matters to both of us. And that is…"

The music changed.

An old Motown hit came on.

Brad pointed to the jukebox. "Can't beat these old songs for saying it just right."

Lucienne smiled and sang the words to "My Girl."

26

Roya felt like a spectator at Wimbledon as ideas were smashed and lobbed across the conference room table between Nick, Addie and Cynthia. She wondered if any of them knew she was in the room.

"I'm telling you, babies are the way to go," Adrienne said. "Next to the bridal industry, it's a billion dollar concern. If we can figure out a way to tap into that market."

"Babies?" Nick pondered the idea thoughtfully. "I like it."

"You're kidding?" Roya shook her head. Had they lost their minds? Thus far they'd rejected her ideas to concentrate on refrigerated trucking contracts for food, raw dairy products and local delivery of catered foods. Her ideas to expand into hauling steel from the Indiana steel mills had been shot down equally as fast. All had seemed viable conduits.

Nick had been the first to veto her.

Roya realized as the exchanges between Nick and Addie became more animated, more electric, that his censure of her thoughts had hurt her pride—if not her heart.

It wasn't that Roya thought her ideas were all that brilliant, it was that she'd wanted Nick's approval. It bothered her even more that she was unable to stem her emotions. Like invisible bands, they clutched at her throat. To appear professional, she chose silence.

"They need to be sweet babies, cherubic. Right, Aunt Addie?" Cynthia smiled. "Maybe with a stork."

"Storks are mystical. Symbolic and spiritual. I like the

angel angle, Cyn. All of these are emotional hot buttons of today's consumer," Addie agreed.

Cynthia beamed.

Nick snapped his fingers. "Roya, you know that fleet of eighteen-foot delivery trucks and vans Bud bought in the fall before he died?" Nick asked.

"Yes."

"We'll paint them white. Cynthia can work up a graphic of a stork delivering a baby. Classy, though. Very art deco. That would work. Maybe flying over the Chicago skyline at night. Moon and stars."

"Great going, Nick," Addie said enthusiastically. "Celestial motifs are everywhere right now."

"And just what do we do with these trucks?" Roya asked.

Nick's mind hit warp speed. "We call our delivery service Special Delivery. We offer it to every baby-related business in the city. This will boost our local delivery market, which is our weakest leg. We go to every retailer, food store, baby furniture store in Chicago. We'll advertise their business when we advertise our Special Delivery for new mothers. We'll get women hooked on having that special delivery man or woman show up in their neighborhood." Nick drummed his fingers. "We need a sharp uniform."

"Black and white," Adrienne said. "To go with the art deco idea. Then another gimmick for why our delivery is so special."

Cynthia cut in. "That's easy. Twenty-four hours a day, seven days a week. Christmas. Holidays."

"Cool!" Nick said appreciatively.

"The minute the baby is born our guys are on the road delivering flowers to the hospital, baby clothes to the baby shower."

"Fantastic idea, Cyn!" Adrienne said.

"And," Adrienne continued, "given time, it could get

to where the arrival of our Special Delivery truck is synonymous with the birth announcement."

The energy in the room was explosive, Roya thought as she watched the trio work. They played off one another's ideas like a symphony working up to the crescendo. Jealously, she wished she were part of it.

Roya didn't understand advertising. She'd never thought much about the science of ads on television or in magazines. Roya's mother had taught her classic good taste when she and Adrienne were children. Roya had seldom been swayed by ads, what other people owned or had. She relied on her natural talent for putting clothing ensembles together, blending colors, striking a balance of weight and functionality in a room. Roya didn't need others' opinions of what she should like or want. Roya had always thought for herself when it came to such things.

She was fascinated by the nuances a word or color meant in the minds of the consumers whose decisions would spell the economic future of Pulaski Trucking.

"But a service like this will cost money to the consumer. Don't they all want discounts these days?" Roya asked.

Adrienne shook her head. "They want service. They want to be treated as special. And they don't want it to cost extra."

Roya threw up her hands. "I rest my case."

"I didn't say that's what they get. Just that their perception must be that it costs no more to have special handling."

"How do we do that?" Roya asked.

Nick winked at Adrienne.

Roya felt as if she'd been set up and she didn't like it. She looked from Adrienne to Nick and back again.

There was no mistaking the conspiratorial look they exchanged. And for the first time, she noticed appreciation in Nick's eyes as Addie explained. With every sentence, the respect in his eyes for her sister's ideas grew.

Roya discovered she was profoundly jealous—jealous of Adrienne for the years of experience in advertising and marketing that molded her mind, restructured her thought patterns and ultimately won the admiration of businessmen like Nick.

Roya found herself suddenly regretting, not her years of child-rearing and the irreplaceable joyful moments with her children, but the lost chances to have continued her education, embarked on a career and focused her creativity.

She and Adrienne had the same genes, the same blood and brains. She could have been the one to make Nick's mind shift into overdrive.

Instead, it was Addie who turned him on.

Roya felt left out.

Nick answered Roya's question. "We do that by giving bulk discounts to the retailer. The more times they employ us, the less it costs. We show them how to cover our costs in the price of the goods they sell. My first suggestion is that our costs are automatically covered in the shipping-and-handling category. Most stores have a delivery service as it is. Instead of using their own guys for baby or related items, they use us. The co-op on advertising benefits us both and lowers their cost. There're a million and one ways to do it."

Roya wasn't convinced. "It still sounds like this campaign is going to cost us an awful lot up front."

Adrienne answered her sister's concerns. "I've got a couple of artists who are really good and really, really hungry. You could pick one. Have him paint two trucks. Cover his materials and then give him billing. Use his name in the logo. Print his name on all the advertising.

Make him part of the advertising. I know one young man—" she motioned toward Cynthia "—not but a year or two older than Cyn who would do it for trade-out."

"Wow!" Cynthia rolled her eyes. "Let's do it, Mom!"

Roya crossed her arms. "I want to think about it."

"Do better than that," Nick said. "Let's test it."

"How?"

"You and I take our concept to somebody big, say BabyLand. Or Field's, for all I care. Someone really, really tough. We pitch them and see where we land."

"You'll need to work up some numbers," Adrienne warned. "You can't go in there blind. If you screw up, you'll be stuck with giving away our product."

"That could take months," Roya groaned. "I need something now to bring in revenues."

Adrienne was nonplussed. "I'll feed some preliminary numbers into my computer. I can have a bare-bones proposal for you by Monday."

"I'll help you," Nick said quickly.

Too quickly. Too eagerly. Roya looked from Nick's smiling face to Adrienne's. *Why, she's preening! Flirting!*

"Don't you and Gavin have plans?" Roya asked hopefully, reminding her sister about her fiancé.

"Sure we do. But it won't take as much time as you think." She looked away from Roya to Nick. "I'm game if you are, Nick."

"Great! I haven't got any plans at all. Nothing to cancel."

Adrienne rose and gathered her pen, legal pad and briefcase. "I'm excited, Nick."

"So am I, Adrienne. This project has huge potential if handled correctly." He held out his hand and she took it.

"Special Delivery. I really like it. It feels good. Right here, you know?" She put her hand on her solar plexus.

"My feelings exactly." Nick's smile was megawatt.

Cynthia was on her feet. "This is so cool! I can't wait to get started. So do you think I could work with the artist? When can I meet him? Does he go to the Art Institute? Where does he live, Aunt Addie?"

Adrienne laughed as she pushed in her chair. "I'll give him a call later. Why don't you get to that computer and put together concepts. Things your mother could take with her on her first presentation."

"No problem!" Cynthia replied.

Adrienne turned to Roya. "I'll call you later, sis." She kissed her cheek.

"I'll walk you to your car," Nick said, whisking out of the conference room after Adrienne.

Roya rose slowly, feeling like the tortoise who'd just been passed by the hare.

When Nick and Adrienne were gone, Cynthia hugged her mother. "You are the most wonderful mother in the world."

"How's that?"

"Letting me do this, be a part of this team. Nick says no business can survive today unless there's absolute teamwork. I never knew this was what he meant."

"Teamwork."

"Man! What great vibes! We were electric! All of us. Isn't it just about the coolest day of your life, Mom?" Cynthia practically bounced out the door. "I can't wait to get to my Mac."

Alone, Roya tried to feel the electricity, but it was gone.

Feeling useless, she sank into the chair once again. She replayed the conversation, the glances and eye exchanges between her sister and Nick. There was no question Nick found Adrienne attractive, intelligent and exciting.

Who wouldn't? Addie is all those things.

She supposed she couldn't blame Nick for being attracted to Adrienne. Chemistry was a powerful element in a relationship. It either existed or it didn't.

Roya had chemistry for Nick.

Once, at a party, when he hadn't known who she was, Nick had had chemistry for Roya.

But Nick had willfully killed his.

It made sense he would pursue Adrienne.

And there wasn't a damn thing Roya could do about it.

27

"Don't be nervous," Nick said, parking his car at the Randolph Street parking garage.

"I'm not," Roya countered, picking lint off her black wool coat.

"You're fidgeting. You only do that when you're nervous."

Roya put her nose in the air and got out of the car.

"Or anxious," he added, taking the ticket from the valet, who jumped in the car and raced up the dangerously narrow incline.

Nick's back arched up when he heard his tires squeal.

Roya held out his briefcase to him. "Forget this?" She smiled smugly.

"Okay." He put his hand out pleadingly. "So we have a lot riding on this. So we could get dusted."

Roya walked in front of him. "I wish to heaven I hadn't let you and Addie talk me into this."

"Cynthia, too."

"Right. A kid. I really am nuts." She stopped abruptly, looking up at the old Marshall Field's clock on the corner of State and Randolph. "I used to love coming here. It's not the same at Water Tower, you know."

"I agree."

"I'm glad we're having this meeting here. That way, if we blow it, I can always remember that my own sister and her *friend* gave me a historical setting so I'd remember my humiliation for the rest of my life."

"Friend? You said that like I was her...lover."

Silence.

Roya walked up to the revolving door. She didn't go through; Nick was pulling her back onto the sidewalk.

"What is this?" he demanded.

"What's what?"

He looked at her. Her eyes were filled with pain—deep, scalding emotional pain. He hadn't realized it until this minute, but her eyes were bloodshot, as if she'd been crying. There were some things makeup couldn't hide.

She turned her face away from him once she saw he'd seen the truth in her eyes. She could tell him she was crying over Bud, but he wouldn't believe that. She'd told him several times she'd cried over Bud in the beginning and that they were mostly self-pitying tears.

Roya hadn't wanted Nick to know she felt anything for him one way or the other. She didn't want him to know that he was beginning to matter to her.

"I called her apartment several times over the weekend. The line was always busy. Like it was off the hook."

"Oh, for God's sake." He lifted his briefcase. "You saw all this stuff. The layouts. The budgets. The company history and the pitch letter. It took one hell of a lot of work, Roya. On Addie's part and mine. We worked night and day."

But I saw how you looked at her.

Nick was venting. "I can't believe you think so little of me and that you don't even trust your own sister. How could you think she would betray you like that?"

He put his hands on her shoulders. "Roya, the phone was busy because it was just that—busy. She was faxing me. I was faxing her. When we weren't using the line for the fax, we were calling each other. I spoke with Gavin at least a half dozen times. He made pasta for her while she worked. He invited me over, but then I knew if I did that, we'd all start bullshitting about various things and never get this done on time. She gave up her weekend for you, Roya. So did I."

"She's my sister."

"And I'm your general manager. We both want what's best for you. For the company, I mean."

"Thank you," she replied, embarrassed now by the thoughts she'd had over the past week and a half, knowing Nick and Adrienne worked closely.

"You can't do it, can you."

"What?"

"Trust men."

"After Bud? I don't think that's possible."

"It has to be sometime," he said.

"Why?"

He ground his fingers into her shoulders ever so slightly as he fought the impulse to shake her, make her come to her senses.

If you don't trust me, we'll never have a chance.

He wanted to kiss her then, kiss her deeply. Bring her to tears the way he had the first day they'd met. He wanted her to move his soul again. He'd never felt like that before, or since. It had been hell working with her everyday—watching her struggle against Bud's screwups, his addictions, his mistress's greed and legitimate legal claims. It must be hell for her, writing out a check to Kitt Cabrizzi every month, knowing how desperately she needed the money for Cynthia and Lucienne.

But Roya did it and never complained to anyone.

Nick admired her for that. It was just one more reason why Roya had gotten under his skin.

When she looked at him like this, as if she were seeing right down into his core, he was terrified to kiss her.

It was all too possible that that first kiss had been a dream. That it would never happen again. And if it did? Where would he go after that?

If it did, he knew he would never want to stop. He'd be insatiable.

And he didn't believe Roya was ready for that. She was

just discovering what life was about. She was learning to think on her own, be on her own, know herself.

He wanted her to have all the chances and time he'd had to discover and create himself over a lifetime. Roya had lived in a shadow for twenty years.

She'd only just begun to see the light of day.

"Because...you just do, is all," he finally said.

"Is this a self-serving wish of yours, Nick?" she asked tauntingly.

He wanted to answer her truthfully but knew if he did, he'd tip his hand. To lie was defeating his purpose. "What do you think?"

She smiled and wagged her forefinger at him. "Clever, Nick."

He dropped his hands with a chuckle.

You're free again, Roya.

She walked toward the building. "What do you say we trust in each other? Trust that we'll get a positive response."

"I'm ahead of you on that score," he said, following her inside the building. "I brought a company contract...just in case."

The meeting lacked the excitement Roya had witnessed when Addie, Nick and Cynthia had conceived the idea. The department heads listened intensely, complimented them politely and asked probing, exact questions which Nick answered matter-of-factly.

When the hour appointment came to an end, Roya was shocked that time could move so quickly.

No one had asked to sign a contract.

Nick left a large envelope containing pricing, start dates and business cards.

"We'll get back with you."

"May I expect a call within a week?" Nick asked.

"We'll try," the elder of the three men said. "Most definitely within two weeks. I'm inclined to think we would test this concept in this market first. If it catches on, we'll expand into other cities."

"That's all fine and good, but understand that we are not giving an exclusive with this and that we have filed patent papers."

"Of course you have. Perhaps if we gave you a decision this week we might discuss exclusivity?"

"We might," Nick replied. "But only for a test period. Our company needs to move forward, gentlemen. As swiftly as possible."

They bade their farewells and left.

Roya's mood was downcast in the elevator. "I'm sorry, Nick. Maybe I should have insisted Adrienne make this presentation."

"It's more impressive to have the president of the company at meetings like this. After this, you can remain in your ivory tower. They've met you. They have a face, a name and a voice. It was good. In fact, it was an outstanding meeting."

"What? How can you say that? They didn't lift an eyebrow."

"They're twitching in their wool suits. They thought the idea was dynamite. I nailed them when I told them about the patent."

"Tell me we did talk to Brian...."

"It's handled. I promise."

"God, I hope so."

"Trust me," he said.

She looked at him. She held her breath.

Weeks were too long to wait. Months were unbearably painful working with her every day. Seeing her pass his office time after time, never lifting her head to so much as glance his way. Most times, she didn't know he was on the grounds. When he worked at home and didn't come in, Roya never mentioned his absence.

Many times he'd worked at home because he knew if he'd gone into the office he would have seen her. Would have wanted her to notice him, grant him an audience, speak to him. When she was too busy, he would have gone away, hurting again. Aching again.

He'd tried to stay away. Keep her at a distance. Keep his heart locked up tight.

But he was failing—miserably.

"It's late. Let's celebrate. Rivers Café is close."

"Never heard of it," she said.

"It's new. In the Merc Building. You can watch the sunset over the buildings. See the reflection of the colors in the river."

"Sounds romantic."

He smiled. "It is."

"The food was divine," Roya said after finishing a seafood pasta dish with smoked scallops and mesquite grilled shrimp. "I guess I'm guilty of ordering takeout or pizza delivery so much for myself and the girls, I'd forgotten food could, and should, taste like this." She leaned back in her chair and folded her napkin. "I actually used to cook like this. But I'd take all day or all week to prepare special dishes."

He propped his elbows on the table and steepled his fingers. "Your life has changed a great deal since then."

"Yes." *Not the least of which is your presence in it.*

She felt the scrutiny of his gaze. Three months ago she would have wriggled under it, feeling as if she were being dissected and categorized as to her usefulness. That was the way her father and mother had always made her feel when they stared at her for any length of time.

She felt she'd been born in the judgment seat.

But Nick didn't make her feel that way.

Nick wasn't judging her, but rather observing her, she realized. "What are you waiting to see, Nick?"

The corner of his mouth turned up. "Caught me red-handed."

She leveled a cool gaze on him. "That's what you are doing, isn't it? Waiting."

He hadn't expected her to dare him. "Yes," he replied honestly, his voice low with aching sincerity.

She traced her finger through the water ring from her glass, but she kept her eyes unmercifully on his face. "Am I getting there?"

"Where?"

"Wherever it is you think I should be before you kiss me again."

In all his imaginings he'd expected a lot of responses from this elegant and beautiful woman, but this was not one of them. "Excuse me?"

"Shouldn't you pay the bill now, Nick?"

She didn't smile. Her eyes held no anticipation, no desperation and no hope. She didn't need him in her life if he didn't want to be there. She wouldn't allow her ego to overshadow reality. She was in a place. He was in a place. She would not force him to come to her if he wasn't ready.

Nick's surprise so overwhelmed him that he nearly did not perceive the one thing her mind-set had tried to eradicate from her eyes.

Desire.

Nick knew she didn't simply lust after him. He would have seen that long before this.

She didn't look to him to be her savior. She could have asked for a loan earlier.

She didn't expect anything from him in the least—not loyalty and certainly not trust.

He wished that she had.

He would have given her those unconditionally. Forever.

But Nick knew that if he ventured the slightest provocation, everything between them would change irreversibly. He could never go back to being Nick, the general manager. If he let her see his vulnerability, his own need for her, he might possibly lose his chance at having her when she did complete her metamorphosis.

The rest of his life lay at stake.

It was the biggest gamble he'd ever taken.

He'd never acted heedlessly except for the day he'd kissed Roya.

"Yes, I think I should pay the bill. Then I want to show you where I live, Roya."

"I'd like that, Nick."

28

◀━ ━▶

Roya never dreamed Nick wanted her.

She knew he didn't still think she was immoral. Time working with her, getting to know her had shown him the truth.

Until he suggested they come to his apartment, he'd kept his distance. She'd been just as focused as he on the demands of the business and the frightening imbalance of debits and credits. She never knew where the next payroll was coming from. She'd been shooting from the hip for three months. She wondered how many bullets she had left.

All this time, thoughts of Christmas party kisses had been relegated to her nocturnal imaginings.

Now he was asking her to think about it consciously.

"Martini?" he asked.

She wrinkled her nose. "Do you have something less caustic?"

"Chardonnay?"

"Perfect. Very cold."

"Coming right up," he replied, dimming the lights to candle glow. He went to the kitchen saying, "Make yourself at home. The stereo is on the bookshelf. Just push the power button and the CD player comes on automatically. Then push Play."

Roya executed his instructions and stood back as Tony Bennett's voice filled the rooms. The music was romantic and suited her mood. She was surprised. She'd expected something more impersonal and certainly less sentimental. It made her wonder if there was someone in his past whose memories were evoked with each song.

She thought it best not to play Pandora. Some things were best left to rest.

Like Bud. The past is dead. It's the future that counts.

Nick returned with their drinks.

"Great lights," she said, turning away from him toward the windows. Above all, she wanted the moment to last.

"I bought this place for the view. And the potential resale. My Realtor said—"

She cut in, "I don't want to hear about your investments, Nick. I don't want to talk about work. Or Bud. Or the presentation or any of a hundred things we talk about every day. I want to talk about you."

"What about me?"

She faced him. "Everything about you. Do you like peanut-butter-and-jelly sandwiches when you get depressed? Do you like your cookies with warm milk or cold? Do you ride horses? Play chess? What's your favorite color? Where is your favorite city? Have you ever been to Europe? How do you like your steak? Bloody rare, I bet. What's your pet peeve? Have you ever been in love? Do you dive? Ski? Play tennis…?"

"Whoa. Back up."

"To where?"

"The one about being in love," he said, taking the onion-stuffed olive out of his drink and feeding it to Roya.

She hadn't realized she'd asked the dangerous question. "You don't have to answer that."

"I don't mind. Yes, I have," he replied.

"Fine. Good." She sipped her wine, focusing her eyes on the view.

"She was the cutest girl in my second-grade class. A foot taller than everyone. She told me her father had been transferred to the city in the middle of the year. She wasn't slow, just unlucky. She was always alone. Never fitting in. I adored her."

"What happened to her?"

"She left with her parents at the end of the year. I never saw her again."

Roya smiled inwardly. "And that's it?"

"Afraid so. Now your turn," he said blithely, then held his breath. Was he nuts asking her that question? He didn't want to hear about Bud. He knew too much already. "Don't answer that."

He put their drinks on the coffee table.

"I'm going to kiss you, Roya. That's what I brought you here for. You know that...don't you?"

She nodded.

"So, if you've changed your mind, I'll walk you to your car now."

"I haven't changed my mind."

Nick pulled her to him, fitting her body to his. She could feel his heart pounding. She was surprised its rhythm matched hers.

She realized she was afraid. Afraid this kiss would be nothing like what she remembered. Afraid she'd imagined the emotions she felt with Nick that day at the party. Afraid she'd read too much into her response to him. Afraid she'd used Nick that day to fill the emptiness inside her. She remembered being afraid then, too, but for other reasons. She'd been afraid Bud was having an affair. Afraid Bud didn't love her. Afraid her life with Bud was over.

And she'd been right.

What if she was right about Nick?

"On second thought, I think I should go," she said, pushing away from him.

"Too late," Nick said, and kissed her.

His lips were strong and eagerly aggressive. There was nothing soft or inquisitive about this kiss. Nor was there anything chaste.

Nick translated his passion and desire for her with his lips. He demanded that she respond to him.

And she did.

It was as if she'd been the one who'd died, not Bud. Nick was resurrecting her. An electric maelstrom exploded inside her heart, its current shooting down her nerves to the extremities of her body. She felt as if she'd been hit by a thunderbolt.

And she had.

Nick's demanding lips parted hers, his tongue plunged into her mouth. She accepted him. She participated with him. She became his equal.

In perfectly rationed parts, they shared their ravenous desire for each other.

He gave all of himself.

She gave all of herself.

Roya clamped her hands on either side of his face as she slanted her mouth over his. She was the aggressor.

He followed suit, holding her face. Pleading with his lips that she never leave. Telling her with his hands she was the most precious treasure he would ever hold.

"Oh, God, Nick," she whispered breathlessly. "How can this be happening?"

"Again?" he groaned sensually. He was as shaken as she.

He'd traveled the gamut of human emotions over the past months of being around Roya. He'd gone through the phase of struggling to negate her impact on him. The self-denial mechanisms he'd tried could fill a book. When none of that put a halt to his dreams about her, his lust turned to desire and desire to longing.

Nick had never needed anyone in his life. Never wanted anyone *in* his life.

But he wanted Roya with all his heart.

Her eyes were suffused with passion and hope when she looked at him. "Have you thought about what happens after this?" she asked.

"I have. Have you?"

"No. Not because I didn't think about kissing you. Being with you. I'd convinced myself that our first kiss wasn't real. That I'd made too much of it."

"And now?" he asked softly, his hand on her nape, his eyes devouring her swollen lips.

"I didn't make enough of it," she replied.

His mouth captured hers again. Nick crushed her to him, his arms strong, supportive and willing to keep her or let her go.

Roya responded to the intensity of his heat with that of her own. For the first time in her life, she realized her body was communicating the emotions etched on her soul.

Roya wanted to be loved.

That was why she'd married Bud.

Though she'd only been eighteen, it wasn't youth or naiveté that had led her to believe Bud was her soul mate. It was that she was hoping he loved her.

Kissing Nick, feeling his thoughts, his passions, with her body, she knew now that wanting and hoping didn't make something so.

She had tried to make Bud love her. She had tried to love Bud. She had thought she was doing the right thing.

But she'd been wrong.

Her head told her that Nick demonstrated all the qualities in a man she'd tried to see in Bud but couldn't. They weren't there to see. Nick was ethical, loyal, giving and honest.

Her body craved him. Her heart wanted to love him.

"I won't make love to you, Roya," Nick whispered against her ear.

Roya's body froze. She pulled away from him, her eyes filled with shock. "I'll go…"

He pulled her back. "I seem to have a problem expressing myself to you."

She strained against him. "I wasn't begging."

"What I meant was that I don't want to take you to bed just tonight."

She felt her heart closing and her hopes dying. She'd miscalculated with him. Badly. She was torn between saving her pride and walking out the door, and staying long enough to prove to him that what he really wanted was her, but that his fears deterred him.

"We're kissing. Who said anything about sex?" she asked, watching his discomfiture grow with each new statement.

"I've been thinking about it for months and you know it. I want you so badly I can't put my words together, and that has never happened to me. Ever." He placed his hands on her hips and pressed her pelvis into his erection. "But I should take you home."

She felt a pang of rejection touch her in the deepest recesses of her heart, where not even Bud's betrayal had struck. If he wanted her, then why did he want her to leave?

She had to know. She'd come too far to allow misunderstandings to stand in the way of possibly the most wonderful event of her life.

"Do you think I'll hurt you, Nick? Is that why you want me to leave?"

"Yes, I am afraid. You should be, too."

"Maybe I don't have your kind of success in business, Nick, but I've lived through the birth of two children, my husband's betrayal and his suicide. I'm willing to take a chance on you."

Nick was stunned. She was more courageous than he'd ever been. Her challenge humbled and excited him.

His hands were on her waist at the same moment he kissed her again. This time his kiss was more greedy than ever before.

Roya felt as if she'd been swept out to sea.

Everything happened so fast.

He peeled off her suit jacket and unzipped her skirt. It

whooshed to the floor and puddled at her feet. He unbuttoned her blouse, unhooked her bra, and while he filled his hands with her breasts, she was fumbling with his shirt buttons.

She'd never felt this incredible urgency, as if a time bomb were about to explode and they only had seconds before detonation.

She grappled with his belt. He unbuckled it and unzipped his suit pants.

He kicked off his shoes while she peeled off her panty hose.

Their naked bodies were silhouetted against the backdrop of city lights. He led her across the wood floor to the bedroom.

The room was large, with little furniture—no dresser, no armoire, no mirrors, which told her that his closets were most likely filled with built-ins. However, the room was ringed with floor-to-ceiling bookcases. In the far corner was an overstuffed club chair and a reading lamp. A pile of opened books and magazines were clustered haphazardly around the chair. The bed rested against the far wall, over which was suspended an enormous gold-framed Impressionist painting. In the dim city lights, she couldn't make out its colors, but it appeared to be a turn-of-the-century Chicago street scene.

"This is where I bring all my lovers," he said.

Glancing at the thousands of books around her, she smiled. "And you have many."

"Scores," he said. "Joan Didion, Joyce Carol Oates, whom I especially adored. She's a head trip."

He put his hands on her shoulders and pressed her to the bed.

Roya was smiling when she kissed him. Nick had made her feel secure just by being himself.

This time their embraces were tender, their passion attenuating into more profound emotions.

Roya felt it all: adoration, as he decorated her breasts

with dewdrop-size kisses; respect, as he cupped her face with his palm and moved his body over hers; love, as he entered her.

Nick didn't close his eyes as he made love to Roya. Watching the nuances of her reactions, he learned what she liked, what thrilled her and how far he could go to bring her to the pitch of ecstasy without bringing her to a full climax. Then he would build to a crescendo once again, pull back, and then begin all over again.

He wanted her to feel the ebb and flow of her body's response to him. To learn about her body with him. He wanted her to understand his needs and desires at the same time.

"Together, Roya." He propped himself on his elbows, pulled his body away from hers. "Look at me inside you."

She opened her eyes. "Oh, Nick."

When she looked up into his eyes, she saw a tear fall from his eye.

"I never thought it would be like this," he said, with so much emotion in his voice, it awed her.

"This?"

He plunged himself deeply inside her, slaking himself against her. She arched her back, raising her breasts to his mouth. With his arm under her shoulders, he pulled her to a sitting position until she was sitting in his lap, their arms wrapped around each other. He cupped his hands under her buttocks and guided her rhythm on him until finally she burst into an orgasm.

Nick smothered his face with her breasts, pulling on her nipples with his lips.

Roya screamed with pleasure, thinking her joy had peaked.

Nick continued to press her down on him, then push her away, forcing her pulses to come at an even more rapid pace.

She was caressed with perspiration as she struggled to

catch her breath. She thought surely the pounding of her heart would crack her ribs.

"Hold me, Roya. Don't ever let me go."

In all her life, in all her imaginings, Roya had never thought a man's desires, his words, could touch her soul. But Nick's did.

When he threw his head back, a guttural animal groan escaping his throat, he filled her. Roya's orgasm was cataclysmic. She felt as if she were falling, spinning down a deep, warm tunnel. She clung to Nick. He would catch her. He would be there to keep her from harm. He would be there. Always and forever. He would never let her go.

They spiraled for an eternity before they ascended to the light. Joy filled her heart, and when she opened her eyes Nick was there.

She knew, even if he did not, that he would be with her forever. Neither age nor time nor space would ever keep them apart.

She knew it in that place inside her that spoke to her in her dreams at night and sparked her intuitions in the day. What she felt for Nick was divine.

Destiny wasn't a place or a career. It wasn't a thing. Destiny was people.

Roya had waited a long time.

She'd found her destiny at last.

29

—►◄—

Cynthia held her logo sketches tightly as she walked outside the office building toward the bay where the two eighteen-foot trucks were parked. She was to meet the artist from the Chicago Art Institute, who had signed an agreement with her mother to paint for free.

His back was to her as she walked up. She knew instantly she wouldn't like him, what with all that thick dark hair hanging below his shoulders and tied in a ponytail with a leather thong, as if he were playing artistic Bohemian or an Indian brave. Or something.

"Hi. You must be Randy."

"Randolph Miller," he corrected her in a voice as deep as the ocean. He faced her.

"I'm Cynthia. This is my project."

"So I heard," he said dully.

His eyes were charismatic blue, clear, icy and ringed in dark lashes looking far too much like a high fashion male model and not enough like any artist she'd ever envisioned. She was almost disappointed he didn't have a beard. It would have helped cover his rugged jawline and sensual mouth.

His eyes dropped to her hand, but not before they plummeted down from her face to her neck, her breasts and to her hips. "That mine?"

"It's mine," she replied with due possessiveness. "But I'll let you see it."

"You'll have to if you want me to paint these vans."

Cynthia felt not only stupid, but stupefied. She didn't

know why her hand had grown clammy when she handed him the roll, but it had. It didn't make any sense, this dryness in her mouth, the ache in her eyes when she looked at him.

He unfolded it, took a quick peek and rolled it back up. "Here." He started walking away.

"What's wrong?"

"I don't like them. The deal's off."

She was incredulous. "What do you mean you don't like them?"

"They don't make sense." He kept walking.

"I didn't hire you to make sense of my logo. Just to paint it. It's not your job to have a brain."

He stopped dead in his tracks. He put his hands on his hips and dropped his head. He stood looking at the ground for an inordinately long period of time, as if counting to ten to hold in his anger. "Excuse me, Miss Pulaski, but I do happen to have a brain. I have so much of a brain that I thought I was being smart to trade my expertise and time to your mother for the privilege of being mentioned in all your advertisements."

He turned to her and began walking toward her. "You see, she sold me a bill of goods. She told me you were a genius. You were great on the computer. Now, I ask you, why would I want my name on some stupid logo that any five-year-old could dream up?"

She glared at him. "This is for babies. Baby deliveries. It's supposed to be juvenile."

He stopped walking. "What?" He blinked once. Then twice, as if taking a reality check.

It was Cynthia's turn to be indignant. "Surely Mother told you that."

"No. She said Special Delivery. I was thinking FedEx. Overnight. High-tech stuff, like that."

"I figured as much."

"You did."

She smiled. "I did. I'm not trying to assault your artistic sensibilities. I'm trying to make money."

His face softened when he chuckled. "Oh, that old thing," he said, coming to stand next to her.

She realized she had to look up to him. Was it possible his shoulders were so wide? She felt surrounded by him.

"Wanna look at it again?"

"I think I should take a very long second look. Don't you?"

She swallowed hard. Cynthia had never been the object of a blatant sexual attack, but she got the distinct impression Randolph was making plans.

She held out her sketch. "Be my guest."

He unfurled the roll as if it were precious parchment. His eye was as keen as an eagle's, taking in every minute detail. "I like the art deco slant you've given it. The angels are too Rubenesque, however. I can fix that. I think the skyline would have more impact if we did it in indigo blue rather than flat black. Gives depth and romance." He raised his eyes to her. "You like a little depth with your romance, I can tell."

Before she could shoot back a quip, he'd turned back to the drawing.

"It needs a full moon and the stork should be flying across it. He should be wearing a top hat. What if we cut the cherubs altogether and put in some art nouveau adult angels—goddesses in diaphanous gowns, swirling upward, holding the stars in their hands."

She gasped. "Art nouveau is my favorite."

His smile was tainted with mischievous seduction. "You see? I hardly know you, and I can tell from your work what you like."

"Can you tell who I am?"

He instantly rolled the paper. "Not necessarily. No."

She reached for the drawing.

He pulled it toward his chest and held it close. "Can I keep this? To study it overnight, I mean."

"Sure."

"Cool. I'll see you tomorrow."

She stuck her hands in her jeans pockets. "Good."

She watched him walk away. His pants were old cotton twills, and though they'd seen a lot of wear, she noticed they were clean and recently pressed. His shoes were new Top-Siders, and the hunter green sweatshirt was an obvious favorite.

She liked the way he walked, comfortable in himself, with himself. He was sure of his talent in a way she wished she would someday be.

She hadn't known what to expect of him, but she'd not been prepared for his arrogance. Yet he'd quickly dropped it when he realized there had been a mistake.

She was shocked Randolph Miller had made such an impression on her.

He was almost to the chain-link gate when he called back to her. "Cynthia!"

"Yeah?" she shouted back.

"Will you be here tomorrow?"

"Yes. I'm always here. Eight to five. Every day."

"Every day?"

"Except Sunday."

He whistled. "I'm impressed. I don't think I could do that."

"I love it," she said.

"That's all that matters." He smiled at her.

She felt as if she'd been hit by a laser blast.

Randolph returned the following day toting a bag of painting clothes and a boxful of paints. He went directly to the bay where he would be painting the trucks, without informing Cynthia he'd arrived.

It was Marjorie who tapped her on the shoulder while she was immersed in a project on the computer. "That painter you wanted is out there going to town."

"Painter?" Her hand flew to her mouth. She checked her watch. "Randolph is here?"

"Been here two hours now."

Suddenly, she was rattled. "How can he be? He doesn't even know where the paints are."

"Brought his own, he told me," Marjorie said, but before she finished her statement, Cynthia was out the door, smoothing her hair on the way down the hall.

Marjorie watched after her. "What the devil's gotten into her?"

Cynthia had worn a skirt that day, one she'd borrowed from Lucienne's closet, and a white blouse. She wore her contacts, too. Funny how no one had noticed that. Not even Marjorie.

Randolph had measured out his spaces, blocked the letters and had begun roughing in the largest silhouettes. He appeared to be more engineer than artist.

Cynthia was impressed.

"Hi, Randolph. I didn't know you were here."

"I know," he said sternly, not looking up from his work.

She looked down at the floor and realized these tubs and cans were half-empty. There were dozens of colors. "You need all this to do a black-and-white logo?"

"Indigo blue," he said flatly. "I thought we'd discussed this."

"Yeah, but…"

"I need all this to give it shading, depth, light, tone. The angels must be ethereal. It takes a lot. Your mother can just reimburse me."

"But I've already bought…"

"Take them back. Obviously, they're all wrong for this project."

"How can you say that?" she asked. "You haven't even seen them."

He expelled an extremely frustrated breath. "My dear young woman, if you don't know why I would need all these colors, how on earth would you know what to buy previous to our meeting yesterday?"

"I guess…I wouldn't."

He threw her a sidelong glance. "Now, please, I'm very busy.…"

She started backing up. "Fine." She backed farther away. "I'm leaving. I'll be inside if you need me."

"I won't."

"Fine," she said under her breath, wondering why she felt a stinging in her stomach, as if someone had hurt her feelings. She didn't know Randolph Miller at all. How could he hurt her? He was no one—just a hired painter. In a day or two she would never see him again. And that would be that.

"Not until I finish." He turned to her, gifting her with one of his luminous smiles. Then just as quickly he went back to his work.

Cynthia stormed away. "It's true what they say about artists. They're not only temperamental, but very strange."

30

Driving home from shopping, Kitt Cabrizzi turned up the volume on her car radio at the stoplight while students from Our Lady of Mount Carmel High School meandered along the crosswalk. The sight of backpacks slung over their shoulders and of boys wearing the same navy-and-gold letterman sweaters and khaki slacks they had back when she was in high school caused her to shake her head.

"Back then the pants and skirts were corduroy. Today duck twill. Some things never change."

There was even a young couple kissing under a lamppost a block from the school. The boy was tall, athletic-looking and wearing a letterman jacket. The girl looked at him adoringly. "Just like Bud and I…"

She watched them as if she were time-traveling through a hole in space. She was with Bud once again.

Kitt shivered and hugged herself. "Nonsense."

The couple parted slowly. The girl was smiling, the boy intent on kissing her again. This time he put his hand on her breast. The girl did not flinch, as if she were used to his touch—just the way Kitt had been familiar with Bud's body when she was only sixteen.

The light changed and Kitt drove forward. Coming closer to the couple, she realized the blond-haired girl looked vaguely familiar.

Like a younger version of Roya.

Kitt nearly slammed on the brakes.

That girl wasn't Roya, but Roya's daughter!

"What is she doing here? Do they live around here now?"

Kitt's hands were shaking.

"Oh, God. She isn't that stupid, is she? To invade my space?"

Kitt slammed her fist on the steering wheel. Her self-centered brain could only function in one mode. Kitt believed the world revolved around her. She was unable to understand that other people had their own life agendas. That they did not spend time choreographing their actions around Kitt never occurred to her. She was paranoid and delusional enough to believe that they did.

It was in terms of others' dealings with her that Kitt explained and validated her own existence. Therefore, her natural deductive reasonings told her that Roya had purposefully placed her youngest daughter at Our Lady of Mount Carmel as a kind of karmic taunting.

How dare she make fun of me as if Bud and I were nothing more than a high school fling! I'll make her wish she'd never thought of taking me on!

Kitt kept her eyes on the couple in the rearview mirror. The girl was beautiful and cool, sure of herself in that same manner Kitt had seen in Roya.

The boy walked close to the girl, with his arm around her shoulder, kissing her neck with every other step. Kitt could tell he was saying all the right things that the girl wanted to hear because her young face was filled with happiness.

The couple blurred in the mirror.

Kitt's eyes were full. She immediately turned the corner and parked the car. Then she leaned her head back on the headrest and let the tears sear her cheeks. They were filled with anger, jealousy and regret.

She ground the wet remains with her palms.

The boy walked the girl to the school parking lot and they approached a ten-year-old black Buick. The boy leaned the girl against the door, pressed his body to hers and kissed her again.

Then he opened the door and waited for her to get in. He went around to the driver's side, got in, and before turning the engine over, he kissed the girl deeply again. She leaned her head on his shoulder as he backed the car out of his parking slot and drove away.

Kitt's emotions died in the wake of revenge.

She quickly turned the car around in a residential driveway and sped up to the corner. The couple was still in sight.

Kitt turned the corner in time to see the black Buick head east.

She followed them for seventeen minutes, and when the car pulled up to the tacky ranch house and the girl unlocked the front door with her own key, Kitt knew she'd found Roya's new home.

She waited while the boy drove back the way he'd come. Kitt assumed he was probably going back to the school for practice of some kind. Bud had always gone back to the school for football practice or wrestling. On days when he did not have practice, he went inside with Kitt to her bedroom to make love to her.

Kitt could tell this couple was no different.

She glanced down the street. Cars came and went in driveways as mothers brought kids home from school. Spring had not yet arrived in Chicago and the yards were still muddy from melting snow, forcing the younger children indoors. Within twenty minutes the street was quiet again.

Kitt locked her car and walked up the cracked concrete to the house. She rang the doorbell.

The girl came to the door.

"Yes?" Lucienne gasped and nearly choked on the cookie she'd been eating. "You! What are you doing here? How did you find us?"

Before she gave Kitt a chance to reply, she stepped back and started to shut the door.

Kitt threw her body into the doorway, stopping the door. She didn't care if her entire backside was bruised. It would be worth it to screw with Roya. She was amazed at the thrill that ran through her body. She felt it again—power. The rush was as good as drugs. No, it was better.

"I wanted to see what you looked like up close. I wanted to know if my daughter might have looked like you."

Lucienne's indignation turned to shock. She looked in the woman's dark, mesmerizing eyes. She felt as if the blood had seeped out of her body. She was cold, her shock turned to fear.

"What daughter?" Lucienne heard herself ask.

"The one I had with your father."

"What's her name?" Lucienne's tongue felt as if it was rubbing against gravel in her mouth. But her curiosity was more determined to possess her mind than her fears.

"I never named her. She died."

Lucienne's hand flew to her mouth. "You killed her?"

"I had an abortion."

"Then how do you know you had a daughter?" Lucienne's mind cleared as she watched Kitt's expression. There was no question the woman was filled with hatred and jealousy. But of one thing Lucienne could tell—she was smarter than this old hag.

"I just know."

Lucienne felt her blood return. She finished off her cookie and wiped her hand down the side of her jeans. She was surprised how clammy her palms had gotten. "Well, thanks for the info. You better go now."

Lucienne shoved Kitt's shoulder, pushing her backward.

"Your father never loved your mother. He loved me," Kitt ranted.

Lucienne didn't know where her strength came from at

that moment, but she felt as if she could take on the devil himself and win. "I'm calling 911 if you don't get the hell outta here in two seconds."

"Don't you understand? This is damage control. I'm trying to help you. I don't want you to make the same mistakes I did. I saw you with your boyfriend at school. I followed you from there."

"What?"

"I'm your friend. More than you can imagine. I know the pitfalls. I screwed up my life because of your father. I see you starting to do the same thing." Kitt smiled benevolently; it was one of her best expressions.

Lucienne couldn't believe her ears. "Get outta my face." She shoved her body against the door, pushing Kitt Cabrizzi out of the threshold, out of her space.

Lucienne quickly locked the door and slid the bolt, then hooked the chain lock. She raced to the back door and checked the lock there. She darted back to the living room and drew the ugly drapes her mother was going to replace with the elegant cream silks from their old house. Lucienne flew down the hall to the bathroom and peeked out.

The old hag was standing on the front step just staring at the closed door.

Lucienne held her breath. Her heart thundered in her chest. She'd never felt this frightened in her life.

What if the old hag pulled a gun? Tried to break down the door? What did she want from her? From her mother? What kind of sicko was she?

That was when it hit Lucienne.

"She's certifiable. An out-and-out nutcase. And she hates me. Us. All of us. Me, Mom and Cyn. And now she knows where we live. Where I go to school."

Cold sweat broke out on Lucienne's upper lip. "What if she comes back?"

Kitt waited on the front stoop for a full ten minutes before taking a step back. She knew the girl was watching her from the bathroom window, for she'd seen the mini-blinds part.

She was banking on the girl's fear to make this moment count.

Kitt was making her statement loud and clear.

She could only hope that Roya would tremble even more when her daughter related their encounter this afternoon.

It was time for Roya to be in the hot seat. Kitt knew precisely how to make it very hot, indeed.

The day of reckoning was approaching. It was time for Roya to pay for stealing Bud.

Kitt turned slowly so as not to slip on the faulty concrete as she walked back to her car.

She hit the remote control and unlocked the doors of the Cadillac.

When she drove away, she leaned down and took a very long look at the house through the passenger window. She made certain the girl saw her scrutinizing the house.

Kitt smiled to herself, knowing she'd accomplished her first goal.

She had successfully infused Roya's house with fear.

She envisioned herself as the Angel of Death seeking revenge on the House of Israel. Yet, Roya had not swabbed her doorway with lamb's blood. She was unprotected.

At that moment, Kitt realized her destiny—she would smite the House of Pulaski.

31

Roya had wanted to tell Adrienne the good news in person.

She stood in her sister's kitchen measuring dark French roasted coffee for the cappuccino maker. "We got the Field's account!"

Pulling oversized Spode cappuccino cups from the cabinet, Adrienne shrieked, "I don't believe it! I mean, I believe it, but I don't! My God! I've never gotten to them. For twenty years my timing with them has been about as lousy as it gets. And the one time I do a gratis job, it works!"

"Gosh, I'm sorry, Addie. I thought you'd be thrilled."

"I am thrilled." She beamed. "I'm shocked and a bit disappointed. I would have loved—" she pressed her jaw together just enough to give her words grit "—to throw this up to Freddie. But because I'm on his payroll, he'd kill me."

Roya's face fell. "That's not fair. It was your idea."

"Some of it. Not all of it. Your daughter is no slouch," she said, foaming skim milk.

Roya watched her expertly concoct the best cappuccino she'd had in years. "I've got to learn to use one of these machines." She sighed, taking another long drink. "Later. When I have time."

"You know, Roya, Nick deserves a great deal of credit on this."

At the mention of his name, Roya's eyes lit up.

Adrienne saw it. "You think so, too."

"You should have seen him at the presentation. He knew exactly when to push them, when to pull back. How to maneuver their thinking to his next point before they had the slightest idea what he was doing. When we left, I thought we'd blown it, but he told me he thought we'd get it. He's incredible."

Adrienne smiled to herself. "You knew he was capable, Roya. That's why you hired him. Right?"

"Only because Daria thought so highly of his reputation. When I went over his résumé, I knew I had to talk him into staying."

Adrienne watched Roya closely while she talked. There was no mistaking the faint blush to her cheeks and the softness in her voice. She'd never seen Roya like this. "Does he know you're interested in him?"

"Interested?"

"Yeah. As a man. As a lover. That at minimum you have a crush on him?"

"Addie, really. We aren't in high school."

"Mmmm. So, you're already lovers."

Roya put her cup down with more force than she'd intended. "Is there no keeping anything from you?"

"Damn!" Adrienne's mouth gaped in a circle. "I was just shooting in the dark. I...God, are you really?"

Roya nodded sheepishly, then corrected herself. "I haven't the slightest idea how I'm supposed to act now. I mean, if I'm supposed to feel guilty or immoral. I just don't, Addie. In fact, I've never felt so wonderful in all my life. Sometimes I think it's impossible to be this happy. Even when the outside of my life looks like it should be the pits, it's not!"

"I'm really, really happy for you, Roya...."

The doorbell rang.

Adrienne put her cup down. "I'll be right back."

"Is it time for Gavin to be here already?" Roya looked at her watch. It was only four-thirty.

"No. I can't imagine..."

Adrienne opened the door.

"Hello, Ms. Monier," Lieutenant Dutton said. Two plainclothes detectives stood behind him. Adrienne thought she remembered seeing them at Roya's house the night Bud died. *Or was killed.*

She shivered.

"Good afternoon, Lieutenant," she answered.

Upon hearing their voices, Roya got up from the bar stool and walked to the foyer. She stood behind her sister. "It must be important for you to have followed me all the way here," Roya said. "What did you want to see me about?"

"Actually, I didn't know you were here. I came to speak with Ms. Monier."

"Me?"

"Addie?" Roya's shock rattled in her voice. "That's preposterous. What would Addie be able to tell you?" She looked at her sister.

Roya didn't like the veil of guilt that descended over Adrienne's face. Suddenly, she felt weak in the knees as the atmosphere in the room metamorphosed. Fear huddled in the corners, watching, waiting to pounce on her like a preying panther.

"Do we have to do this here, Lieutenant?" Adrienne asked.

Lieutenant Dutton didn't blink an eye. "Downtown is fine."

"I want my attorney present," she replied flatly, as if she'd been prepared for his request.

"Fine."

"May I call him now and have him meet us there?"

"Certainly." The lieutenant nodded.

Roya felt the world tilt ever so slightly, upsetting her balance. "Addie, what's he talking about? Why does he want to talk to you? What can you tell him that you don't want me to hear?"

Roya followed her sister to the bedroom.

Adrienne lifted the receiver and punched out a number. "Hi, darling." Her voice cracked when she spoke. "The police are here." She paused. "Not yet. Will you call him for me? I...I can't even remember where I put my Day-Timer with Peter's number."

Roya's eyes were vast, unbelieving orbs in her face. She wrung her hands. She didn't want to hear what Adrienne was telling Gavin or the way she said it. She didn't want to see the tears in Adrienne's eyes. And she certainly did not want to see the way her own sister was avoiding eye contact with her, as if she had something to hide.

"Addie?" Roya pleaded as she hung up the phone.

Adrienne drew in a deep breath. She turned to Roya and put her hands on her shoulders. "It's okay, Roya. I didn't kill Bud, if that's what you're thinking."

"I wasn't thinking that!"

"I love you, Roya."

"I love you, too, Addie. Just tell me what's going on."

"I'm not sure, yet."

"But—but you knew he was coming. The lieutenant. Maybe not precisely when, but you knew eventually he would get around to you. You've already prepared your attorney. Gavin knows! Please, Addie... I'm scared. Tell me."

Adrienne looked away. Her tears were running in thick streams. She hugged Roya quickly, then rushed to the closet, grabbed her coat and fled from the room.

The lieutenant was inspecting an antique Ming vase on the sofa table when Adrienne entered the room.

"I'm ready," she said.

Roya was fast on her heels.

"Lock up for me, will you, Roya?" Adrienne asked, without looking back at her sister. "This won't take long. But the coffee will get cold."

"Addie..." Roya stood in the foyer as the officers closed around her sister, blocking her view, closing off their access to each other.

In a matter of seconds Roya was alone in the apartment.

Cynthia was immersed in her work at the computer when Randolph walked in. She didn't hear him behind her, gazing over her shoulder at the screen.

He cleared his throat to announce his presence, but Cynthia didn't notice.

"Uh, the secretary outside said I could just come in," he said.

"What?" Cynthia nearly leaped out of her chair; it went spinning off on its rollers behind her. She grabbed the armrest to steady herself more than to rescue the chair. "Do you always sneak up on people like that?"

"I knocked on the door. You didn't respond."

"How long have you been there?" she asked, pushing her glasses up on the bridge of her nose.

He smiled with that cocky sensuality she remembered more vividly than she cared to admit. She looked down at her faded jeans and old turtleneck. She wished to heaven she'd had time this morning to put on makeup. But she hadn't planned on seeing Randolph again...ever. She felt self-conscious, remembering how she'd tried to look pretty for him and he hadn't paid the slightest attention to her.

"You didn't call to tell me what you thought of the painting I did."

"Was I supposed to?"

"I was hoping you would."

"Really? I didn't get that impression the last time we talked," she said, folding her arms in front of her protectively. "In fact, I got the distinct impression the less you saw of me, the better. For your work, that is."

He looked around sheepishly, making an arc with his shoe on the floor, not looking at all like the arrogant young artist he'd portrayed himself to be. This Randolph was different.

It hit her then that he, like many creative people,

needed approval. The fact that it was her approval he sought pleased her a lot. She smiled. But she remained silent. She wasn't above milking the situation for a while, anyway.

"I'm sorry about that. When I start working, my mind just goes off somewhere and I can be rude at times. I don't mean to be, honest. It just happens. I try to work on that, but it's not enough, I guess."

"You're young. There's still time," she joked.

He smiled appreciatively.

Cynthia felt as if she'd been knocked back; the force of his attention on her was like a blast of energy. "Just so you know, your work is incredible."

"Incredible." He ran the word around his mouth, as if it were fine wine. "No one's ever said that before."

"Unique." She timidly took a step toward him. "For me it was more than that."

"No kidding?" He held his breath.

"It is divine. I've never seen anything like it. The way you captured the blues of the night sky, the lake water, the angels ascending, and the stars and the shading of the moon is perfection."

"You think that?"

"Everyone here does. Mother. Nick. Marjorie. And the calls have been coming in ever since we sent our first deliveries out. Nick is talking about a billboard."

"A billboard! Why, I'll be…"

"Famous," she said, liking the fact that she was the one giving him this joy. His face was beaming.

Randolph put his hands at his temples, splaying his fingers through his thick hair. "My God, this is incredible!"

"I told you." She giggled.

He expelled a deep sigh. "All of it thanks to you."

"To Mother, you mean. She hired you.…"

In two strides he was next to her, holding her hands in his. Tightly. "But you convinced me to stay. I was so bull-headed I was ready to walk out. You stopped me. It was you, Cyn," he said quietly.

Cynthia was so overcome by his nearness she thought her heart would explode. She didn't know why she should be reacting so strongly to him, since she didn't know much about him.

Is that what this is? Am I in love?

"I didn't do much," she finally said. "Just knocked some sense into you, is all."

"I needed that," he said. "Thank you."

"Any time," she replied, looking deeply into his eyes. Then an electric pulse shot through her, making her jump a fraction out of her shoes. The room went black when she shut her eyes.

He's kissing me. Really kissing me.

Randolph Miller had intended his kiss to knock Cynthia Pulaski's socks off. He'd meant it to be the kiss of her lifetime. He captured her lips with his and pulled her close to him so that he could feel her heartbeat.

He hadn't intended for the kiss to be as sensual as he found it. Nor had he thought she would know anything about kissing. But she kissed him back with a passion he could only equate to his deep-felt need to paint. He had intended to be the master but discovered he was the student.

Cynthia slipped her fingers around his nape and pulled him closer to her. She couldn't imagine one single reason why this pleasure should ever end.

Randolph moaned deep in his throat and pressed his body into hers. "Cyn," he breathed softly as he kissed her earlobes and throat. "What are you doing to me?"

Cynthia opened her eyes, but her glasses had fogged over. She quickly removed them so she could see. She didn't want to miss seeing his expression. "You were kissing me."

"That I was," he replied between planting tiny raindrop kisses on her lips, chin and cheeks. "And you like me to kiss you, don't you?"

"Uh-huh." She closed her eyes.

"Tell me I kiss you best."

"Best."

"Better than you've ever been kissed before."

Her eyes popped open. "That would be a lie."

"Huh?"

"I've never been kissed before."

Randolph blinked twice before her words registered. "No way."

She tried to look down, but he was holding her face in his hands so that all she could see was him. "Does that frighten you?"

"Me? No way," he replied nervously.

"It's okay, Randolph. It was just a kiss. I'm not holding you prisoner. You're free to go."

His eyes probed hers, looking for clues to the mystery he'd found. "I don't want to go anywhere."

Cynthia didn't believe him. He seemed too good to be true. It was more than his talent, his intelligence and his handsomeness. It was his spirit and energy she could feel surging through his body. Randolph impressed her as a man who wanted to make a mark on the world. He would want to take his bites of life in huge chunks. Nothing small or pedestrian would do for Randolph. He would want to see the world, taste it, chew it and spit it out. He was the kind of adventurous, passionate man that frightened most women.

But Cynthia had never thought of herself as one of the crowd. She liked being different, being blessed with brains and purpose. She didn't want to spend the rest of her life in Illinois working for the Pulaski Trucking Company. She still wanted to go to college. She still wanted to pursue graphic arts. But now she realized she wanted to know more about Randolph Miller.

"There's a Russian art exhibit opening next week. Why don't you take me there, Randolph?" she asked.

He chuckled deeply and threw his head back. Then he kissed her soundly on the forehead. "Sweetie—" he reached in his back pocket "—I've already bought the tickets."

Cynthia gaped at him, then shrugged her shoulders. Something told her her life was taking a major turn. She struggled with herself, not wanting to give in too soon. After all, she didn't know anything about such relationships. She'd never dated, hadn't even hung out with the guys at school to know how their minds worked. She'd only known what she'd observed from the way her father had treated her mother—and it was a bad example.

Cynthia had always felt abandoned by her father, and tried to make up for his absence by performing well in school or whatever task she took on.

For some reason fate had decided to throw her a curve. Randolph's exuberance for life intrigued her. She could become addicted to his fire, and as she looked into his eager eyes, she couldn't help wondering if that really was such a bad thing.

She took the tickets from him, acceptance glowing in her smile. "But of course you have."

Roya had been home for two hours pacing the living room, but still she hadn't heard from Addie.

She walked down the hall. "Lucy, please get off the phone! I'm expecting a very important call."

"This is important, too, Mom," Lucienne said, holding her hand over the mouthpiece.

Roya knocked on the door and opened it. She stuck her head inside the room. Her eyes were steely as she looked at her daughter. Roya didn't notice that Lucienne was equally as frazzled. "I mean it. I'm waiting for the police to call."

"God, Mom, why didn't you say so?"

"I'm saying it now."

"Two minutes." Lucienne held up two fingers.

Roya held up one finger.

Lucienne nodded and Roya closed the door.

"Brad, I have to go. My mom is freaking. No, not over that. I haven't told her about that hag and I'm not going to. She's got enough problems. Besides, the old bat hasn't come back and it's been over two weeks."

"I don't like you being at home alone with that crazy woman on the loose," Brad said. "I want you to come watch me practice in the afternoons. I can drive you home afterward. Or just stay in the library and do your homework. This kind of thing winds up on the six o'clock news."

"I can handle it," she said.

"Lucy, if you don't tell your mom soon, I'll tell her."

"You wouldn't!"

"Hell I wouldn't. I love you. I don't want anything to happen to my girl. Okay?"

"Okay," she said, smiling to herself. "I better go, Brad."

"Tell me you love me first."

"I love you, Brad. I'll see you tomorrow." She hung up and joined her mother and Cynthia in the kitchen.

Cynthia was taking prepared meals out of the microwave.

"Who's cooking tonight?" Lucienne asked brightly.

"Wolfgang Puck," Cynthia announced. "Yum. Sundried tomato lasagna. Better than yours, Mom."

Lucienne took the plastic dish and smelled the garlic. "Nobody beats Mom's cooking. When she cooks, that is."

The phone rang, startling Roya. She grabbed the receiver before Lucienne could get to it. "It's for me. Promise," she said, swallowing hard.

"Lieutenant?"

"No, Roya, it's Addie."

"You're home?"

"Yeah."

"I...I didn't think you'd call me," Roya admitted.

"I figured that out when Lieutenant Dutton told me you'd called four times. I asked him not to talk to you."

"Why not?"

"Because I know you'll insist upon hearing this. You won't rest until you do. That doggedness of yours can be a real pain in the ass sometimes, Roya."

"I already know I'm not going to like any of this, but before you tell me, I want you to know I'm glad it's you telling me."

"At least that counts for something." Adrienne steeled herself for what could possibly be the last time she ever spoke with her sister. "They called me in because they found out about my relationship with Bud."

Roya had prepared herself for a myriad of possible scenarios Adrienne could tell her. This had been the first one she had naively negated.

Not Addie. Never Addie.

But her heart had warned her. Addie was precisely Bud's type. Addie was elegant and classically beautiful. Her sexuality wafted around her like an invisible veil of expensive perfume. Addie was enticing where Roya was cool and reserved.

Roya knew Bud well. He wouldn't have been able to keep his hands off Adrienne.

Roya's mind was flooded with visions of Adrienne and Bud in bed together. The thoughts lanced her heart.

So immersed in her pain, Roya barely heard Adrienne's explanation. "I c-can't listen to any more of this." Her hand was shaking when she slammed down the receiver.

"Mom! God! What is it?" Cynthia asked, dropping her fork.

"Mom?" Lucienne looked from her mother's terrified face. "Is it that Cabrizzi woman? What's she done to Aunt Addie?"

"Cabrizzi?" Roya's eyes stung as she tried to focus on Lucienne, but all she saw was Addie and Bud.

Roya felt numb as she left the table. "I have to lie down."

"What can we do, Mom?" Cynthia asked.

"I'll be fine," she said, and closed the door to her bedroom.

Cynthia looked at Lucienne. "What's going on?"

"I'm clueless," Lucienne replied, dropping her eyes immediately. She speared the lasagna but didn't eat. She put the fork down.

"Why did you ask if it was Kitt? Nobody has spoken her name in months around here."

"Because…" Lucienne took a deep breath. "Kitt Cabrizzi was here."

"In this house?" Cynthia was stunned.

"She followed me home from school. She came to the door. I didn't check the peephole first. Dumb, I know. She's a crazy person, Cyn. She went left but quick. Half of what she said didn't make sense."

"What exactly did she say?"

"It was stuff about me and—" Lucienne quickly stopped herself. Until now she'd been careful never to have Brad call her when her mother or sister were home. She had effectively kept the knowledge of his existence to herself. His presence in her life had been her secret for almost a month. She had liked having him all to herself. Bringing him out into the open would bring an end to their idyll. Suddenly, their relationship would be public. And much, much more real.

"And who, Lucy?" Cynthia probed.

"Nothing. I mean, nobody." She lifted her shoulders in a cavalier fashion that told Cynthia she was lying but which Lucy thought hid the truth.

"Fine. Play it your way. I'll ask around. I'll find out."

"Brad. Brad Eastman," Lucienne replied with pride and an impassioned intensity in her eyes.

Cynthia sat back in her chair. "He's important."

"Yeah. He's got a full basketball scholarship to college.

Honor roll, too. He's not a jock. He's—" Lucy's voice held rapture.

"Important to you," Cynthia cut in.

Lucienne lowered her eyes. "Very."

"Does he love you?"

"He tells me so about fifty times a day."

Cynthia wiped her hand across her forehead. "Where have I been?"

"In your head. Working. Supporting Mom."

"Yeah, wrapped up in my own world. I'm sorry I didn't pay attention to you."

"There's nothing to be sorry about. I was keeping him a secret until…"

"Until what?" Cynthia asked, knowing she was guilty of the same sin. *Until I'm sure about Randolph.*

"I dunno," Lucienne said. "The secrecy kept it kinda special. Oh—" she sighed heavily "—it's hard to explain. Especially to you."

"You didn't think I would understand?"

"I suppose. Mom said you were a major part of the reason she got the Field's account. If you hadn't worked so hard, been so concentrated…"

"I've met someone, Lucy."

Lucienne's face was suffused with incredulity. "No way." She threw her hands over her mouth.

Cynthia winced.

"Cyn," she said, reaching for her sister's hand, "it's just such a shock. You were never interested in boys. I mean…"

Cynthia shook her head. "I'm still not interested in boys. Men, on the other hand…" She chuckled.

Lucy cocked her head, observing her sister. "That's it, isn't it? You were too brainy for the kids in school."

"I think so," Cynthia looked down at her hands. "He's an artist. Graduate artist."

"How old?"

"Twenty-two."

"What's his name?" Lucienne was nearly bouncing off her chair with questions.

"Randolph Miller. He painted the logos for Special Delivery."

"Oh, my God! And I thought I had a secret. Mom will bust!" She giggled.

Cynthia expelled a huge nervous breath and looked away. "I sure hope not. To use your words, I think he's important."

"But you're not sure?"

"We're just getting to know each other. I don't know what kind of person he is yet, really. Time will tell. And I intend to take my very sweet time. I don't want to rush into anything, like Mom did."

"You don't?" Lucienne chewed her bottom lip thoughtfully.

"I have my whole life to fall in love. I want to be prudent about this. I mean, I don't want to…to…"

"To what?"

"I don't ever want to lose someone I love."

"Me, neither," Lucienne replied, and touched Cynthia's shoulder. "Don't worry, Brad's not going to die on me. Or Randolph on you, like Daddy did."

Cynthia's head jerked back as if she'd been hit. "How did you know what I was thinking?"

"I didn't. It was what I was thinking."

Because Cynthia's only relationship with a man had been her father, her contact with the male species had been limited and wanting. Until Cynthia met Randolph, she'd never seen any purpose in seeking out a man. She knew too well her mother's disappointment, pain and humiliation these last months. Cynthia just wasn't sure what good a man could possibly serve in her life. Except for children. Cynthia did want children someday.

Everything about her relationship with Randolph frightened her. She was afraid when she didn't hear from him and even more so when he appeared. She seemed to lose her mind whenever he was around—which was incredibly unsettling.

Lucienne, she observed, didn't seem to have any of the same misgivings. She couldn't help wondering if her sister knew something about the mysteries of love that she didn't.

"What makes this guy so special?" Cynthia asked.

"He's very sweet to me. He gives me lots of attention. He *thinks* about me, about my feelings, and he's protective. He was majorly pissed when I told him about the hag showing up here and what she did."

"What did she do?"

"It was weird, Cyn. She told me I was like her when she was with Dad in high school. She said she was saving me from myself. And she acted like some crazed kind of preacher you'd see on television. She was creepy. Really."

Cynthia sensed there was more. "What exactly did she say that was so creepy?"

Lucienne didn't know why her face crumpled at that point, but it did. It was as if the truth, or the lie, that Kitt Cabrizzi had told her would haunt them all. Hurt them. "She said she'd had Daddy's baby."

"No way."

"Yeah. But she aborted it. She said it was a girl. And she wanted to know what I looked like up close in case I looked like her."

"How awful!" Cynthia reached for her sister's hand. "Know what, Lucy? You're right. You can't tell this to Mom. It would freak her out."

"Major."

"Yeah. We gotta protect her. I don't know what's going on between her and Aunt Addie, but it's not good."

"Cyn, we can't let that happen. With the hag out there lurking around, we don't need problems on the inside of our family. Maybe we can help Mom with Aunt Addie."

"Yeah," Cynthia agreed. "I guess the first thing to do is find out what the problem is."

"I'm not going to ask her!"

Cynthia straightened her shoulders. "That's okay. I'm the oldest. It's my responsibility to take care of things like this. I'll talk to Mom."

"Do you think she'll tell you?"

"Probably not at first. But if I bug her enough she will."

Lucienne glanced sadly down the hall. "I just want Mom to be happy. Like me."

"This guy actually makes you happy?"

"He's that special."

"I'm glad for you," Cynthia said. As she hugged her sister, Cynthia couldn't help saying a little prayer for Lucienne, hoping that Brad was all Lucienne wanted him to be.

32

Daria awoke choking on smoke.

It billowed above her head like a dark phantom, past the open door of her bedroom to the hall, down the narrow staircase to the small foyer and the living room. She stumbled, coughing, her eyes stinging with tears from the caustic fumes.

"Dad!"

Silence.

She'd feared his Alzheimer's for months as the slumbering monster it was. When she'd quit the business world and spent more time at home with Oscar, she'd discovered the truth.

Roya had hidden the severity of his disease from Bud and herself. Pride kept Daria from speaking to Roya about it. She told herself that Oscar was her responsibility, and anything that Roya had handled without complaint, so could she. Daria was out to prove to herself, if not the rest of the world, that she was as patient, kind and understanding as her sister-in-law.

By February Daria thought she'd go out of her mind listening to Oscar's inane ramblings, his horrendous gaps of memory and loss of time, his whining and his abject stubbornness that there was nothing wrong with him whatsoever.

By March, when the weather began to break somewhat, Oscar wandered out of the house. He didn't come back.

The police found him, and because Daria had had the

good sense to notify them first and the hospitals second, they brought him home unharmed.

By May, Oscar seldom lived in the present. He lived in a world she barely remembered and he ranted constantly about the inequities in his world. He wanted to know why Whitey Ford wasn't playing baseball anymore. Where was Jack Brickhouse, his favorite announcer? Why had Daria sold his Ford Fairlane? But most important, he waited for hours on end, sitting in his favorite chair by the picture window, for Bud to come home and tell him about the business.

No matter how much Daria explained, reasoned or ignored him, Oscar never understood and he was never happy with her.

For Daria, her life with her father was like being thrust back to her childhood. She was the daughter who screwed up everything. She was back in Bud's shadow.

Just when she'd come to realize she was living in hell and that things could not possibly be any worse, one serious mishap after another occurred.

Oscar fell down the stairs and broke his hip on the first of June. Daria didn't tell a soul that he was in the hospital. When Roya called, Daria checked the caller ID and let the machine pick up the message. Daria had not returned a single call since the day she'd walked out of her office. And she'd never told Oscar that Roya called.

The only thing that had registered in his feeble mind was the fact that his daughter-in-law didn't love him anymore. Finally, he stopped asking about Roya and his granddaughters.

Smoke curled around the walls like the insidious memory of Roya that Daria had sought to purge from her life. Her tactics had failed. Just that night Oscar and Daria had argued about Roya once again.

"She's not coming to see you, Dad. Not tonight. Not ever again. Now that Bud is dead, she has no ties to us."

Oscar banged his fist on the end table, making his pipe

jump in the ashtray. "Why do you insist upon lying to me? I spoke with Bud only an hour ago. He said he'd drop by to see me on his way home. Did you buy the beer like I asked you?"

"Dad," she groaned with exasperation, "Bud hasn't had a beer since he married Roya twenty years ago. Bud died at Christmastime. This is June. Look out the window. See? Leaves. It's hot!"

She had stormed from the room, cursing under her breath.

She needed a vacation. She needed to get away. Far, far away. She didn't know how much more she could take.

Daria stumbled down the hallway, tears from the smoke and regret filling her eyes. Her path was illuminated by what she thought was a living room lamp. By the time she reached the last step, she realized the horrifying truth.

Fire!

Flames leaped up the draperies and seared the ceiling. The walls were aflame, the wallpaper pockmarked by sparks. The arm of the overstuffed chair in which Oscar slept was on fire. She saw his pipe on the arm of the chair, a ring of burned fabric and kapok around the pipe bowl. The ashtray had fallen to the floor.

Oscar had slumped to the opposite side of the chair, overcome by smoke inhalation. Flames encircled his body like a halo.

"God almighty!" She raced toward her sleeping father.

She grabbed him by the lapels of his robe and ripped the burning fabric from his body. She dragged him out of the chair, his dead weight even too much for her to carry.

But she could pull him.

In the distance she heard sirens.

A neighbor must have called the fire department!

"Dad! Wake up!"

She kept pulling him toward the foyer. She saw burns on his forearms where the fire had devoured the sleeves of his robe. She could tell his face was unharmed, though his hair was singed nearly to the scalp.

The acrid smell of burning flesh and hair terrified her. If she didn't get them out the door, they would both die.

"Help me!" she screamed.

The dining room windows were open, as well as the east side living room windows. It was a balmy summer night; the breezes fanning the flames made the room feel like a tropical inferno. The fire seemed to prance ahead of her, impeding her escape. Then it bolted into the foyer. The draperies crashed to the floor.

Daria screamed again.

The falling drapes blanketed Oscar's chair in shooting fireworks. Had she been only a minute later, he would have burned to death.

"Dad! Wake up! Please."

Oscar did not flinch. He was beyond consciousness.

The heat in the house intensified as the flames swallowed the ceiling above. Paint sputtered, sending off a new array of sparks that dripped like long molten fingers down to the sofa across the room from Oscar's chair. Electrical sockets exploded like bombs.

Daria clasped her hands around her father's upper chest, forming a locking hold. Using all her strength, she managed to drag him through the small foyer to the front door. She started to reach for the door handle and abruptly stopped.

The handle was brass—metal—and would undoubtedly scald her.

She grabbed a sweater from the peg on the wall to protect her hand and opened the door.

From behind her she heard what she thought was a train coming down a tunnel. She pulled her father onto the front porch.

The sound of sirens blared through the summer trees. Smoke billowed from the open windows and flames peeked around the corners like mischievous children. They retracted, then burst outside with a vengeance.

Oscar moaned as Daria began descending the front steps.

From behind her she heard voices. A neighbor child was crying. Other familiar voices swooped across her lawn.

"Daria! God in heaven! How did this happen?" Willie Abrams asked, his strong hands moving over hers.

"Let me help," another neighbor, Chuck Piatroski, said. Oscar was lifted out of her hands.

A fire engine pulled to a halt at the curb. More neighbors gathered. Another truck came into view. Paramedics surrounded her. Two men wheeled a gurney toward Chuck and Willie.

They placed Oscar on the gurney as a paramedic strapped oxygen over Daria's nose and mouth.

"I'm okay," she protested, but the paramedic insisted. Daria couldn't take her eyes off her father. "Is he going to be all right?"

"We can't tell. His heart is very weak."

Daria blinked incredulously at the man.

There's nothing wrong with his heart. It's his mind that's weak.

Her eyes were filled with terror as they flew back to her father. These men were telling her that he could die. They were telling her that she might be all alone very soon. They were telling her that the only person left in this world who needed her was vanishing from her existence.

"Dad?" She fled toward the gurney. "Daddy...please. Hang in there. For me. Do it, Daddy. For me. I...I need you."

The paramedics wheeled Oscar toward the ambulance so quickly he looked like a rocket shooting across the lawn. In a blink he was inside the ambulance. They were taking him away.

Daria felt incredibly small and powerless.

Her life was being altered by a fate she hadn't asked for.

A paramedic prevailed upon her to lie down on a gurney.

"Please, Miss Pulaski. We have to check your vitals and tend to your burns."

"What burns?" She looked at him quizzically.

"The ones on your face and arms. Are you in pain?"

"Pain?"

Daria winced. The only pain she felt was in her heart. "Don't let my father die." She clasped the man's hand with a strength she didn't know she had.

"We'll do our best."

Daria demanded they be taken to Northwestern Hospital where their family physician, Paul Koslowski, was on staff.

Dr. Koslowski treated Daria's minor burns after Oscar was taken to the burn unit.

"How bad is it, Paul?" Daria asked.

"Several of his burns may need grafting. The pain will be intense, but I'll keep him medicated as much as possible. Fortunately, you got him out of there before anything worse happened. He's got second-degree burns on his arms and head. Only his hand is badly burned. It was a matter of seconds, Daria. How in God's name did you waken when you did?"

Daria had gone to parochial school with Paul. Their backgrounds were nearly identical. He was an older brother to his younger sister. Paul was the shining star in his family, just as Bud had been.

"I guess my guardian angel woke me up," she said flippantly.

Paul's face was serious. "I've had two similar situations myself," he said.

"I was kidding, Paul," she said.

He didn't blink an eye. "I wasn't."

Paul took off his plastic gloves. "I'd better see to your

father. You need to get some rest. You can stay here tonight, though you don't need monitoring."

"Thanks, but I despise hospitals."

"I remembered that about you," he said.

"How's that?"

"Your father told me that was why you never brought
him in for his checkups. Roya always came with him."

"Oh."

"Will you be staying with Roya, then?"

Suddenly, Daria realized she couldn't go home. She
hadn't the slightest idea how much of the house they'd
saved. Surely there was something left, though it would
be uninhabitable for some time to come. Her clothes, the
furniture, rugs—everything would be smoke-damaged
and unusable.

She couldn't go to Roya for charity. Not after she'd
treated her sister-in-law so icily. Pride had nothing to do
with the fact she hadn't called Roya to come get her. Daria
was ashamed.

She looked down at her hospital gown. "How can I
leave? I have nothing to wear. My nightshirt was ruined.
I was barefoot when I came here."

Paul laid his hand on her shoulder. "I thought of that.
My wife is on her way with some clothes for you. You're
about the same size."

"That's sweet of Anne. It reminds me of something
Roya would do."

"So would you, I'm sure," Paul said.

*You think too highly of me. Giving hasn't been my strong
suit. I've always been the one taking.*

Clarity struck Daria. All her life she'd complained
about being Bud's little sister. He always got the breaks.
He and Oscar had the power, called the shots and made
the decisions for her.

Yet for the life of her she couldn't remember ever reaching out to another human being with no thought of what
was in it for her.

She'd always thought her actions were calculated. Smart. Discerning. In actuality, she'd been a selfish bitch.

She'd stolen pleasure when and where she could get it. Which wasn't often. She'd hated Bud while he was alive and hated him now that he was dead. She'd accused Roya of murdering her brother when she knew deep down that Roya didn't have the heart to swat flies. She'd attacked Roya for doing the very thing she would have done had the tables been turned. Daria hadn't wanted to admit it, but she knew exactly what Roya was doing.

She was taking the blame for Bud's screwups.

If anyone was going to shoulder the cloak of bankruptcy it was going to be Roya.

For months, Daria hadn't wanted to admit it, but Roya was a better person than she.

"God bless you, Paul. Anne, too," Daria said.

"It's not a problem at all. Glad to do it," he said. "Do you want me to call Roya for you?"

"No! I'll get a room near here so I can see Dad in the morning. After all, Roya's got her hands full what with the girls and running the business now."

"Roya is what?" Paul's eyes were incredulous.

"She's a trouper, that one," Daria said. "It was time for me to take a break. Besides, Dad needed me."

"Good plan," he said. "Let me know if I can be of any more help."

It was an unfamiliar smile that filled Daria's face. She realized that gratitude sat more easily with her than she'd thought. "You've already done it. You saved my dad."

Paul's mouth crinkled. "He's a tough old goat. I've always liked your father."

"Yeah? Why?" Daria always found little to like in Oscar. She loved him because he was her father. She'd never actually thought of him as a person one would like or want to be around.

"He has an irascible sense of humor. At least, he used

to. Obviously, the Alzheimer's has progressed rapidly since I last saw him in November."

Daria looked at the floor. "Yes."

"What have you and Roya decided?"

"Decided? I don't follow you."

Paul took a deep breath. "For two years I've pressed Roya to talk to Bud and you about putting Oscar in a nursing home. She was adamant that you and Bud wouldn't agree to that. She told me that she didn't mind caring for him. With Bud gone, things have changed."

"A nursing home? She never said…" Daria stopped herself. Of course Roya never said anything about a nursing home. Roya always took double duty with Oscar. Roya always volunteered to take him to the grocery to buy his favorite foods, to the bank, to the barber, to the pipe shop, to the magazine stand. Roya checked on Oscar daily.

Now that she'd spent so much time with her father, Daria realized all that Roya had done for Oscar these past years. She'd cleaned up his messes, smoothed over his frustrations and fears. She'd talked to him when he made no sense, and made him feel important and vital in a way that Daria couldn't.

Daria knew all this because Oscar had told her. The neighbors had told her. The butcher at the grocery had told her how Roya often had to put back foods that Oscar had hidden in the grocery cart. The mailman told her that Roya had personally gone down the street redistributing mail that Oscar had taken from everyone's mailboxes. Roya had returned a mountain of newspapers the neighbors had never received that Oscar had gathered in the predawn hours.

The list of Oscar's escapades seemed endless.

Yet, Roya had never complained of the time or energy she'd spent giving Oscar back his dignity.

I, on the other hand, have bitched every chance I've gotten.

"Do you have a list of places you recommend?" Daria asked.

"Yes. Some excellent ones." He put his hand on her shoulder. "I'm glad you can see the time has come. This is a progressive disease and it will only worsen. The next time, Oscar might succeed in killing you both."

"I know," Daria said, and turned away.

Something had changed inside her. The world was suddenly different. She saw things differently.

Bud's death had completely altered her daily life, her work schedule. It had forced her to live every hour with her dying father. Never before had she faced mortality the way she had in the past six months. One minute Bud was her excuse for her failures and the next minute he vanished.

Her life with Oscar was tedious, frustrating and oddly poignant. He would sit for hours on the front porch in winter and spring and watch the birds searching the snow and slush for the birdseed he flung at them every morning and afternoon. She watched him wait for the children to come home on the school buses.

She'd thought it odd he would sit wrapped in coats and an old Hudson's Bay blanket and wave to the children. The younger ones waved back, the older ones ridiculed him and called him names. But Oscar didn't seem to mind.

His pastime drove Daria to distraction. She couldn't understand why he would subject himself and her to neighborhood gossip.

Oscar's eyes had been clear as glass, unfettered by his disease when he said, "I don't do this for them. I do it for me. Life goes on, Daria. Because of that fact, I tell myself there is a heaven."

Daria hadn't wanted to hear metaphysical drivel from a man who only possessed half a brain and little memory.

She hadn't wanted to face the fact that her own life was dwindling. She was past the halfway mark of her life.

She'd never live to be a hundred, which meant that when she turned fifty next month, she had fewer years to look forward to and more to look back on.

Daria's past seeped behind her—a lifetime of mistakes. Suddenly, she didn't like the person she'd become.

Daria had never been one to look at the bright side of things. She was no Pollyanna, like Roya. She was a realist. But for the first time she began to see a flip side to her tragedies.

Bud's death had forced her to take stock of her life. She'd made lists of her talents and accomplishments, and realized she was one hell of a bookkeeper and knew as much or more about accounting and corporate taxes than most accountants. She just didn't have the degree, was all.

She could go back and get her degree. Shoot for her CPA. Maybe start her own practice. She knew plenty of former trucking clients who would be interested. People she'd worked with in the past had admired her efficiency. Even Sol had said that about her work habits.

Sol. Yes. And there is Sol.

How odd it was for her to think about another person as part of or even sharing in her life. She'd been so self-absorbed for so long, she'd literally canceled out the possibility of a man in her life.

What would it be like to pursue something more than just a friendship with Sol?

He cared about her, but he'd never said anything about love. He'd never tried to kiss her. He complimented her, but she didn't know how he would feel about taking things a step further.

She wasn't one to want a man to come along and rescue her. She'd always cast herself in the role of the savior.

The fire tonight had purged her life of the remains of the past. Whatever memories haunted her childhood home had been choked out of existence by the smoke. She doubted even a bed linen or bath towel had survived.

Oscar was too ill to make decisions about rebuilding. It would all be left up to her, and rightfully so.

Daria would build a new house, one that reflected her altered psyche. This new house—this new life—would be far different from the one she'd built based on a loveless childhood.

This time around, she would love herself.

This time she would fill her house with light and love and laughter. Maybe there would even be a place for Sol.

Suddenly, she remembered Sol talking about his house, a brownstone he'd renovated to include a chef's kitchen. She'd never asked to see it before. She'd been too focused on herself.

She realized she didn't have to stay in the old neighborhood. She could move somewhere else. She could do anything she pleased. She could make anything she wanted out of the rest of her life.

For the first time, Daria realized the limitlessness of her future. It was awe-inspiring.

It was after midnight when Daria stood outside the coffee shop. The place was packed. She shoved her bandaged hands into the pockets of Anne Koslowski's jogging suit and walked inside.

Sol was behind the counter joking with customers. She sat on a bar stool at the green marble counter observing him.

He'd lost weight and the shirt he wore was new and more expensive than she was used to seeing him wear.

When he turned around, he stopped abruptly and smiled.

"I shoulda called," she joked. She felt light beaming in her own eyes. It felt good.

"Not necessary. You know that."

"Yeah." She glanced around. "Did you have another brainstorm? The place is jumping."

"Coconut mocha breeze. Best frappaccino around. That

and the simple fact it's summer in Chicago. The town never sleeps. But you know that." He wiped his hands on a towel.

In the past twenty years, I hadn't noticed.

"It's good to see you again, Sol."

"It's better seeing you," he said, standing close to the counter.

"I've been thinking about you," she said, discovering a lump in her throat. She'd never been one to participate in intimate conversations. It was more difficult than she'd thought to break old habits. But she was going to try. And try hard.

He reached for her hand. "God! What happened?"

"A fire. I burned myself pulling my father out of the house."

"Are you sure you're all right?" He inspected her bandages.

"I'll be fine. They don't hurt at all anymore," she said, looking down at the gentle manner in which he cradled her hands.

"And your father?"

"Not so good. His burns are much worse. They'll let me see him again in the morning."

Sol looked in her eyes. "You must have been terrified."

"The old Daria would have thought only of saving her own neck."

I grew up tonight, Sol. I had a mind-blowing experience that even LSD hallucinations couldn't envision. I saved myself, all right, but in a different way.

"And this is the new version I'm seeing?" he asked.

"New and vastly improved. I almost died tonight, Sol. I decided changes are called for. I want to be near my father while he's in the hospital, so I want to rent a place in the neighborhood."

"How close?" he asked, holding back his anticipation, his delight.

"Two blocks. I saw a sign in a window on my way over

here. I'll probably bug you to death coming in here." She chuckled nervously.

"You could never bug me."

"Maybe you'll change your mind."

Sol's voice was barely a whisper when he replied, "I'll never change my mind about you."

Daria felt the warm glow inside her spread. "I was hoping you'd say that, Sol. You see, tonight I realized that my father won't be around much longer, and when that happens, I have no family left. No one. Ever since my mother died, I've been afraid of being alone. I was so terrified of it that I made certain I never extended myself to anyone. I thought I'd be safe that way.

"I was jealous of Roya all these years because she seemed to do it so easily. To me she seemed so courageous in the way she gave of herself. She didn't seem to care if people shut her out...especially me. No matter how I treated her, she was always kind to me. I have to make it up to her some way."

Sol's voice was suffused with compassion. "I believe you'll know just how to do it. And when the time is right, you will."

She peered deeply into his eyes. "I hope you're right. I really do." She paused thoughtfully. "You know, I was sitting in that hospital and I realized there wasn't a single thing about my past worth taking into my future. Except you."

Sol's eyes teared slightly as he bent and kissed her cheek. "That's just about the sweetest thing I've ever heard." He untied his apron. "Missy," he said to the waitress, "take over for a while, will you?"

"Sure, Sol. What's up?" she asked.

He walked around the counter and put his arm around Daria's shoulder. "I'm going for a walk with this pretty lady."

Daria rose and smiled at him—her friend.

33

The sting of Adrienne's betrayal poisoned Roya's working hours and weekends. She repressed her anger and let it roil until it turned into depression. Then she pretended it didn't exist.

Not used to this dark behavior from her mother, Cynthia probed her endlessly. "What is going on with Aunt Addie? Grandma said the police were asking her questions, Mom. What kind of questions? They don't think she had anything to do with Daddy's death, do they? Why can't the police just drop it? He killed himself."

"I don't know any of these answers, Cyn," Roya answered sharply. "Why don't you ask your aunt Addie? Call Lieutenant Dutton for all I care."

"Mom, I was just asking."

Roya dropped her face to her hands. *And I don't want to think about this anymore. I just want it all to go away. Why can't it all just be over? Like Cynthia, I want a definitive answer. I don't even care if it's the truth anymore, just put closure to it.*

"I'm sorry, Cyn. I've been under a lot of pressure."

"You're stressed to the max, Mom. Everybody says so."

"Everybody?"

"Nick, then."

"Oh," Roya replied quietly. "I haven't been myself lately."

"No joke. I would have thought getting the Field's account would make you happy."

"To tell the truth, I never thought we'd really do it. I

thought we'd have more time to pull it all together. I wasn't prepared to have to move this fast. I hope we aren't making any mistakes in our rush."

Cynthia crossed her arms over her chest, her eyes scouring her mother's face. "The new account isn't what's got you down. You forget, I was a kid all those years when you had fifteen different charity meetings in a day. Even then I marveled at your stamina. I couldn't keep up with you if I tried. The only time I've ever seen that pinched look in your face is when you're mad at me or Lucy. Something's eating you, Mom."

"I don't want to discuss this anymore, Cynthia."

"Have it your way," she said, pushing herself off the doorjamb.

Roya rubbed her temples, searching her memory to place the timing of Bud's affair with Adrienne. She knew she was on the verge of obsession, but she couldn't help it. And she was damned if she would let her sister know she was bothered by any of it.

However, she came up with nothing. Even with Kitt Cabrizzi, Bud had never acted any differently. He never displayed the telltale signs of sex, affairs and illicit meetings like she'd seen in the soap operas or movies. There had never been the slightest clue.

Roya realized that, at this point, she didn't even care about Kitt Cabrizzi anymore. Or if Bud had had a hundred women.

What she cared about was that her sister had committed the most damning of all betrayals. Roya believed she would never, ever be strong enough, mature enough or loving enough to forgive Adrienne.

Roya knew she'd been distant with Nick ever since Adrienne's inquisition. He'd asked Roya to confide in him.

"I'm here for you, Roya," he'd said. "Anytime you want to talk, I'll listen."

"I'm fine. I'm dealing with it," Roya had said.

"I don't think so. You can't hide that pained look from me."

"Just leave me alone!"

Nick had persisted. "Now I really know you're in trouble. It must have been damned awful."

Tears had stung her eyes. "I'll be fine."

"Sure. No problem," he'd said, and left her alone.

Roya wished she could open up to Nick, but the truth was just too awful, too humiliating, to share with him. She didn't want him to think she was angry at Bud or his ghost.

Roya needed time alone.

Unfortunately, she was at her worst when she was alone. That was when bitterness festered inside her the most.

The days became weeks. June moved into July and still Roya had not returned Adrienne's phone calls. The one time she had decided to confront her sister, Marie had telephoned with her usual weekly banter and offhandedly informed Roya that Adrienne had gone to New York for a week on business.

Roya pretended to her mother that nothing was amiss between herself and Adrienne. The less said, the better.

Roya had been so immersed in her own emotions, she'd almost missed the changes taking place with her youngest daughter.

Lucienne bounced into the living room wearing white shorts, white Keds and a long tunic top. "Brad and I are going to the beach," she said, sticking a pair of white plastic sunglasses on her face.

Roya was poring over the last set of bank entries for the company. She couldn't believe it. The start-up costs for Special Delivery had added up to a third more than she'd forecasted. If she didn't get more revenues in this week, she wouldn't make payroll.

No matter what she did, it seemed she was perpetually short of working capital. The bankruptcy harpies fluttered around her. Depressed over the situation with Adrienne, her mood was spiraling down quickly.

She rubbed her forehead. "Cynthia is at Oak Brook with her friends?"

"Gayle and Trish, Mom. They all took Accounting 101 together last year."

"That's right. Gayle and Trish."

Lucienne shook her head. "I'll be home about ten. Okay?"

Roya looked up. "Why on earth would you stay at the beach that late?"

Lucienne sighed heavily, as all teenagers do when their parents are clueless. "During sunlight hours I'll be at the beach. Then we're going to a movie. Then supper."

"Right."

Lucienne kissed her mother's cheek. "If I'm a little late, don't worry. Brad is a good driver. Maybe I should get a pager."

"What for?" Roya asked, thinking of the cost.

"So you could page me when you get worried. You do that a lot lately. Worry." She snapped her fingers. "Better yet, a cellular phone."

"Don't even think about it!" Roya exclaimed. "Have you any idea how much they cost?"

"Yeah. Thirty bucks a month plus the minute charge. The phone is free if you sign up before September 1. I read an ad in the *Tribune*."

Suddenly, it didn't sound so expensive, but given her circumstances, even a dollar a month was too much. "I'll learn not to worry."

Just then a car pulled into the driveway.

Lucienne pulled the drapes apart. "Brad's here!"

Brad sprinted to the front steps, and before he could ring the bell, Lucienne opened the door.

"Hello, Mrs. Pulaski," he said politely. "How are you?"

"Fine, Brad. And you?"

He looked at Lucienne with youthful, sparkling eyes, eyes that hadn't seen life and knew only to expect fulfillment. "I'm great," he said.

Lucienne slipped her arm around Brad's back, returning his smile.

Was I ever that young? Was I ever that happy?

"You two have your suits?" Roya asked.

"Suits?" Brad asked.

Lucienne elbowed Brad. "Bathing suits."

"Yeah." He patted his jeans. "I'm wearing mine."

"Me, too." Lucienne quickly lifted her shirt, revealing a fire-engine red one-piece suit.

"Be careful, then," Roya said. "Don't swim out too far."

"Mom!" Lucienne laughed. "You said you were going to quit worrying."

"Sorry. Habit." She waved as they left.

Roya watched them get into Brad's car. She liked how he held the door for Lucienne. She didn't know boys did that kind of thing anymore. She certainly hadn't seen it for a long time.

Then she saw Brad get in the car, lean over and kiss Lucienne for an inordinately long time. There was nothing chaste about his kiss. She also noticed the way he held her daughter's face, the words they spoke afterward to each other. She didn't know what they were saying, but she realized that this was not a high school crush.

This was something more profound—this was her daughter's future unveiled.

Roya held her breath as Brad drove away.

Suddenly, she felt fiercely alone.

While Roya had chosen to mire herself in her dead husband's financial problems, her sister's betrayal and her own inability to address her feelings about Nick, Lucienne had grown up. She'd fallen in love and she'd done so without confiding in Roya.

Roya had missed it all.

Lucienne had gone to the spring formal, wearing Cynthia's old dress, the night Roya and Nick had worked late devising a new round of cold-call soliciting.

The day Lucienne had asked her mother to go with her to Brad's graduation party at his parents' house, Roya had been seeing a client.

The signs had been there all along, but Roya hadn't paid attention. She'd thought Lucienne was "dating" a "cute boy." She'd assumed he was part of a high school experience, a passing thing like braces and acne.

Roya rubbed her eyes and realized she was crying. She felt cold inside. She remembered feeling this same way when she'd put Lucienne on the bus for her first day of school.

This was a moment of passage as significant as that of birth, baptism, graduation, marriage or death.

Today was the day she realized her youngest daughter was going to leave her.

Roya hugged herself.

She'd told herself she was trying to rebuild the business for the girls. Their future had driven her.

But what if her daughters weren't there to motivate her?

"Then who am I doing this for?"

Life turns on a dime.

"Nick had said that," she remembered.

Nick.

Roya looked out the window, wondering when it had become summer.

Nick paced with a cup of cold coffee he should have tossed out hours ago. It was like that for him most Saturdays thinking about Roya.

He didn't need a barometer to know that Roya's mood had become inexplicably depressed over the past weeks.

To his thinking, she should have been soaring over the Field's account. Their challenge now was making Special

Delivery a reality. Then it was up to him to make it profitable.

Nick personally saw to the truck painting and the fine detailing. He ordered stationery printed with the logo and set up a separate phone line to handle orders. The only aspect that had bothered him was the cost. Though he'd given Roya actual cost figures when they'd originally presented their proposal, he hadn't figured on the closing of McKinley's retail chain of stereo and electronic equipment. The announcement was a stunning blow for Roya and Nick and a loss of seventy-five thousand dollars a year.

The loss of profit from McKinley's alone could cause Special Delivery to be stillborn.

Business aside, Nick knew that Roya was strong enough to handle the challenges. Whenever he asked her what was troubling her, she denied the problem. If it weren't for Cynthia telling him that Roya and Adrienne had had some sort of falling out, he would still be in the dark.

However, he couldn't let Roya know that he was privy to the truth. He had to play dumb. He had to wait until she came to him.

But she never did.

And it saddened him that she didn't trust him enough to confide in him.

Perhaps it was because Roya didn't think he could be of any help. He'd never had brothers or sisters, and therefore didn't know much about siblings, but he did know that if he'd had a severe break with his mother, he wouldn't be able to sleep at night. Nick believed Roya was of similar character.

He'd taken it upon himself to act as mediator and elicited a promise of a date with her for lunch.

Nick glanced anxiously at his watch. It was noon. "Finally!"

* * *

Nick arrived at Roya's house at one o'clock. "You're not dressed," he said when she answered the door in jeans and an old sweatshirt. She wore no makeup and her hair was pulled back in a ponytail. She didn't look a day over fifteen.

"Nick!" She checked her watch. "Oh, God, I'm so sorry! I was cleaning out the pantry." *I was trying to get my mind off Lucienne. Off Addie. Off bankruptcy.* "Please, come in."

He decided to keep his tone light to counterbalance the heaviness in her eyes that she struggled to hide. "Not that I don't like this look, because I do. I like it a lot," he said, stepping inside.

He closed the door and pulled her into his arms, kissing her passionately.

"Thank God," he said, holding her close. "I was afraid it was me."

"What was?" she replied, eyes closed, her hands around his neck.

"This change in you. Something has really gotten you down."

"It's really nothing to concern you." She avoided his eyes.

He lifted her chin with his forefinger. "Everything about you—the girls, the business, everything—is my business now. I want to be a part of your life, Roya. The good and the bad. I want that to be one of our rules. We'll talk about everything. All our feelings, problems, concerns and silly, stupid things that wouldn't matter to anyone else but us. How else are we going to be a team?"

A team.

Roya had never been on an equal footing with a man—not with her father and certainly not with Bud. She'd always been a child to both men. Nick was asking her to grow up.

Sharing emotions with another human being carried responsibility and risk. What if Nick chastised her? Ignored her? Thought less of her?

She realized these were thought patterns from the past, when she was Bud's wife. The old Roya used to think like this. She was perpetually fearful of not pleasing others— Bud, her parents, her sister.

Roya realized her depression carried regression. She didn't want to go back to that place where she'd spent far too many years. Living in the present was positive and good. She was happy here.

"It's Adrienne."

"What about her?" *Thank God she's finally confiding in me.*

"The police called her in for questioning the day I went over to tell her about the Field's account. Later, when I asked her why they would want to question her, she told me that they must have found out about her affair with Bud."

"Did they arrest her?"

"No."

"She didn't go to jail?"

"No."

"She didn't have to go back for more questioning?" he asked.

"Not that I know of."

"Then she's not in immediate danger?"

"No."

Suddenly, Roya saw his point. Nick thought she was worried about Adrienne's physical and mental well-being. That her concern was *for* her sister. Not *because of* her sister.

"Damn it, Nick, she had an affair with Bud!"

"I heard you the first time. And when did she have this affair?"

Roya blinked. "When?"

"Yeah. Last year? Five years ago? A decade ago? When?"

"I don't know," Roya replied suddenly, feeling more stupid than hurt. "Our conversation was short."

"Or was it that you assumed it was recent?"

"Recent?"

"Tell me if I'm wrong, but Bud died six months ago. This affair could have been a decade ago. Maybe two decades ago. My question is, why does this bother you now?" *Now that you know me. Now that I thought I was becoming part of your life.*

"She betrayed me!" Roya felt hot from the inside out.

"So, where do I fit in your emotions, Roya?"

"You?"

"Odd man out, if you ask me. You're so busy filling yourself up with negativity, you're not seeing what's going on around you. You're living in the past, Roya. Not here. Not with me. Not with your daughters. If you think about it, it's like you're the one who is dead."

"And I have no one to blame but myself," she said, glancing out the living room window where Lucienne and Brad had been only an hour ago. She looked back at him. "You're right, Nick. I have been doing it all wrong, haven't I?"

"Not all of it."

Out of the corner of her eye she caught a glimpse of the kitchen wall phone. "Addie called here this morning."

"Not to mention a dozen times at the office this past week alone. I saw the stack of pink slips on Marjorie's desk next to my phone messages. You must have quite a collection by now."

He lifted her face to his. "Let's give her a call. You and I."

Roya felt the first smile her lips had known for days. Hope was always a good feeling. "Okay."

Roya went to the kitchen while Nick routed around in the refrigerator for something to drink.

Roya waited while her sister's phone rang.

Nick opened a soda and walked into the living room to give Roya privacy. He wanted her to come to him on her own. He knew there was a chance he could be wrong, human nature being what it was. He didn't believe there was much in the world that could surprise him anymore, but that was before he'd met Roya. Before she'd changed his perspective on just about everything in his life. Especially his future.

Roya hung up the phone. "There's no answer."

"Does she have a machine?"

"Yes."

"Good, then call her back and tell her that we're coming into the city for a matinee. We can meet her at six for cocktails at the Drake. She can call us back on my cellular number."

Roya brightened and made the call.

When she walked back into the living room, she felt lighter.

Nick took her hand. "Tell you what. Why don't you go grab something to wear later to the Drake." He yanked playfully on her ponytail. "And whatever else you feel you need. It's a gorgeous summer day outside. Perfect for a drive down Lake Shore."

"I thought you wanted to go to a movie."

He moved closer, his eyes plunging into hers. "I changed my mind. I think I'd rather take you home to bed."

Her mouth formed a small O.

This time his kiss was a promise of seduction.

"I'll only be a minute," she said breathlessly.

"I'll time you," he teased.

The drive down Lake Shore was lovely. The trees had budded, forsythia, lilacs and fruit trees blossomed. Huge white clouds billowed across a crystal sky and the lake shimmered in the afternoon sun. It was the kind of day that all Chicagoans endured the blistery winter for.

It was heaven.

But Roya didn't relax until she got the call from Addie.

"I was so glad you called me, Roya. I've wanted so much to talk with you."

"Nick says I was silly not to return your calls."

"Thank God for Nick," Adrienne said. "Is it possible you could meet me now? I don't want to put this off another minute."

"We're not far from your place."

Nick stopped at the red light. "Tell her you'll be there in ten minutes," he said. "I'll get a cup of coffee while you go up."

Roya listened patiently while Adrienne explained.

"I can't believe how this has gotten so misconstrued. I mean, to have the police come to my house and take me with them like I was some criminal was bad enough. But seeing your face when they showed up was awful. I knew what you had to be thinking. I know I'd have thought the same thing if the roles were reversed."

"When was it, Addie?" Roya braced herself.

"Two years before you met Bud."

"Two years! He…he met you first?" Roya's eyes were saucers.

"It was at a charity gala on the lakefront. He had just started going to them at the time. My assignment was the invitations, printed materials and such. I was a novice in my job. A novice at life in general. He thought that by dating me he would get a foothold into society. Bud was big on that—even then. It was as if he thought he'd be a failure if he didn't get accepted by the 'in' crowd."

"I don't get it. Why didn't he marry you?"

"Actually, he asked me. I even accepted. He gave me a ring."

Roya's imagination had conjured several scenarios about her sister and Bud. This had not been one of them.

"Did you love him?"

"The person I was back then did. He was charming, as only Bud could be. Handsome. But when he met you, Bud flipped. You were his dream woman, he told me. And frankly, you had that sweetness that I've never had. At least not until I met Gavin. I guess I was always trying to attack the world rather than live in it. Gavin showed me that being alternately offensive and defensive was exhaustive and nonproductive.

"I challenged Bud too much. It made him nervous. Even if he hadn't met you, I'm convinced we never would have actually married."

"Yes, Bud was looking for someone he could manipulate. I certainly filled that bill."

"Don't be hard on yourself. You were only eighteen. Everyone is...untested, shall we say, at eighteen. Look at all the mistakes I made at eighteen. Twenty-three. And thirty-five. Thirty-nine!" She laughed at herself.

Roya couldn't help thinking how incredibly strange it was to be discussing her husband with her sister as a person they had both loved, slept with, been in love with.

It smacked of the profane. She felt as if she were committing a sin.

Adrienne reached for Roya's hand. "This is more difficult than I thought. Maybe we should leave the past alone."

"Yes. I think we should. You see, I thought..."

"You thought I was having an affair with Bud after you married him, right?"

"Yes," Roya admitted. "I did you a terrible injustice not trusting you." She wiped her face with her hands. "I feel like I'm walking upside down on the ceiling. Nothing I'd ever thought about my life is real. My husband was not who he purported to be. His business was not my security. My children have to rethink their futures. I'm working in a world I don't know anything about, and somehow, some way, my guardian angels keep giving me the right answers to parrot back to clients, attorneys and bankers. I don't know which end is up. And then, when the police were here..."

"You figured I had betrayed you, as well."

"I'm so sorry, Addie. What hurt most of all was that we had just found each other. As equals, I mean. I was just learning how to be a true friend to you. I didn't want to let that go."

"I think you've done pretty well, actually. The Roya I used to know would have crawled in her shell, blamed me, never confronted me to learn the truth, and would have pretended anything she needed to in order to keep her perfect little world perfect."

"I guess I haven't grown up that much, because it was Nick who pushed me to call you."

"But you made the call."

"Yeah."

Adrienne smiled warmly. "And you're here. That took guts, Roya. I don't know if I would have done it."

"Sure you would." Roya smiled.

34

Kitt Cabrizzi's plan to destroy Roya Pulaski reached the fail-safe point when she enlisted Charlie Ledner's help.

In the office of his gambling casino riverboat moored in Joliet, Illinois, Charlie cocked a bushy but discerning eyebrow at his thirty-something bodybuilder secretary. "Are you sure you got the name right? Cabrizzi?"

"That's what she said."

"Kitt Cabrizzi would never come here," Charlie said, slicking his hand over his dyed black hair. He adjusted his Versace tie and yanked slightly on his French-cuff shirt so that his eighteen-carat-gold monogrammed cuff links peeked out ever-so-discreetly from the sleeves of his slate gray summer wool suit.

"She didn't have an appointment. I told her you were booked all day, sir."

The corner of Charlie's mouth turned up. "She knows she never needs an appointment with me. Smart girl."

"Sir, may I remind you that the president of American Steel is expecting you for lunch? The helicopter is on standby."

Charlie stood, buttoning his jacket over his flat belly. At fifty-seven, Charles Anthony Ledner had the body of a thirty-year-old, thanks to massive workouts with a personal trainer and a fat-free diet he followed rigorously except on Saturday nights, when he indulged himself in a Texas Black Angus steak, salad with blue cheese dressing and a baked potato with all the trimmings. On his one night of indulgence he drank no less than two martinis and an entire bottle of red wine followed by a deep cognac. The only thing in the world that could make his Saturday nights any more hedonistic would be having sex with Kitt Cabrizzi.

"Cancel my lunch, but not the helicopter. Get me on the afternoon flight to Vegas. The three o'clock out of O'Hare is perfect."

The secretary scribbled on his pad. "And your return?"

Charlie grinned. "I'll let you know."

"Yes, sir."

"Show Miss Cabrizzi in," Charlie instructed.

Kitt Cabrizzi was nineteen the first time Charlie met her. She was wearing a white satin gown so tight he could make out her belly button. It was cheap fabric, and cut even cheaper, but the body inside the dress would have made a gunnysack look like haute couture. She'd been standing at the bar of the Chicago Yacht Club during a formal dance around the holidays.

He remembered it was freezing cold outside, but when he saw Kitt, his temperature soared.

"I'm with someone," she'd said.

"I should think you would be," he replied, realizing the cowl neck of her gown made her look covered only from a distance. Up close, he could see every inch of her voluptuous breasts.

When she smiled at him, he thought he'd been knocked over. "What's your name?" he asked.

"Kitt Cabrizzi. But I'm changing it to Pulaski. Mrs. Bud Pulaski," she said with such pride and triumph he was stunned a man could mean that much to a woman. "What's yours?"

"Charlie Ledner."

"Are you sure?"

"Yes." He nodded.

"You look like Peter Lawford. That's why I was staring. He's one of my favorite movie stars."

"Lucky for me," Charlie said.

The bartender handed her a pink drink with a paper umbrella. Charlie instantly snatched the drink from her.

"Hey! What gives?" She pouted.

Charlie wagged his finger seductively at her. "You're far too classy for that." He signaled the bartender. "Two martinis. Don't stir. Don't shake. Just pour. Onion only."

"You know a lot, huh?" she asked him.

He reached in his pocket. "I know enough to give a beautiful woman my card."

"Why would I need that?"

"In case Mr. Pulaski doesn't pull through. You call me, doll."

She laughed at him and tossed her dark waves over her shoulder. "That'll never happen. I'm Bud's girl."

"Take the card. You never can tell."

Kitt looked at his card. Then traced her finger over the expensive engraving. "What do you do, Charlie?"

"I'm the guy your mother told you to watch out for." He chuckled at his private joke. "I'm a bookie."

"You don't know my mother."

She laughed with him, not at him, and Charlie never forgot that about Kitt. She knew then she and Charlie had a connection, a link, a psychic bond.

And so did he.

Kitt walked into Charlie's office wearing the designer suit she'd worn to Bud's funeral. She'd left the hat at home.

"You look like a million bucks, Kitt," he said. "How long's it been?"

"Charlie, you told me you counted the days when we were apart."

"You caught me. It's been ten months, two weeks and four days."

"You're right. I looked it up in my date book. That's when Bud and I drove out here to see you."

"Bud lost a bundle that night." He motioned toward the leather sofa near the window.

"Yes, he did."

Charlie liked the sensual sound of leather against Kitt's stockinged legs as she crossed them. Flesh and leather— the sound of lovemaking.

Charlie felt the room grow warm, though he knew the thermostat was set on sixty-eight.

"His passing must have been hard on you, Kitt. I know how much you loved him."

She looked down. "I've had a lot to think about since the funeral, Charlie. It's been kinda depressing knowing that my whole life is a series of regrets."

"That is tough," he said, inhaling her perfume.

Kitt slowly uncrossed her legs again, then recrossed them.

Charlie bit his lower lip.

Kitt had always had power over Charlie, but she'd never exercised it before. She'd always had Bud.

She needed to know just how far she could push Charlie. How much she could manipulate him. One wrong word, one miscalculation, and she'd blow her gambit.

Charlie was her trump card.

"One of my regrets, Charlie, is you."

"Me." He said it flatly, not daring to let his imagination go where it wanted.

"That I didn't take you up on your offer."

"Offers, Kitt. It was more than once." He touched her knee, intending a patronizing pat, but instead his fingers clamped around her flesh. He squeezed it.

It held a promise of greater things.

He swallowed hard. "You're just lonely now that Bud is gone. Bored, maybe. That's why you came out here."

"That's true, Charlie."

His dark eyes probed her exotic face. Even when she was a hundred Charlie knew he would want Kitt Cabrizzi. Perhaps it would be best to screw her and be done with it. On the other hand, Charlie had held his fantasy for almost forty years. There was something sad and dangerous about profaning the divine.

Charlie had built a temple around this goddess in his mind. The reality could never measure up.

"Maybe it's best that you go, Kitt," he said.

She smiled indulgently, then rose. She went to the door, looked back at him over her shoulder. "I thought you'd say that. I figured you'd be scared to touch me."

She threw the bolt and locked the door. Then she faced him, unbuttoning the top button of her suit. "You think because I stayed true blue to Bud that I never thought about you, Charlie? Well, I did. Not very often. You had that right. But sometimes when I'd get really, really mad at Bud for not seeing me, or like those horrible months after he first married Roya and kicked me out, I used you to get even with Bud. Bet you didn't know that, did you, Charlie?"

"How'd you do that?" His eyes were glued to her hands as the last button was unfastened and she dropped her jacket on the floor.

She was wearing a black French lace teddy that looked to be two sizes too small. Her flesh spilled over the top, rising and falling as she breathed.

"Magnificent," he said, awe filling his voice.

"Thank you, Charlie. That's the most wonderful compliment a man could ever give a woman."

She unzipped her skirt and it fell to the floor. She stepped over it, wearing nothing but black garters and stockings.

She placed her hands on the sides of his face.

He was trembling.

"I got Bud back but good by using you, Charlie. It was your voice I heard inside my head when I made myself come, Charlie. Your face I saw. Not Bud's. I used to tell him that. It made him crazy."

She peeled the thin strap off her shoulder. The lace fell away from her breast. Her nipple was taut.

"Now open your mouth, Charlie."

She put her breast to his lips.

Charlie groaned.

"Put your hand right there. That's right." Kitt closed her eyes. "And if you're really good, Charlie, as good as Bud, I'll let you do this to me any time you want. Wherever you want. As often as you want."

She pressed her flesh into him. "That's right, Charlie."

Charlie slid down on the couch and pulled her on top of him. He unzipped his pants.

"Don't you want to take your clothes off, Charlie? This is an expensive suit."

"I'll buy a new one," he said, cupping his hands around her buttocks and guiding her onto him.

"God, Charlie, is that all you?"

He smiled. "You've made me very happy today, Kitt."

"And you'll make me very happy when you ask Roya Pulaski to pay back the ten thousand dollars she owes you."

Charlie should have been angry, but he wasn't. He should have stopped, but he didn't. Charlie considered himself a wise man.

Instead, he pressed himself farther into her.

She moaned loudly.

"I'll do it," he said. "And you'll keep your promise to me. Anytime. Anyplace. Anywhere."

"Yes, I will, Charlie. I keep my promises."

"Good," he said, placing his hand on her breast.

Charlie knew then that his fantasies hadn't come close to reality.

35

━━━━◄━━

"Marry me, Lucienne," Brad pleaded as they stood looking at an illuminated Buckingham Fountain.

A full moon hung over the lake, and in the distance Lucienne heard strains of Rachmaninoff being played by street musicians. If she'd been at the Trevi Fountain in Rome, Lucienne couldn't have been in a more romantic place.

Brad took her hand. "I don't have enough money for a ring right now, but I do have enough to get us to Kentucky."

"Kentucky?"

"There's no waiting period there. I found a guy who'll get us a fake birth certificate showing that you are eighteen. We'd both be of legal age. We can leave on Friday. Say yes."

Bewildered, Lucienne said, "You're moving a little too fast for me."

He pulled her close. "I love you, Lucienne. I can hardly get through the day at work without thinking about you. Please marry me."

"I love you as much or more, Brad," she said as a cool lake breeze fluttered her blond hair around her face. "Are you sure?" she asked.

"More than sure. I didn't know I could ever feel like this. I used to make fun of guys who acted like me."

"Brad, your father will kill you."

"That's why I want to go away. Then he won't know."

"All our parents will find out eventually, won't they?"

"Yeah, when we're not here anymore. We'll leave notes explaining that we're okay. We'll live someplace far enough away that we don't have to listen to them try to talk us out of it."

He kissed her.

As always, Brad's kiss was magic. He made her tingle, and at the same time, he made her very dreary world light up again. She'd felt displaced ever since her father had died. She'd hated their new house and she still didn't like the school.

She was glad summer had come. She was enjoying her job at the neighborhood bookstore and used the money she earned to buy pretty clothes to wear when Brad took her out.

It wasn't until Brad had showered her with affection and attention that she'd realized how empty her world had been all her life. Now her life was full.

"Mrs. Brad Eastman," he said, with a smile radiating love.

"Doesn't that scare you, Brad? Having a wife?"

"Not in the least. But it scares you, doesn't it?"

She was thoughtful for a moment. "Not as much as not having you in my life."

Gently, he pressed her head against his shoulder. He gazed up at the stars. "Everything has been so natural between us, Lucienne. We're meant to be together. I just know it."

"How do you know it?"

"Don't you feel it? Right here?" he asked, placing his hand on her solar plexus. "Close your eyes and concentrate on us. On our future. Does it feel heavy or light, right here, where I'm touching you?"

"Light. Very light and happy."

"That's how you know."

"Who taught you that, Brad?"

"My dad," he said proudly.

"If that's true, then he would know that our getting married is a good thing. He would feel it, too."

Brad frowned. "I don't know if I'd go that far. He's pretty set on my going to school."

Lucienne felt a tear in her eye. "And training camp starts next week."

"That's why I want to get married instead. Then he can't say anything."

"How will we live? How will we support ourselves?"

"It's a lot cheaper to live in Kentucky. I've been reading everything I could get my hands on. You could work in a bookstore just like you are now. Maybe just part-time so you could finish high school. I don't want to be the cause of you not finishing high school."

"I agree. It's important," she said, thinking of Cynthia and how much she dreamed of nothing but going back to her classes and her friends. Cynthia missed being in college as much as Lucienne missed being with Brad.

Brad continued. "I'll find a job. I know computers and could sure as heck get a data entry job. There's a million things I could do."

"And you won't miss basketball?"

"I'd miss you more," he said, kissing her deeply.

Lucienne folded into his arms. "I wish we were older so we wouldn't have to go through this. I can't possibly go a whole day without seeing you. If I knew you were going away for months on end, I don't know how I'd handle it."

"I know I can't," he said. "Tell me you'll marry me, Lucienne. Now."

"I'll marry you, Brad."

"Thank God," he said, closing his eyes and kissing her one last time before he took her home.

* * *

"How are you going to tell your mother, Cyn?" Gayle asked.

"I don't know," Cynthia said, dipping her plastic spoon into a mound of frozen yogurt.

"Well, you better think of something quick. Registration is this coming weekend." Trish sighed. "You've been planning this since June."

"I have been planning it ever since you two came up with the idea for me to ask your dad for a loan."

"I," Gayle said. "I came up with the idea."

Trish smiled. "Yeah, but my father was the easiest to persuade."

"That's because you're an only child, Trish," Gayle said.

"It's not," Trish pouted. "It's because he wouldn't be able to spend all his money in two lifetimes. Heck, I bet he doesn't even ask you to pay it back."

"Oh, no. I'll pay him back!" Cynthia replied. It was bad enough that her father had thrust them into near bankruptcy. If it was the last thing she did, Cynthia intended to make the name Pulaski honorable. "If I'm as good as I think I am, I'll be making plenty of money."

"Yeah, but as a graphic artist and not as a business major."

Cynthia shook her head, her eyes filled with wonder. "It's the darnedest thing, isn't it? I mean, I went into business because my father wanted me to. It was his dream for me. It was what he thought a firstborn should do, never mind that my talents definitely lie elsewhere. He didn't care about that. All he cared about was my accomplishing what he should have done with his life. He always talked about getting his master's, but he never did."

"From the looks of things, he could have used it,"

Gayle said. Then, looking sheepishly at Cynthia, she added, "I shouldn't have said that."

"It's the truth," Cynthia said. "I was so busy trying to get some kind of attention from him that I almost missed finding myself. So, he goes and kills himself, and because of all his screwups, I figure out what my future is really supposed to be."

"Weird," Trish agreed.

"Totally," Gayle chimed in.

Cynthia was thoughtful. "The bad part is, my Mom counts on me at work."

"She can hire somebody else," Trish said.

"You don't get it, do you? I'm a body. A free one. I don't get paid. The burden of an extra salary right now could spell disaster."

"Okay, so fine, Cyn. Turn my Dad's offer down. It won't come around again. You've already lost all last semester. If another goes by, then you're a year behind. Before you know it, we'll be graduating and you won't have started."

"That's why I *am* going to do this. I want to learn this stuff so bad, I lie awake at night. Even Lucienne says I act crazed sometimes, staying up all night working on the computer. I get so frustrated because I don't know enough. It's like being blind and the seeing eye dog is only a few steps away, but I can't see to get to him."

"God, Cyn," Gayle said, scooping out the last of her no-fat hot fudge sundae. "Even I don't have it that bad. I mean, I love medicine, but it's not keeping me awake nights."

Trish laughed. "You're going into obstetrics. Just wait. It will!"

They all laughed and kidded, but when they departed for the night they wished Cynthia luck.

"You'll need it," Gayle said.

"I know," Cynthia replied, and went into the house.

36

⟶ ⟵

Late Friday afternoon, Charlie Ledner was accompanied by two of his assistants as he walked unannounced into Pulaski Trucking Company. Though all three men were well dressed in conservative dark business suits, there was no mistaking their predatory command as they marched down the hall toward Marjorie's desk.

"I'll call you back, Ruth," Marjorie said, hanging up the phone. "May I help you?"

Charlie smiled winningly. "I'm here to see Mrs. Pulaski."

"She's in a meeting."

Undaunted, he replied, "Explain to Mrs. Pulaski that Charles Ledner of Joliet is here to see her. I regret I did not have an opportunity to make an appointment." He yanked on his French cuff for emphasis. "But then, I never make appointments."

Marjorie looked at the two young thugs behind this slick-looking man. Their eyes were vacant. "Of course. Would you like a seat?" She gestured to the Chippendale sofa and two wing chairs across the room from her desk.

"No, thanks. I won't be staying that long."

Marjorie instantly picked up the receiver and buzzed Roya's office. "I'm sorry to disturb you, Mrs. Pulaski, but there's a Mr. Charles Ledner from Joliet here to see you. He doesn't have an appointment, but he promises it won't take long. Um, I think you should see him now if possible."

Marjorie hung up. "She'll be right with you. Would you follow me, please?"

"Very good." Charlie smiled once again.

When the trio of men stood in the doorway to her office, Roya thought she'd never seen shoulders so wide.

"I'm pleased to meet you, Mr. Ledner."

Charlie shook hands with Roya. "Myself as well. These are my assistants, Mr. Dunn and Mr. White."

"Please, have a seat," she said.

"I'm not here to chitchat, Mrs. Pulaski."

Roya swallowed the lump that had suddenly formed in her throat. She didn't like this man whose crackling energy filled her with fear. He'd had a lot of practice wielding intimidation. She'd had little learning on how to defend herself, much less attack. All she could think to do was disarm him quickly and worry about fear and consequences later.

"You knew my husband."

"Yes. I guess you could say I was his banker."

"Joliet, Marjorie said. You're a bookie."

"Among other things," he said.

Roya felt her intestines freeze. If he'd been holding a gun to her head she couldn't have been more afraid.

Something snapped inside her brain. She distinctly heard a click. Instantly, her perspective changed. Her fear vanished.

There are just times when you have nothing to lose. You have to take a stand, Roya. It's now or never.

"Bud owed you money. How much?"

"Ten thousand. I don't take checks."

"Then it was a gross miscalculation on your part to even make this trip, Mr. Ledner," Roya said. "I haven't got that kind of money in cash around here. Hell, I don't even have that in my checking account. The fact is, I'm on the verge of bankruptcy. I seriously doubt there'll be that kind of cash flow around here for months. Not only have you wasted my time and yours, but I can tell you this, I'm not going to pay Bud's debt to you."

"Oh, we'll see about that," Charlie replied icily.

Roya shrugged her shoulders nonchalantly. "The fact is, I don't even have life insurance on myself. So, even if you shot me, you'd still have nothing."

Charlie clasped his hands complacently in front of him. "You're good, doll. Real good. But, correct me if I'm wrong here, you have two daughters, don't you?"

Roya went as white as a sheet, but she wouldn't back down. Her mind was racing. "Is that a threat?"

"No, it's a question."

"Don't ask questions I can relate to the police, Mr. Ledner. In case you don't know it, my husband's death has not been verified yet as suicide or a murder. Your two associates there might have the same shoe size as the imprint the police found in my backyard the night of the murder. Maybe I should tell Lieutenant Dutton of the Chicago Police Department that he needs to start looking in Joliet for his suspects."

"You're more than good," Charlie said with healthy respect in his voice.

Steeling him with a determined look, Roya said, "I think our meeting has concluded, Mr. Ledner. If you'll excuse me, I have business to conduct."

Charlie held her gaze for a long moment as he weighed his options. *No wonder Kitt is riled over this woman. She could walk through a snake pit and not get bit.*

Until now, Charlie had written off the ten grand as a bad debt when Bud died. He realized his dick had gotten him into a trap. If he didn't push Roya Pulaski for the money, he'd lose Kitt, and he wasn't finished with her by a long shot. However, if he did carry out his threats to Roya Pulaski, she'd call down the police on him, which in turn would start some serious heat he didn't really need.

Charlie needed time to think.

"Perhaps we could discuss a payment schedule. Something on a monthly basis. Something you could easily handle, until the debt was paid up."

Roya gritted her teeth. "I don't think you understand my position, Mr. Ledner."

"Please do explain."

"I'm angry as hell that my husband dumped a lifetime of bad decisions in my lap. He left me not only to clean up the mess of his suicide—"

Charlie cut in. "Oh, so it's suicide? I thought you said murder?"

"I think it was suicide. It was like Bud to be that selfish. The police, however, are convinced it was murder. Especially since there are witnesses who claim an unfamiliar Cadillac was parked outside the house that night, witnesses who place it at the same time the shot rang out."

"I see."

"I hope you do. Frankly, I'm sure my deceased husband's debt to you is genuine. I'm just fed up paying his bills. I've filed for reorganization, Mr. Ledner. That would include you. But if you continue to harass me on this, I'll go ahead and bankrupt the company and everything that's left of what Bud ever touched. I may decide it's not worth it."

"I understand."

"I hope so. Now, I do have to get back to work," she said dismissively.

Charlie had no alternative but to leave. Just as he got to the door, he turned back to Roya. "Mind me asking one last question?"

"No."

"You know, I've seen a lot of pissed-off dames in my life, but you're really hot. What did Bud do to make you so mad?"

Glaring at him, she replied, "He had a mistress."

Charlie lifted his chin, then lowered it solemnly. "Oh."

He left the office knowing just how he would proceed.

* * *

Charlie Ledner was driving away in a black Mercedes limousine as Roya trembled in Nick's arms.

"Why didn't you buzz me? I could have handled him," Nick said.

"Oh, I handled him," Roya said. "I just don't know how long we've got until he retaliates. When I looked at those two goons, I got the impression they were the ones who killed Bud."

"Bud killed himself," he reminded her.

"You should have seen their eyes. When I talked about my house, there was knowing in their eyes. They looked at me as if they knew every room as well as I did."

"Roya, don't let your fear color your perspective."

"I wasn't afraid of them. Not then, anyway."

Nick kissed her forehead. "I'll call Lieutenant Dutton."

"Do you think we should? Wouldn't they just make matters worse? This Charlie is not a person I'd want to see angry. In fact, I bet he never gets angry. He just kills, thinks nothing of it and moves on to the next victim."

"You think he's really a killer?"

"You should have seen his eyes. He takes. And takes. Forever."

"He's a bookie, Roya. That's his job."

"Are you on his side?" she gasped.

"No, just getting this into perspective," he said thoughtfully. "What I don't like is his unannounced arrival."

"Me, neither. He gave me the creeps." She shuddered.

Nick laughed. "Obviously, he didn't spook you too much. It sounds to me like you took care of him."

"I didn't know what else to do," she said.

Nick didn't want to delve any further into the situation. If Roya knew his true feelings, she was sure to be frightened. Nick knew some of Charlie Ledner's reputation from his first days with Bud when he'd done his preliminary investigations.

There was no question in Nick's mind that Charlie Ledner's henchmen had been putting a great deal of pressure on Bud that last day Nick had argued with Bud in the office.

Bud's face had been ashen. He was sweating profusely and it was twenty degrees outside. Bud had been rattled—terrified.

Nick had never said anything to Roya about his take on Bud's death. It was always best to bury the dead, he'd believed.

But Nick had to go along with the police. He believed Bud was murdered, too. And someone had definitely been outside on the patio that night. Someone had been following Bud for days.

Something major had set Bud off, and Nick believed that Charlie Ledner's appearance here today was confirmation.

However, Nick also believed that if Roya did go to the police, Charlie Ledner was just the kind of crazy bastard who would terrorize her. He might smash up the offices, hijack a truck or two, buy off some drivers and harass the others. Maybe even cause accidents that could be potentially deadly.

Nick didn't want to think they were being lined up in a murderer's sight, but…Bud was dead. Who was next?

All this over a measly ten grand?

No, they had too much to lose if Roya naively went to the police believing she was doing her civic duty. Nick had to think of a way to defuse her until he could formulate a plan of action.

"I want you to stay at my place tonight."

"What for?"

"Safety. Go home, get the girls. Bring them as well. I'll stay at my mother's if this offends your sense of propriety."

"I never said anything about that. I'd feel better if you were there, frankly," she said, her smile forced but sincere.

"I'll alert my mother just in case you change your mind. I don't want the girls thinking I'm trying to replace their father. I have enough problems trying to convince you that we should be together. Not just on the weekends," he said, kissing the tip of her nose fondly.

"You really feel strongly about this?"

He leaned over the desk and grabbed her purse. "So much so, I've changed my mind. I'll drive you. Leave your car in the lot. If they come back they'll think you're still here."

"I hate running away like this. I'd rather fight them."

"That macho crap works in the movies but not in real life. Better to be safe than sorry. Besides, I want to get to your house before…"

Roya's hand flew to her mouth. "Oh, God, Nick. I hadn't thought of that. They wouldn't dare."

"Dare?" he snorted. "These men don't dare. They act."

"Let's go," she said firmly.

They left.

37

Roya arrived home with Nick just as Cynthia pulled up in Trish's Mustang behind them.

"Mom, what are you doing home so early?" Cynthia asked, a deep blush coloring her cheeks while she stuffed her registration papers into her purse. "I didn't expect you till much later."

Roya was so focused on her problems she didn't pay any attention to Cynthia's flustered state.

But Nick did.

Trish leaned over to the passenger's window. "Hi, Mrs. Pulaski. How are you doing?"

"Fine, Trish. Fine."

"Great. Well, I gotta be going, Cyn. Call me later and let me know how it goes."

"Sure, Trish. Bye." Cynthia waved as her friend drove off.

"Long drive for your friend to get home," Nick said.

"Yeah, but Trish has stuck by me through all this. That's more than I can say for Mom's friends. Even for Lucy's. Guess I'm lucky."

"Yes, you are," Nick said. "You must have been a good friend to her, too."

They walked into the house.

"Yeah, her parents got divorced when we were in grade school. It was pretty tough. The kids made fun of her and…"

Roya stopped abruptly. "Tell her how what goes, Cynthia?"

Cynthia rolled her eyes. Then she looked at Nick as if he were an intruder. "I was meaning to tell you." She looked down at the floor.

Nick put his hand on her shoulder. "Do you want me to leave? I could go get some ice cream or something."

"Or something," Cynthia said. "And thanks, Nick."

He looked at Roya. "Just so you know, I'm going to that little place two blocks away. I'll stand outside the front door till you're finished, but I'm not leaving for any longer than that."

"I understand. We'll be fine."

He looked at Cynthia, wondering if her sense of bad timing was going to change as she matured.

When Nick left, Cynthia pulled her registration papers out of her purse. "Things have been moving so quickly this summer that all this got away from me before I realized what was happening. Then it was just here and there was nothing I could do. I had to move forward, Mom. I felt it was what you would have done in my shoes."

"What is this?" Roya looked at the papers. "The Art Institute?"

Cynthia still got chills every time she heard the name out loud. To think she'd been accepted at the famous Chicago Art Institute seemed like a dream come true. "I've enrolled for the fall semester, Mom."

"Oh, Cynthia." Roya felt like crying. "I know what education means to you, but I just can't afford…"

"I got a loan."

"What?" Roya eyes were as round as plates. "You have been busy. How?"

"It's pretty unconventional, actually."

Roya instantly thought of sleazy Charlie Ledner. Steel bands of fear clamped around her heart. She glanced out the window. No traffic. She breathed easier. "How unconventional?"

"Trish's father."

Roya opened her mouth to protest, then closed it. "That took courage to ask him."

"Trish and I did it together. She said he'd give her just about anything she wanted. He told her he was doing it because he wanted to show his trust in her judgment. And he said his money was better spent this way than on the trip to Hawaii Trish had asked for the month before."

"So, Trish gave up her trip for you?"

"Yes."

"My, she is a friend."

"So, you aren't mad?"

"How could I be?" Roya hugged her.

"But, Mom. Now you'll have to replace me at work and that will cost more money. I know how difficult it is to bring the bucks in." Cynthia didn't want to muddy the issue about her education by telling her mother about Randolph and his considerable influence on her decision. Her mother seemed to have enough to deal with as it was. Besides, Cynthia realized she would eventually have gone back to school and finished her education. It was just that Randolph had convinced her to move up her timetable by a few years.

"Don't you worry about it, we'll manage somehow. You've been able to put all this together on your own. Get accepted. God, honey. I'm so proud of you. It never occurred to me to go to the private sector for loans." Roya stopped. *The private sector. I wonder if...*

Just then, Nick returned with the ice cream. "I'll put this in the freezer while you two pack."

"Pack?" Cynthia asked. "Are we going somewhere?"

"Yes, to Nick's for a few days. Longer, if necessary."

"Why?"

"I'll explain on the way over," Roya said, taking her daughter's hand and going toward the bedrooms. "Where is your sister?"

"I don't know. I just got here myself."

"She's probably out with Brad," Roya said. She looked at her watch. "I'll try her pager," she replied, glad now that she'd allowed herself the monthly expense.

"Okay. I'll grab some things," Cynthia said, and went to her room.

As she passed by Lucienne's room, she glanced inside. Something was wrong. Half her posters had been taken down from the walls. Her pink bear was missing from the bed. Her closet door was open.

Taped smack in the middle of the mirror was an envelope addressed to Roya and Cynthia.

Cynthia froze as visions of the night they'd found her father dead in the kitchen filled her mind. "Mom." Cynthia's voice was high-pitched as it cracked.

Roya knew panic when she heard it. She raced to Lucienne's room, where Cynthia plucked the envelope off the mirror.

"My God." Roya took the envelope from Cynthia, who was looking at it as if it would explode.

Nick slowly approached Roya. He had the feeling she might keel over in a faint. He wanted to be ready.

"It's a note," Roya said to Nick, opening the envelope.

Dear Mom and Cyn,
By the time you read this, Brad and I will be in downstate Illinois, I would imagine. We're getting married tomorrow. I know if I were ten years older you'd be really happy for us, but I'm not. I know you're going to worry about us, but don't. We are both incredibly happy. I wish with all my heart you could be happy for us, too, but that's probably too much to ask for. I love him. He makes me happy. Please try to understand. I'll call you in a few days. Maybe you'll feel like talking to me then. I love you both.

Lucy

"Has she gone and lost her mind?" Cynthia railed. "I can't believe this! Of all the stupid, ridiculous moves she could make, this is it! Maybe we can force her to get it annulled. Mom! This is insanity!"

Roya looked from the note up to Nick. "She's safe."

"I was thinking the same thing."

Cynthia was incredulous. "How can you be so calm?" she demanded, flinging her arms in the air.

Roya's voice was calm when she spoke. "I didn't tell you not to go back to school, yet you did all that behind my back."

"That's different. I was thinking about my future! My decision is a positive one."

"And who is to say Lucienne's is not? I've met Brad. He seems very nice. Bright. He appears to love her. She definitely appears to love him. All I can do is pray they get there in one piece."

"Have I walked onto the set of 'Star Trek'? Did some alien being take over your body? Mom, you've done nothing but preach education, education to us since we were in diapers. You said that because you didn't get your degree, you'd learned a lesson. A degree would set us free, you said."

"Give you freedom is what I said. Freedom to make choices. I also know now that making the right choice in relationships is even more important. You chose correctly by putting energy into your friendship with Trish."

"That's different. She's just a girlfriend."

"But at this point in your life, she's all you've got."

"Mom! Lucy is getting married, for God's sake, and—" She stopped. "Why did you say 'she's safe.'"

Roya looked at Nick.

"We're wasting time," he said. "We need to get going."

Cynthia saw the guarded look they exchanged. Something was going on and it had more to do with her mother's strange reaction to Lucienne's elopement than she was saying. "Mom?"

"Pack your things. Enough for a week. And all the things you'll need for school. Nick will drive us."

"Where's our car?"

"Never mind, Cyn. I'll tell you on the way."

Nick went back to the living room window, drew the drapes and turned off the kitchen lights. He watched the street while Roya and Cynthia packed.

He'd never liked the way the hairs stood up on the back of his head when he was anxious. It reminded him of being afraid of thunderstorms when he was a kid.

On the drive to his apartment, Roya explained part of the situation with Charlie Ledner to Cynthia. She didn't go into all the details for there was no need to frighten her daughter. Cynthia had been through enough the night Bud died.

"Nick simply thought we should take precautionary measures where the three of us were concerned. At least until the police can get a handle on things."

"This Mr. Ledner, he just wanted the money, right?"

"Yes," Roya answered. "He made some vague veiled threats. They were probably nothing, but Nick and I thought, to be on the safe side, we'd stay with him for a few days."

"I understand. Besides, now that I'm starting at the Art Institute, Nick's place is much closer. I could even walk."

"That's right," Nick said. "You'll find living in the city quite convenient. I always have."

Cynthia shrugged her shoulders. "I never thought about it one way or the other."

"Now you will," he said as Roya reached over, squeezed his hand and mouthed the words "thank you" for keeping the subject light.

"Cool place, Nick," Cynthia said as she entered the apartment. "My God, look at that view! Okay, I've changed my mind. I never want to live in the 'burbs again. I like this. I like it a lot."

"Your life is changing, Cynthia," Nick said. "The Art Institute, new, though temporary, digs."

Nick winked at Roya.

"I saw that," Cynthia said, investigating the extra bedroom. "I like this. Is it mine?"

"Sure," he said.

"Are you bunking with me, Mom?"

"No," Nick said. "She's taking my room."

Cynthia's mouth gaped. She snapped it shut. "Sorry."

"Don't be," Nick replied. "I'm not staying here." He picked up the telephone, punched out a series of numbers and then replaced it.

"Roya, I've forwarded your phone here. Should Lucienne, your mother or anyone else call, it'll ring through. You answer all the calls. Take messages for me. Then tell your family you're at home, but that if they want to see you, you'll come to them. I'll drive you."

"I understand, Nick."

He went to his bedroom and packed a hanging bag with a clean suit, shoes, shirt, underwear, cologne and toiletries. "Where are you going, Nick?"

He closed the bag and carried it to the front door.

Roya followed him.

"To my mother's," he lied.

"Will you call me when you get there?"

"Sure. I'll have my cellular on if you need me."

He took her in his arms and kissed her tenderly. "I thought you were pretty terrific the way you handled Lucienne's elopement. I would have gone ballistic like Cynthia if it were my daughter."

"I learned a long time ago that if you do that, you alienate your child forever. She's my daughter. I want her to come back home. But for right now, I can't think of a better place for her than to be far, far away. It's Cynthia I worry about now."

"I can still call the cops. They could have her followed, just for protection."

"Fortunately, her enrollment is a secret. I'll keep her away from the plant, in case there's a leak there. No one will know where she is."

"Good point."

He kissed her again. Roya was certain it tasted bitter and sweet at the same time.

He opened the door. "I love you, Roya. Remind me to ask you to marry me when I get back."

Her eyes met his and held him. "You're not going to your mother's, are you?"

"Of course I am."

"You're going to meet Charlie Ledner."

He winked at her again. "I'll call you when I get to Mother's. You sleep well."

"I'd sleep better if you were here with me," she said.

"What about propriety? Cynthia seeing us and all that?"

"Seems petty when I realize you might not come back."

He kissed her forehead. "Better watch out. I may take you up on your offer."

She felt a pang in her heart. She realized she'd never loved anyone as much as she loved Nick. "You're doing it again, Nick."

"What's that?"

"Being my Sir Galahad."

"Shucks. With all this practice, I might get good at it."

"Please be careful, Nick. I love you. I don't want to lose you. Nothing is worth that."

"I love you more," he said, and was gone.

38

Lieutenant Dutton normally assigned stakeouts to his staff. After eighteen years with the force, such work was best delegated to underlings while he tended to important matters. However, as far as he was concerned, Kitt Cabrizzi was the key to the Pulaski case.

Although he'd uncovered Bud Pulaski's gambling and drug habits, he hadn't been able to nail down his supplier. He'd guessed that Kitt bought the drugs and made betting calls to a bookie, but he discovered she was smart when it came to covering her tracks.

Not once since the funeral had Kitt purchased any drugs that he'd known about. He'd used high-tech surveillance equipment to tap her phones, but he'd turned up nothing.

Because Kitt didn't hang out in the streets, Lieutenant Dutton's snitches didn't know a thing about her. As far as he could tell, for all intents and purposes, Kitt Cabrizzi was a recluse.

Until today.

Kitt was dressed to the nines when she'd raced out of her apartment. She was clearly going somewhere where the need to impress was critical.

Lieutenant Dutton couldn't help whistling to himself when he saw her get in her car and drive away.

"Patience is a virtue, my pappy always said," he mumbled to himself with a satisfied grin. "And he was always right as rain."

Lieutenant Dutton followed Kitt down the neighborhood streets, the farther onto I-94. She headed out on the Dan Ryan Expressway. When she took the turnoff for Joliet, they passed directly beneath a billboard for the *Indian Princess.*

He snapped his fingers. "Well, I'll be."

Knowing exactly where she was headed, he hung back a few car lengths so as not to alarm her. This was the first move his pigeon had made and he didn't want to blow it.

The ride seemed endless, and the wait outside Charlie Ledner's casino even longer. It didn't take a rocket scientist to figure out what was going on inside.

It was after midnight when Kitt finally surfaced. She was accompanied out the door by two of Charlie's henchmen. One of the men went to Kitt's car and drove off. The other waited with her while a black stretch limousine pulled up. He held the door for Kitt as she got in. The man scanned the area looking for police.

Lieutenant Dutton slid down in his seat.

The limousine drove off toward Chicago.

"Whoowee!" The lieutenant whistled to himself. "Whatever that woman's got, she not only knows how to use it, but she gets results."

He started his engine and pulled away from the jammed casino parking lot. He wouldn't be following Kitt into the city. He knew everything he needed to know.

Charlie Ledner was Kitt's connection for Bud Pulaski's gambling and no doubt the drugs. It was the lieutenant's bet that the two thugs he just saw had the same shoe size as the prints he'd found in the snow outside Bud Pulaski's house the night he died.

The last thing he would allow himself was overzealousness. He would get a search warrant and a subpoena for Charlie's records before he returned. If Charlie had ordered the hit on Bud Pulaski, Lieutenant Dutton wanted to see the man prosecuted. He didn't want any foul-ups due to legal technicalities.

Lieutenant Dutton smiled to himself.

* * *

It took less than twenty-four hours for Lieutenant Dutton to return to Joliet with two of his assistants carrying tote bags filled with forensic materials and all the properly filed legal work to make Charlie Ledner's life hell…if he was guilty.

He walked up to the tall henchman dressed in an expensive Italian suit. "Are you Alan Dunn or Bartholomew White?"

"Who wants to know?"

Lieutenant Dutton pulled out his badge. "Lieutenant Dutton. Homicide. I'm here to see Mr. Charles Ledner."

"He's not in," the man growled.

"I asked you politely. Are you Dunn or White?"

"Dunn," he replied with the expected sneer.

"Buzz your boss. Or I'll just help myself to the place," Lieutenant Dutton said, flashing the search warrant in the man's face.

"He's in a meeting. Can't be disturbed."

"I'm losing my patience, Mr. Dunn." Lieutenant Dutton lifted the phone receiver. His eyes held determination.

Alan Dunn yanked it out of the lieutenant's hand. "Okay," he said, and announced the trio of law enforcement men.

Charlie came to the door himself. "Please, Lieutenant, come in. I certainly don't know what all this is about, but I want to do everything I can to help."

"It's about Bud Pulaski and his mysterious demise."

"Ah, yes, Bud," Charlie said, gesturing for the men to be seated.

"Thanks, we'll stand. Now, about Bud."

"I really don't know much about him, except that he has excellent taste in women."

"That and the fact that he owed you ten thousand dollars when he died."

Charlie adjusted his French cuffs. "Have I got you right about this, Lieutenant? You came here with a search warrant and whatever else you have there because you think I snuffed Bud Pulaski over a measly ten thousand dollars?"

"It's a lot of dough."

"It's peanuts to a man like me." He rocked back on his heels. "Do you have any idea how much it takes to make this place run? How much I have to gross in a day just to break even? Half a million, Lieutenant. And I've never been in the hole."

"Proud of that, are you?" the lieutenant asked, baiting him.

"Pride is highly overrated these days, if you ask me."

"Really? Then it wouldn't hurt your sensibilities if we took shoe imprints of your two goons out there?"

Charlie swallowed hard. He turned away, pausing for effect. He lifted the lid of his burled wood humidor. "You'll need more than that to take me to court, Lieutenant. Your case is flimsy and you know it."

"I wonder what we'd find if we pulled your records? Enough to call in the IRS? Close you down for a few months? Say six or seven? You'd be in the hole then, wouldn't you?"

Charlie was losing patience. "What's your beef with me?"

"I don't like drug dealers and I don't like loan sharks who think they can rough people up. Or kill them. Did you kill Bud Pulaski, Charlie? Because if you did, I will nail you."

Charlie clipped the end of an illegal Havana cigar. "No, I did not murder Mr. Pulaski. I did not order a hit. My men didn't even have firearms with them that night."

"So they were there."

"Yes. They were. I won't lie to you. I have nothing to hide. They were supposed to meet with Pulaski to collect the ten thousand. I figured it was a nice Christmas bonus I hadn't planned on. I'd written Bud off over a year ago.

I'll admit I liked playing with him from time to time. Making him sweat. Watching how he drove Kitt crazy."

He blew out the smoke. "By the way, I don't peddle drugs, either."

"Like hell you don't."

"Prove it." Charlie leaned back confidently. "You can't because I don't. I don't want the heat. I'm getting on in years, and frankly, I make a good living doing what I do legitimately. Like they say, there's a sucker born every minute. I rake in over half a million a day from suckers. Why would I want to mess my hands with drugs? I'll leave that to the immigrant gangs."

"Let me get this straight. You didn't try to collect the money from Bud Pulaski?"

"Not really. I liked jackin' with him too much. Man, he squirmed like a scared rabbit every time I called. So, go ahead, waste your time poking around here. You won't find a thing. Give my associates lie detector tests. Pulaski was dead when they got there."

"That's what they told you?"

"Yeah. And I believe them. They have no reason to lie to me."

Lieutenant Dutton glared at Charlie. "You're wrong about one thing, Charlie. You may not have murdered Bud, or even ordered the hit, but you killed him all the same. Bud's mind snapped that night. He pulled the trigger and killed himself because he thought he had no way out. He thought your men were there to kill him."

"That's possible. But then, we'll never know." He blew out a mouthful of smoke. "Will we?"

Lieutenant Dutton didn't answer. He turned his back on Charlie. "C'mon guys. Let's get out of here before the air gets any more polluted."

They left without making their search because Lieutenant Dutton believed Charlie Ledner. Ten thousand might have been the moon to a man like Bud at the helm of a sinking ship, but Charlie was on top of the world. He didn't need money.

As far as Lieutenant Dutton could tell, the only motivation Charlie would have had to kill Bud Pulaski was to win Kitt Cabrizzi. However, had that been the case, Charlie would have made a move toward Kitt months ago—right after the funeral, for that matter.

It had been Kitt who had put the moves on Charlie.

It didn't make any sense.

There was something missing in the puzzle Lieutenant Dutton was putting together, and for the very life of him he didn't think he'd ever unearth it.

39

Nick made fast time to Joliet. The riverboat was still docked at the pier. Nick had never been to Joliet, but he'd seen the billboards around Chicago for the well-known *Empress* and for Charlie Ledner's *Indian Princess*.

Charlie's establishment was an authentic replica of a pre-Civil War Mississippi gambling boat. The lobby and all the staterooms were decorated with antique furniture and paintings, and the kitchens boasted a French chef. The "gaming room" boasted everything from blackjack to billiards. If a bet could be wagered, Charlie had the equipment installed. On the lower decks were bowling lanes, basketball alleys and batting cages. Bets were wagered electronically before play began.

Nick was amazed at the new computerized slot machines that banked the main room. In the middle were crap tables, blackjack tables and roulette wheels manned by French-speaking croupiers who, like the waitresses and other staff, were dressed in period costumes.

He inquired as to the whereabouts of Charlie's offices and was led to an elevator that took him to the second level. The elevator opened onto a blue-carpeted vestibule studded with French antiques.

An expensively dressed young man sat at a rococo desk. "May I help you?"

"Mr. Charles Ledner, please."

"Do you have an appointment?"

"No, but he is expecting me, I believe."

"Well, he's not here."

"When will he be back?" Nick looked at the man's nameplate on his desk, which read Mr. S. Ellsworth. "Steve?"

"It's Sam," he said. "There's no telling. Mr. Ledner flew back to Vegas an hour ago."

"Back? He lives there? I thought he lived here."

"He has homes in many cities. Vegas is just one," Sam said, going back to his paperwork.

Nick took out the check he'd written for ten thousand dollars. "I'd like a receipt for this."

"This?" Sam looked at it as if it were refuse.

"It's payment in full on the Pulaski account. I'd like a receipt."

"I can give you the receipt for the check, but I can't write that it is paid in full since I'm not privy to that information. There may be interest."

"Interest?"

"Of course," Sam said.

Nick leaned over the desk so that his face was squarely in Sam's. "You tell Mr. Ledner there better not be any interest or I will call the cops down on him, and he knows what I'm talking about. The owner of this debt is dead."

"That may not matter to Mr. Ledner."

Nick's eyes were steely. "You make damn sure it does."

"Are you threatening me or Mr. Ledner?" Sam shot to his feet, now keeping his face squarely in Nick's. Their eyes were unrelenting.

Nick was ready to go to the mat for Roya. He felt fearless, just as she had. It made him feel omnipotent.

Nick grabbed Sam by the collar. "I don't give a damn which one of you makes this happen. You tell Mr. Charlie Ledner that if he ever threatens Mrs. Pulaski again, he's got me to answer to."

Sam was not impressed. He wrapped his fingers around Nick's wrist like a vise.

Nick didn't flinch. He went for Sam's throat, his thumb on the man's jugular. "Like I said, I'll call the cops down on Charlie. For ten thousand bucks, it won't be worth it. Neither will the call I'll make to the IRS."

Sam relented.

Nick dropped his handhold.

Sam coughed and his face lost its azure hue. He rubbed his throat. "I'll give him your message."

"See that you do," Nick said. "I'll take that receipt now."

Sam scribbled his name across the bottom of the paper.

Nick took the receipt, leaned across the desk and hit the remote button he'd seen Sam operate when he came into the office.

The elevator door opened instantly.

He walked on, then smiled back at Sam and said, "Tell Mr. Ledner he's got a nice place here. I'll bring my mother some time."

The elevator door closed.

Charlie Ledner returned to the suite he'd had arranged gratis for himself and Kitt.

She was waiting for him dressed in a black silk-and-lace peignoir, lace bra, garter belt and silk hose. The seal on the bottle of Chivas had been cracked. From his calculations, she'd had two Scotchs, no more. She would be pliant but not drunk.

That was good—he wanted her to remember everything he said to her tonight.

"You're back," she said with anticipation in her eyes. She leaned back on the gold sofa, bending her knee just enough for the peignoir to fall away.

Charlie sucked in his breath. "Yes, just. Any calls for me?"

"Business at a time like this, Charlie?" she purred.

"You'll get used to it. Business is always number one with me."

She laughed heartily. "You are my business, Charlie."

"That I am," he replied, dialing Joliet. "Give me Sam."

"Mr. Ledner, did you have a nice flight?"

"All flights to Vegas are nice."

"Yes, sir. I have only one message for you. A Mr. Petros delivered a check to you for ten thousand dollars. I gave him a receipt but told him I wasn't sure about the interest charges."

"That was good thinking."

"Not when you consider his threat to call the cops down on our operations if we pursued that tack."

"That's fine. Any other calls?"

"None," Sam said. "Good night, Mr. Ledner. Enjoy your trip."

"I will, Sam, and a good evening to you."

Kitt inhaled the Cartier perfume Charlie had bought for her just prior to his trip back to Chicago. She'd been glad she'd persuaded him to leave. He was getting on her nerves, always wanting sex, demanding so much from her when he hadn't given her anything she'd wanted.

She'd never had a man spend so much money on her. She wasn't used to pampering, as Charlie called it. Even Bud at his zenith, before Roya came along, didn't spend money the way Charlie did. But it bothered her that Charlie got that sappy look on his face sometimes when they made love or had dinner in a romantic restaurant. She knew some women would kill for a man to treat her the way Charlie did.

But Kitt liked her sex more savage. And her life more dangerous. Bud had given her peril. Excitement. He'd given her life. Charlie was just too civilized.

"Did you get the money?" she asked, licking her lips voraciously.

"Yes."

Of all the things Kitt wanted to hear, a positive reply was not it. She wanted to know that Roya had sweated over the payment, that Charlie's demands had put her company in jeopardy. She wanted Roya to explode. She wanted to torture Roya. She wanted to hear anguish and pain. She did not want this whimpering ending.

She would have liked to jump on Charlie's case about his methods, but she knew better than to pry. Charlie was a private man. He wasn't flashy. He claimed he was a legitimate businessman. For all she knew, he was, but she doubted it. Charlie exuded too much power, and one did not come by that kind of power playing by the rules.

"Tell me everything," she said, moving her hips seductively.

"I told you, I did what you asked. I did you the favor, but it's the last one I'll do. You must learn, Kitt. I don't do favors for people. They do them for me."

Kitt barely heard his babble. "She gave you the money?"

Charlie shook his head. "Not her. One of her employees. Wrote a check. It's good."

"But that was too easy! It shouldn't have been that easy...just having some friend put up the money. She was supposed to have..."

"What difference does it make? I got the money," Charlie replied coolly. "Books are closed. It's in the past."

He unbuttoned his jacket and carefully placed it on the back of a French chair. He took off his tie and stepped out of his shoes. "I'd like a back rub."

"I'm not good at that sort of thing," she replied offhandedly.

"I think it best you learn. I'll have the masseur come from downstairs. He can teach you."

"Ha! I'm too old to learn that kind of thing, Charlie."

His eyes were cold when he looked at her. "It would

please me to have you give me a back rub from time to time, Kitt."

She didn't like the way he lowered his voice and chose his words deliberately, as if delivering a eulogy. "From time to time?"

"Yes."

"But Charlie, I thought we were having a fling. You know, like a week or so and then…"

"Why would you think that?"

"I…"

"You know I've always wanted you. There have been times I've wanted to take you away from Bud so badly, I would have killed for you."

"Killed?" She swallowed hard. Was he confessing? Or warning?

"Bud is dead now. I'll take good care of you. I guess you could say, in my own way, I love you."

"Charlie, I hadn't bargained for this."

"Then what exactly did you think you were doing? Playing me for a fool?"

"Oh, no, Charlie. Never that!" She realized she'd fallen into a trap. If she said the wrong thing, he would retaliate.

"Don't think you can go back to Bud. He's dead. And don't think I don't know you pretend it's him making love to you and not me. You slipped last night and whispered his name when you were coming. I know what's in your head. A woman like you doesn't give up easily on a man. On love. You're just an old-fashioned romantic. That's what I like about you."

He took off his shirt.

"Tell me what you like about me," he said seductively.

"You do have a magnificent body, Charlie," she said.

"You bet I do. If Bud were here, I could rip him apart and you know it."

He stood over her and unbuckled his alligator belt.

Kitt found what she was looking for as she probed his

dark eyes. Hidden in the darkest recesses of his soul, she found the recklessness she'd been searching for.

The glint in his eyes was ominous and threatening as he stripped off the remainder of his clothes. Placing his hand on the dainty black satin bow at the cleft between her breasts, he shredded the fabric from her body in one movement.

"Is this the last of it, Kitt?"

"Of what?"

"Of the clothes you wore for Bud? That Bud bought for you?"

Her laugh was taunting. "You'd have to burn everything I own to do that. Bud touched it all. Made love to me in it all."

"I've already taken care of that."

"You what?"

"My men took it all. I donated it to charity."

She wanted to cry, but shock froze her tears. "Everything?"

"Everything Bud ever touched. Including the furniture."

"How could you? I love those things."

"I won't live in another man's shrine," he said.

"Bastard!"

She struggled to rise, but Charlie held her down. His hands clamped around her wrists and he yanked them over her head. The more she wriggled away from him, the easier it was for him to pin her down with his body. In seconds he was inside her.

"Get off of me!"

"I don't think so, Kitt. From the day you walked in my office, you were mine. You didn't know that, but you sensed it. You like walking on the wild side, and baby, this is as wild as it gets. Bud wasn't half the man I am."

"You're insane."

"Hardly." He laughed. "I'm just taking what's mine.

You wanted a favor from me. I did it. Now you owe me. That's how it works, Kitt."

She stopped squirming and lay perfectly still. "Fine, take me. Get it over with. You won't like it."

Charlie's laugh this time was menacing. "I'm not a fool like Bud Pulaski. I don't want you part-time, Kitt. I want you all the time. Every day, every hour, every minute. I want to marry you."

"Marry?"

"Why do you think we're in Vegas? I've planned this since the day you walked into my office. You know me better than anyone. You've always known I'm not a man for half measures. I'm a plotter and a planner. Some say I'm a schemer. I'm just practical. And I always, always, get what I want." He peered deeply into her eyes. "What you need to finally admit to yourself is that I am what you want."

"But...I don't want to marry you."

"Of course you're going to marry me, darling." His eyes were granite. He placed his hand on her jaw and squeezed ever so slightly, warning her. Slowly, his strong fingers increased their pressure.

Kitt realized she was terrified for the first time in her life. "You're hurting me."

"But I thought you liked it like that. Rough. And just a bit perverse. That was the key to you and Bud. Perversity. Two peas in a pod."

Kitt held her breath. *How did Charlie know that Bud always said that? What else did he know?*

She was trapped.

Charlie's eyes were hard, but his voice was honey-smooth as he said, "I can adapt. After all, my job is to please you."

A tear fell from Kitt's eye.

"What's this? Emotion? From my goddess?"

"I'm not a goddess. All I wanted was for Roya to suffer.

I wanted you to shut her down. Scare the shit out of her. I wanted the books closed, but not this way."

He shook his head. "It's not good to store up so much bitterness, darling. It creates toxins in the body. I'll have my masseur explain that to you as well. Foot and hand reflexology would be beneficial, as well. I'll have Sam call the nutritionist in L.A. who has changed my life. Oh, you have so much to learn, darling. I want so much for you to be very, very healthy so I can do this to you every day. Several times a day."

Charlie's kiss tasted acrid. She despised the feel of him inside her. The thought of being with him more than just a day or two was more than she could stand. She would go insane if she were to be married to Charlie for the rest of her life.

She realized that all her life she'd had freedom. As much as she protested to the contrary, she'd never been tied down to a husband or children or a job. She slept when she wanted. She ate what and where she wanted. She read all night and went to the beach on Tuesdays. She'd never set a routine for herself, because she never knew when she was going to be with Bud.

She'd never had to cater to anyone else. She never thought of anyone else but herself. Charlie talked of her giving him back rubs and foot massages. He intended for her to be his beck-and-call girl.

Charlie had enough money to keep her under lock and key twenty-four hours a day. Even now, there were two bodyguards at the door. She would be a prisoner.

Charlie continued pumping himself into her. "Darling, you're wrong about your not being a goddess. To me you are."

She turned her face from his kiss.

Angered, Charlie yanked her head back so fast her neck snapped. Pain burned down her spine like a cauterizing iron.

Slamming his mouth down on hers, he kissed her in a long, suffocating manner, causing Kitt to beg for air.

When he finished she was gasping and looked at him with fear in her eyes.

"That's better," he said. "I can give you everything you want, Kitt. And even some things you never dreamed."

Kitt stared at him, believing she was looking into the face of death.

40

Lucienne didn't know what she'd expected for her wedding, but this wasn't it.

The justice of the peace's office was paneled in fake knotty pine. The carpet was so threadbare she could see the concrete floor beneath. The place smelled of dog urine from the two blind Prince Charles cocker spaniels that slept on dirty blankets in the corner of the room next to the box fan. Lucienne did not think the dogs had been bathed in a month. Her heart went out to them.

There were no flowers in the parlor and no music of any kind, just the sound of chicken frying in grease in the kitchen.

"You got the license, son?" the fat man asked, hauling his girth around the marred metal-and-Formica desk. He flopped into an office chair and the ball bearing feet groaned, then rolled on the clear plastic mat.

"Right here." Brad produced a handful of papers. "I have it all. Birth certificates, too."

"Just need the license, son."

"Yes, sir."

Lucienne heard the sound of a lawn mower cutting off outside. The back door opened, then a screen door slammed shut. She glanced through the gold-and-orange-decorated kitchen and saw a middle-aged woman dressed in shorts, a No Fear T-shirt and grass-covered Nikes walking toward them. "You need me, Hal? I saw the car parked out front. Illinois plates."

"Cheri, say hello to Mr. and Mrs. Brad Eastman. Or at least they will be when I get through with them." Hal laughed at his joke.

Cheri smiled warmly and her cheeks bloomed into crimson apples. Her blue eyes sparkled as she whisked back an errant clump of strawberry blond hair. "I look a sight for a wedding."

"So do I," Lucienne commiserated. Though her dress was new, it was nowhere near the wedding gown she'd envisioned years ago when she'd watched *Father of the Bride* three times in a row at the theater with her sister.

At the thought of Cynthia, Lucienne felt a burning sensation behind her eyelids. She remembered playing Barbie weddings with Cynthia when they were kids during the long winter weeks after Christmas. Lucienne had wanted to be a wife and mother, and work on charities like Roya. Even then Cynthia had wanted to go to college, study Renaissance architecture in Europe and haunt the Louvre every day. Cynthia had asked Santa Claus for paints, oils and canvases when she was eleven, but never got them. Lucienne had asked for Barbie's camping set and Baby Wet and Cry.

Cynthia had wanted to change her perspective of the world.

Lucienne had wanted to mold a child's life.

"Do I have time to clean up, Hal?"

Hal looked at Brad. Brad nodded.

"Yeah, but don't take forever, Cheri."

She disappeared down the hallway.

Lucienne glanced at Brad, who didn't seem at all nervous, but rather, eager and filled with excitement. When he looked at her he made her feel as if she'd hung the moon.

Brad loved her. That was a fact. He loved her more than she'd ever been loved in her life, and that had to count for something. Despite the fact that she was only sixteen, she'd never seen a man look at a woman the way he looked at her.

Man? Woman? I don't feel like a woman. I still feel like a girl. But my feelings for Brad feel old. Very, very old. Is that what makes a girl become a woman? Loving?

She loved Brad. She loved him so much it hurt. She'd never loved anyone as much as she loved him. She'd never thought much about love, actually. It always seemed as if it were the path to having the family she believed was her destiny, the children she would raise.

She'd never thought about relationships—the bonding, the melding of two individuals becoming husband and wife. As she looked at her life and the patterns her parents had cut out for her, Lucienne realized that they had never had a relationship. What she had experienced in the six months she'd been dating Brad was more closeness than she'd ever witnessed between her parents.

She realized her yardstick for becoming a wife didn't measure up. She could see pitfalls looming before her if she reacted like her mother did in situations.

Just like I'm doing now. Mother married at eighteen. She never got her degree, which she now regrets. She didn't know much about Daddy at all. She was only nineteen when she had Cyn.

In a few weeks Lucienne would be seventeen. In October, she would have been going to her homecoming dance. In her old school she would have been a queen candidate. She would have had a new dress and danced all night with her friends. But that was her old world.

"You okay, Lucienne?" Brad asked, taking her hand and kissing it.

She could tell his eyes had to ache from all the love they held. No one could bear that much caring, that much giving. But Brad did.

He amazed her.

From the gossip she'd heard around Our Lady of

Mount Carmel, Brad Eastman had been more than a super jock, he was a super jerk. They said he was vain and selfish. Egotistical. They also said he was the most talented ball player in Mount Carmel's history. He had everyone's respect—the teachers, the coaches, the kids. Everyone looked up to him like he was a god.

Everyone except Lucienne.

She'd done the one thing no one else had dared.

She'd looked at him as a man. She'd given him the one thing he was lacking—her heart.

"I love you, Brad. With all my heart. I will love you till the day you die. And beyond. Nothing you could ever do would make me stop loving you. If you ever hurt me, I'd cut you out of my life in a second. But I'd always love you, because I know this person deep inside here," she said, touching his heart.

He put his arms around her. "If you love me so much, then why do I have this sinking feeling in the pit of my stomach?"

She took a deep breath, steeling her courage. "Because I don't want to marry you today, Brad."

"Don't say that."

"Listen to me, Brad. I love you enough to trust both you and the future. I want us to go home. I want us to go back to school and at least try this semester seeing each other on weekends only."

His arms tightened, as if he were falling and she were his savior. "I've tried being without you, Lucy. It doesn't work, not for me. My game suffers. I suffer."

"I didn't say forever, Brad. Just one semester. Let's see how it goes." She touched his quivering lower lip. "Maybe we've been together so much that we haven't allowed ourselves enough time for ourselves. I mean, when I wake up in the morning, all I think about is you. Then just about the time I start thinking about schoolwork, intensely, I mean, it's time to get dressed to see you. So, I start thinking about you all over again."

"Oh, great, I'm just part of a vicious cycle."

She smiled. "I didn't say that. And I didn't say I wanted to break up, either. In fact, when we go back, I want you to buy me a real ring, Brad. I want us to spend time making plans."

She glanced at Hal and Cheri, who had resurfaced from the back of the house wearing a print dress. "I want my mother at my wedding, Brad. And my sister, too. I've realized it's more important to me than I thought."

"It's a girl thing, huh?"

"It's a family thing, Brad. Your family deserves all that, too. I want them to be happy for us, not angry at us for whatever reason."

Brad thought about his father finding the note he'd left, knowing there was no way to get in touch with his only son. He could hear his father's voice, raging with disappointment and pain.

Brad remembered times in the past when his father used to get angry at him for losing a game, missing a shot. He'd intimidated the hell out of Brad when he was younger. Brad had been frightened of his father for the longest time. Then he'd started winning. And he kept on winning. He would do anything to avoid hearing his father's anger, even if it meant becoming the best he could be.

Brad realized that though his father's tactics were ones he would never use with his own child, they were also the tools that had honed Brad into the player he was.

But it had been Lucienne who had shown him the side of himself that he'd never known existed.

It was ironic that her initial rejection of him had spurred his interest. She had always spoken her mind with him. She didn't revere him like the other girls, as if he were some god, nor did she see only the basketball star. Lucienne was the first person who'd demanded more of him. She pushed him. She challenged him.

Once again she was making sense.

"I love you too much to let you give up your future. I'll always be here for you, Brad. We can get married next year. Or even the year after that. If you really love me, then you'll see we're not taking a risk at all. I really love you. I don't think that, just because you go off to college, anything will change between us. Truth is, it should get better."

"It'll be lonely," he said.

"Yes. And it won't be easy. But maybe it will. Maybe we'll be so busy during the week that the time will go faster. I think we should at least try."

"You're something else, Lucy."

She smiled and kissed him tenderly.

Brad kept his arm around Lucienne's shoulder when he said to Hal, "I guess we won't be needing you after all."

"Appears that way," Hal replied, smiling. "Here," he said, handing the marriage license to Brad. "You keep this. Souvenir of the most important day of your life."

Cheri clasped Lucienne's hand. "You keep our address, honey. And when you send out those invitations, I'd sure like to be there."

"I'll do that," she said.

Brad and Lucienne left, their arms around each other, happier now than when they'd arrived.

Lucienne knew they'd made the right decision.

So did Brad.

Hal put his arm around his wife as the young couple drove away. "Kinda sad, isn't it, Cheri?"

"Sad?"

"Of all the folks I've married, I never give two bits that even a fourth of them will make it for long. But those two? Now, there's a couple that belongs together."

Cheri patted her husband's huge middle. "They're going to be just fine."

41

"I can't believe Roya expects to get all of us in that dinky little house of hers for Thanksgiving dinner. And just where does she think she's going to prepare that kind of a meal? She doesn't even have a microwave," Marie railed to her eldest daughter.

"Mother, Roya is never going to live in Schaumburg again. She lives in Oak Park now. She likes her dinky house. She's been cooking for two days and the girls are helping. Besides, I bought her a microwave."

"Adrienne, what on earth possessed you to do that?"

"She needs help, Mother. Not criticism. Now, if you'll let me get off the phone, Gavin and I will meet you there."

"Are you bringing the invitations so I can at least see them? I was hoping to help pick out the paper...."

"Mother, it's my wedding. Okay? You've had plenty of input on the other two weddings. This one is special. It's my last."

"Adrienne, I don't know why—"

Adrienne cut her off. "Mother, stop. It's not your wedding. If you want to pick stationery, have a renewal-of-vows ceremony and send your own. I'll see you in an hour at Roya's."

"Addie..."

"I'm hanging up now, Mother."

Adrienne shook her head as Gavin slipped his arms around her waist. "That woman makes me nuts!"

"She wants to be needed, Addie. That's all. You don't need her any longer and that makes *her* nuts."

"I hate a man who makes sense!" She laughed and kissed him.

Lucienne finished setting the table, then looked out the living room window. The trees had long since lost their leaves. She'd raked and bagged them on Saturday while Cynthia worked on homework at the computer and her mother and Nick had talked about business in the living room. She'd had fun making Halloween cookies and taffy apples for Brad at college and she'd sent him a mountain of funny cards to cheer him. They'd made a pact to see each other three weekends out of each month. Two weekends she would drive to Bloomington to see Brad and one he would come home to Chicago.

Brad didn't write, but he E-mailed her on Cynthia's computer. It wasn't much, but every night he'd either call her for a three-minute good-night or he'd send a simple E-mail that always read, "I love you."

The first two weeks had been more torturous than Lucienne had ever imagined. And the yearning she had in her heart to be with him never abated. It got worse. But she never told Brad.

She sensed it was the same for him.

But now it was Thanksgiving and they would have five full days together. He'd gotten home late last night and spent the evening with his parents and only telephoned her. However, his classes didn't start until Tuesday morning, and he'd promised to spend the rest of his vacation with her.

Her anticipation over seeing him, being with him, made her want to jump out of her skin.

He'd called twenty minutes ago and said he was on his way over. He wanted to watch the morning parades with her.

The wind was building as it whipped through the trees. A neighbor was outside putting up lights in an evergreen tree. Another neighbor hung a pinecone wreath on a door. Mrs. Jaworski across the street pulled her old station wagon into the drive, got out, looked up and saw Lucienne standing at the window. She waved.

Lucienne beamed and waved back as Mrs. Jaworski began unloading dozens of sacks.

Lucienne went to the coat closet. "Hey, Mom! It's starting to snow! I'm going to run across and help Mrs. Jaworski. I'll be right back."

"Okay." Roya came out of the kitchen, where she'd been making chocolate mousse, and looked out the window. "Snow! Now it really feels like the holidays."

Cynthia bounced happily out of her bedroom with a stack of holiday CDs, looked at her mother and started laughing. "Mom, you've been away from the kitchen waa-ay too long."

"What?"

Lucienne put her finger to her nose. "You have chocolate on your face."

Roya laughed with her daughters and cleaned her face with the towel.

Lucienne opened the door as a car drove up. She held her breath for a second. "Nick's here, Mom."

"Great! He can help me with this turkey. I swear it weighs a ton."

"No, just twenty-three pounds and twelve ounces," Cynthia replied, going to the stereo. She stopped, looked at her mother and said, "I don't remember Daddy ever helping with the turkey."

"That's because he never did."

Cynthia smiled as Nick walked in the door without knocking.

"Hey, group! I'm home," he said as Roya rushed to him and kissed him.

Cynthia slipped the Aaron Neville Christmas CD on the player. Strains of "Please Come Home for Christmas" filled the room. She was still smiling.

Nick's arms tightened around Roya. "Tell me you love me," he whispered.

"I love you, Nick," she said very loudly. "Cyn, tell Nick I love him."

"Mom loves you, Nick. I love you, too."

"I was just testing." He laughed.

Roya took his hand, pulling him toward the kitchen. "Then come help me test the turkey."

When the phone rang, Cynthia leaped for the receiver. "I'll get it!"

"If it's Randolph Miller, please ask him to join us for dinner, Cynthia," Roya said.

Cynthia stared incredulously at her mother. "How did you know?"

"Mothers know everything," Roya teased.

"No, really, who told?"

Roya rolled her eyes playfully. "Marjorie, James on the docks, Pete in Receiving…need I go on?"

Cynthia shook her head. "I get the picture." She spoke into the phone. "Happy Thanksgiving…" she said tentatively. "Randolph, I was hoping you'd call. Mom wants to know if you have plans for this afternoon. I mean, I do, too. Would you like to come over? You would! That's perfect. The best."

While Cynthia chatted with Randolph, Roya smiled to herself.

Life this autumn had settled into a comfortable pattern for them, Roya thought. At a time when they should have been feeling displaced, damaged and incomplete, they were whole.

When Lucienne had run away, Roya thought her heart would burst from the loneliness she felt creeping around her as her daughters were growing up without her. She knew in her soul that both girls would make the right decisions. She'd raised them to think for themselves, to make their own mistakes, but not to dwell on them.

When Lucienne and Brad had called from the road and found her at Nick's apartment, Roya's heart had flooded with relief and happiness.

She was happy Lucienne had come back, but she was even more thrilled that her daughter had found a loving man like Nick.

When Brad and Lucienne finally arrived at Nick's, Roya had held them both simultaneously. She found it amazing how she thought of them as a unit. Loving one meant loving the other. She supposed that was the way it should be with soul mates.

Roya had found her other half in Nick.

She knew firsthand what Lucienne was going through. Roya couldn't wait for the nights to end and the day to begin, just so she could be with Nick again.

Roya wasn't so sure she'd have the fortitude to endure a separation like Lucienne and Brad's. They were made of stronger stuff. She admired and loved them for it.

Brad's grades at midterm were straight A's. So were Lucienne's. His game had actually improved with the fantastic coaching he was getting at Indiana University. They talked about marrying in June, the day after Lucienne's graduation from high school. Brad would have the two most difficult years of college under his belt, and if things went well at Pulaski Trucking through the New Year, Roya had promised Lucienne she would pay for her college tuition while Brad finished up.

Cynthia had never been as happy as she was at the Art Institute. Roya was glad that her budding relationship with Randolph made her daughter happy. There were no guarantees in life, but so far, they appeared to be on the right course. Roya intended to thank Randolph for being instrumental in putting their Special Delivery project in the black so quickly. Each time they took an order, the client almost always mentioned their sensational billboard and advertising logo.

Cynthia's classes were progressing well and she was creating all manner of things on computers that Roya didn't understand, but the results were amazing. In only a few short months, Cynthia's skills had vastly improved.

Now that Nick had signed a three-year contract with the company and was an official employee, he and Cynthia had already begun devising next year's ad campaign. Through their mutual interests, Cynthia and Nick had bonded more closely than most fathers and daughters.

Nick had told Roya he'd never thought of himself as a father figure, but since knowing her, he'd come to know himself better.

"Whenever I want happiness, I never have to look farther than these walls," he'd said to her months ago.

They'd weathered the threat from Charlie Ledner and Kitt Cabrizzi seemed to have disappeared off the face of the earth, except for Bud's inheritance check that she cashed like clockwork on the first of every month. Though Lieutenant Dutton had not yet been able to close the case on Bud's death, Roya and her daughters had.

Bud was dead.

It didn't matter how. It didn't matter why. None of them wanted to know anymore. They chose to live.

"Grandma and Grandpa are here!" Cynthia announced. "Guess that means I have to turn the carols off, huh?"

"Just turn them down, darling," Roya said, glancing out the picture window. "And here's Gavin and Addie."

Roya went to the door, Nick following.

Marie held her black wool cashmere coat tightly around her middle, blocking the wind from her chest. Roya knew her mother loved the coat she'd bought her more than a decade ago. It was classic in style, tasteful and would last forever. "Quality endures," Marie had said at least once a day every day of her life.

Roya thought of those words as she watched her family's bright smiles as they came toward her.

No matter how much Marie tried to control her two daughters, Roya knew she meant well. She loved them— they were her children. Marie had secretly wished she could have taken away Addie's pain each time she divorced. During Bud's death and funeral, Marie had over-reacted because it had been the end of a dream for her. Of all the things Marie had prayed for in her life, the most important was for her daughters to have an easy life. A carefree life without struggle. Without pain.

Roya knew that feeling. It was her daily prayer.

"Mother, you look wonderful!" Roya said, putting her arms around Marie.

Marie smiled. "Do you like my new hat? Black mink. Your father gave it to me this morning. It was supposed to be my Christmas present."

"She needed it today." Etienne winked at Roya. "It's gotten so darned cold."

"Papa, that was very sweet of you."

Marie embraced Nick. "Tell me you helped with the turkey. I couldn't believe Roya was trying to lift that thing. When I called her at six this morning, she said she almost dropped it on the floor. *Mon Dieu!* What would we eat?"

"Mother, I'm not feeble," Roya said, greeting Addie with a hug.

Nick bit his tongue to keep from laughing. Roya was right, her mother had never heard of take-out. "Don't worry. I'm on the job."

"Roya, who's that?" Adrienne asked, pointing to the white Mercedes.

An elegant woman dressed completely in cream wool walked toward the house carrying a soufflé dish.

"Nick, your mother is here," Roya said.

Nick stepped through the doorway, greeted Adrienne and Gavin, and took the dish from his mother, kissing her cheek. "I can't wait for you to meet the family, Mother."

"If they are anything like Roya, I couldn't be more thrilled," Antigone replied as the brisk wind blew her auburn hair away from her face. "I have a small gift for your engagement announcement. It's in the trunk. I wrapped it myself."

"Shh, Mother. Roya hasn't told anyone yet."

"Not even the girls?"

"Like they haven't figured it out." He laughed. "So, what did you get us?"

"You have to ask?"

"Oil or acrylic? No! Watercolor."

"Nick, you're incorrigible." She laughed as she stepped to the door and embraced her future daughter-in-law.

Cynthia took coats, purses and hats while Adrienne and Gavin reorganized food in the small refrigerator.

"Maybe I should have brought my cooler," Gavin said. "What's all the champagne for?"

Adrienne laughed. "It's Thanksgiving. And if ever I knew a family who had a lot to be thankful for, it's this one."

"I understand, but she could launch a ship with all this."

"It's cold outside. Let's put it on the patio. Maybe stick it in a bowl with some ice."

"Good thinking," Gavin said.

Nick introduced his mother to Marie and Etienne while Roya opened the door for Daria, Oscar and Sol.

Oscar walked slowly, but only with a footed cane. Gone was the wheelchair he'd used at the funeral. Gone were the hideous burns from the harrowing night of the fire.

Sol walked between Daria and Oscar, lending his huge, strong arms as support and respect for both.

Roya could tell, even from a distance, that Oscar was lucid at this moment as he lifted his hand in the air to wave feebly at her.

"Hello, Roya!" Oscar said, joy bursting across his face.

She waved back. Tears filled her eyes. "Hello, Dad."

In all the years she'd known Oscar, he'd never looked at any woman with approval. It wasn't in his heritage.

But he did now as he glanced at his daughter, then looked up at her.

"Thank you, God, for letting him live to give me this day," she said to herself.

Daria was beaming in a way Roya had never seen her smile before. When Roya had telephoned to invite Daria and Oscar for dinner, Daria had chosen the opportunity to apologize to Roya for past indiscretions that Roya hardly remembered. Then Daria had told her about Sol and their new relationship. Roya couldn't have been more pleased for her sister-in-law and immediately suggested Daria bring him Thanksgiving Day. Since then, Daria had made a practice of phoning Roya several times a week, keeping the lines of communication open.

Roya had asked Daria to come back to the trucking company, but Daria explained she was ready to begin a new life for herself.

Roya had begun her new life. Now it was time for Daria to begin hers.

"Roya, I'd like to introduce you to my dear friend, Sol. Sol, this is Roya, my sister-in-law."

Sol's face was warm and inviting. Roya liked him instantly. "I'm pleased to meet you, Sol. Daria has told me so much about you. Welcome to my home and our family."

"Thank you for inviting me. Daria talked me into taking the day off. This is the first Thanksgiving I've closed the coffee shop since 1979."

Daria laughed. "I told him he needed a change as much as I did."

"More," Sol chuckled.

"I'm so sorry I didn't bring any food, Roya. I'm not that good a cook, you know."

"Daria, we have enough to feed us clear through till Christmas. I'm just so happy you're here."

Oscar kissed Roya's cheek. "I've missed you," he said, emotion cracking his voice.

"What are you saying? I came to visit only two days ago."

"Oh, really? I don't remember."

"That's all right, Dad. We understand, don't we, Roya?" Daria said sweetly.

"We most certainly do," Roya replied.

She hugged Daria longer than she ever had. Daria needed it, but Roya needed it more. "It's you I've missed. Thank you for coming."

Daria had tears in her eyes. "Nobody said Pulaskis aren't fools. Guess I was the most foolish. Thanks for inviting us."

Roya sniffed back her joy. "Please, come in out of the cold. Cynthia will help you with your coat, Dad. And I've kept your favorite chair, just for you."

Daria looked into the small living room crowded with more people than things. "My God, you did!" Daria helped her father to the overstuffed chair.

Sol leaned over to Oscar. "I'll get you something to drink, Oscar."

"Okay," he said, twirling his wool scarf away from his neck. "Just make damn sure it's got alcohol in it."

Roya looked across the lawn to Mrs. Jaworski's house. She stepped outside, wrapping her arms around herself to ward off the cold. "Lucy! Everyone is here!"

"Just one more bag, Mom. She must have bought out the store!"

"Okay, but hurry."

Lucienne took the last sack of groceries into Mrs. Jaworski's kitchen. "You start cooking late, huh, Mrs. Jaworski?"

"My family will be here in thirty minutes. It's tradition. We do all the cooking together, then eat later at night when it's dark outside. My sons put the lights on the trees outside for me and my daughters help me put up the artificial tree."

"Tradition is pretty cool, isn't it?"

"Yes, dear. Sometimes, when life gets almost too tough to take, it's tradition that gets us through. I've never understood people who think holidays are depressing. Once you get into the ritual, you can handle anything. Even death."

"Yeah, I know. My dad died at Christmas last year."

"Oh, my God. You dear child. I had no idea. I'm so sorry."

"Don't be." Lucienne smiled at her. "We stuck together. And this year is the best year of our lives. Best year of mine, anyway." Lucienne glanced out the window at her mother's house.

She'd hated this house when they first came to live here. Now she felt as if it were the first home she'd ever had. This was the house that love had built.

"I'd better go, Mrs. Jaworski. My mom needs me."

"Thank you, dear."

Lucienne started for the door. "Could I ask a favor, Mrs. Jaworski?"

"Sure."

"Could I bring my fiancé over to meet you and your kids later tonight? After you have your supper, I mean."

"I would love to meet this boy you're so proud of."

"Thanks."

Just as Lucienne started across her neighbor's lawn she saw Brad's car pulling up.

"Brad!" She screamed his name. "Brad!"

"Lucy!" Brad almost jumped out of the car before he was fully parked. He raced toward her, lifted her off the ground and swung her around three times.

"You're making me dizzy!" she squealed.

"Not yet I haven't," he said, and kissed her while she was still airborne.

She slid downward into his arms. She kissed his eyes, his cheeks, his cold nose and his warm lips. "I've missed you so much," she said.

"Not as much as I've missed you."

He kissed her again, and kissed her as they crossed the street toward her lawn.

When they looked up, the entire family was waving from the picture window. They were all laughing.

Brad and Lucienne burst into laughter and then broke into a run as they rushed into the house to receive hugs and kisses from their family.

Right behind them, Randolph Miller pulled up to the house carrying three bronze chrysanthemums for his hostesses.

Cynthia was beaming.

"I've said it before, Roya, you have no room for us!" Marie said, putting the mashed potatoes on the table.

"Sure we do, Grandma," Lucienne said. "It's the food that's gotta go."

"Oh, Lucy!" Etienne laughed.

Nick carried the golden brown turkey to the table, pretending it was a strain for him. "The groaning sound you are about to hear will not come from me, but from the table."

Lucienne took Brad's hand. "Come sit with me here by the window so we can watch the snow...." Lucienne glanced out the window and stopped abruptly.

Her face went white. Her hand turned to ice.

"What is it?" Roya asked, placing Antigone's spinach soufflé on a trivet.

"A black Cadillac," Lucienne breathed ominously.

"What?" Adrienne watched Roya's face blanch.

Nick put the turkey down. "What's she doing here?"

"I don't know."

Kitt Cabrizzi stood for a moment after getting out of the car. It was the first time in three months she'd escaped from Charlie. He'd had her watched like a hawk. She'd had to play according to his rules twenty-four hours a day, seven days a week since Vegas. It was Thanksgiving and she'd told him she always went to mass at Our Lady of Mount Carmel.

He'd believed her.

It wasn't enough that she was a married woman now. She'd gotten what she'd prayed for—legitimacy, a wedding ring on her finger. But Charlie wasn't Bud. Never would be. No one could ever be what Bud was to her.

This was her moment to balance the scales. This was Judgment Day.

If ever she was going to make her move, this was it.

The drapes were drawn back and she could see the house packed full of smiling faces.

Where had they all come from? Thanksgiving is for family. They can't all be family. Can they?

Kitt thought of her own life, her own Thanksgivings spent alone, the yawning future spent with Charlie.

She recognized the man who'd thrown her out of the church at Bud's funeral and who was now kissing Roya. Roya looked ten years younger, which was impossible given the fact that she had been forced to work for a living now.

She should have looked haggard. She should have been unhappy.

Then Kitt saw the youngest daughter with her boyfriend as they spoke to Bud's father, Oscar. The boy had his arm lovingly placed around the girl's shoulder. He seemed much older than when she'd followed them home from high school.

Her eyes flitted from one contented, happy face to the next.

Then she smiled inwardly.

What a wonderful feeling it would be to see each and every one of their faces change from bliss to horror. To revulsion.

Never in her life had Kitt felt so powerful.

She walked up the cracked concrete. "God, what a hovel. How can they live like this?"

Roya opened the door before Kitt had a chance to knock.

"You have no business here," Roya said firmly. "Please leave."

"I will, soon as I say what I came here to say. You can call the cops if you want. I don't give a damn. They'd like to hear this, believe me."

"I doubt that," Roya said.

Surprisingly, it was Marie who came to stand by Roya. Marie, who had shunned confrontation, run from tragedy and tried to escape unpleasantries at all costs, sensed impending danger like a lioness protecting her cubs. "Trash! You leave my family alone. All you're here for is trouble."

Nick watched Kitt's movements. He didn't like the vacant look in her eye. He watched how she fidgeted with her purse. He didn't trust her in the least.

Nick put his hands gently on Marie's shoulders. "Let Roya handle this, Marie. You come with me," he whispered in her ear.

"No!" Marie tried to shrug off his hold.

"Now," he whispered emphatically, and pulled her away from the door.

Marie stood next to Etienne.

"Say what you need to say, Kitt, and then leave my family alone," Roya said.

"I'm only here to give you the truth."

"I'm not afraid of the truth."

Kitt snarled. "You have no idea how the truth can blister. But I do." She paused. "Every one of you needs to hear this. You all want to know how Bud died. I can tell you how."

"Get on with it," Roya said.

"What's going on?" Randolph whispered to Cynthia. "Maybe I should help Nick."

"Mom can handle it. Trust me."

Roya's family and extended family moved closer to the doorway to hear.

"My story starts at the beginning. I was an orphan. Born into a Catholic orphanage. A family in Palatine adopted me. When I was a freshman in high school, the Cabrizzis moved not all that far from here, actually. I went to Our Lady of Mount Carmel and that's where I met Bud my junior year. I fell in love with him the first time I saw him. It was the same for him. Kismet. We always said fate had brought us together.

"We lived for the day when we could marry. Bud graduated. Then he got into building the business for his old man. He stalled me. He got me pregnant. I had an abortion. I wasn't going to do to my kid what my mother did to me. There's nothing worse on this planet than being an unwanted child. I know. Bud paid for the abortion. And the next one."

Roya gasped. *Two children. Were they boys or girls? What if I'd done that? Marriage or no marriage, I'd never have had my daughters. My life.*

Kitt continued. "I told Bud I never wanted brats. His or anybody else's. I had my tubes tied. Bud was okay with that. He just wanted the sex. And the money. Bud always liked making money. We had a blast building that house."

"I know this," Roya said. "Get on with it."

"You don't know the pain I went through the day he met you. He threw me out. No damn warning. No chance to think about shit. He didn't even know you! He'd only met you! An eighteen-year-old. He didn't love you. He wanted your looks. He wanted a classy blond wife who looked like she sailed in from Hyannis Port. He thought your aristocratic genes would wash away his heritage. Not the Polish part, though he despised that as well, but the stigma of having been an orphan. Of being unwanted.

"That was our bond, Roya. We were both unwanted. That's why he never let me go. You could never in a million years understand where he was coming from."

Kitt's emotions nearly strangled her.

"What's all that got to do with how he died?" Nick demanded.

"The year Bud married Roya, my foster parents died. In their safety deposit box, I found my adoption papers and the letters my foster mother had written to the administrator of the adoption agency. I discovered that I'd had a brother. He was two years older than me. But they'd never said a word. He'd been adopted by a family who lived on the West Side, just like me."

Roya held her breath.

Nick felt as if time stood still.

The entire family clutched one another's hands. Their faces turned ashen one by one.

"Their name was Pulaski."

"Bud...was your brother?"

"It was fate we be reunited. For twenty years I never told Bud the truth. I wanted to get him back for rejecting me. For choosing you."

"My God!" Roya's eyes held shock. "You finally told

him, didn't you. The night he killed himself. You'd told him."

"It was time. He still refused to leave you," Kitt said.

"That's more than disgusting. It's sick! You're sick!"

Kitt felt triumphant until she looked past Roya at the faces of the family behind her. She'd expected shock, derision, horror. She'd wanted them to hurt in the same way she'd hurt the day Bud had thrown her out.

Instead, she saw the one thing she could never, would never abide—pity.

Why wasn't Roya exploding at her? Why wasn't she ranting? Why wasn't she screaming with pain?

Why was she looking at her with real concern written all over her face?

Did this Goody Two-shoes have no brain?

Kitt reached in her purse and pulled out Charlie's gun. "You're all nuts, you know that? I should shoot every one of you for being so damn stupid. You're on Bud's side. That's it. Well, you're fools. So are those idiot cops. You've wasted a whole year trying to figure out what the hell happened that night.

"Bud killed himself, all right. He couldn't take the fact that he was going to have to leave you, Roya. Cuz I told him I'd come to you and show you the papers myself. I told him he either divorced you and married me or that was it. I was taking action.

"Bud always said we were two peas in a pod. Ha! That was the truth.

"That night, Charlie's men were following him. They were told to get the money Bud owed or rough him up. Not kill him, just put some pressure on him. They told Charlie they heard one shot, checked out the house, looked in the windows. They saw the body."

"He killed himself," Roya said flatly.

Lucienne slipped away from Brad with a warning look not to give away her intentions. She went quickly to the kitchen phone, dialed 911 and alerted the police. Whispering, she gave their address, then hung up and eased back next to Brad.

Nick watched as Kitt spoke so quickly, her words ran together and spittle flew from her mouth. She was losing it fast.

He had one chance. But he had to wait for the right moment....

Roya started moving toward Kitt. "Give me the gun, Kitt."

Nick couldn't help thinking Roya had read his mind.

"No way," Kitt growled.

"Kitt, you've loved the wrong man for so long, it's unbalanced you. It must have been wretched for you keeping your secret all those years. Even more horrible was knowing full well the cruel trick God had played on you. And that's exactly what happened, Kitt. I can understand you being angry with Bud, mad at me, but you must hate God with every ounce of your soul."

Kitt's voice was barely audible as she said, "I do."

"I don't blame you. You don't deserve any of this heartbreak. The only thing you're guilty of is loving. I've learned a lot in this past year, Kitt. I've learned that people aren't all good or all bad. They're both. Sort of like night and day blending into each other to make a date on the calendar."

"That was Bud and I. Parts of a whole."

"That's right. You didn't do anything wrong loving him. Even after I was married to him. Even after you knew he was your brother."

"I didn't."

"No. But this—" Roya pointed to the gun. "Murder is different. That's a sin against man. You can't get even with God by killing me. You'd get even with me, but that's not what you really, really want...."

Kitt blinked.

Nick took his cue. He stepped in front of Roya. If the gun went off, he'd take the bullet.

Kitt looked at the gun. Her eyes were dry, but she was crying inside. She loosened her hold only slightly, but it was enough for Nick to take the gun from her.

He handed the gun to Gavin, who shoved it in his pocket, far from Kitt's reach.

The sound of sirens filled the crisp air. Neighborhood front doors opened.

"You called the cops?" Kitt asked Roya.

"I've been here all the time, Kitt. Someone did. Maybe it's time you told your story to Lieutenant Dutton."

Nick put his arm firmly around Kitt's shoulders and walked her away from the house, away from his family.

Roya's daughters rushed to her. "Mom! Geez, are you all right?" Cynthia asked.

"I'm fine," she said, watching as the police took Kitt's wrists and put her in the squad car.

Nick spoke to the officer for a period of time. The officer made a call on a cellular phone. Then the officer got back in the car and drove away. Nick raced back into the house.

Taking Roya in his arms, he said, "Well, that's just about the bravest, most insane moment of my life." He chuckled.

"What did you tell the police?"

"That we'd file a report after our Thanksgiving meal."

"And he agreed?"

"He was ordered by Lieutenant Dutton."

Roya rested her head on Nick's shoulder. "Thank God it's over."

"Yes, it is, darling," he said.

Irascible as ever, still fighting for his moments of clarity, Oscar looked up from his chair. "I've been looking at that turkey for twenty minutes now. Is there a problem finding a carver around this place?"

Everyone burst into laughter.

"No, Dad," Daria said, patting his hand.

Nick looked at Gavin and Brad, and then at Randolph and Sol. "With a bird this big, I think it'll take all of us."

The family gathered around the table, held hands and bowed their heads as they said the blessing.

"Bless us O Lord and these thy gifts which we are about to receive from thy bounty, through Christ, our Lord, Amen."

Nick, sitting at the head of the table, raised his wine-glass. "A toast to Adrienne and Gavin and their New Year's Eve wedding. A toast to Lucienne and Brad, who decided to wait. A toast to Cynthia, Randolph, Daria, Sol, Oscar, Marie, Etienne and my mother, Antigone. I consider you all my family. God bless us everyone."

They drank.

"Hey!" Cynthia said. "You left out Mom."

Nick smiled. "On purpose." He raised his glass to Roya, who sat at the opposite end of the table. "A toast to my bride."

"Mom?" Lucienne exclaimed.

"Roya!" Adrienne grinned. "Am I going to beat you to the altar?"

"No," Roya shook her head. "We thought Christmas Eve."

"God, little sister, I couldn't be happier for you." She squeezed Roya's hand. "Truly."

"I know, Addie. I know."

"Roya!" Marie and Etienne said in unison.

"It's okay, Gran," Cynthia said. "We'll print the invitations on my computer!"

Everyone laughed.

Roya raised her glass.

She's radiant, Nick thought. *I want to remember this moment for the rest of my life.*

"To happiness," Roya said. "We all have all we'll ever need. We have one another."

"Hear! Hear!" the family replied in united chorus.

Roya couldn't help thinking their voices were more joyous than church bells on Christmas Eve. That's why she'd chosen the most miraculous night of the year to marry Nick.

She had always believed love was a miracle.

She had been right.

Turn the page for
an exciting preview of

THE LEGEND MAKERS

Catherine Lanigan's
newest blockbuster

available from MIRA Books
July 1999

M.J. was breathless and anxious as she raced up to the podium and checked in for her flight. That was why she hadn't noticed him watching her.

He wore a battered, sweat-stained white hat with a black hat band, jeans, hiking boots and a khaki safari shirt. His chest was broad and his shoulders even broader. The two-day-old stubble of blond beard told her he'd been flying through the night and into the day to make this flight with her. His blond hair was long in back, scraping his shirt collar. He smiled at her with a quirky, almost mischievous smile and shook his head when she dropped her tote and spilled brand-new tubes of lipsticks and mascaras on her way to the gangway.

Immediately, he bent to help her retrieve her possessions. "Did I hear right? You're M. J. Callahan?" He balanced a square gold-cased lipstick on his forefinger.

M.J. didn't like the smirk he gave her. Nor the flashing sexual broadcasts he was sending with his deep-set crystal blue eyes. But she smiled back anyway. She could feel herself being drawn into his gaze.

"I'm M.J.," she heard her own voice purr. The sun shimmered off the lipstick case. "Thanks, Mr. Hunter," she said, snatching it off his finger and shoving it into her tote.

"So, you know me?" he asked, his cocky smile brimming with a twinge of machismo charm.

"Of you. I know *of* you. Your reputation precedes you." He preened.

She smiled in spite of herself. She'd never flirted so outrageously in her life. She liked it.

"You can't be M.J."

"And why not?" she asked with justified impudence.

"Because he's supposed to be a guy. I mean, you're obviously not a guy."

"I know this," she replied with a hand on her hip. "Nobody said your company was gender biased."

"We aren't. Normally."

"And this isn't normal?" She started walking away from him.

"Damn straight it's not," he chuckled, handing his boarding pass to the attendant. "Travis Kincaid is going to go blind over this."

"What are you talking about?" she demanded as she held out her boarding pass.

He grabbed her hand, stopping her. "You can't go."

"What?" Her face screwed up accusingly. "I damn well am going, so get out of my path!"

"I'm trying to help you...." He started to explain before she cut him off—again.

"Excuse me, but how is stopping me from reaching my lifelong dream helping me? And who gave you that kind of authority anyway? I don't see Travis Kincaid standing here." Her head switched from side to side, peering around him. "I don't see anyone dictating to me but you, and just who do you think you are, anyway?" she demanded.

His eyes narrowed to icy slits. "Pardon me," he replied condescendingly. "It's just that I have a hard time imagining Travis Kincaid hiring a woman for this particular assignment."

"Actually, he didn't."

"What?"

"I mean, I haven't exactly met Mr. Kincaid."

Michael's blue eyes widened. "I was right."

"Half-correct, Mr. Hunter. Mr. Pinchon in the personnel department hired me. I was what you might call a 'rush job.' I had less than a week to quit my job and get to Ecuador."

"This is a nightmare," Michael said, taking off his hat and raking his hair. He set the hat back with a slight backward tilt in order to see her better. "Mr. Pinchon—"

"Was acting on direct orders from Mr. Kincaid," she cut in.

"No way. I know Pinchon. He's one of the best in the field for matching personalities to positions. He would have taken one look at—" He looked at her bangle bracelets, matching leopard print earrings and fashionable shoes. "No way. Period."

The chink in M.J.'s defense screeched as it widened. "I, er, uh… That is, we never actually met. Mr. Pinchon and I."

"Don't stop now," he said, clearly exasperated. "I'm all ears."

"I applied by E-mail. He replied by E-mail."

Michael expelled a heavy sigh. "I really don't want to know any more. I'm convinced. There's been a mistake. A big one."

"Now, wait a minute," she said hotly. "I have every right—"

He interrupted quickly. "You bet you do. And you know what? I can see you're a big girl. Travis Kincaid will be putty in your hands. You'll figure out a way to change his mind. You can take care of yourself. Right?"

"Yes, I can." She smiled reassuringly.

"I was just trying to save you. Save you the bother and embarrassment of going all the way to Ecuador only to have Travis Kincaid send you straight back home."

"What's he got against women?"

He replied quickly. "A lot actually, but that's another story which has nothing to do with business."

"Then what makes you think you know so much about my situation?"

"Experience," he said with a cool twist of disdain and arrogance.

M.J. was consumed with envy. She would give anything to be as smug as Michael Hunter.

And the worst of it was that he was right. She had no experience with Travis Kincaid, the rain forest or larger-than-life men like Michael Hunter, not to mention just about everything else that constituted "experience."

Her shoulders slumped, the fire left her eyes and the venom dissolved in her mouth. She liked herself a bit better when she was shooting for effect. Michael Hunter had done a good job of stripping away her mask.

"Okay. I give. But really, why would he send me back? I have credentials...."

"It's too dangerous for women in the jungle. They get hurt. Physically. They aren't prepared for what's out there."

She was undeterred. "Which is?"

He blinked at her incredulously, then began blasting her with the ingredients of nightmares. "Pythons, piranha, jaguars, quicksand, dangerous mountains, hostile natives...."

"Oh, those," she replied dismissively.

He watched her implacable countenance. He couldn't help wincing at the thought of a charging jaguar. Intelligence shone in M.J.'s periwinkle blue eyes and in the easy yet firm lift of her chin as she looked at him straight on, as if daring him to challenge her.

He got the impression she knew exactly what she was getting into. Yet, something didn't add up.

Michael couldn't remember a woman ever looking at him with such an unwavering gaze. Mysteriously, she held him spellbound.

Michael Hunter had never been bewitched before in his life, and though he wanted to believe it wasn't really happening to him now, there was something about M.J. that made his heart stop.

Dear Reader,

I hope you enjoyed *In Love's Shadow* as much as I enjoyed bringing it to you. Many of you have been my pen pals and friends for a long time and I know you are wondering where the recipe was. Because the suspense was so heightened at the end, there was time only to make reference to the chocolate mousse. This is a recipe I've had for almost thirty years; it was given to me by my college roommate, Ann Marie Duke McNair. It is the easiest holiday dessert, and so scrumptious that, like Roya, you'll have it all over your face!

If you would like a copy of Roya's Quick Chocolate Mousse, my newsletter and an autographed color bookmark, please send a stamped, self-addressed envelope to me, Catherine Lanigan, 5644 Westheimer, #110, Houston, Texas 77056.

Please look for *The Legend Makers,* another romantic suspense novel coming from MIRA Books in July 1999.

**Discover the real magic
of Christmas with**

DEBBIE
MACOMBER

A group of travelers, stranded in a shabby train depot, spend Christmas Eve with strangers instead of their loved ones. Anticipated joy becomes disappointment; excitement becomes despair.

Then the depot's reservations clerk brings them a small, leftover tree. Local kids come caroling. It's beginning to feel like Christmas!

CAN THIS BE CHRISTMAS?

Sharing Christmas cookies, stories and presents, hanging makeshift decorations on the tree, these strangers open their hearts to each other and discover the real magic of Christmas.

**Christmas comes but once a year; a
Christmas like this comes once in a lifetime.**

Available beginning October 1998
wherever books are sold!

Looking For More Romance?

Visit Romance.net